WHEN THE HANGMAN CAME

Joe Caruana

authorHOUSE®

AuthorHouse™ UK Ltd.
500 Avebury Boulevard
Central Milton Keynes, MK9 2BE
www.authorhouse.co.uk
Phone: 08001974150

© 2011. Joe Caruana All righs reserved.

No part of this book may be reproduced, stored in a retrieval system, or transmitted by any means without the written permission of the author.

First published by AuthorHouse   10/13/2011

ISBN: 978-1-4567-7866-8

Any people depicted in stock imagery provided by Thinkstock are models, and such images are being used for illustrative purposes only.

Certain stock imagery © Thinkstock.

This book is printed on acid-free paper.

Because of the dynamic nature of the Internet, any web addresses or links contained in this book may have changed since publication and may no longer be valid. The views expressed in this work are solely those of the author and do not necessarily reflect the views of the publisher, and the publisher hereby disclaims any responsibility for them.

Dedication

To the loving memory of my brother, Charles Caruana, former Roman Catholic Bishop of Gibraltar, who followed the development of this book but who did not get to see the ending.

Acknowledgements

My thanks go to:

My cousin, Mrs Barbara Jurado, who did a splendid job in the initial proofreading.

Dennis Beiso, Chief Archivist, for his help and cooperation.

Charles Gomez barrister-at-law, who read my early manuscript and gave me encouragement and some good suggestions.

Lorna Swift and Robert at the Gibraltar Garrison Library for providing me with the back issues of the *Gibraltar Chronicle* for the years 1930 and 1931.

Michael and Louise Rugeroni for documents concerning the Gibraltar Coal Merchants' Pool.

Eliosa Yome from the Archive of the Cathedral of St. Mary the Crowned for providing Opisso's birth certificate.

Mr Leslie Cardona, who allowed me to photograph from his wonderful collection of photos from the albums of Mr A. C. Carrara, CMG, JP, KC. In particular, a photograph of Governor Godley on horseback at a hunt and a group photo of lawyers in the 1930's that included all the lawyers involved in our story.

Mr Paul Canessa, who provided me with reports by *El Calpense* in Spanish, *The Gibraltar Chronicle* in English and also a copy of the report that was sent from Scotland Yard to the Colonial Secretary in Gibraltar on their meeting with the Chief of Police.

Superintendent of Prisons Mr Richard Aguilera for arranging for me to be shown around the Old Prison at the Moorish Castle and for showing me a few of the original exhibits used in the hanging of Ernest Opisso. Also, prison officer Garreth Combes, who accompanied me and explained many items of great interest, and whose grandfather and grandmother were also prison wardens.

Mr A. B. Serfaty, QC, the grandson of defence lawyer A. B. M. Serfaty, who provided me with a photo of his grandfather and an outline of his varied career.

Mr John Restano (Junior) for providing me with copies of documents he had retrieved from the Public Record Offices at Kew.

Mrs Ave Maria Fava, daughter of PC Macedo, for providing me with a photo of her father and some other personal details.

Mrs L Pereira, daughter of Detective Sergeant Gilbert, again for providing me with a photo of her father.

Dr Cecil Isola for our several conversations and for kindly providing me with a photo of his father as well as material on this case.

His Excellency Governor Sir Adrian Johns for allowing me to photograph a portrait of Governor Godley at the Convent (the Governor's residence) in his full dress regalia.

Clive Mendez for providing a photograph of Judge Beatty from the Supreme Court Chambers.

Mr Richard Garcia for his valuable time and for providing me with many details from his vast knowledge of the history of Gibraltar.

To the Gibraltar Royal Police for providing me with a portrait of Chief of Police Gulloch and two photos of the scene of the crime. Unfortunately I was not permitted to reproduce the photo showing the victim on the floor of the bedroom, the scene of the crime, but was permitted to sketch an outline of the photo, I have endeavoured to come close to the illustration of the photo.

To retired police officer Albert Attias for providing me with the 'First hand report as recorded by PC Tonna who was injured during the riot.'

To Luis of Luis Photo Studio for providing photos of the Old Moorish Castle Prison and other related photos.

To my late brother Charles Caruana who patiently listened to the development of this story and who gave me the photo of the International Red Brigade.

Contents

Dedication	v
Chapter 1: Introduction	1
Fortress and Colony	1
Key to the Mediterranean.	5
7 Market Lane	8
The Opisso Murder Case	9
Chapter 2: Visit To Scotland Yard	12
The Mystery	12
The Coroner's Inquest	18
Inside Scotland Yard	23
The Scotland Yard Report	24
Chapter 3: The Arrest	31
Under Suspicion	31
The Police Court	34
An Angry Crowd	35
Forced Entry to the Scene of the Crime	37
The Bread Boy	44
Vital but Belated Evidence	47
The Medical Evidence and the Bloody Footprints	49
The Key	52
The Bedroom	54
Was the File the Murder Weapon?	55
Chapter 4: Life in Gibraltar in the Years 1930-31	64
An Active Society and a Colonial People	64
The First Tourist Bureau	66
Entertainment by the Military	67
The Good Old Days?	68
St. Vincent de Paul Bazaar	71
Entertainment High on the List	71
Chapter 5: The First Trial	78
Trial at the Criminal Courts	78

Busy Morning of the Accused	87
The Case for the Defence	90
Opisso Testifies	93
Prosecution Winds Up	95
Judge's Summing Up	97
The Hung Jury	98

Chapter 6: Spectacular Parade and Naval Review — 101

Grand Mediterranean Fleet Visits Gibraltar	101
The Spanish Revolt	103
The Calpe Hunt	106
High Society	107
The City Council of Gibraltar	108

Chapter 7: The Retrial — 112

The Moorish Castle in Ancient Times and Today	112
The Special Jury	117
The Retrial Begins	120
Abridged Evidence by PC Bacarese	120
The List of Articles of Evidence	120
Abridged Evidence of Superintendent Brown	121
Abridged Evidence of the Chief of Police	122
Abridged Evidence of Doctor Griffiths	126
Abridged Evidence of Mr Joseph Canessa	129
Abridged Evidence of Joseph Busquet	130
Abridged Evidence of the Bread Delivery Boy	131
Abridged Evidence of PC Eliot Macedo	131
Abridged Evidence of the Hairdresser	132
Abridged Evidence of PC S. Wahnon	132
Abridged Evidence of Mr J. Caetano	133
Abridged Evidence of Doctor James Durante	133
Statement by the Defence	136
Abridged Evidence of the Accused, Ernest Opisso	136
Ernest's Movements	137
Evidence of Dr James Giraldi	150
Guilty Of Murder and Sentenced to Death by Hanging	155

Chapter 8: A Mother's Plea — 164

The Public Petition	164
The Request for a Medical Board	166

The Governor's Concern	168
The Medical Board: Normal or Abnormal?	169
Eleventh-Hour Appeal by Father Salvador	175
Mother's Plea to the Governor for Mercy	177
Petition by Mr Serfaty and S. P. Triay	178
Appeal from Casablanca, Morroco	179

Chapter 9: Preparations For The Hanging — 183
The Governor's Warrant for the Execution	183
The Hangman, Mr Baxter	185

Chapter 10: The Riot — 188
The Bishop's Activities	189
Governor's Report to the Secretary of State	193
The Duffield Story	196
The Arrests and the 'Red Brigade'	197
A Spark of Gibraltarian Identity	198

Chapter 11: The Day of the Execution — 202
The Execution	202
3rd July 1931	204
No Flags, No Bells Tolled	206
The Coroner Gets into Trouble	207
Recognition of the Jailers	208

Chapter 12: Where Was the Motive? — 212
First Possible Motive: Jealousy	212
Second Possible Motive: Money	218
The Third Possibility: Persons or Persons Unknown	223

Chapter 13: What Was the Evidence? — 228
The Special Jury System: Fair or Unfair?	228
Mystery that Shrouded Scotland Yard	230
Mystery of the Time of Death	231
Was Opisso the Murderer?	233
The Question of Third-Degree Methods	234
Mystery of the Timing of Ernest's Movements	236
Who Else Could Have Done It?	240
The Late Witness	240
Was PC Macedo's Account Accurate?	242
Mystery of the Bread Boy	245

Mystery of the Man Who Answered the Door	246
Mystery Of the Stopped Clock	247
Mystery of the Keys	247
The Fingerprint Mystery	248
The Footprint Mystery	249
Mystery of the Hair	251
Mystery of the Washed Clothes	251
Mystery of the hairdresser.	252
Bishop FitzGerald and Father Salvador's Appeals to the Governor	253
Should the Governor Have Granted a Reprieve?	253
Mysteries about the Chief of Police	255
The Mystery of the Black Book.	257
Mystery of The Iron File and the Bone	258
One Last Observation	261

Chapter 14. SHORT SEQUEL ABOUT SIR ALEXANDER GODLEY, GCB, KMC. **263**

Appendix 1: *The Royal Gibraltar Police 1830–1930*	267
Appendix 2: An Unsubstantiated Rumour—True or False?	267
Appendix 3: History of UK Capital Punishment and Its Abolition	268
Appendix 4: U.K. Press reports	271
Appendix 5: Telex to Malta requesting a hangman	272
Appendix 6: Letter of Public Petition of 3,000 signatures	273
Appendix 7: Medical report	274
Appendix 8: Medical report	275
Appendix 9: Negative report from Scotland Yard	276
Appendix 10: Mother's Plea, letter to Governor	277
Appendix 11: Acknowledgement of Public Petition	278
Appendix 12: Second Negative report from Scotland Yard	279
Appendix 13: Hand written note from Colonial Secretary.	280
Appendix 14: Opisso's Baptismal details.	281
Appendix 15: Executive Council's decision on Medical Report	282
Appendix 16: Court's Warrant for Execution	283

Bibliography and Sources **284**

About the Author **285**

Chapter 1: Introduction

Fortress and Colony

This is the true story of a murder, the trials, and finally the hanging of Ernest Opisso. The crime took place on Saturday, 29th November 1930, at 7 Market Lane, a narrow alley between Main Street and Irish Town, in the British colony of Gibraltar. The victim was 59-year-old Maria Luisa Bossano. The motive was unknown.

The London *Times* reported the scene on the eve of the hanging, once all prospects of a reprieve had been refused:

> Scenes of wild disorder were witnessed tonight when crowds surged through the streets demonstrating against the execution fixed for tomorrow morning of a carpenter, Ernesto Opisso, who has been sentenced to be hanged for the murder of an elderly woman. It will be the first execution in Gibraltar since 1896. A reprieve was refused by the Governor in Council. The crowds thronged the streets demanding a reprieve and forced cafes and places of amusement to close. No taxis were to be had, as the drivers are on strike.
>
> So ugly was the situation that troops turned out and are patrolling the streets armed with hockey sticks.

It was Gibraltar's first execution of any kind since 1896 and remains to date the last peacetime execution on the Rock. (Two Spanish citizens were hanged for wartime offences in 1944.)

1930 was a year marked with various important events. Astronomers discovered the planet Pluto. Equally important, an American, Karl Landsteiner, discovered the essence of human blood groups, a gigantic leap in medical science.

In sports, Uruguay beat Argentina 4-2 in the World Cup. The First World War epic *All Quiet on the Western Front,* released by Universal Pictures, won an Oscar award and was showing at the local Theatre Royal.

In its own way, Gibraltar was small, peculiar, and quaint. It was different to any other place in the Mediterranean except Malta. It was distinguished by its highbrow British colonial customs and idiosyncrasies, an outpost of a diminishing and soon-to-disappear British Empire but, nevertheless, a bastion of British maritime power. In fact, a Round-Table conference was taking place at the time between many of the remaining British colonies where the future of the vast British Empire, especially in Africa, was being debated.

In schools, colleges, and universities, a huge map of the world was pinned to the wall, and all those countries that belonged to the Empire were coloured in red. This red mass covered about two thirds of the surface of the map. Large countries like Canada, Australia, New Zealand, South Africa and huge areas of the Continent of Africa plus India comprised this collosus of power.

India was one of the first large colonies to go. Mahatma Ghandi, with his policy of peaceful resistance, defeated the might of fire power and much bloodshed.

Winston Churchill for one, denounced the deliberations and aims of this conference as a demeaning political act of cowardice on the part of Britain. His fears would come true, and the reality of the day had to be faced. The British Commonwealth would eventually emerge out of this Round-Table conference. The local newspaper, the *Gibraltar Chronicle and Gazette,* first published in 1801 and the oldest British newspaper after the *London Times,* carried a daily account about this staggering, empire-shaking conference on its front page. The Gibraltar Chronicle's front page carried letters from London and summary reports from the UK media. Local news always appeared on the second page. Even so, the new British Commonwealth would be of great and vital value to the war effort of World War Two.

There was in Gibraltar at the time, a civilian group of wealthy merchants who carried much influence and who had the ear of the Governor. The Governor was the King's representative in Gibraltar. This was the only group that was invited to the many official functions and the only group that would be listened to—unofficially, of course. They were known as the 'Irish Town Barons' and most of them had made their fortunes in shipping, salvage work, some dating back to before the Napoleonic Wars, and (later) coal.

A second tier of influential personages, few as they were, belonged to the legal and medical professions. Other Gibraltarians were white-collar workers— clerks and bookkeepers with the War Ministry, the City Council, the telegraph companies, private shipping firms, and banks. Quite a few of the civilian population of the fortress were small to medium-sized traders of whom many owned shops and invariably employed Spaniards as shop assistants. Close to 12,000 Spaniards crossed the border daily to work in Gibraltar. Thousands were employed as manual workers at the naval dockyard and military workshops. Others worked in ship repair and stevedoring and related shipping activities. Many were of Genoese, Portuguese and Maltese descent. A survey of the time stated that 20% of the population was totally illiterate.

Only three apes resided on the Rock at this time. This was an alarming situation that prompted Governor Godley, a retired British general who had returned from the Boer War in South Africa, to import seven more apes from Morocco in an attempt to make them breed. (Talk by Richard Garcia)

Though disliked, trade unionism was strong in the 1930s in Gibraltar, and notices appeared in the press urging workers to join. Young trade union leaders, including Alvarez, Risso, Hewitt, Bardaquino, Balloqui, and many others, set the foundation for future political emancipation. There were also other radical extreme-left members who were activists within the unions. These persons formed the main spearhead of those wishing to have a greater say on local matters. They were pressing for general elections to be held for the formation of a Municipal Council of locals. Up until then, the council was principally composed of military personnel and British civil servants.

A notice in the *Gibraltar Gazette* reminded everyone that the gates at the frontier closed promptly at 10 p.m. every night and that any non-resident found within the city would be arrested and fined or imprisoned.

Those of high rank in the Army and the Navy, as well as British senior employees at the Colonial Office, ruled in this small piece of rock. They were extremely socially active.

Joe Caruana

The military strength of the garrison numbered about 10,000. The Mediterranean and Atlantic squadron of the Royal Navy was the biggest in the world and would often assemble in the harbour and the bay of Gibraltar. Often the American Fleet also made an appearance and used the services of one of the best and most modern naval dockyard facilities in the world. The four dry docks in the harbour were constantly in use and rivalled the activity of Portsmouth and Plymouth.

The undisputed and uncontested ruler of the roost on the Rock was His Excellency the Governor, Sir Alexander Godley, GCB, KDMC, General and Governor of the Garrison and Fortress of Gibraltar. His commands were final; and, he and he alone had the last word. However, on serious diplomatic issues he would naturally consult with the Secretary for the Colonies in London. In this particular period, the official exchanges between Gibraltar and London were few and far between, and urgent matters were handled through telegraphic messages.

So strong was the Governor's hold on the reins of power that he even extended it to the much-respected Calpe Hunt Society. Governor Godley wanted the master of the hounds to be an Englishman, but some of the local members, such as Paul Larios, with the title of Marques, thought otherwise. A feud took place between them over this question, and the two factions became known as 'The Godleys and the UnGodly.' Eventually it was decided that Lady Godley should be the master of the hounds. Apparently, Lady Godley was quite a character. The story went around that she rode down the stairs of the Governor's residence sitting and sliding on top of a tray. (*The Hounds are Home,* Gordon Ferguson).

The Montague Bathing Pavilion was opened in 1930, with segregated bathing facilities for men and women, and work started on the Luxury Rock Hotel to be owned by the Marques de Buttes, both projects considered to be of the highest importance for the future of Gibraltar.

In this year too, a cold wind of change was sweeping politically through Spain shaking the very foundation of the monarchy in that country. It would put Gibraltar in the limelight again, not quite as much as during the Peninsular War that liberated Spain from Napoleon, but nevertheless significantly so. The new republican government of Spain, following elections and a political revolution, ousted the King and with him the monarchy from Spain, On abdication from the throne, the King of Spain went to Paris, but his son, the Prince, came to Gibraltar and stayed there for a few days using Gibraltar as a stepping-stone on his way to exile in Portugal. Hundreds of Spanish nationals, supporters of the monarchy escaped to Gibraltar for safety and exile fearing persecution. Gibraltar's next-door neighbour, the town of La Linea, became a hotbed for socialist and communist elements, and this too was to have an effect on our story.

Even then, there was relative peace in the world, although rumblings of unrest from the Portuguese colony of Madeira, from Germany, and from nearby Spain appeared in the press. Germany held its general elections in 1930, and the Nazi Party gained a significant success, winning 18.3 per cent of the votes and becoming the second largest party in the Reichstag. Heinrich Himmler became chief of a new military corps called the SS, and soon afterwards in 1933, Hitler, a one-time painter and decorator, became the new Chancellor of Germany.

Winston Churchill, then a Conservative MP in the House of Commons and an arch-imperialist backbencher, annoyed many in the House with his fiery speeches and his distrust of Germany's ultimate intent of 'expansionism'. Churchill was one of a minority group of politicians advising military preparation and re-armament against the threat of a highly militarised Germany. His warnings fell upon deaf ears.

Key to the Mediterranean.

Gibraltar's lifeline was shipping. The port and the bay were very active.

In these pre-war years, my father was busy working his bumboat in the bay and had a lucrative business in partnership with my mother's father, Antonio Jurado. My father's multilingual ability (he spoke five languages) helped him in dealing with the captains of the many steamships that came into port.

With great foresight and vision, the first tourist bureau was established on the Rock in the hope of attracting tourists. Relations with Spain were friendly, so much so that a Spanish tourist bureau was also set up in Gibraltar. Tourists came on cruises, they came for long stays, and they also came on their way to Spain. Similarly, they came overland, driving or travelling by train through France and Spain.

Gibraltar became known as the 'Key to the Mediterranean,' a slogan created by James Adamberry in a competition held by the new tourist bureau. (Talk by Richard Garcia) Virtually all the big passenger-carrying shipping lines stopped at Gibraltar, since Gibraltar was a strategic coal-refuelling stop. The stiff competition between shipping lines made them call at Gibraltar as they had to be where the competitors were.

A novel form of transportation was developed by the Lloyd Sabaudo Shipping Line, a frequent user of the Port of Gibraltar. On 6 December, they introduced the first air service from Italy, using a seaplane that flew their passengers from Genoa via Barcelona, on their way to New York. Passengers were picked up at Genoa The plane was refuelled in Barcelona, and then it would land outside the harbour in the bay of Gibraltar, close to the passenger ship. The transfer of passengers was carried out in less than half an hour to the waiting cruise liners. The transatlantic crossing to America was thus reduced for travellers from Italy and the sea trip would now take seven days instead of the regular ten days. This took place three to four times a month. The seaplane would not go back empty. Usually, it would carry several hundred kilos of mail to Italy. However this service did not last long; it ended in 1931.

No doubt picking up on this idea and thinking that this was a great form of travel, the local shipping company H. M. Blands, owned by the Gaggero family, started a seaplane service, Gibraltar Airways, with the route from Gibraltar to Tangiers and Casablanca. (Ibid)

Many years before in 1917, the coal merchants of Gibraltar had organised themselves into a pool, known as the Gibraltar Coaling Depot. The Senior Superintendent Naval Stores officer, Mr Edgar Charles Watts, OBE, was appointed controller of the coal pool and helped in organising this pool and the purchasing of coal from Wales. The coal was unloaded and piled up in the North Mole and in Coaling Island. Not only the Royal Navy's fighting ships but also all other shipping relied on steam power, and therefore plentiful supply of coal was imperative—hence the great interest taken by the Naval Dockyard in appointing Mr Watts,

After several years of operation, the local coaling depot pool found itself with a tremendous surplus of cash. They had invoiced more coal than they had imported! It appears that the coal heavers, who at one time loaded the coal in huge baskets that they had to carry upon their shoulders, in order to make their work lighter and easier, had got into the practice of filling the baskets with less coal than the supposed measure. Each basket load was predetermined to carry a certain weight, and the tally clerk would tick each basket as it was emptied into the holds of the ships. X number of baskets should contain Y weight in coal, but it didn't. After thousands of baskets had been unloaded into the steam ships, the weight that had been dispensed to the ship owners was considerably short, and the ship owners were being overcharged by this short weighing.

At some particular point in time when it was hard to find work of any kind in Gibraltar, my father found it necessary to work as a coal heaver and he used to recount that the heavers got calluses on their shoulders from carrying the wicker baskets of coal.

The coal owners were not aware of this practice, so it came as a wonderful surprise to the coal pool members when an audit was carried out of the accounts and they found a significant surplus. In cash terms it was a windfall! All the members agreed to mechanise and economise on labour costs by purchasing new coal handling equipment in the form of bucket cranes and to split the rest of the surplus money.

All got their share—all, that is, but one. The firm of Joseph Rugeroni & Son claimed their share, but the chairman of the pool, Mr John Mackintosh, informed the members that the Rugeroni brothers, although engaged in the coal business, were not members of the pool. They had stockpiled their coal at the same place as the coal pool but had invoiced directly from their own stock.

This lead to a very serious challenge in court with the coal pool defending itself against the challenge from Joseph Rugeroni & Son, who were represented by three notable lawyers who also appear in the body of our main story. These were Mr A. C. Carrara, KC, Mr A. R. Isola, and Mr S. P. Triay. Representing the defendant were Mr Naisby and Mr A. B. M. Serfaty, who was also representing Mr King, who was absent at the time. Mr Watts, controller of the Gibraltar pool, had to be recalled from his posting in Malta, because he had been present when the coal pool had been formed. He was brought in specially to give evidence as a prime witness for the coal pool. The named defendant of the coal pool was none other than Mr John Mackintosh. After a long court battle, he won the case. (From private papers of M. & L. Rugeroni)

Joe Caruana

Gibraltar's strategic position was ideal, and shipping activity was so great that the *Gibraltar Chronicle* dedicated one whole page inside their daily edition to notices of shipping movements. The Ellermans Westcott & Laurence Line, Lloyd Sabaudo of Genoa, John Carrara and Sons, Rotterdam Lloyd, Navegazione General of Italy and Genoa, NYK Line, Anchor Line, Peninsular and Oriental Steam Navigation Co., Orient Line of Mail Steamers, and Papayani Steam Line were but a few of the shipping companies announcing their arrivals and departures. For more than one reason, they all included Gibraltar in their itinerary. Coal refuelling and victualling was a major reason, but they were also using a well-run port that was neither Spanish nor Portuguese but British, where British maritime law prevailed. (*Gibraltar Chronicle*)

The well-known firm of the Rugeroni Brothers and Co. announced a notice of a change of address. The notice read:

These Offices will be removed to Premises No.142 Main Street, (The premises previously occupied by SPQR) as of the 1st December1930. (*Gibraltar Chronicle*)

7 Market Lane

It so happened that whilst all of these things were going on a rare but brutal murder took place during this year in this peaceful but dynamic British fortress and garrison, the Rock of Gibraltar. The event shook, as if by an earthquake, the tight social fabric of this British colony and friendly community. The murder took place on 29 November at 7 Market Lane.

Why was this short street called Market Lane? It was not remotely close to the public market. However, it was closer to another market. In fact, only one street away was situated the Jews' Market, the location of which was initially known as Commercial Square and is now the Piazza or John Mackintosh Square. But this was not why it was called Market Lane. The true name derived from the times around the 1800s when the meat market was situated at a location called *El Zoco,* which in older times extended west from Market Lane and the Irish Town district up to the fortification walls. Beyond that was a drop of about ten metres to the sea. The block of buildings that today houses the police station had not yet been built. The area was all open ground, next to which was a fresh water fountain. In later years this place became known as Fountain Ramp. During the British occupation the new fortification became known as Zoca Flank, which was derived and borrowed from the Moorish name for market, *the meat Zoco*. 'Zoca' has no other origin.

The meat sellers or butchers set up shop in this open area where the slaughtering and quartering of the animals took place. Conveniently, on the other side of the walled fortification was the sea, and the butchers of those days found it handy not only to draw water from the sea below but also to throw the meat waste over the fortification's walls, feeding the crabs and fish in the area. Regrettably, it also created a tremendous health problem. The stench was unbearable, and this habit was soon stopped on grounds of hygiene. (Conversation with R. Garcia).

The Meat Market disappeared but Market Lane, which now joined and met with Irish Town, lived on. Why was this street called Irish Town? The story goes that the Irish contingent in the British Army was barracked outside the usual army compound, which seems to have been the standard practice of segregation within the British Army. Therefore, the Irish troops with their families were heavily exposed to the bombardment from the enemy when they got close to the fortification walls. It appears that the Irish constituted a frontline buffer zone and became cannon fodder. The street that was Irish Town was the only street in Gibraltar that was paved with wooden cobble blocks, when all other streets had cobble stones as paving. (Conversation with R. Garcia).

After Main Street, Irish Town was one of the busiest streets in town. Most of the shipping companies had their main offices there, as did the coffee and tobacco importers and processors. There was a great traffic of mule-drawn carts loaded with sacks of coffee and bales of tobacco.

The Opisso Murder Case

It was not known who had killed the 59-year-old lady. A frantic police search followed and notices asking the public for help were placed in public places. It was a brutal murder and a complex one, so the assistance of Scotland Yard was requested. In late January 1931, almost seven weeks after the murder had taken place, a suspect was identified and an individual was eventually charged, one Ernest Opisso. But was he the murderer?

The case was to be known to generations of Gibraltarians as the Opisso Murder Case.

However it was not a straightforward case. There was the usual coroner's inquest, then a magistrate's court to determine if the accused was to be committed for trial to the Supreme Court. Then there was a trial with a Grand Jury that reached a split verdict and ended with a hung jury. Therefore, the Chief Justice ordered a 'Special Trial.' This special retrial by law required a 'Special Jury.' A special jury was a twelve-man jury with a difference because it was picked from the general jury list that had been selected by the Chief Justice. These persons were qualified for the special jury because of their integrity and social standing and because they were property or land-owners, businessmen or professionals. Alongside their names on the published general jury list was the annotated suffix 'SP.' The special retrial took place on 8th June 1931, six months plus one week after the murder took place.

The story of the murder itself and all the details, together with the main characters in this saga, are true and factual unless there exist files or records held outside the local archives that I have not seen though I also managed to obtain several documents from the British Public Records Office at Kew. I have endeavoured to remain faithful to the facts of the story to the best of my ability. The opinions expressed are my own.

Some of the court transcripts are not explicit. In fact, at times they are very brief, economical in the recordings, and almost in shorthand.

The details of the hanging are those specified in the *Official Memorandum for Executions, 1892*.

I visited the old Civilian Prison at the Moorish Castle and walked about the location where the gallows once stood, and I entered the condemned man's cell. I touched the walls and breathed the air and closed my eyes and allowed my mind to go back to the days when Ernest Opisso was a prisoner awaiting execution.

I have not found an eyewitness account of the hanging, but have read a first hand account recorded by a policeman, so I presumed that the official rules were followed rigorously as I have recounted them.

When the Hangman Came

Certain details have been included with literary artistic license to enhance and unfold the circumstances and the flow of the story. However the details of the case and quotations are totally factual

I have researched the newspapers of the day to follow the sequence of events of this crime and the details as reported by the various media, the *Gibraltar Chronicle*, *El Calpense* and *El Anunciador* newspapers. I have examined letters to and from the Governor to the Secretary of State at Downing Street, police reports, and Judge Beatty's trial reports to the Governor, as well as the Governor's report to the Secretary of State who wanted to closely follow this case.

I have spoken with the Supreme Court registrar, the Royal Gibraltar Police records and with several family members of some of the individuals who took part in this case.

The name Opisso is no longer in use in Gibraltar and all but a first cousin lives to this day, To my great surprise and joy he turned out to be a close and dear friend of mine who's name I have no need to mention.

Tourist Board postcard of 1930's of Gibraltar

Chapter 2: Visit To Scotland Yard

The Mystery

The Chief of the Gibraltar Police Force, William Sutherland Gulloch, and Sergeant Gilbert leaned on the railings of the P&O Liner *Ranpura* that regularly called at Gibraltar and was now taking them to London. They contemplated the crests of the white waves as the wake of the ship broke the surface of the dark blue Atlantic Ocean. The rhythmic effect was rather mesmerising. Both men were deep in thought. Luckily, the weather was holding fine as they sailed close to the Bay of Biscay, renowned for its rough passage. They were conscious that, if they were delayed for any reason such as bad weather or fog, they would not arrive on Christmas Eve as scheduled but rather on Christmas Day, but if the weather continued as at present they would arrive as planned though their patience was under trial.

Once again, maybe for the hundredth time, they were going through the mystery of the murder case that was taking them to Scotland Yard for expert assistance.

Sergeant Gilbert was attached to the CID branch of the Gibraltar police force, and his experience as a detective was being put to the test. Murders were very uncommon in peaceful Gibraltar. The local police's daily routine was mostly taken up with minor infringements of the Law—stealing, drunkenness, disorderly conduct, street brawls, short changing on weights and measures, and illegal street gambling.

But their blissful and comfortable colonial way of life had been suddenly and rudely interrupted. They had been landed with a full-blown and devastating, bloody and ghastly murder case!

On 9 December, because of the serious nature of the murder, the Chief had requested, verbally and in writing, from the Governor of Gibraltar, that an expert from Scotland Yard be sent from London to Gibraltar to assist the local police force in solving the murder case. He felt that they could help with fingerprints in particular and with other items of evidence that they had found at the scene of the crime. They needed help to determine who had killed the lady in Market Lane. The local police force was totally inexperienced in dealing with forensic work of this nature, and this case was way over their heads.

Since they were supposed to arrive on Christmas Eve, they were hoping that the Scotland Yard officials would be waiting for them as had been intimated in the telegram to the Governor's office.

The Chief was telling the Sergeant what had transpired during the previous few days before they had left Gibraltar. He said that he had looked up the shipping schedules and had read that a P&O steam liner was sailing from London on 12 December and that a Scotland Yard expert could reach Gibraltar by the 16th or 17th. He had personally communicated this to the Colonial Secretary, who in turn passed the information to the Governor.

'Promptly,' the Chief continued, 'the Governor telegraphed the Secretary of State's office in London with Gibraltar's request, and by the 10th, the Governor had a telegraphic answer from the Secretary of State, that said 'I regret that the present organisation of Scotland Yard is not such as to enable officers of requisite rank and experience to be spared for the purpose you seek.' This was signed by the Secretary of State himself.

'So, Sergeant, here we are. We have several pieces of evidence that we desperately need to look at—fingerprints to check and compare, bloody smudges left on a bed mat—and we have no experts to analyse them. As time was of the essence, I eventually suggested to the Colonial Secretary that there was only one solution. If the mountain would not come to Mohammed, Mohammed should go to the mountain, meaning that if Scotland Yard could not come to Gibraltar, then we ourselves would have to go to Scotland Yard in London. So here we find ourselves'

'Pity that there was not an earlier vessel from Gibraltar to London,' observed Gilbert. 'We've had to delay our departure till the 20th, which means, if we arrive on schedule, we will get to Scotland Yard on the 24th. That's Christmas Eve—damn awkward time to arrive! Surely the folk at Scotland Yard won't be very happy about this?'

The Chief smiled a knowing smile. 'In any case, Gilbert, we could not leave earlier. We needed to stay till the inquest was finished. Yes, I feel for the poor buggers at the Yard, but don't worry. H.E. has sent a telegram to the Secretary of State informing them of our urgency and our arrival and telling them that he would be grateful if they would arrange for Scotland Yard to give us every facility. I'm sure they will cooperate with us, and if everything goes according to our plans, we should catch the next steamer back on the 26th, which is, of course, Boxing Day.

'But back to the murder, Gilbert. Don't you find it strange that the door of the flat was locked when Mr Joseph Canessa, the deceased's relative knocked? Luckily, he met with that carpenter fellow who knew the place well, and he and Canessa tried keys in the lock to no avail. So they decided to call at the police station, which, as you know, is round the corner. PC Bacarese immediately borrowed a ladder from the fire station close by at Commercial Square and succeeded in entering the flat through the street window, which luckily is not very high.'

'Yes, Chief, I've been wondering about this Canessa fellow. He's related to the victim, and the victim happens to be very well off. Bit of an inheritance there, I should imagine. I think we must keep an eye on him. But no, Chief, to be totally correct, it was the carpenter who climbed up the ladder and got to the window first. PC Bacarese told him to stay at the window whilst Bacarese went into what was the in fact the bedroom.

'It was fairly dark inside, so the carpenter lit a match and called to the PC to have a look. Then he entered the flat after the PC, who tried to switch on the electric lights, but with no results. He then lit his own match to have a look around and saw that the room was in complete disarray, with a basin full of water and blood, as well as bloodstains on the floor. Then, as he entered the next room, he saw the horrible scene. He saw the body on the floor there in the sitting room. He tried to open the front door, but this was locked and there was no key, so he quickly left the flat the way he had come in. It was at that point that PC Bacarese placed a call to Superintendent Brown'.

Gilbert continued, 'Yes, Superintendent Brown did some quick thinking. The moment he arrived and was told what had been seen inside, they tried everything to push the door open, but eventually he ordered the door to be broken down. This same carpenter fetched a hammer from the next-door neighbour, and after a few minutes they succeeded in forcing an entry.

The noise caused much excitement amongst the occupants of the various flats in the building.

'The door led to an extremely dark, small lobby, and the three rooms led one out of the other. The place was in complete darkness. They tried the light switch, but nothing happened. This carpenter fellow, who knew the place well, went to the fuse box and tinkered about, and the lights came on. The body of Miss Bossano could be seen fully clothed, lying face downwards on the floor of the centre room of the flat. She was in a pool of blood with her head towards the door. A blood-stained towel and a pair of eye glasses were lying close by.' Gilbert stopped for a breather and lit a cigarette. Then he continued, 'This is when you and Dr Griffiths were summoned by telephone.

'As you know, we carried out an exhaustive examination of the premises and of the body that lasted two hours. Since there was a trail of blood from the bedroom to the sitting room, we searched for blood trails in the outside corridor and on the stairs, but we found none. In the meantime, we called the photographer, Mr Benjunes, who luckily happens to live in the same block of flats. He took some magnesium flash photos of the scene and of the body of the victim.

'When Dr Griffith, who happens to be assistant colonial surgeon, finally came, he said that he saw the body of an elderly woman lying on the middle room in a large pool of blood and that the carpet was soaked in blood. He examined the body and found a large wound on the crown of the head, which had pierced the skull. The body was quite cold, and death appeared to have occurred many hours before. The injuries were very severe and were not consistent with a fall, unless the deceased had fallen from a height head downwards. It appears that a blunt weapon and not a fist must have caused the wound on the head, but we found no weapon at the scene of the crime.

Gilbert continued, 'Yes, Mr King, the coroner arrived at 11.45 p.m. and finished his examination at 12.30 a.m. Then he ordered the body to be taken to the Colonial Hospital. The city council ambulance arrived, and the body was moved there.'

The Chief, in a thoughtful mood and gazing at the far horizon, said into the ocean darkness and to no one in particular, 'Person or persons unknown, I guess.'

'Yes, indeed,' said Gilbert. 'For the moment person or persons unknown, but if the door and the window were locked and there was no key on the inside of the lock, how did the killer get in and out of the flat?'

'That is the question, my dear Mr Gilbert. How did the killer get in, leaving lots of smeared blood on the floor and no traces on the outside of the flat? Whoever it is, is a clever murderer. But where is the murderer? Did he or they know the victim? And what was the motive, since, according to the relatives, nothing of value was stolen? Do you think, Sergeant, that the inquest was thorough enough?'

'Only in so far as to the cause of death,' replied Gilbert

'Yes,' said the Chief. 'Bloody messy operation that! The skull was cracked open and the brain visible. So fierce were the blows that a piece of the skull had been broken and lay close to the corpse. Can you imagine the force of the blow? Poor lady! Judging from the damage done, she must have received several blows.

'When you examined the scene of the crime, Gilbert, did you notice the duster and towel near the body and the handkerchief almost in her hand, all of which were soaked in blood. Did she have time to pick up a towel?'

Thinking this question over for a while, Gilbert replied. 'I doubt it, Chief. The towel was probably used by the murderer to dry his hands, and the duster was used to gag the lady. Why else would the duster be where it was found? But what struck me most was that there was also blood in front of the dressing table, the walls, and the glass door partition, with several splashes of blood about ten feet high up. Except for the blood, the bedroom seemed to be in good order, although the wash basins were on the floor out from under the wardrobe and the bed apparently had not been slept in. But why had the clock on the bedside table stopped at 3.55 p.m.?'

'Most probably, because the lady forgot to wind the clock when she got up in the morning. What about the wash basin? There was blood in with the water,' added the Chief.

'It appears that someone tried to wash the bloodstains off. There was also soap in the wash basin. The lady must have attended to her wounds with the towel close to the dressing table carried it with her as she continued to be attacked and went from the bedroom to the sitting room and dropped the towel there.'

'Yes, Gilbert, that may be the case, but robbery does not appear to be the motive. We found the lady's handbag in the chest of drawers, which was totally undisturbed with a considerable amount of money in it. Funny thing is that we found a bunch of keys on the chest of drawers, but none of them fitted the lock on the entrance door, though I might add that, although the culprit was in a hurry whoever did this took time to lock the door on leaving. The two photos on the chest of drawers had fallen down, maybe a sign of panic or struggle?'

'Very strange Chief a handbag full of money? And we have yet to find the keys to the victim's flat and no sign of a murder weapon either. '

'Even so, we have not learnt anything new. All we have at present are several fingerprints and other evidence found at the scene of the crime and the fingerprints taken from those persons who knew the victim, all of which we are taking to Scotland Yard for analysis. So, Sergeant, what else have we learned from what transpired at the inquest?'

'I think, Chief, that it would be a good idea if we went through the proceedings again, don't you think? We seem to have more questions than answers.'

The Chief and the Sergeant went into the lounge of the liner, found comfortable seats in a quiet corner, ordered tea and a plate of wedged sandwiches, brought out the transcript of the inquest, and proceeded to review the proceedings of the inquest.

Prior to the Inquest, ten days later on 9 December, DC Wahnon located Ernest and told him that he had an order to search his house but that no charges had been made against him, so Ernest accompanied him to his house at 2 Castle Street.

'Listen Ernest I have been told to get some things from your house to take to the police station, nothing personal you understand, just mere formality.?'

'Ye-e-ss oof co-u-rse,' replied Ernest, 'Come I'll take you there myself. W-w- h-at ex-a-ctl-y do yo-u want?' He asked.

'Oh just a few things, the clothes you were wearing the day the lady was killed, your trousers, shirt etc. purely routine you know,' put in DC Wahnon.

'Ye-es o-f cou-rse.' Replied Ernest.

The detective took away with him a pair of trousers, a shirt, and a raincoat. He noticed that even though it was a fine day, the coat was wet. This made him suspicious, and he pointed it out to his superiors. Incidentally, these three articles, were the only things available to the police at the time and were obtained after the coroner's inquest had taken place but before the visit of the Chief to Scotland Yard.

The Coroner's Inquest

The Chief read the proceedings.

> The Coroner presiding was Mr H. J. King, with a jury. The inquest was held on 11 December 1930 at the police court.
>
> The first witness called was Dr James Durante, who stated that he assisted Dr Griffith in the *post mortem* examination of the deceased and described the various wounds and injuries that were found. Witness corroborated Dr Griffith's evidence and finally stated that the cause of death was consistent with the result of repeated blows on the head with a blunt weapon, which in his opinion must have been about 18 inches in length.
>
> Miss Amanda Amar stated that she has her flat near that of the deceased and on Friday, 28 November at about 3.45 p.m., she left her flat, as she usually did, and then passed in front of the deceased's window that opened to the common corridor. The latter called out to her, 'Are you going, Miss Amar?' and she replied, 'Yes, goodbye.' She did not actually see her but she distinctly heard her voice. The witness did not live permanently at that flat and only went there regularly every week but she knew the deceased well. A Spanish woman, who also sells flowers, cleaned her house every week, but the witness did not know whether this woman knew the deceased or not.
>
> In reply to a question from Mr A. C. Carrera, KC, who was present as a representative of the family of the deceased, the witness stated

that the corridor of her flat was rather dark at about 4 p.m. and that she did not see anything abnormal or see anybody in the vicinity when she left her flat, but she did add that in April this year her flat was broken into and two watches, an opera glass, and several Argentinean coins were stolen, but the thieves were never traced.

In reply to the foreman of the jury, the witness stated that she was sure it was the deceased who asked if she was going out.

Mr Joseph Caetano stated that he lived in a flat adjacent to that of Miss Bossano and that on the day in question, he noticed that smoke was coming out through the kitchen window of her flat. He had remained in his house all day because he was not feeling well and had heard nothing unusual. On Saturday morning, he came out of his flat and saw a small boy who was selling bread, knocking at the door of the deceased and as apparently he could not get a reply, the boy asked him if he knew whether the lady was in. He told the boy to knock harder in case the lady was in an inner room. He had also stayed in his flat that day and had heard nothing.

The witness explained that the rooms of his flat are parallel and adjacent to those of the deceased and that the wall, which separates his flat from hers, was very thick and rendered it impossible to hear anything that happened in the adjoining rooms.

In reply to Mr A. C. Carrara, the witness stated that he had seen the deceased very seldom, perhaps three times in three months, and that even if shouts were in the deceased's flat they could not be overheard from his flat.

Replying to the foreman of the jury, the witness stated that the window of the kitchen of the deceased's flat was closed when the boy was knocking at the door on Saturday morning and that eleven persons altogether lived in the building. He had however seen a lady hairdresser and a charwoman going now and then to the deceased's flat.

Inspector Brown informed the Court that his police had made exhaustive enquiries and they had failed to find the boy referred to above. He further stated that there were about 18 more witnesses to be called.

At this stage the proceedings were adjourned until Tuesday next.

Joe Caruana

The Chief put the script down as if wishing to change the subject. He lit a cigarette and said, 'Amazing, Sergeant. Our department and the coroner's have been kept rather busy these days. Why, only the day following that of the murder on the 12 December, the coroner, poor fellow, had to attend to two other incidents involving deaths.

'The first involved one individual, a Maltese, who was found on Thursday afternoon hanging from a beam in the roof of a stable. Dr Deale confirmed that in his opinion the hanging must have been self-inflicted. The poor fellow was over eighty years old, and he used to sleep often in the stables. The fellow was well known in Gibraltar and could be seen daily in the streets selling milk. When his son went to look for him, he saw his father hanging from a beam in the roof.'

'Yes, it certainly has been busy lately, Chief. Our boys have been doing a great job, not a moment's rest for anyone. We have a full squad on the Bossano case besides all the other altercations.

'There was a rather nasty fight at the Universal Salon. Our boys had to assist the Naval Shore Patrol and the MPs in that fray, and a couple ended behind bars at the station after the Shore Patrol detained and carried away several others.'

'Then on top of this,' the Chief continued, 'we had that Spanish fellow found floating in the sea and obviously drowned off Commercial Wharf. The poor coroner, Mr King, had to attend to this case as well in the afternoon. The fellow was a shop assistant who had been born in Ronda, and his relatives had reported him missing. Apparently, he had threatened the family with taking his life. A case of drowning was recorded by the coroner.'

The Chief picked up the Coroner's Court transcript again and continued where they had left off.

> When the Inquest was resumed on the 16th. Mr King, the Coroner and the Jury continued to hear evidence from witnesses summoned by us.
>
> A number of neighbours gave evidence that they had not seen or heard anything abnormal.

Mr Joseph Canessa, a relative, stated that the deceased had sufficient money to live on comfortably and as far as he knew she did not have any enemies.

Miss Rosario Villatoro, a Spanish hairdresser, stated that she had attended Miss Bossano for the past 13 years and the last day she saw her alive was on Thursday, 27 November. On Friday she had called at the deceased's flat at about 2.30 p.m. and, after knocking several times and obtaining no reply, she went away. She came the following day and again got no reply.

Mr Ernesto Opisso, a local carpenter/handyman, stated that on Friday the 28th he saw the deceased for the last time at her window as he passed by through Market Lane, and she called him to her flat and told him to measure the cistern of a house that she owned. The deceased gave him a cord with a lead weight attached to it, which he later kept at his store. He said he knew the deceased very well and used to do odd jobs in her flat.

'Then you Chief,' interjected Gilbert, 'stated that the police had no further evidence to produce at that stage which might help the jury in arriving at their verdict. The police were following up certain lines of enquiry, but they were not yet completed.

'The coroner then addressed the jury and summed up the evidence, after which they retired to consider their verdict' continued Gilbert.

'After a short interval they returned a verdict of wilful murder against some person or persons unknown and added that "they considered that owing to this unprecedented murder and recent robberies committed in such a short time, which have so far been undiscovered, vigilance at night is insufficient as it is actually done by the police."'

When the inquest had finally terminated, the Chief of Police and Sergeant Gilbert had anxiously left for London the following day, 20 December, 1930. Their vessel eventually reached Southampton in the early hours of the morning of the 24th.

It was a cold and wintry day in England, and they soon regretted leaving the warm Gibraltar weather. They hurriedly walked down the ship's gangplank. On disembarking, they saw a man bearing a placard in one hand and an umbrella in the other. The placard bore the name 'C.o.P. Gulloch.'

Leaving the other disembarking passengers behind. and carrying their overnight bags and a large suitcase that contained the various items of evidence, they briskly walked towards this individual, who touched the rim of his trilby as if in a mild salute and guided them to a waiting Scotland Yard car.

Their host got into the driver's seat and, as the vehicle was warm inside, they both unbuttoned their overcoats. The driver immediately set off on the A30 Southampton to London road to their appointment at the Yard.

In an attempt to break the dead silence, the Chief said to his companion, 'You know, Gilbert, I missed the annual dinner, I guess my wife went along with my eldest son in my place.'

'Which dinner was this, Chief?'

'The Gibraltar Yacht Club annual dinner, of course. All the VIPs must have been there—H.E., who is the vice-patron, and Rear-Admiral Barwick Curtis, who is the commodore, and many more.'

'Your one consolation, Chief, is that you missed all those long-winded speeches. Do you actually sail yourself, Chief?'

And so, it seems, the social activity in Gibraltar continued unabated. The yacht club's main table was occupied by, but for a few locals, expatriates on tour duty in Gibraltar. The one notable local personage was Mr A. C. Carrara, KC, who proposed a toast to the health of the visitors. The Chief remembered that there was also to be a performance by the Lincolnshire Regiment's band at the Kingsway (Alameda Grand Parade) bandstand, to which he had also been invited, and this would be taking place between 3.00 and 4.30 p.m. the coming Saturday. The programme stated that nine tunes were to be played, together with a *paso double*, the regimental marches, and ending with 'God Save the King.'

'Can't forget, Gilbert, our centenary celebration last August of our police force,' said the Chief. 'It seems as if it was only yesterday. What a turn out our men put on at Casemates Square! What a joy it was to see some of the pensioners, especially retired Inspector Bob Randall, who turned up dressed in his old police uniform with his top hat and everything else that was worn 100 years ago by the pioneers of the police force.

'Proud as a peacock I was, as we marched from Casemates down Main Street to Alameda Parade ground to the tune of the band of the 1st Battalion of the Lincolnshire Regiment. We were complimented by the acting governor, Brigadier Buxton. We'll never forget how the crowd cheered our boys as we marched back to Casemates.'

'I rather enjoyed the dinner that night,' added Gilbert. 'Whoever organised that event deserves a medal. What a show! What with the singers and the clowns from the Spanish circus next door, Tedy and Pompoff I think they were called. They got huge applause. Of course, they were surpassed by J. F. Brew's singing his milongas accompanied by Guillem and Diaz. I guess, Chief, you never expected to be carried around the room in your chair by the men, did you?'

'Indeed it was most unexpected. The moment the Acting Governor left the room and was cheered off with 'For He's a Jolly Good Fellow,' they came in a rush and lifted me and Superintendent Brown shoulder high, and then the action started. Yes, indeed, I'll never forget that particular centenary celebration,'

The Poppy Day organisers, of whom his wife was a member, had announced the result of their collection in November of the monumental sum of £80. The Chief's daughter formed part of 'The Our Day Poor Fund Committee', which had also announced a concert at the Theatre Royal for Monday, 22 December.

For his part, Gilbert said that the Chief was not the only one to be missing out. He and his wife had tickets to the operatic show put on by the *Agrupacion Artistica Calpense,* the comedy *El Rosal de las Tres Rosas.* And in the interval, it had been announced that Mr H. Smith and Mr. J.F. Brew would be singing. Likewise, they had planned to take a weekend visit to Morocco over Christmas, where Messrs M. H. Bland and Co. had announced the services to Tangier and Casablanca by *SS Gibel Zerjon.*

Inside Scotland Yard

The Chief was familiar with London, and when he looked out of the window, he noticed that they were on Victoria Street and would soon reach Scotland Yard. He said to Sergeant Gilbert, 'Can't wait to get this all over! Hopefully, we can get some joy from the few pieces of evidence we have brought over.'

Finally, the car brought them to the courtyard outside Scotland Yard. The Metropolitan Police Chief Constable, Mr Ashley of the CID, together with several senior individuals, welcomed them cordially. Considering it was Christmas Eve, they were rather pleasant and made them feel at home.

Without much ado, they got down to business. The visitors brought out the excellent flash photographs taken at the scene of the crime by local expert photographer Mr. Benjunes, as well as the victim's black journal book, the hand basin, and all the sets of fingerprints of the various individuals familiar with the victim.

The experts got around the table comparing fingerprints, those at the scene of the crime and those of others. Based on a gut feeling, the Chief had one fingerprint in particular he wanted scrutinised closely, that of Ernest Opisso. Bloody fingerprints taken from the dresser and the glass door panel, where the crime had taken place were compared with those willingly provided by Opisso, relatives of the victim, neighbours, and several police officers who had entered the flat.

After several hours of analysis and discussions, the group at Scotland Yard could not come to any conclusion, and so London's Chief Constable Ashley suggested the Gibraltar delegation visited Dr Roche who was the Scotland Yard's expert pathologist and fingerprint expert.

The photos and the fingerprint slips were viewed under the latest fingerprint comparator microscope.

The Scotland Yard Report

A report dated 29 December was received from Scotland Yard signed by Chief Inspector A. C. Collins and addressed to the Metropolitan Police's Chief Superintendent.

In it, Collins said that he had met with the Gibraltar delegation and was accompanied by Chief Constable Ashley and Superintendent Nicholls and that they had previously been seen by Chief Inspector Battley of C3 Department.

When the Hangman Came

This eight-page report contained the following important data.

Though the body had been found in the sitting room which adjoined the bedroom, the 'apparent footprints' on the bedroom mat led them to believe that the assault had taken place in the bedroom and that either the lady had walked or had stumbled her way to the sitting room, or else she had been carried there, where she probably collapsed.

Sixteen or eighteen blows had been struck, with a blunt instrument, on the poor lady.

The lady was described as having a peculiar temperament and was very methodical in her ways and had a 'religious turn of mind.'

Death had probably occurred not later than 4 p.m.

The Chief of Police told them that Ernest Opisso had been seen 'leaving' the building at around 1.45 p.m.

They state that the only key in existence, as identified by the cleaning lady, was that found in the bunch of keys at Opisso's store

Found clasped in the hand of the deceased was a small quantity of black hair. This was part of the assailant's, since the deceased had grey hair some of which was intermingled with blood on the linoleum.

There was no trace of any weapon or instrument in the flat.

Mr Gulloch suspected that he did not have sufficient evidence to prove his case, and that the important witness was the baker's boy who saw him (Opisso), at 12 p.m.

The Chief of Police had taken with him to Scotland Yard a) the rain coat, b) the trousers, c) the black book, d) several pieces of linoleum, e) the key and lock.

They had sought expert advice on the examination for fingerprints on the basin and the book.

Footprints on the linoleum and bloodstains (if any) on the clothing.

The experts reported on each of these as follows;

The impression on the book and other articles submitted for examination reveal insufficient clearly defined ridge characteristic data for the purpose of analysis or comparison with other fingerprint impressions.

The clothing, particularly the raincoat, was carefully examined by Chief Constable Ashley and other Officers present at the conference. By its appearance and smell it had been recently washed, and had not since been worn.

Trousers also had been washed but had been worn since, this had upon them marks to be either of red paint, rust or blood.

The soles of the lady's shoes had ample evidence of blood.

The pieces of linoleum and bloodstains coincided with the shape and size of the shoes. The theory advanced was that in all probability she had been first attacked in her bedroom and had either walked or been assisted to the sitting room where she was again attacked and had finally collapsed, which would account for the blood footprint impression.

This theory was rather supported by the fact that a towel was found by the side of the body in the sitting room and a 'number of blood splashes' found on the wall in the sitting room would be accounted for by the fact that a second attack took place there.

Chief of Police Gulloch stated that he relied principally on the expert examination of the footprints, but as these proved negative it was agreed that the other points did not carry the case much further 'so far as the suspect was concerned.'

Gulloch mentioned that 'he had not brought with him the black hair found,' which was the same colour as the suspect's hair, because he did not attach much importance to this as nearly every other person in Gibraltar, being of Spanish extraction, had black hair.

The advice of Dr Roche Lynch was sought at his residence and an appointment was arranged for the following day, the 26th, at 11 a.m. at St. Mary's Hospital.

The fingerprints on the book and basin were too smudged to give conclusive answers.

He determined that the footprints coincided with the woman's shoes.

The clothing was left with him for further analysis, and he would report if the results were positive.

On hearing the full story, he was of the opinion that after the first attack she could have attended to her wounds, which would account for the basin of water and blood.

She then proceeded to the sitting room, carrying in her hand the towel, and there received the final blows.

After the admitted negative assessment of all the tests and analysis, and its admission that 'Mr Gulloch suspected that he did not have sufficient evidence to prove his case, that the important witness was the baker's boy who saw him at 12 p.m.,' the report ended with this strange concluding note.

'We formed the opinion that very little more, if any, was required to justify a charge against him on the facts already disclosed.'

Chief Inspector

    A. C. Collins. (Metropolitan police memo supplied by P. Canessa)

Even with this last note, the Chief and the Sergeant stood crestfallen, apologised once again to all for intruding on their Christmas Eve celebrations, and bade them all farewell and a happy Christmas. The Chief Constable assured them that his secretary would call the shipping line and make all the arrangements for their return.

There was only one thing for them to do—return to Southampton that same day if possible and catch a liner that was leaving for the Orient and would be stopping at Gibraltar to take on coal.

The Scotland Yard car and driver were waiting for them when they reached the cold outdoors. They both felt the chill—the chill of the London air and the chill of the frustrated visit.

The car took them to Victoria Station, where they took a direct train to Southampton. The Chief of Police was silent and morose throughout the trip. He wondered if Opisso would still get away with it He had made some pretty damning statements to Scotland Yard about his suspicions of Opisso

Anxious to get back to Gibraltar, they spent Christmas in Southampton and New Year's Day on board the liner SS Rampura. The return trip took five days, and this put their patience to the test. They arrived back in Gibraltar on 3 January 1931, and the Chief handed Governor Godley his report of his unsuccessful and inconclusive proofs.

This was a big setback for the Chief. He called his top men and urged them that everything possible must be done to resolve this mystery. He had a suspect, but the evidence at hand was not conclusive. It was now 1931, and he had not ventured to issue a warrant for the arrest of his main suspect. With no additional evidence there was a chance that the case would surely be thrown out the window by the judge.

He decided on taking some urgent steps.

(Footnote. In 1936 the P&O liner *SS Ranpura* ran aground in the shallow waters of the beach in the north end of the Bay of Gibraltar when her anchor dragged during strong gales. When the storm finally abated the liner was pulled out into deep waters by a team of four tugs from the Gibraltar Dockyard).

When the Hangman Came

†

Apostolado de la Oración

Centro de Santa María la Coronada

Las Misas de 8 y 12 y demás cultos propios de primer Viernes que serán celebrados mañana Viernes 5 de Diciembre en la Santa Iglesia Catedral, serán aplicados por el eterno descanso del alma de la señorita,

Da. Maria Luisa Bossano,

Celadora que fué de este Centro

q. d. D. g.

———

El P. Director y Celadores de ambos sexos suplican á los asociados y fieles en general la asistencia á los indicados cultos y apliquen la Sagrada Comunión por el alma de la finada.

Dic. 4.

El Calpense Dec 1st 1930 to Jul 7th 1931

Notice of Funeral Mass for the repose of Miss Maria Luisa Bossano.

Detective Sergeant Ernest Gilbert. Now Detective Inspector.

Ernest Gilbert was born in 1896 and joined the Civil Police Force in 1922 at age 26.
He always served was in the CID in the Detective Division. He was involved in several important criminal cases. The most important one was the discovery of a bomb in 1942during World War II by a Spanish saboteur who had hid the bomb in a fruit basket in a fruit store in Main Street. As a consequence the saboteur was
Hanged at the Moorish Castle gallows and is buried there.
He played a mayor part in the investigation of the Opisso Murder Case and features in our story.
He was also instrumental in the discovery of a cross that was stolen from Bishop Fitzgerald, the thief was arrested and prosecuted.
A notable distinction of Ernest Gilbert was that he was appointed personal bodyguard to the Emperor of Abysinia. His Majesty King Haily Selassi when he took refuge in Gibraltar after Abysinia was invaded by Italy in 1937.
He finished his career as Detective Inspector and head of CID he retired in 1951 and died shortly after in 1951 at the early age of 61.
He was awarded the highest Honour of the Police Force, The King's Police Medal.

Detective Sergeant Ernest Gilbert – In Inspector's uniform.

Chapter 3: The Arrest

Under Suspicion

At this point in the story, no one had been charged or arrested for the murder of Miss Luisa Bossano. From the information leaked to the public and reported in one of the local newspapers, it would have been natural to think that the criminal would have left in a rush or panic and that his clothes must have been stained with blood and his face transfigured following such a barbaric crime. No doubt the criminal had killed the lady to stop her from identifying her murderer. Yet the killer had sufficient serenity after the crime to wash his or her hands carefully and to take the key of the flat so that no one could find the body for a long time.

The crime had caused a lot of commotion and unease amongst the people, and it was the topic of conversation everywhere. Not since the tragic murders committed by Jose Calvo and an attempted murder of another gentleman, had there been so much anger and furore in the colony. These murders had taken place many years earlier, and the Calvo murders were called the 'Double Murder Case.'

Jose Calvo had established a friendship with a gentleman who was very wealthy and kept an imprudent amount of money in his house. The friendship grew to the point where Calvo had the protection of the family, and he even stayed to sleep at the victim's house. One day he attempted to steal from his friend, and the child of the house saw him. Calvo hit the child violently and killed him. The child's cries were overheard by the father who rushed in to find Calvo with the child at his feet and the money in sight. Calvo attacked the father brutally and killed him also.

The other case that had created a lot of commotion amongst the public was a murderous attempt on the life of a Mr Cabedo. Mr Cabedo happened to be in his shop, where he too kept a lot of money. A stranger knew about the hidden money, and this provoked the individual to attack and steal from him. A timely intervention from Police Inspector Hope prevented another murder.

It appears that the present crime had no such motive. The lady was a fragile person, incapable of defending herself, and although she did have money, it was not considered to be sufficient to provoke a murder though there was plenty of money in her hand bag none had been taken.

The police were still groping in the dark. There was still no definite and official suspect or suspects to the murder of Miss Bossano, but experience and gut feeling led the Chief of Police to ask Detective Constable Wahnon to take an interest in Ernest Opisso. When DC Wahnon had gone to the scene of the crime on the evening of Sunday, 30 November, Ernest was still there with Mr Canessa. DC Wahnon made as if to lean against the wall near a light switch, and Ernest abruptly stopped him and told him to be careful since the switch was broken and that he had orders to repair it but had not yet got round to it.

As yet, the police still did not have a murder weapon or a motive for the murder, even though the police had two apparently strong eye-witnesses, who for various reasons had not testified at the inquest. These were the baker's boy and PC Macedo.

The Chief of Police and Superintendent Brown were pressing their men to come up with a solution to the mystery, and they indicated that an arrest was well overdue. Their main suspect was still Ernest, the carpenter who had helped Brown in breaking down the door to the flat wherein had been the murdered lady, but as yet he had not been charged. Ernest was, to them, a logical suspect. He knew the victim because he had done odd jobs for her, had visited her flat often, and rented a store from her in Cornwall's Lane. The experts in London were still examining the few new clues, which the Chief of Police had taken with him to Scotland Yard and which they hoped would point to Opisso and perhaps be crucial to the case. Though significant pieces of evidence had not proved positive at Scotland Yard, all the results were not yet known.

On 26 January 1931, Detective Constable Wahnon stopped Ernest in the street and asked him to accompany him to the police station. Ernest thought nothing of this, since he had cooperated fully with them and had even been questioned at the inquest. He had allowed his fingerprints to be taken and had taken the police to his house, had opened his store to

When the Hangman Came

them on a number of occasions, and had answered numerous questions. He was not at all concerned as he limped along to the police station with the detective. On that same day, even though Ernest had not been charged, the detective went back to Ernest's house at 2 Castle Street and took another three pairs of shoes, another pair of trousers, and a shirt from Ernest's room where his mother assisted them. The CID personnel were being very thorough.

On 27 January, DC Wahnon, accompanied by Superintendent Brown, went again to search Ernest's store. Technically, it was their obligation to inform the accused's lawyers of this, but they went ahead without doing so. They were continuing their search for further evidence subsequent to the arrest. One item that they took away was alleged to have been the murder weapon, a course carpenter's file.

Ernest Opisso lived in Castle Street, though Castle Street was actually a thoroughfare of wide steps. It had once been a steep hill, but to make it easier to walk up, it had been converted to wide steps, each step ranging from three to seven feet wide. If these steps were followed uphill, the stroller would eventually reach the Moorish Castle district, hence the street's name. During Spanish times, this street was known as *Calle de la Comedia*, 'Comedy Street.' This was because down at the bottom of the steps at Cornwall's Parade, there was a theatre adjoining the steps. Parts of this theatre are still in existence, albeit hidden under the more modern buildings. Cornwall's Parade itself was known as the 'Green Market' or *Plaza de la Verdura* because most of the street fruit and vegetable vendors tended to congregate there with their donkeys and carts to sell their produce. (Conversation with R. Garcia).

To Ernest's great surprise and horror, he was not allowed to go home. Instead, he was held in jail at the police station in Irish Town. The following morning, the

27 January, he was taken to the upstairs police court to appear before the magistrates and be formally charged with the murder of Miss Bossano.

The Police Court

Word of his arrest spread like wildfire through the town, and by 10 a.m. a large crowd had amassed in Irish Town in the hope of obtaining admission to the police court. When the doors finally opened at 10.15 a.m., the crowd far exceeded the accommodation available. Many disappointed persons had to remain outside in the street, where they awaited the outcome of the proceedings.

Ernest, who was described as a handyman, was now formally charged with the murder of Miss Bossano and was remanded in prison until the charges were placed before the magistrates. Being a Friday, the proceedings were short and were adjourned until 2 February.

One newspaper, printed in the Spanish language, *El Calpense,* noted that the arrest went to show the good work done by the police and stated that this gave the lie to those who had said that the police would do nothing and brush this matter under the carpet.

On 2 February, Mr E. P. Griffin sat as the justice of the peace. There was a large and curious crowd outside the police court, waiting to get a glimpse of the accused. Representing Ernest in his defence were Mr A. B. M. Serfaty and Mr H. J. Galliano.

Superintendent Brown gave formal evidence of arrest and of charging the prisoner in the presence of Mr Serfaty on 27 January on a warrant for murder. He stated that when the warrant was read to the prisoner, he was cautioned in the prescribed manner and the prisoner made no reply. Mr Brown then applied for a remand, and this was granted for seven days. Quite naturally, the accused did not answer on advice from his lawyer. It was obvious that the prosecution and the police needed time to prepare their case. Even at this stage, their evidence was neither strong nor conclusive.

There was much speculation and talk in the streets and the various neighbourhoods. Both Ernest and the victim were well known persons in the town area. Miss Bossano, who came from a well-off family, was known as a respectable and methodical prim lady, who went regularly to the cathedral to attend mass and was also known for her charitable nature.

Ernest too was well known in the district as a handyman, working on odd jobs for many people in the neighbourhood. In particular, he had lately been working for the victim and her relatives. He was also known because he was lame and walked with a limp, and those familiar with him knew that he was also deaf and spoke with a speech impairment that made him difficult to understand. It is not known whether his deafness was the result of the illness that affected his left leg and made him lame. If so, since this illness overcame him at the age of seven, it would explain why he could vocalise some words that he had heard prior to his hearing being impaired. Furthermore, those closely related to him knew that he was a bastard child.

Since the police department was frantically working on the supposedly new pieces of evidence, the prosecution asked for an adjournment until the following day.

An Angry Crowd

On the following day, 3 February, the accused was about to make his reappearance in court. A taxicab conveyed the prisoner from the Moorish Castle civil prison in the custody of two police constables. As the taxi drew near the courthouse, the crowd rushed towards the taxi to get a glimpse of Ernest. It was a frightening rush that rocked the taxi. When the taxi finally made its stop, a squad of policemen came out in quick time, since the constables on duty had great difficulty in keeping a passage clear for the accused and his escort to pass into the building. Shouts of 'murderer' and obscene insults were directed at the prisoner by some of the crowd.

Even though it was raining heavily, a huge crowd, larger than the one on the previous day, had gathered outside the police court, making so much commotion that they had to be ordered to remain silent. The crowd got denser as the time for the hearing drew nearer. A notable point made in the newspaper reports was that amongst the crowd there were many women.

The purpose of this court hearing was to determine whether, after the charge of murder had been made, sufficient evidence existed to refer the case to the criminal court, where the accused would be tried by a judge and jury. With the small court room packed to full capacity, Ernest stood waiting to hear the continuance of the charge of murder against him.

The Attorney General Mr H. C. F. Cox appeared for the prosecution. To everyone's surprise, he immediately applied for a further remand of yet another week and stated that he wished to make it clear that it would not be possible for him to proceed with the case the following week either. He said that there had been very important developments recently, which he could not at present disclose.

Mr Serfaty, Ernest's defence lawyer, strongly objected to this application on the grounds that the alleged crime had been committed as far back as the previous November and that, since then, the prisoner had given every facility to the police, who had interrogated him several times and carried out a number of searches. He asked why, if the police were not ready with their evidence, they had arrested this man. They had no right, he submitted, to arrest a man and then try to find proof against him. He added that it was public knowledge that the Chief of Police had gone to England to consult with Scotland Yard. Therefore where was the evidence?

The defence then applied for bail, but the Attorney General objected. The bench refused the application and ordered a week's adjournment until 13 February. Mr Serfaty drew the attention of the court to the rowdy scene outside the street and pointed out that the crowd had rushed the cab in which the prisoner arrived, which he considered a very menacing move towards his client.

His Worship said that he was sure this would have the attention of the Chief of Police. The Chief of Police, who was in the court, immediately left the room. He ordered his men to form a cordon around the entrance to the court to hold the crowd back at a prudent distance. Although it was raining hard, the crowd had persisted outside the police station. A full cordon of constables urgently pushed the crowd back and, holding hands, formed a formidable barrier around the police station. They made way for the passage of the prisoner, and the crowd shouted at him as he passed by. He got into the taxi and was driven back to the prison at the Moorish Castle.

The steep ride up to the streets of the rock and the isolated area where the Moorish Castle Prison was located was a hair-raising affair. Torrential rain came down, and drains were overflowing and spouting water. Negotiating the rushing rainwater that flowed in cascades downs the steep hilly roads was a nightmare.

A bewildered Ernest waited in the damp cellar of the prison until his next day in court. His poor broken mother was allowed to visit him and took food and extra warm clothes and blankets. Conditions at the prison were deplorable. She wondered where she had gone wrong with Ernest. Why was he again in trouble? Apart from his physical disabilities, Ernest was also known to be somewhat mentally slow and had been a source of concern all his young life. If it had not been for the fact that Ernest was somehow very useful with his hands, he would be considered a misfit. In fact, the kids at school would tease and make fun of him, which led him to drop out of school before his time. But soon Ernest was doing odd jobs for neighbours and friends and was getting paid for it. She had supported him with what she earned as a midwife, an occupation that kept her busy. She herself, Amanda Opisso, was loved and respected by many people. After all, she had helped to bring countless babies into the world, and her name had become a household name.

As a mother, she naturally thought that Ernest must surely be innocent and that he was incapable of killing anyone, even though at times he tended to be short-tempered; but this was mainly because of his frustration at not being able to communicate verbally.

Forced Entry to the Scene of the Crime

The morning of 13 February dawned perfectly, but it started to rain at 11.30, the precise time at which the hearing was to start, and it continued to rain throughout the day.

The proceedings started with Mrs Leticia Prescott Bossano This lady lived at 114 Irish Town and, therefore, was a close neighbour of the victim. She told the court how on Saturday the 29th, the morning of the day of the murder, she looked out of her window, from which she could see all of Market Lane to Main Street, and saw Miss Bossano at about 10 a.m. walking down from her house in Market Lane and then turning left at the corner of Irish Town, just as Barclays Bank was opening its doors for business. The bank was conveniently located opposite the police station. She saw Miss Bossano continue her walk towards Market Square (also known as Commercial Square and Jews' Market). Many stalls stood in this market selling bric-a-brac and second-hand items. She knew Miss Bossano very well, so there was no mistaking her; Miss Bossano was a rather elegant lady and walked confidently and with poise. She immediately thought that

Miss Bossano was on her way to the cathedral for the 10.30 mass. Leticia had nothing further to add.

The Revd. Bonifacio Soler, a priest at the Cathedral of St. Mary the Crowned, stated that he had known the late Miss Bossano for many years and, when not ill, she went every day to the Cathedral. He believed that she did go to the church on the Saturday morning but was not very sure.

Ernest had remained standing in court all this time and was shifting from his bad foot to the other. He whispered to his lawyer, Mr Serfaty, 'Can I please sit down?' The lawyer took pity on him and requested the magistrate to allow Ernest to be seated, given that he had a bad leg. Permission was immediately granted for Ernest to sit.

The next witness was the victim's hairdresser and manicurist, Rosario Villatoro, who lived in La Linea in Spain. She stated that she had been attending to the late Miss Bossano at her residence for several years and that she came daily to Gibraltar. Miss Bossano had been living at the present address for the last three months. She had last seen Miss Bossano on the previous Thursday, but only for five minutes. At about 2.30 p.m. on Friday, she knocked at Miss Bossano's door but got no answer, so she went away. The following day, she went again at the same time and knocked hard twice, but again there was no answer and again she went away. She said it was raining very heavily.

She said that the deceased was a very quiet lady and that the only person she ever saw there when she attended to the lady was a cousin of the deceased. She used to do the lady's hair in the bedroom at the dressing table, and she described in detail the items that were normally on the top of the dressing table. In particular, there was a set consisting of a round silver mirror with a handle, a brush, and two small photographs. She added that she attended to Miss Bossano's hair several times a week and that the lady paid her weekly.

When asked if she had seen a bottle of ink or a black book on the dressing table, Rosario answered that she had never noticed a bottle of ink or a black notebook there. Rosario then added that she often saw around the place the charwoman who cleaned the late Miss Bossano's flat.

Mr Joseph Canessa was married to a niece of the deceased and said that the lady lived alone, that she was a lady of means, and that, prior to her moving to Market Lane three months earlier, the deceased had lived at his house. He confirmed that the charlady went once a week on Wednesdays to his relative's flat, and he was aware that the hairdresser went to the house almost daily. He also confirmed that Ernest Opisso the handyman went to the lady's house when she had work do be done at her flat or at her property in Cornwall's Lane.

During the early days of the case prior to anyone being charged with the brutal murder, Mr Canessa, because of the continued interviews and interrogations, went through a very stressful period, since he had the impression that he was on the suspect list as a possible murderer.

When giving his evidence, he mentioned an interesting detail. He said that the deceased herself would measure the level of water in the underground water tank at Cornwall's Lane. However, after the murder Opisso had told him that he had measured the tank for her in her property in Cornwall's Lane, no doubt because it was a rainy day. He added that Ernest did odd jobs for him as well and in fact, he had done painting and electrical work in his house.

He knew that the deceased was a very religious lady, very quiet and reserved. She was generous as far as her means allowed. He reckoned that, as far as he knew, she had no trouble with anybody. The last time he had seen her was the day before the murder.

Mr Canessa continued his account. At midday on Sunday after church, he and his wife and a Mrs Carrara had missed her presence at church that morning, and, thinking that something strange was happening, they called at the deceased's door, but the door was locked. He knocked but got no reply. They could see through the kitchen window in the outside corridor that everything inside was in darkness. In an attempt to open the door, they tried several keys, but the keys would go right through the lock and would not fit.

They decided that the ladies should go home and he would go to the house agent. However, on the way there he met with the accused on the corner of Pitman's Alley. Thinking that this was a fortuitous meeting, he asked the handyman to stay with him, as he might have some work for him. He asked whether the accused was busy, and the accused replied that he was not. Canessa was already thinking that somehow Ernest would be able to help him enter the flat.

The house agent gave them some keys, and they both went straight back to Market Lane with them but when they tried them, none of them fitted, so they went to the police station to try to borrow a ladder. The police station was round the corner opposite Market Lane. PC Bacarese was on duty at the time. He told them that he did not have a ladder, so they went to the fire station that was situated close by in Commercial Square, where they borrowed a ladder. It was now late afternoon.

Ernest carried the ladder, and PC Bacarese accompanied them. Canessa then dashed to his home in Irish Town, which was only about 150 yards away, to tell his relatives what was going on, and then he immediately returned to Market Lane. On his return, he found that the ladder was already up against the wall under the bedroom window of the first floor flat. He saw that the constable was inside the room and the handyman was on the ladder, leaning on the window sill and looking in. The entire place was in darkness. Canessa then added that the handyman also went in, and he himself went up the ladder as far as the window.

This exact sequence of events, although not of a serious nature, was, however, not corroborated by later evidence given by PC Bacarese and by Ernest Opisso.

PC Bacarese's account was that when he arrived at Market Lane, the ladder was already up, which meant that Ernest went up to the window on his own. PC Bacarese said that the handyman was climbing up and then he followed, but the handyman made room for him to go past him, and then Canessa followed them both.

The place was in total darkness, so the constable asked the handyman, 'Where can I find the light switch?'

The handyman replied with a strong stammer and in barely audible, halting speech, 'O-over th-there to the r-right of the gla-a-ss door.'

The constable groped forward in the dark and tried the light switch by the door without success. 'This doesn't work!' shouted the constable over his shoulder.

'J-just wait. I-I'll s-s-strike a m-m-a-tch,' answered the handyman, again in his halting and almost unintelligible stammer.

When the Hangman Came

By this time, Canessa had also gone up the ladder and could see into the bedroom. He saw that the bed had not been slept in and said, 'She is not here.'

The handyman looked around and drew Canessa's attention to a basin with blood in it. He pointed and stammered, 'Th- th- there is blood there.' The basin was against the wall to the right of the window. There were two windows that looked out to the lane. Against the wall in between these two windows stood the dressing table, and to the side of the right window stood a stand with its hand basin and towel rack.

Neither the handyman nor Canessa had followed the constable through the glass door into the next room, the sitting room. Canessa attempted to go in, but the constable, pale faced, put his arm out and barred his way forbidding him to go through. 'You stay there. Don't come in here.'

The constable went further and tried the front door, but there was no key in place. The door was securely locked and would not open. Both Canessa and the handyman looked surprised at the constable's abrupt action. Something in his look and his voice said there was trouble on the other side of the partition. They noticed he was excited and nervous. The constable ordered, 'You two, please go down the ladder and on to the police station and fetch the superintendent. He'd better come here straight away.'

Canessa and the handyman immediately went out of the window, down the ladder, and into the street, where a crowd of curious onlookers had gathered. Murmurings and speculation was rampant. Someone said, 'The lady has had a heart attack!' Another said, 'The lady has fallen and has passed out!'

However Canessa, instead of doing what PC Bacarese had ordered, turned to another constable, who was now standing at the foot of the ladder preventing some curious individuals from climbing up, and told him, 'Constable, your colleague upstairs needs help. Would you kindly go to the station and fetch the superintendent I suspect there is trouble in the flat up there.'

Superintendent Brown, with his swag baton under his arm, strode hastily up Market Lane with two other constables trailing behind. PC Bacarese saluted him at the bottom of the ladder and immediately told him, 'Since I couldn't open the door from the inside, sir, I came out the window to wait for you here. Something horrible has happened in the flat. There's a lady above lying on the floor with blood all around her.'

'Okay, Constable, let's go up and see for ourselves and try that door.'

They went up. They pushed and kicked at the door to no avail. A couple of neighbours had come out to witness the commotion that was taking place. Outside the flat, the superintendent, PC Bacarese, Canessa, and the handyman all tried in vain to force the door open.

'We'll need to break the door down. Are there any tools about?'

'I am a-a carp-p-enter,' said Ernest, 'but I do not have my tools with me.'

The next door neighbour, an old gentleman, said, 'Wait, I have a hammer in my flat.'

Brown gave the order to break down the panels of the door. The carpenter, though small in stature, was strong and started to pound with the hammer at the door. He soon had the panels off and the lock broken. They turned the doorknob, and the door flew wide open.

'Everyone, stay right here,' ordered Brown. 'Constable, you come with me.'

The place was still in total darkness. 'Where the hell is the light switch?'

'T- t- to your r-right sir,' replied the carpenter, who understood English perfectly well.

The superintendent tried the switch. 'This damn thing doesn't work! Must be off at the mains! You, there,' Brown said, turning back to the carpenter, 'any idea where the mains are?'

'*Si.* Y-Yes, sir, I know where, b- b- but I am frightened to go in. T-here might be s-some-o-one still hiding in there.'

'Don't be frightened, Ernest. We are here behind you,' the constable reassured him.

After hesitating a little but feeling somewhat braver, the carpenter went in, fiddled around inside, and soon the lights came on.

When the Hangman Came

The constable noticed that a broken porcelain fuse carrier stood on top of the fuse box.

'Constable, make sure no one comes into the flat,' Brown said, addressing another constable who had joined them on the first floor.

Brown went into the flat, followed by PC Bacarese.

The kitchen was to the left as they entered, and then the entrance hall led to the sitting room through a glass door that in turn led to the bedroom through a second glass door. The flat consisted of three rooms and a kitchen.

Canessa, who was straining to get a look, saw the body on the floor past the first glass door. Everyone else, including the carpenter, stood outside in the corridor at the entrance to the flat.

Brown crept forward slowly and carefully and went into the sitting room where the body was. He was taking great care not to step on anything. The body was lying in a pool of blood with the head pointing towards the glass door.

Brown called out, 'Mr Canessa, would you step inside please. Since the lady is your relative, can you say if anything of value is missing? '

A shocked Canessa looked around. The place was in a mess. He saw his relative's body on the floor and noticed all the blood scattered around the place. He was sick to his stomach and bewildered, not quite believing what he was seeing, but he did what the superintendent asked and noticed that the valuable silver items and some jewellery in a glass plate on the dressing table were still in place.

He opened some drawers. In the top drawer he found the lady's handbag. He picked it up and opened it. 'See here, superintendent,' he called out surprised. 'There is money in it still, plenty of money. This could not have been a robbery, don't you think? There is more money here than I expected. Everything appears to be intact. There doesn't seem to be anything missing.'

Aghast, he noticed that there was blood all over the place, on the floors and walls, everywhere.

Now in court, Canessa added that he remembered that on Saturday morning, the morning in question, Ernest had been working at his house till about 12 noon or 12.30 p.m. He had certainly left before one o'clock.

Thinking about this, he was slightly confused as to when the handyman had told him he had gone to measure Miss Bossano's water tank at her property in Cornwall's Lane. Was it Sunday night or the following Monday? He said that the handyman had told him that he had seen Miss Bossano at her window on Friday morning when he was passing by. She called out to him and asked him if he would mind measuring the water level in the tank at her property.

Many of the details being revealed that day in court had not been told at the time of the inquest, and therefore the defence lawyer, Mr Serfaty, asked Constable Bacarese why he had not reported some of this information at the inquest hearing. In an incredibly simple and naïve reply, the constable stated that he had not been asked. All he had given at the time was a simple statement.

The Bread Boy

The boy was not certain whether it was Monday, Tuesday, or Wednesday that he had first gone to the police station. It was certainly four or five days after his visit to the lady's house when he heard about the crime. Antonio Carrero Arjona, aged 13, had recently got a job at Danino's bakery in Engineer's Lane, which also happened to be the property of the family of the victim Miss Bossano. Antonio had taken the job of delivery boy and was new to the job and not yet familiar with the customers or the district. He came from a very poor family in Spain and had never been to school. He was street-wise but not very intelligent.

On the morning in question, he went with his boss to Market Lane to deliver bread. They went to the second and third floors. However, one of the ladies on the second floor wanted a brown Spanish loaf of bread. It so happened that on that day they were only selling English bread, so the deliveryman said he would get one for her and would have it delivered later.

When the Hangman Came

Following their other deliveries, they went to a bakery in City Mill Lane and got a Spanish brown loaf. Then the baker got young Antonio to deliver the bread to the lady at Market Lane with this instruction:

'Remember, it's the lady in the flat opposite the toilet.' The boy ran back and went up one flight of stairs to the flat opposite the toilet. It was about 12 noon or 12.30 p.m. He knocked three times, but there was no answer.

An old man, Mr Caetano, who lived next door to Miss Bossano, came out of the toilet and saw the boy holding a basket with bread in it. The boy asked the old man if he knew whether the lady was in.

'Call again,' said the old man. 'Maybe she is inside and does not hear your knocking.'

The boy knocked again. This time a man opened the door. The man did not speak at first. The door was now ajar. The man was wearing a dirty jacket and striped black and white shirt. He half turned and said aloud over his shoulder 'It's the bread man' to someone inside.

One or two minutes later, a middle aged lady wearing eyeglasses came to the door, looked at the boy, and said, 'I have not asked for bread today young man.'

Sheepishly, Antonio realised that he had made a mistake. His employer had asked him to deliver the bread to a lady there, and he had called on the lady on the first floor instead of the lady on the second floor who also lived opposite the toilet. All he could remember his employer telling him was 'Remember, it's the flat opposite the toilet.'

He alleged that the man who came to the door was the man sitting in the dock in court. four or five days after his visit to Market Lane that he reported this fact. He had heard of the crime when he picked up a pamphlet in the street that told about the murder and mentioned him, 'the bread boy.' Scared, he had told his employer about this.

He had not heard any mention of the prisoner's name. Though he had heard about different persons being under suspicion, Antonio added that he had heard nothing about a lame man and that no one had tried to influence him in any way, though he had walked up and down the street with a detective in the hope that he could identify the man he had seen at the door.

The boy's evidence was incredibly crucial to the case, because it could place the alleged culprit at the scene of the crime close to or within the time frame given at the time by the doctors of the time of death of Miss Bossano. As he walked the streets accompanied by a detective, his attention was directed to various people, and one man in particular was pointed out to him, but he said that that was not the man he had seen opening the door to him.

On further questioning, Antonio said that on Sunday he had again gone to Market Lane to deliver bread, and there he saw two policemen outside the lady's house. He did not make anything out of this and continued with his delivery rounds, since he had not yet heard about the crime.

As his memory was prodded, Antonio also added that he had seen the prisoner in the dock. In fact, he had seen him at three places—in the street, in the inspector's office, and in the guardroom in the police station. Detective Sergeant Gilbert took him to the outside of the office to look through the glass door and asked him, 'There boy, have a look. Is that the man you saw at the door?'

'Yes, sir, that is definitely him.'

It seemed that there was now corroboration from an eyewitness. There were now grounds to bring a charge of murder against Ernest the handyman.

Not long afterwards, the next-door neighbour, Mr Caetano, was called in to testify and was asked to identify the young boy. He confirmed that, although it was very dark in the corridor, this was the boy he had seen in the corridor although dressed differently. Mr Caetano apologised for not turning up at the time of the inquest, but he had been in bed under doctor's orders. The police had served a subpoena on him.

Other individuals who moved about the neighbourhood were called to give evidence. Two particular individuals stood out from the rest. Diego Valle said that he sold miscellaneous things at the Jewish Market and had seen Ernest the handyman working in Miss Bossano's flat on several occasions. In fact, one day she had bought two curtain poles from him and had paid two shillings for them. He believed that she bought them shortly after she moved to Market Lane in August. Juan Bravo also worked at the Jewish Market, and he had been the person who had delivered the two curtain poles to the lady's first floor flat in Market Lane. When cross-examined, Juan claimed total ignorance about the affair and said that he did not know anything about anything (which brought laughter from the gallery).

Vital but Belated Evidence

PC Macedo had not given evidence before, but now, two and a half months after the crime, he was taking the stand as a witness to add some incredible evidence that also placed Ernest at the scene of the crime on the day in question at a critical but different time to that of the bread boy. In fact, he was now confirming the approximate time that the Chief of Police had deduced earlier as to when the crime had been committed. But this late report was an unbelievable omission by an officer of the law.

Macedo stated that he remembered that on November 29, he was coming off duty down Market Lane. It was a Saturday, and at about 2 p.m. he had finished his point duty in Main Street and was walking down Market Lane towards the police station at the end of his shift.

During the many years that I lived at 7 Market Lane, I often looked out of the window to watch the people going by. We became accustomed to seeing policemen coming on and going off duty, and we could tell the time accurately by the policemen's routine point duty changes.

PC Macedo said that as he passed the entrance of number 7, he looked inside because there was a money-changer's shop next door that had its rear door inside the patio. He said that when he looked inside, he saw a man wearing a light coat hanging from his shoulder in Spanish fashion; he was walking in with his back to the constable. The man turned round to look before reaching the stairs at the end of the passage. He stated that the man was the accused.

Recognising the fellow with the coat, he waved at him and said *adios*, though the man did not reply but merely nodded at him. He said he had known Ernest for many years, so he was positive it was Ernest, and he was sure of the date and the time.

On cross-examination, Macedo told the court that whilst the inquest was still going on, he had had an interview with the Chief of Police on the matter but that the Chief of Police decided not to introduce Macedo's evidence at that time. Macedo added that although he had known Ernest for many years, he had not seen him at Market Lane before. He certainly knew that Ernest was lame.

The Chief of Police had put notices in the press and on the radio and had distributed posters appealing to the public to come forward with any information they might have, or to report any suspicious thing or person they might have seen on November 29. The strange thing about this evidence was that Macedo had still taken almost a week to mention his observation of Opisso.

But the problem was not just Macedo's oversight in reporting. The other question was why the police's higher command did not itself ask the policeman on point duty at the suspected time of the crime to report every detail about whom and where or what he may have seen on that day of the murder. Macedo's stated reason for not reporting this earlier was that 'at first he did not think it important.' Yet the reason given by the Chief of Police was that in the first place he 'did not have Opisso under suspicion' and that 'Macedo was not an experienced policeman.'

In any event, this evidence by Macedo was seriously incriminating. His evidence helped the prosecution's case immensely.

Now came Consuelo's turn to give evidence. Consuelo was Miss Bossano's charwoman, and she said that she had never seen Ernest inside Miss Bossano's flat. Consuelo added some colourful details about the interior of Miss Bossano's flat. She expanded on what the hairdresser had already explained. Miss Bossano's dressing table was situated against the wall between two windows that looked down on Market Lane itself, and the light was good there during the morning. On the dressing table, there were two framed photographs a silver mirror and brush, both with long handles, a large comb, a cut-glass tray on which the lady placed her rings and jewellery, and a piece of decoration. This described the arrangement of the dressing table very nicely.

There was also a chest of drawers in the bedroom, and on it stood an inkwell and pen. Miss Bossano kept her account book and another book inside the top drawer. When she wanted to write, Miss Bossano transferred the inkwell and pen from the chest of drawers to the dressing table, which stood close to the window where the light was much better. There was also a wardrobe, and under the wardrobe she kept three basins, one inside the other. Two of the basins were enamel, but on a stand stood another washbasin and water jug of coloured porcelain.

The Medical Evidence and the Bloody Footprints

Dr James Durante was a well-known local family doctor. He had assisted Dr Griffith in the *post mortem*, and he now had his report to make to the court. His evidence was brief and to the point.

They had noticed that there was a tear on the left breast of the victim's outer garment. The garments were bloodstained, especially round the neck and forearms. The injuries consisted mainly of several lacerated wounds that perforated the skull and they varied from five to one and a half inches in length. They were chiefly situated at the back of the head towards the left. There was one severe wound on the top of the head that had obviously been caused by severe blows to the same place; consequently, a piece of skull had been completely dislodged.

One fracture implicated the left eye. Bone and hair had been driven right into the brain. Dr Durante made a diagram of the skull showing the injuries and explained these in detail to the court.

The *post mortem* revealed the remains of a partly digested meal in the stomach. The meal was taken within two hours before death.

Great force was necessary to inflict those injuries. From the *rigor mortis* he concluded that anywhere between forty and forty-eight hours must have elapsed since death to the time he saw the body.

Death, he said, had been caused by shock and haemorrhage caused by the lacerations to the brain and fracture of the skull. These injuries could not have been self-inflicted, and death must have taken place soon after the injuries were inflicted. He added that the wound running across the skull to the left ear was the first inflicted. It would have stunned her. A blunt rounded instrument caused the wounds.

Witness after witness was called to give evidence on various other matters: the photographer Mr M. Benjunes, a Frenchman, who was a tenant at the deceased's property; Helen Bossano, a cousin of the victim; and Mrs Juana

Bonfiglio from Catalan Bay village, who was a washer woman. All of them contributed something to the increasing drama.

Of all these witnesses, Juana Bonfiglio was the most important because she had washed a shirt and pair of trousers for Ernest. The washed clothes were produced in court as evidence. Did the shirt or trousers bear bloodstains, and when did she wash these items? The dear old lady could not remember either point. Was she being truthful?

The Attorney General had exhausted the presentation of the evidence he had for the moment. He produced the statement given by Ernest on 3 December prior to his arrest, but His Worship ruled that before this was presented, the circumstances under which the statement was made should be given.

The Chief of Police, Mr W.B.Gulloch, said that he had interviewed many persons in connection with the crime and had taken fifty to sixty statements, but the statement of Ernest Opisso had been taken by Inspector Santos at his orders, since Ernest was not under suspicion at the time and, furthermore, the statement had been taken in Spanish.

The Chief stood down and Inspector Santos took the stand. He said that Ernest had made his statement to him in Spanish. He in turn wrote it in English and then read it back to Ernest, because, he said, he knew English slightly and understood it well. (Neither the archives nor any of the reports contain Opisso's statement.)

The Chief of Police had several meetings with Opisso. The first was on 6 December at midday and lasted five minutes. Again Inspector Santos was present as translator. They had Macedo in the room and confronted Opisso with what Macedo had said— that he had seen him go into 7 Market Lane on the day of the murder at 2.00 p.m. The Chief of Police admitted that they did not take any notes of that interview, because even then he had not given much importance to Macedo's report, since Ernest was not under suspicion.

There was another interview with Ernest on the 9th. Again the Chief of Police admitted that no notes were taken by them. Ernest was also interviewed on the 15th and the 16th, but no mention is made of whether or not notes were taken of these meetings.

Dr Griffiths, the assistant surgeon at the Colonial Hospital confirmed that he had arrived at the scene of the crime with the Chief of Police, and the first thing he saw when he entered the flat was the body of the lady lying on the floor of the middle room on the linoleum. The bloody footprints made a trail from the bedroom to the sitting room. About eighteen inches from her head were found a gold pair of spectacles, and nearby a towel and a duster, which were coloured with blood. At the time when he examined the body, he had formed the opinion that the body had been dead approximately twenty-four to thirty hours. He performed a *post mortem* the following morning, 30 November, on the body at the Colonial Hospital in the company of Dr Durante.

A housecoat that the deceased was wearing was torn on the left side of the breast. The shoes were not clean, and the left one was more or less covered with blood on the tread. All the articles of clothing that the deceased was wearing without exception were stained with blood.

There were no signs of strangulation, and death might have occurred about an hour after a meal. One of the wounds to the head was consistent with having been caused when the body was lying on the floor. He remembered that splashes of blood on the wall of the sitting room were consistent with the lifting of a weapon saturated with blood.

The Chief of Police had given him a mat with footmarks in blood on it on 16 January for examination. The mat in question was produced, and he identified it in court. It was the same mat that was near the bed at the scene of the crime. The footprints were those of a right shoe or boot, and he was able, with the assistance of a magnifying glass, to reconstruct the whole of the footprints.

He was asked by the Chief of Police to take notes of how Ernest walked. He noticed that Ernest trod with his right foot turned inward and did not take the same length of step with his right foot as with his left. The right stride was two inches longer than his left. Ernest had been examined before, and the Chief of Police had been with him at the time.

Then a file was produced and handed to the doctor. He said the file presented a rounded surface and a flat surface and had two cutting faces. On the piece of bone handed to him, which was the piece of skull found dislodged next to the body, there was a depression with an apparently straight edge and a rounded edge. He had taken the point of the file and had introduced it into the depression in the bone, and it fitted well. The file had been examined under the magnifying glass.

He had observed that the edge on the bone corresponded with the teeth of the file. On one side the teeth were rather worn away, and even these missing indentations corresponded to the part of the bone. There were also two vertical depressions in the bone, which corresponded with the ridges or lines of the file. There was another depression near the cut, which corresponded to the plain surface of the file.

He had also examined the file under the magnifying glass, and it corresponded. There was a mark on the surface of the file more or less on the centre, and he had examined this too with the microscope, and in his opinion it was a scale of bone fractured in three parts, one large part and two small ones. He could not say whether it was human or animal bone. There were also other marks on the file, but he could not swear what these were. The tiny piece of bone was deeply embedded in the teeth of the file.

The Key

As the case unfolded, much new evidence was being gathered by the police.

A Spanish egg vendor said that he came daily to Gibraltar with his young son. One day at about 8 a.m., whilst they were walking with their baskets of eggs along Engineer's Lane close to Danino's Bakery, his young son, Leonardo Bueno, found a key in the street. This could not have been the Sunday morning, because they would not work on that day. He believed that it was on Saturday morning when this happened. They took the key to the bakery, and the owner, Mr Danino, told him to take it to the police station, which he did.

The question remained, was this key the missing key of Miss Bossano's flat? Did the police link this key with the missing key? It could have been, and for a while the police thought it was, but the time of day it was found did not coincide with the timing of the crime—the murder had not yet taken place.

Superintendent Brown was now giving evidence for the prosecution. He recounted how, about 9 p.m., PC Benvenuto had come to him saying that he was called urgently by PC Bacarisa to go to Market Lane. Bacarisa had made a quick report to him, and he had given immediate instructions to the constable there. He told how they fruitlessly tried to open the door, how eventually they got a hammer from the next-door neighbour, and how the carpenter, Ernest, broke the four panels of the door down. The superintendent described how Ernest finally repaired the electrical fuse. Ernest had stood on his left, and he had held everyone else back. He had entered the house alone and gave details of the whole scene. The victim was lying with her head facing the door. He reckoned that the woman was quite dead. He described the bloody scenario.

Brown ordered a constable to call the Chief of Police and Dr Griffiths to the scene of this brutal crime. They arrived twenty minutes later. The Chief of Police, Dr Griffiths, and the superintendent entered the flat together. He and Dr Griffiths went out and examined the entrance to the flat, the corridor, and the staircase outside looking for bloodstains. They saw none.

The superintendent noted that the body was fully clothed. The head, the linoleum nearby, and also a towel were soaked in blood. A pair of gold spectacles was also nearby, likewise soaked in blood. He observed there were large clots of blood between the body and the wall and blood splashed on the east side of the wall both underneath and above a small table that was against the wall. The furniture of the sitting room did not appear to have been disturbed. The glass panel door also had splashes of blood on its surface and its edge. He also noticed what appeared to be a thumb mark on the glass door. The door leading to the bedroom was ajar, and before he entered the bedroom, the doctor came out and certified that life was extinct.

At about midnight, photographs were taken. These photos were produced in court and explained. They showed the position of the body after they forced their entry into the flat. (See outline sketch of the corpse on the floor, Chapter 7).

Joe Caruana

The Bedroom

It was patently clear to the superintendent that the bedroom had been the scene of the crime. Whoever killed Miss Bossano had entered into her private bedroom. Why?

The bed was properly made and had not been slept in. There was a clock standing on a night table near the bed. The clock was stopped, and the time indicated was 3.55 p.m. Strangely this stopped clock was not the topic of further discussion or debate, yet it could have been crucial in the overall direction of the trial.

There were mats on the floor, a dressing table, a chair, a wardrobe, and a chest of drawers, on which they found a bunch of keys. There was also a washstand with clean water in the jug and smudges of blood on one of its edges. He found a coloured handkerchief on the floor near the wardrobe, and near this four enamelled basins placed one inside the other. The top one contained a very thick mixture of blood and water. Near the basins on the floor, there was a large pool of blood, and the basins were about one foot from the dressing table. A chair near the dressing table had splashes of blood on it. There were two photographs on the dressing table and also a few coppers, a hairbrush, two combs, a small bottle of ink, a black-handled pen, one pencil, a glass tray for pens, and a small black book. (See actual photo of the crime scene).

In the kitchen he found five cooked sardines on the kitchen table. There were no dirty plates or dishes. A small loaf and another half loaf were found in a cupboard. All the cooking utensils were clean, and no stains of blood were found in the kitchen. No doubt, this methodical lady had cleaned and cleared up after her lunch, which, according to Mr Canessa, she would normally take at around 1 p.m., and she then put everything away in its proper place. This cleaning up would probably take her between ten and fifteen minutes. It was very important and critical to take account of this fine timing therefore every detail and every minute prior to the murder needed to be taken into account.

From the foot of the night table to the bed, there were diagonal footprints in blood. Part of the linoleum in the bedroom was photographed and taken to the police station. The superintendent found a piece of skull on the edge of a carpet and several hairpins in the sitting room. He observed that there were footmarks of blood in the sitting room as well.

He added that it was not until 26 January at 6.50 p.m. at the police station that Ernest Opisso was arrested on a warrant for murder. That same evening, he ordered Opisso's house to be searched. The search took place in the presence of his mother, his sister, and Mr Galliano, who was one of the defending lawyers. He also searched a store belonging to Ernest situated in Cornwall's Lane.

The superintendent commented that, even in the daylight, the flat of Miss Bossano was very dark, and he had to turn on the electric light on so as to see clearly.

On more than one occasion, the accused had protested at being arrested during the investigation and had said that it was getting late for his lunch.

Was the File the Murder Weapon?

The superintendent continued his account. Whilst searching the store, they found three files and a piece of brass tubing, which they took. All of these were handed to the Chief of Police. The Chief had given Dr Durante the file for him to examine and give his comments.

Dr. Durante had examined the piece of skull that had been found by the body as well as the file. The skull bone showed two depressions, which fitted the file very exactly. One depression was on the edge and the other on the flat. In the middle of the file on the flat surface, a little piece of bone was firmly lodged. He had examined it under the microscope and had no doubt that the matter was bone.

A further expert was called to give evidence about the file and the bone. This was Dr J. E. Deale, assistant surgeon at the Colonial Hospital. This doctor had had seven years' experience in biology, and from 1920 to 1925 he had been a demonstrator in physiology and histology at the School of Medicine at Trinity College, Dublin. During that time, he had also been engaged in research work on those subjects. From 1923 to 1926 he had been an Assistant Professor of Physiology and Histology, subjects that dealt with the microscopic examination of tissues.

About the end of January, Dr Deale had examined the piece of the skull and the file, and he had noticed then that the end of the file appeared to fit exactly into a depression in the bone, which looked like a fracture. He had examined it purely with the naked eye. He had also removed a minute piece of cloth from this file and had carried out experiments with these fragments in search of blood, but he had been unable to detect its presence. Then in the middle of February, he had made further experiments, but with the same result.

However, in his opinion, the bone fragments on the file were consistent with being those from a skull, but he could not state definitely whether they were human, unless he examined them off the file. In his opinion, the bone had been on the file from about four to eight weeks.

Superintendent Brown was recalled and added that on 26 February he went to the accused's store in Cornwall's Lane and took away from there a large bunch of keys, sixty-seven keys in all, which were hanging underneath the counter. In answer to cross-examination, Brown said that, when he went there the first time, he had advised counsel for the defence, but in this particular instance he had not done so.

The court called the accused's attention several times for interrupting.

The Chief of Police was next, and he recounted what he had done on arrival at the scene of the crime. He had taken many notes and done many examinations. He had noted a bloody fingerprint on the glass door separating the sitting room and dining room. This would be the second glass door in the flat. He took several bloodstained articles and a bunch of keys. He had tried the keys in the lock. None worked at first, but when the back plate of the lock was removed, one key worked.

He had opened the chest of drawers as well as the wardrobe, and as far as he knew, there was nothing missing, and the flat was surprisingly in order. He took most of the evidence he found to the police station.

Various articles were produced in court for the Chief of Police to identify, amongst which was a black book. Counsel for the defence, Mr Serfaty, objected to the production of this book on the grounds that he had no knowledge of this book until now, but His Worship ruled that the prosecution was merely tendering something that had been found on the deceased's dressing table.

A piece of linoleum from the bedroom was produced, and the Chief of Police explained the position where the basins had stood on it and also pointed out the footprint of a right shoe or boot and that of a left shoe nearby. The footprint had been measured, and it was a man's shoe with a hard sole about eleven inches in length and worn down at the back of the heel. A second piece of linoleum that had been removed from the sitting room was shown in court. The Chief indicated footprints on it and two of these footmarks appeared to be those of a woman.

Then the accused's raincoat, shirt, and trousers were brought in. The raincoat was damp all over the outside, and the inside also appeared to be uniformly damp throughout. The raincoat was full of wrinkles and was clean even at the neck. The Chief said he had questioned Ernest as to when he had last had his coat washed.

Following his instructions, Superintendent Brown had brought a bunch of keys from the accused's stores, and one of these keys turned the lock of the victim's flat.

When the Chief had shown the accused the photograph with the deceased lying on the floor, the latter had turned his head away saying, 'I can't look at it.' The Chief told the accused, 'Take it. It will not bite you.' Then he asked the accused if had been to the deceased's flat on Saturday, to which Ernest replied that he had not. The Chief added that the accused had a peculiar walk and that he stepped shorter with his left foot than with his right and turned his foot inwards.

The Attorney General then proposed to put in evidence the black book that was found on the dressing table. The defence lawyer forcefully objected to this, saying that it was inadmissible since he was not aware of it and that the prosecution kept bringing up one surprise after another. He had been kept in the dark about this book. This being a capital offence, he felt it his duty to make all objections against anything that, in his opinion, might go against the rules of evidence.

The Attorney General argued that the book should be admitted and, in support of his argument, quoted the case of *Rex v. Podmore* (known as the Garage Murder Case) of 1930.

His Worship overruled the objection, and the book was handed to the Chief of Police, who was still the witness under oath. He said that there were items showing that the accused owed rents to the deceased, and on other pages there were details of work done by him for the deceased. There were tiny blood marks on some of the pages of the black book, even though the book had been found closed. On one such page there was an entry showing that the accused had paid the rents of his store for August and September. There was no entry that he had paid the rent for October and November. Another entry showed that Ernest had worked at Cornwall's Lane, and that page also had tiny blood spots. The page that recorded that Ernest had done the measuring of the cistern was also blood-stained.

Why were the pages that recorded the rent and work done by Opisso opened and exposed to the splashes of the blood? Obviously, the open pages were the last entries the victim had worked on, hence the inkpot and pen on the dressing table. These pages were the ones that had caught the blood-stains, perhaps as the attack on the lady took place. But was this enough to point a finger at Ernest Opisso?

Several other strong points of evidence needed to be considered by the magistrate before he referred the case to the Supreme Court for the next sessions of the Criminal Court.

Was the bread boy's evidence about seeing the accused at the victim's door, reliable?

It was shown that one key from the bunch of keys found in the accused's store turned the lock of the victim's flat. Had the victim given the handyman a spare key for some good reason? Or had the handyman worked for the previous tenant of the same flat and kept a spare key? This was a possibility.

It was said that the file removed from the accused's store bore similar shape to the indentations on the fractured skull, but was this the only file in Gibraltar with such a shape? It was a very common file, and the question was how many similar files existed in Gibraltar at the time.

Also in question was whether the bone in the file was human or animal.

Did the bloody footprints on the mat and the linoleum belong to the accused, or was it possible that another man and woman had been inside the flat at the time of the crime, whose footprint dimensions were the same as those of the accused and the victim?

Indeed, the picture looked pretty dim for Ernest Opisso. The evidence against him seemed overwhelming, but was it?

When the Hangman Came

With all these questions in mind, the magistrate declared that there were ample reasons before him to refer the case to the next Criminal Session of the Supreme Court. This was scheduled to take place in June of 1931. Ernest was cautioned and removed once again to the Moorish Castle Prison to await the main trial by a grand jury for murder, where, if he were to be found guilty, he would be sent to the gallows.

CHIEF JUSTICE, SIR KENNETH JAMES BEATTY Kt.

Sir Kenneth Beatty served in Gibraltar from 1931– 40.
He was born in Australia

Was educated at Melbourne University, Barrister-at-Law Middle Temple.
He served in the South African War; Natal and Zululand Rebellion
In 1906 he was Public Prosecutor, in Transvall, from 1903- 7.
Was Police Magistrate in Sierra Leone 1908.
Served in the European War of 1915 – 18.
He was urgently appointed as Chief Justice in Gibraltar to take charge of the Opisso murder trial, which was his first and immediate assignment on arrival from his tour of duty in Bermuda.

Barrister-at-Law.

Mr. A.B.Serfaty became extremely well known for his defence in the murder trial of Ernest Opisso. As he himself put it, *"I am fighting against a most formidable and experienced Prosecution team with the full force of the whole Police force against me, assisted by the most junior of members in the law fraternity"*.
He was born in Gibraltar in June of 1884.
He had three children, Moses, Olga and Norah. At the time of the crime he lived at 16 Parliament Lane. He worked as a Law Clerk for A.Carrara Q.C.
He wrote for the "Anunciador" and "El Calpense" newspapers signing as Sidney Graham. He took interest in theatrical productions and operatic Zarzuelas.
He started to study Law and at age 39 and was admitted to the Honourable Society of the Middle Temple in October 1923. And called to the Bar on the 16th June 1926. He died at 77 years of age in Tangiers and buried there.
A notable legacy of his was a small booklet called "The Jews of Gibraltar - Under British Rule". Written in 1933 with forward by Lt. Col. The Honourable A.E.Beattie, The Colonial Secretary.
The book was one of the first attempts to write the history of the Jews in Gibraltar.
He states in it how the Jews lived in peace with its neighbours except on Easter Saturday, when some people in the upper areas of town made an effigy of a man with a hat, this he says was set alight and carried down Castle Steps to the proximity of the Shaar Ashamayim Synagoge. Complaints were made about this disrespectful behaviour, but he noted that very little came from the protest, given that the custom was so established and was difficult to eradicate. To his credit this practise was eventually stopped.

Defence lawyer Mr. A.B.Serfaty.

MR.A.ISOLA , Q.C. , J.P.
LAWYER FOR THE PROSECUTION.

Mr. A.R.Isola was born in 1899 and died at the age of 61 in October 1960.
He went to Stonyhurst at the age of 15 years of age and studied there for four years.
He was called to the Bar in 1920, made a Justice of the Peace in 1931 and
King's Counsel in 1951. For several years he was Leader of the Bar in Gibraltar.
Was appointed 'Unofficial' member of the privileged Executive Council.
In 1950, following the New Constitution of that year he became the first Gibraltarian to be elected to the Legislative Council, topping the votes in the polls.
Politically he was an 'Independent' by inclination and stood alone fearlessly as advocate to causes he believed in.
He was President of the Gibraltar Jockey Club as well as President of the Mediterranean Rowing Club.
In 1930 he was awarded "La Medalla de la Paz", 'The Medal of Peace', by the Spanish Government.

Prosecution lawyer Mr. A. Isola Q.C. JP.

Top: John Discombe - A.B.Serfaty - S.P.Triay - A.P.Isola - P.G.Russo - A.F.Verano - ?

Seated: ? - Capt.Anderson - C.J.Sir Sidney Nettleton - A.C.Carrara - ?

Group photo of learned members of the Bar during 1930.

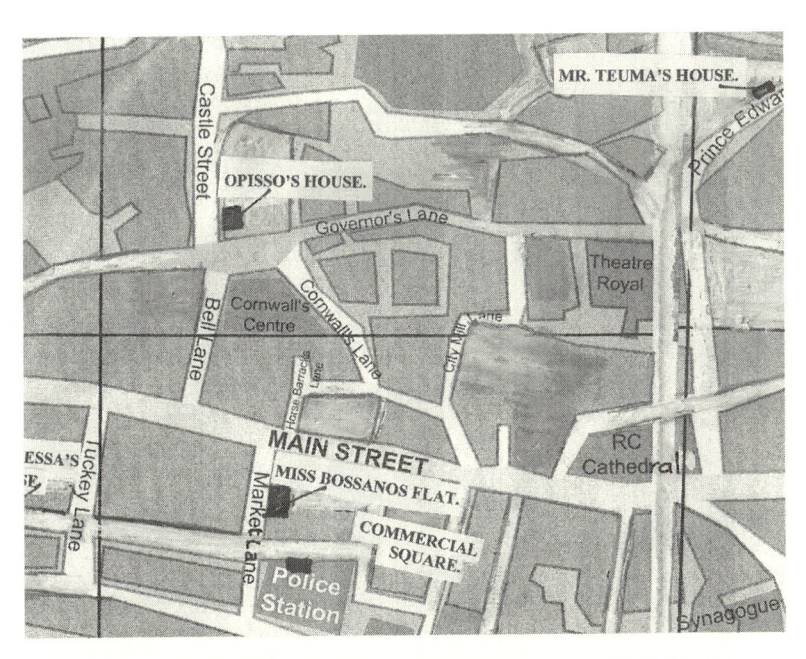

STREET LAYOUT SHOWING, MARKET LANE – CASTLE STREET – IRISH TOWN & MR. CANESSA'S HOUSE – COMMERCIAL SQUARE – POLICE STATION – MR. TEUMA'S HOUSE

Street plan of Town area.

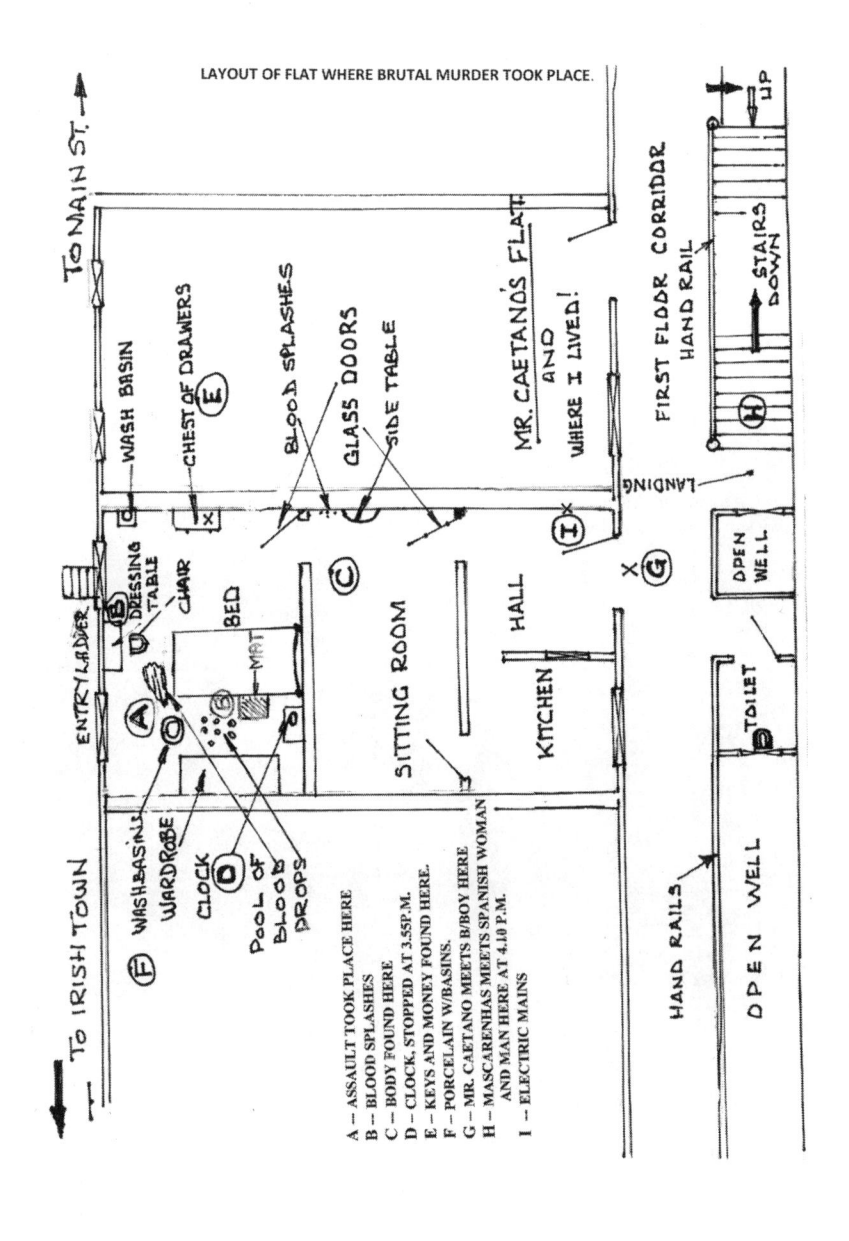

Author's Layout of flat where murder took place.

Chapter 4: Life in Gibraltar in the Years 1930-31

As the trial unfolded, the public was becoming aware of many unsavoury details that filtered through. The strait-laced *Gibraltar Chronicle-Gazette* was not very explicit in the gory details, but the court was always full to capacity, and the spectators' comments and descriptions of the events in court events spread. Among those who knew Ernest, there was incredulity and denial that Opisso could have committed such a crime. Yet those close to Miss Bossano were sure that Opisso was the culprit.

An Active Society and a Colonial People

However, life and business carried on as usual. The affairs of the community continued to function without interruption, and everything in the colony proceeded in a normal way.

The following extracts of news items and short reports were borrowed from the daily copies of the *Gibraltar Chronicle* and *El Calpense* of 1930 and 1931 (exclusively those copies that covered the trial), because it is imperative to relate the background of the drama. In this way, the reader can get the feel of the period, the place, the mood of the people, and a glimpse inside the culture and habits of the inhabitants of Gibraltar at the time.

If we are to understand the many and varied things that made Gibraltar tick and to feel its extremely dynamic spirit, it is important to give a brief insight to the colonial and social setting of the time. To borrow someone else's phrase, 'the Fortress came First.' Colonialism was everywhere, but the civilian population in certain quarters were struggling for representation, for a voice to be heard to address injustices and concerns. People power was in the making, but only just. The full emancipation of the civilian population had not quite yet taken place either socially or politically. This was to happen as the consequence of World War Two and the evacuation.

Looking at the examples mentioned below, we can deduce that there was a high level of participation in a number of activities by normal working-class individuals in Gibraltar, but the military forces were most active in them at the time. I should add that many of the activities that were going on during 1930-31 did have a high level of participation by the ordinary working-class individuals, but only as spectators. There were some sports, such as football and cricket, where locals participated competitively as teams. Other activities involved only a handful of locals. Nevertheless, the number of such activities was extremely high.

Gibraltar was very much a colony in every respect, and therefore the Rock was not without the typical colonial types of entertainment. For example, the Assembly Rooms were a large and popular dance hall that stood at the start of Europa Road and at the entrance to the very popular Alameda Gardens. These gardens, which were much in demand, extended in width from Europa Road to Jumpers Road, long before the Humphrey's Housing Estate was constructed and ate up at least a third of the gardens.

A very popular photographer had a special place somewhere at the entrance of these Gardens, close to Southport Gates. His name was M. Benyunes, and he played a part in our dramatic story. He would stand around with his tripod stand and square box camera, wearing his brown coat. He would insert a glass-plated negative into the side of the camera and would then hide his head under a short, dark cloth, hold the cadmium flash in one hand, and press the long wire-trigger with the other.

On the day of the murder, the *Chronicle* reports the birth of three male and seven female civilian babies. Only one male baby was born on that day to the military.

On Monday, 1 December 1930, the Calpe Philharmonic Orchestra held its dress ball. This meant that ladies would wear their elegant long evening gowns with full apparel, and men would wear their tails or tuxedos.

The Royal Calpe Hunt announced its meet at the 1st *Venta* in Spain on the 2nd and 6th of December. Dozens of riders and their horses, together with a large pack of hounds, would trot down Main Street into Spain for these outings. Although there were several well-known local members, the majority were military men and their wives. The Royal Calpe Hunt was indeed Royal, since the King of England and the King of Spain were its joint patrons. The Hunt Club had its origins when the Garrison's chaplain had brought with him from England a couple of foxhounds sometime in 1812. From this small beginning, it grew until 1939 and continued to hold its meets even during the Spanish Civil War.

The Gibraltar Golf Club met for their monthly award of medals, and two more dances was announced at the Assembly Rooms for the 9th and 10th. One was an evening dress ball in aid of 'Our Fund,' and the other a dance for commissioned and warrant officers of the Royal Navy.

The First Tourist Bureau

A couple of days after the murder took place, a comprehensive report appeared in the *Gibraltar Chronicle* of 2 December 1930 concerning the efforts that had been made by the Executive Council to improve many of the amenities in Gibraltar. Amongst other things, it reported:

Work had been started in what were to become two of Gibraltar's great tourist sites, the Rock Hotel and the Montague Bathing Establishment, a facility which had been built by the City Council, and was said to stand comparison with any that can be found at the most popular seaside resorts either in this part of the world or elsewhere.

The Gibraltar Museum is at last an established fact and though only opened a few months ago is rapidly acquiring a valuable and interesting collection of objects connected with the Rock and its famous history.

Many of these existed in the Colony before but were not accessible to the general public, being in possession of private individuals or institutions, such as Regimental Messes, the Garrison Library or City Council. By the generosity of their owners these objects have been either given or lent to the Museum so that all may see them.

The Rock has always been rich in historical associations and places but in the past tourists, on account of the difficulties of obtaining permission, could not visit these sites, and if permission was obtained, finding competent guides to take them where they wanted to go was almost impossible.

With the establishment of the 'Tourist Bureau' all this has been altered There is no longer any difficulty in the way of the visitor who wishes to visit any place of interest such as the Galleries Under the auspices of the government, a corps of trained guides is in the process of information.

Though much has been done in the short time since the scheme was started by the Government, and much more will be done in the future to attract tourists to Gibraltar, it was felt from the outset that something further was needed if they were to be induced to do more than pay the Rock a fleeting visit, and that was the establishment of a first-rate modern hotel, run on the most up-to-date lines and placing the satisfaction of its guests as the first and only consideration.

Here again, for a long time, there were many who held that such an institution would never be seen in Gibraltar, and it was not until work on the clearing of the site on the Europa Road, overlooking the Alameda Gardens, was begun a few months ago, that doubt gave way to belief. Even now there has been much uncertainty in the Colony as to what the completed hotel would be like but this will be dissipated by the view of it published above.

The site will give a beautiful view from the windows across the bay whilst its internal arrangements will be of the most modern type.

> There will be 75 bedrooms, most with private bathrooms and cold and hot water. Spacious dining rooms, lounges, drawing and writing rooms and an American bar, will be situated on the ground floor, whilst there will be shady wide verandas downstairs and good balconies to the bedrooms. Several suites will be available. In the plans consideration has been given to an extension when found necessary for another block with a further 25 bedrooms. It is hoped to arrange for tennis courts in the 13 acres of land that will be the terraced gardens of the hotel.

It is expected to open in January 1932.

Entertainment by the Military

The Fortress and Garrison of Gibraltar was well manned. Over 10,000 military personnel served the town. Casemates Square held the largest of the barracks. A couple of thousand men lived in the arched chambers in the second fortification the casemates of the fortress walls. Then there were South Barracks, Wind Mill Hill, Buena Vista Barracks, and hundreds of married quarters scattered in the upper rock and south district for non-commissioned officers.

The military provided a lot of entertainment for the civilian population, and naturally this served the military well, because it kept its troops occupied and busy. It was a wonderful experience for youngsters to witness the troops marching along Main Street and at the two great parade grounds, Grand Parade and Casemates Square.

On Saturday and Sunday afternoons, mothers would push their prams, and the young and old enjoyed their walk along the various beautiful paths in Alameda Gardens. There they took their seats to listen to the military band in the Alameda's big bandstand playing their repertoire of Sousa's military marches, with drums, trumpets, clarinets, cymbals, and French horns blazing away, filling the air with melodic and resounding grace. These regular shows were an occasion of great excitement and always produced much applause. Local bands also displayed their musical talents at the Alameda Gardens and entertained the crowds.

The Good Old Days?

The civilian population had its deprivations, but it enjoyed a luxurious service, rare in modern times, of door-to-door deliveries. People would hand in their grocery list to the shop, and their orders were then delivered to the front door. Charcoal, bread, fruits and vegetables, olive oil, fresh cheese, fresh goat's milk, fresh fish, and fresh water were delivered daily almost to your door, each vendor voicing had his sing-song call to announce his presence.

A deprivation of the day was that there was no electric cooking, and gas cooking was almost non-existent and a luxury. You either used a 'primus' oil stove, which you pumped to regulate the flame's intensity, or else you continued to use the charcoal fire built into every kitchen top.

Communal toilets for a block of flats were to be shared between four to six neighbours, and toilet paper was also a luxury, strips of old newspapers being much in fashion. Running fresh water was virtually unavailable. Almost every building in the town area depended on an underground water cistern. Water was drawn via a pump and then carried in buckets to your home. Those areas that did not have an underground cistern depended on the delivery of water by watermen, who would push a wheelbarrow loaded with small water barrels that they would carry on their shoulder to your house.

In far-off districts, the water would be delivered in huge barrels loaded on horse-drawn carriages. They would stop and shout *'El Agua!* Water!' The neighbours would come down with their buckets and be served under the tap from the huge water barrel.

Knives and scissors would be sharpened on a regular basis by the sharpener who would scream at the top of his voice *'Afilador!* Sharpener!' As he travelled around the district, he would blow on his penny whistle, which would warble loudly in the distance. One sharpening device was a converted bicycle that, with the motion of a treadmill, would rotate the grinding wheel. Streams of sparks would pour forth as the edge of a steel knife or scissors was sharpened.

One particular street vendor would roam around announcing the sale of *'calentita.'* He carried a huge round flat pan, which he balanced on top of his head, containing a delicacy made of a mixture of baked chickpeas, olive oil, water, egg, salt, and pepper. He would slice this thick pancake-like delicacy in small sections and serve it on a piece of old newspaper.

Another fellow could be heard crying out 'Paris, sweet Paris!' and this individual would serve you delicious flavoured creams on a coned wafer.

Yet another fellow, the peanut vendor, pushed his cart along the way stopping at street corners. On his cart were a variety of nuts, peanuts in the shell and off the shell, almonds and hazel nuts fresh or roasted Almonds were also sold caramelised, just like the toffee apples and the kids would gather round and get their penny's worth of goodies.

During the summer months, the homemade ice cream vendors would sit on the street corners on their bicycle-cum-icebox and would ring the bicycle bell to call attention with the chime. The ice cream was kept frozen inside these iceboxes with the help of huge chunks of ice.

The Prescott family was the owner of the ice and ice cream factory. Years later, when I was a young boy, I would offer my services to help at the ice cream factory, which was located, luckily, at street level almost below our flat. I would help the young ladies there by dipping ice cream squares on a stick into a very hot chocolate pot. Somehow I managed to get a fair portion of the spoilt chocolate bars on a stick.

In winter the chestnut vendors stood at strategic locations in town, roasting their chestnuts in a stack of cooking pots placed one on top of the other. They did not have to announce their presence; the smoke and the smell of roasting chestnuts by itself would attract the crowds. The majority of these vendors were Spanish nationals.

Education had come mostly from church bodies. The Catholic schools had the Christian Brothers and the Sisters of the Loreto Order. The Methodist and the Jewish communities had their own schools as well. By 1930, the colonial government had taken an interest in the education field and a director of education, who also came from the UK, had been appointed. This was an important development in setting standards for the education system in Gibraltar.

Government-run social services had been virtually non-existent. They had merely reacted to specific needs and problems, but slowly the colonial government was starting to take an interest in social matters. However, here again the churches had been in the forefront. The Catholic Church in particular, through the St. Vincent de Paul Group, helped the poor. There was always a soup kitchen. They also ran the Gavino Orphanages for girls and the St. John's of God (Benso's Home) at 7 Palace Gulley Steps. The Sisters of Mercy, through the St. Francis Clinic, relentlessly made house calls to the sick, lonely, and elderly. The nursing sisters, *Les Soeurs de Bon Secours,* at Library Street had their own home and moved around the town as well.

The Asylum for the Aged was run by the Little Sisters of the Poor. The *Haz Dalim* was the Jewish Poor and Sick Benevolent Society. There were also the Protestant Poor Fund, the Soldiers, Sailors, and Air Force Family Association, and the Hebrew Poor Asylum at Beriro's Home. Additionally, Gavino's Asylum in Prince Edward's Road and the Gibraltar Home for the Sick and Aged served the peoples' needs. (Directory of *Gibraltar Chronicle,* 1930)

What a spectacular list of outstanding endeavours! One wonders how many kind and charitable persons, religious and lay people alike, gave of their time and money. Many made a life-long career of these charitable activities. There have always been people who care, and for this reason an executive committee for the inauguration of a branch of the National Institute for the Blind was formed in this year (1930), and His Excellency the Governor attended and presided. This, no doubt, ensured the enrolment of plenty of supporters.

St. Vincent de Paul Bazaar

One particular event was the annual bazaar in aid of the Society of St. Vincent de Paul, the biggest and most dedicated of the charities to the poor, that took place in the presence of a distinguished gathering of patrons and representatives of all classes of Gibraltar society headed by The Right Reverend, Dr R. J. Fitzgerald, DD, Roman Catholic Bishop of Gibraltar. The organising committee, with Mrs J. A. Patron, at the bazaar received the Governor's deputy, Colonel Hon. H. C. Maitland-Makgill-Crichton and Mrs Maitland at the entrance to the convent.

The bazaar was the principal source on which the society depended for funds, and unfortunately the need was great, and the struggle became more difficult every year.

There were a number of attractive stalls, amongst which may be mentioned those presided over Mrs L. Imossi and the Miss Larios (flowers and vegetables), Mrs E. Imossi and Mrs Rooney (chocolates), Miss Patron (leatherwork, etc.). The tearooms were in charge of Miss R. Imossi, while Miss P. Gaggero had done excellent work in procuring 1,000 prizes for distribution.

At one stage on the day of the bazaar, Mr Manuel Linares Rivas performed a comedy in three acts '*No Quiero, No Quiero.*'

It was hoped that the funds of this excellent charity would have greatly benefited as a result of the bazaar and the theatricals. (*Gibraltar Chronicle*, April 1931)

Entertainment High on the List

The Garrison Cinema stood where Ince's Hall now stands, but the most popular local cinema then was by far the Rialto Cinema. It appears that live shows were much preferred to the 'magic box.' The Theatre Royal showed both live shows and films. There was also the Naval Cinema, where they were showing at this time two great comedy films *Silver Comes Through* and *Three Kings*.

When the Hangman Came

The amount, the frequency, and the quality of the shows that were continuously being shown at the Theatre Royal are extremely impressive—English and Spanish plays, dramas, comedies, and musicals. There was no lack of variety at the Theatre Royal, and it certainly stood out as one of the most popular places of entertainment.

Second in line for entertainment were the Assembly Rooms and the Racing Hippodrome, where both horse races and dog races were much frequented.

And there were also moving pictures shown at the Theatre Royal—'Talkies! Talkies!' A futuristic film produced by Fox's Grand Productions was showing about life in the 1980's. 'Come to the 1980s,' said the advertisement! It was an English film with Spanish subtitles. A variety of theatrical companies came from all over Europe to perform at the Theatre Royal. Dancing companies from ballet to Spanish flamenco dancing performed in this beautifully decorated theatre of three levels, with private booths on either side of the stage on the first two levels.

The Great Caruso sang in the Theatre Royal. Lola Flores, the Russian Chorus and Ballet, and many others also took their turn to visit the Theatre Royal or *Teatro Real*.

In one issue alone of the *Gibraltar Chronicle*, dated 10 February 1931, no less than three write-ups of three different shows appear. The first write-up was of a play that received great acclaim and half a column's report. A cast of actors from the forces club must have performed the show, since none of the names are recognisably local. This English-language play was called *Braltar Brightoned*. The names of the main characters in the play were Sir Orange Bastion, Miss Jago Hargraves, Miss Rosia Parade, and Mr Town Mayor. One particular actor was hailed highly for his versatility in quadrupling the parts of a P&O Steward, a policeman, the master-at-arms, and a guide. The stage scenery had the Alameda Gardens as its backdrop, and the company boasted of an excellent chorus, whose dancing and singing was extremely good.

The second performance that week was one presented by the Association of Musical Culture. Pilar Bayona gave a piano recital on Sunday of three parts. The first part was taken up with renditions from the works of Beethoven. The second part was wholly taken up by Spanish music, and the third part with pieces form Saint Suer's and Liszt's *Polonaise*.

The next show that week at the Theatre Royal was by Sugrane's International Review. It had come straight from the *Teatro Comico* of Barcelona and was composed of seventy artists. The review had a line of English girls that would appeal to the English-speaking audiences in Gibraltar. The first performance took place at 10 p.m., but it was hoped that on future days it would be shown earlier, since 10.p.m. was too late for many members of the fleet to be able to attend.

The *Chronicle* also records that yet another great performance at the Theatre Royal was The Forbes-Russell Comedy Company's rendition of *Bluebeard's 8th Wife*. The early part of the performance was somewhat marred by the arrival of latecomers to the theatre; otherwise the play was enjoyed by all.

The Man in Possession was to go on stage the following day; this play had recently had a successful run at the Ambassador's Theatre in London and was much anticipated on the Rock.

Some of the advertisements in the newspapers boggle modern-day thinking. Medical science, it seems, was far in advance of the times. We have often heard that a glass of wine is what the doctor ordered, but the following advertisement that appeared in the 1930s beats them all. 'How to Assist the Digestion' was the slogan for an advertisement for White Horse Whisky. It told the public:

> Thus many a man has found a virtue in WHITE HORSE, taken just before or just after lunch or dinner. And, of course, you know that WHITE HORSE WHISKY is non-gouty. See that your medicine chest contains a bottle of WHITE HORSE WHISKY. Because it is so safe and so sound and so certain in the good it does. (Obtainable in flasks of varying sizes.)

But that was not the only recommendation for good health. There was another excellent advertisement that took the health of the public seriously: the advertisement for Craven A cigarettes said, 'It is specially made for you to ease sore throats.'

And from across the Atlantic, the international news from Chicago reported:

> The notorious gang leader Al Capone appeared in court for the first time for years, charged with contempt of court in connection

When the Hangman Came

with the non-payment of income tax. The case had been pending for two years. Foot and mounted police guarded all approaches to the court and, with the greatest difficulty, cleared a way among the hundreds who surged in. Capone had arrived in the city secretly to participate in the nomination of Big Bill Thompson as candidate for the Mayoralty.

The British Ambassador to Rome sent an urgent message to the Governor announcing the melancholy news of the demise of His Holiness Pius VIII, which took place at 9.30 p.m. on the 30 November.

Closer to home on the treacherous coastline of the Straits of Gibraltar, the Yugoslavian steamer *Drima* ran aground on the rocks off Tarifa Point. The salvage steamers *Rescue* and *Express* belonging to Messrs H.M. Bland went to its assistance.

The busy firm of H. M. Blands put up notices giving details of a temporary modification of its service to Tangiers and Casablanca by the *S.S. Gibel Zerjon*, which service came into force from 1 January 1930.

At the police court, Francisco Ruiz Garcia, a Spanish vegetable vendor, was charged with overloading his donkey and was fined ten shillings or ninety-five hours imprisonment. Inspector Vella of the GSPCA had brought this to the attention of the authorities. Yet another offender, a Spanish chauffeur, was fined two shillings and six pence or two and a half hours imprisonment for carrying more than the authorised number of passengers in the motorbus.

The Calpe Tennis League was now coming to the end of its season, and the Gibraltar Tennis Club needed to gain a decisive victory in their next and final match to prevent the Royal Engineers Tennis Club from displacing them from their position as holders of the trophy.

Another form of outdoor entertainment was horseracing. The Gibraltar Jockey Club had a very active season with regular race meetings. The highlight of the season was the Empire Cup. A particularly interesting race announced for the month of February 1931 was the inter-regimental point-to-point horse races. No less than fifty-one horses took part in these point-to-point races. The contestants were the Royal Navy, the Royal Artillery, the Royal Engineers, the Lincolnshire Regiment, and the Calpe Hunt Club. It seems to have been a rather confusing race, because the team with the lowest points wins the race. The horse that comes first gets one point, the second winner two points, the third three, and the fourth four points. Only the points of the first four horses to cross the line from each team get counted. It was impossible to find who won the race because it was cancelled due to rain.

One particular race, announced for a sunny weekend, consisted of ten races with about sixty horses participating. The local newspapers gave a very detailed account of the condition of the horses, the jockeys, and the trainers.

Horse races in both Gibraltar's racecourse and the Campamento Hippodrome were extremely well attended. Next to the Gibraltar Race Course, Victoria Gardens, was a favourite for family outings.

Football was a very popular pastime, and the local civilian team would often play against the garrison's eleven. In one such game, the match ended in a 1-1 draw. The civilian team was composed of Navas (goalie), Verano (capt.), Gaetto, Raffo, Bado, Torres, Alvares, Cardona, Joselle, Jones, and Balbuena. The referee was J. Noguera. The civilians would also face teams composed of members of the visiting naval fleets.

In the face of so many activities, the trial of Ernest Opisso continued, and the public got glimpses of the developing story from the local newspapers, in particular the *Gibraltar Chronicle*, the *Anunciador,* and a very eloquent *El Calpense*.

Assembly Rooms Dancing Hall

Castle Steps Opisso's House 1st on Right

Ice Cream Vendor

The Honky Tonk

Chapter 5: The First Trial

Trial at the Criminal Courts

It was now 27 April 1931. An escort of two prison officers brought Ernest Opisso from the Moorish Castle Prison to the criminal courts for judgement by a jury. In judgement sat the Chief Justice, His Honour Sir Kenneth Beatty. Sir Kenneth had been sent an urgent cable whilst he was on vacation in the Caribbean and he arrived just in time from a tour of the West Indies to attend to this case.

It did not take long for a jury to be formed. Capt. A. Patron, was selected foreman of the jury. Messrs Andrew J. Ferrary, John Joseph Hayes, A. M. Hassan, W. Piccone, W. S. Roscoe, Charles Povedano, Angel C. Rugeroni, Albert Bacarisas, Charles B. Beanland, Lionel Imossi, Isaac R. Massias, Charles Imossi, Alfred Vasquez, Hector Posso, Charles Gaggero, Joseph Noguera, George F. Imosi, Charles Savignon, Joseph A. Rugeroni, Harry C. Reynolds, Horatio Scullard, and Edward Bassadone, a total of twenty-three jurors, were selected.

The judge asked the jury to take their oath and instructed them that their duty was to deal with the evidence given as presented before them and to come to a decision according to the oath which they had taken. They were cautioned as to discretion and secrecy.

The prisoner's two escorts brought him in and showed him to the dock. The officer of the court read out the charge of murder against him: 'that on 29 November 1930 the accused had wilfully caused the death of one Maria Luisa Bossano.'

The Attorney General first called Mr Joseph Canessa, who was a relative of the victim and who had gone to the flat at Market Lane where Miss Bossano lived on Sunday the 30th. Joseph Canessa lived at 53 Irish Town. Irish Town was one of the busiest streets in town. Canessa lived in an apartment block sandwiched between several tobacco and coffee-processing factories.

Mule-led carriages would come along Irish Town to unload the huge bales of tobacco. The fine Virginia tobacco, *El Rubio* or 'Golden,' went into making English cigarettes, and this came all the way from the United States, though its importation went back to before the American War of Independence, when Virginia was very much a part of England and was governed from Westminster. In fact, after the War of Independence, when American ships were banned from using many European ports, they were nevertheless allowed to come to Gibraltar. This waiver made Gibraltar a priority destination for the import and exportation of tobacco. The strong black tobacco, *El Negro,* came in leaf form in huge bales from Brazil. The leaves were crushed into tiny flakes and packed tight into quarter-pound packs that were a favourite in Spain.

It was said that 'from the high-born to the low-born,' everyone in Spain was involved in smuggling. The fine Virginia tobacco was smuggled to the Cadiz region. Naturally, the black tobacco reached Portuguese ports from the Portuguese colony of Brazil. Therefore, the black *El Negro Picadura* from Gibraltar was only smuggled into neighbouring regions and the Malaga area. It is understood that Mr Emanuel Viales gave a detailed account to the Governor of how these smuggling operations took place.

The cocktail of aromas in the Irish Town area was a rare mixture that pleased some and displeased others. As you walked past the coffee factory, the pleasant smell of the roasting coffee greeted the passer-by, but a few paces further, a curtain of pungent tobacco dust filled the nostrils and throat, forcing pedestrians to hold their breath for a while. Mr Joseph Canessa, one of the principal witnesses, happened to live at 53 Irish Town. To the right of his entrance stood the famous coffee dealer, the Sacarellos. To his left a few doors down were two tobacco-processing factories.

All this was far removed from Mr Canessa's mind because now he was taking the stand in the Opisso murder case. Mr Canessa said in court that he and his relatives were worried that they had not seen Miss Bossano during the previous two days. This, they felt, was unusual. Maybe, they thought, she was ill and needed attention. He had knocked on the door without success and, getting no answer, he decided to go to the house agents and try to get a key. On the way there, he met with Ernest, who had done some work for him and for Miss Bossano, so who, he thought, would be better than him to help him with the opening of the lady's flat.

Constable Bacarese said that, with the help of Ernest, they lifted the sash of one of the windows of the flat. The shutters were wide open, and the room was in darkness. Ernest stood astride the windowsill. He struck a match and then saw a basin full of water and blood.

The details of the sequence of events followed very closely the details given at the inquest and the police court hearing.

PC Bacarese said that he noticed that when Ernest finally broke down the door, he hesitated and looked doubtful about stepping in and moved slightly back, but the accused did not appear to be trembling or excited and had not hesitated about breaking the door down. The superintendent was the first to enter the flat followed by himself, then Mr Canessa, and then the accused.

The superintendent then gave evidence and said that he ordered Ernest to break down the door. The superintendent added that when he had given evidence at the police court, he had mentioned that he had seen what appeared to be a thumbprint on the edge of the glass door and that at that moment Ernest, the accused, had said *'Mentira,'* which means 'It's a lie.' But neither the translator, nor the defence lawyer, nor the clerk of the court heard him say this.

Superintendent Brown said that he had been in the police force fifty-four years and had been second-in-command of the Gibraltar Civil Police Force since his arrival in the colony about twenty years ago.

The Superintendent clarified that when he had retrieved a large bunch of keys from the accused's store, on orders from the Chief of Police and at the suggestion of the judge, the defence counsel had not been informed and therefore was not present. He had shown the large bunch of keys to the charwoman Consuelo, who cleaned the victim's flat, and she immediately picked the right key from the bunch that worked on the victim's lock. But so did one of the keys found inside the flat on the victim's dresser when matched the lock.

He corrected the statement he had made at the inquest that it was he who had turned on the electric mains. In fact it had been Ernest Opisso who had done this.

He also added that he had been present at the police station when Dr Griffiths and the Chief of Police made certain observations about how the accused walked. The accused's counsel had not been asked to be present during these observations, and he further added that he had not interviewed the accused before his arrest, although he was present during one of the interviews.

A rather unorthodox series of events had occurred whilst the inquest was in progress. Brown said that whilst the inquest was still on, PC Macedo had an interview with the Chief of Police, six or seven days after the deceased was found, to inform him of the extremely important observation that he had seen the accused going inside the patio where the victim lived at about 2 p.m. Yet Macedo for some reason had not brought this out before and had not been brought forward as a witness to give evidence at the inquest. He added that the bread boy too had made a statement at the police station and that he too had seen the accused at the door of the deceased, but because he was not precise about the date, he was not called to give evidence at the inquest either.

When asked, Brown said he could not say why the accused's store was not searched before his arrest. Brown had been present when the photograph and the lady's bloodstained coat belonging to the deceased were shown to the accused.

Following an allegation by the accused that Sergeant Gilbert had put his hand on the accused's breast to see if the accused was palpitating when questions were put to him about the photos and the coat, Brown said that he had not seen this done, even though he had been present at this interview. However, he heard Sergeant Gilbert saying to the accused, 'You did not return with the cord after measuring the cistern because you had killed her.'

This was apparently an accusation made before Ernest was actually arrested. The fact that the lady had asked him to measure the water level in the cistern on a Friday afternoon and that Ernest had done the job and not returned the cord and weight used for measuring the water level was not indicative of anything. Maybe Ernest thought, ' the water tank is not full, so why bother the lady on the weekend? I'll wait till Monday morning.' This was a very logical consideration. Brown continued that the accused had not objected to the taking of his fingerprints and that he the Chief of Police, Dr Griffiths and Sergeant Gilbert, Sergeant Reyes, were all present when this was done. Brown said that it had not occurred to him to advise counsel for the accused when the bunch of keys was removed from the store or when the experiments as to how the accused walked were made.

Nothing special, he claimed, was prepared for this observation, but it so happened that the patio outside the cell was wet and the charge room was dry and swept, so as the accused walked on his way to the courtroom upstairs, he left his footmarks on the dry floor. It later transpired that the patio had been purposely wetted by throwing a bucket of water over it. He said he never had the accused's footmarks photographed.

He had also made experiments of how the accused walked by throwing sawdust on the floor of the civil prison, but it was very difficult to verify whether it was the woman's footprint on the linoleum or the deceased's because the mark was very faint. He added that he had carried out his observations of how the accused walked to ascertain the direction of the tread and also to see if there was any peculiarity in his walk.

In his statement, the Chief of Police said that he did state at the inquest (and this appeared in the *Gibraltar Chronicle* on 20 December) that he had made a reservation that should be borne in mind. He reminded the court of his precise words at the inquest which were, 'The police had no further evidence to produce at this stage that might help the jury in arriving at their verdict and that the police were following up certain lines of enquiry but they were not complete.'

In this way the Chief thought he was covered, since he had not asked either PC Macedo or the young bread boy to give evidence at that time. Holding this information back was a strategy that did not favour the defence, who had been kept in the dark about these two crucial witnesses.

When the Chief of Police asked the accused to look at the photograph the accused said, 'Take it away. I cannot look at it.' The Chief then repeated to the accused 'Take it. It will not bite you.' Ernest's disinclination to look at a gory photo of a bloody corpse was not an indication of guilt and this would be a natural reaction of any person who is affected by the sight of blood.

The Chief of Police also showed the accused the deceased's overcoat, which he had previously confirmed as being the one worn by the lady when he had seen the body at the hospital on the 30 November.

He gave a practical demonstration to the court by trying one of the keys from the bunch brought from the accused's stores, to show that it turned the lock.

When the Chief was cross-examined by the defence, he added that one of the short interviews he had with the accused was concerning the fact that PC Macedo had reported to him that he, Macedo, had seen the accused entering the patio on the day of the murder. He added that he had not taken notes of what the accused had said because he was not then under suspicion. He was asked why PC Macedo had taken so long in reporting seeing the accused at the scene of the crime. The Chief said that in the first place, the accused was not under suspicion, and secondly, he did not think that Macedo had been slow in reporting to him the information, as he was not a very experienced constable, but by the time the accused was giving evidence at the inquest, he personally had the accused under suspicion.

The Chief of Police said that when the photograph showing the deceased on the floor in a pool of blood was shown to the accused, it was not intended to frighten him.

He had closely questioned the accused as to the visits he had made to the deceased flat, and all the questions were put in English and to the best of his abilities were interpreted by Sergeant Gilbert. He had not noticed that the accused had been angry when he was questioning him, but he knew that he had been grumbling because he had been kept waiting for some time before he was interviewed. He added that neither he nor anybody else in his presence had pointed at the accused saying, 'You, you have murdered her.'

This statement was later shown to be a lie, because the police accused Opisso on a couple of occasions that he had killed the lady.

As the trial proceeded with the Chief of Police as witness, he was handed portions of the linoleum from the victim's flat to view and he stated that the footmarks in blood on them were, in his opinion, those of the right toe of a woman's shoe. Both shoes of the deceased had blood on the tread.

When the Hangman Came

Then the Attorney General re-examined the Chief of Police about the raincoat, and the Chief of Police replied that he was surprised at the dampness of the raincoat because the weather had been dry at the time.

The Chief clarified that the key found by a small boy in Engineer's Lane was, according to his information, found on the window sill of a Mr Cohen's shop, but he was still in doubt as to the date when it was found.

As to the fingerprints on the black book, he was now satisfied that they did not belong to any particular person from whom they had obtained fingerprints. These were the fingerprints the Chief of Police had taken to Scotland Yard in London, but this in itself was an amazing statement, since it had been determined in London at Scotland Yard through examination by experts that the prints did not belong to any particular person that they knew of, so to whom then did they belong? The Chief of Police did not mention this piece of important information during the trial.

In reply to a question from the judge, the Chief said that he had measured the shoes that were removed from the accused's house and had also made comparisons with the footprints in blood found on the linoleum, and they were of the corresponding size.

He categorically denied having used 'third-degree' methods.

Police Inspector Ernest Santos stated that on 2 December he had acted as interpreter at an interview between the Chief of Police and the accused. The Chief of Police questioned him at length, and he had also been sent with the accused to another room to take down in writing what the accused had said. He took down his story as he gave it to him. The accused had given his statement in Spanish, and he himself put it into English. Because the accused had said that he knew a little English he had read the statement to him both in English and in Spanish. The inspector had no difficulty in understanding what the accused was saying, as he had known him since childhood and knew about the impediment in his speech.

Ernest Opisso's statement was read. The accused described how he had met Mr Canessa, how they had obtained the ladder, how they had climbed to the flat from the street, and then how he had broken down the door at Inspector Brown's orders. The accused stated that on Friday, 28 November the deceased had called him as he was passing under her window and asked him up. He went up to the deceased's flat, where she asked him to measure the water cistern of her property at Cornwall's Lane. The deceased had given him a cord with some lead attached to it, and this he had kept in his store after using it. He had measured the cistern on Sunday, 30 November, and his intention was to inform the deceased on the following Monday. He added that he knew her very well and used to do odd jobs in her flat for her.

Inspector Santos added that he had been present when PC Macedo had made a statement to the Chief of Police in the presence of the accused and when the accused heard this, he had interjected, saying 'That is not true.' Macedo's statement to the Chief of Police had been that he had remembered having seen the accused entering the patio in Market Lane on Saturday, 29 November at about 2.00 p.m.

The next witness to be called was Dr Gilbert Henry Collin St. George Griffiths, assistant surgeon at the Colonial Hospital. (The name alone gives a fair idea of the double-barrel names typically used by those posted to the colony.) He described how he was called and went to Market Lane and saw the body of the deceased. His description was similar to the one he had made at the inquest, but he did add that the wounds on the head and the position of the body were consistent with the blows having been inflicted when the body was lying on the floor.

Dr Griffiths went into detail about the injuries that were found on the deceased and also about the measurements of the footprints in the blood found on the linoleum. He then produced paper specimens of these footprints, which were examined by the jury. He explained that he had been able, with assistance of a magnifying glass, to reconstruct the whole of the footmark, which was that of a right shoe or boot. He then gave a practical demonstration with paper specimens of the footprints in blood on the mat found in the deceased's bedroom.

He had observed how the accused walked at the police station. His right stride was two inches longer than his left, and he trod with his right foot turned inward and did not take the same length of step with his right as with his left. The footprint on the mat turned inwards.

Then an iron file and the piece of skull were handed over to the doctor. He stated that there was a depression in the bone with an apparent straight edge and a rounded edge. He had examined it, and the outline of the file with its teeth fitted exactly into the depression in the bone. There were also two vertical depressions in the bone, which corresponded with the ridges of the file, and another depression near the cut, which corresponded to the plain surface of the file. He had examined the file very carefully under the microscope and had found embedded in the teeth a scale of bone fractured in three parts, one large part and two small ones. He could not say whether it was human or animal bone. He further gave a practical demonstration with the file and the bone to the jury. The accused asked to see the demonstration and the doctor showed it to him.

Defence lawyer Mr Serfaty then cross-examined the doctor. The doctor said that before entering the flat of the deceased, he made an examination outside her flat and had not rushed to inspect the body, because he had already been informed that the deceased was dead. When he finally saw the deceased in her flat, he had formed the opinion that she must have died not later than 10 p.m. on Saturday, 29 November and that the same weapon he had just shown must have caused the wounds on the deceased's head. He had examined the edges of all wounds very carefully, and the weapon that caused these wounds must have been nine inches long or more and could not have been five inches long.

Sergeant Gilbert took the mat, which he had examined, to his residence. Gilbert and he had examined it some six or seven weeks after the murder had been discovered. He could have taken an impression of the footprint by cutting the mat. On the mat there were also other marks in blood but he could not say what they were. A piece of linoleum was shown to him, and he stated that the footprint on it was that of a woman's right foot, and on another piece of the linoleum there were two prints, one that of a man's left shoe and the other what appeared to be a man's heel.

The judge asked him to clarify what in his opinion was important about these items. The doctor said that he had carefully examined the file and also the piece of skull and that the depression found in the piece of bone fitted with the teeth of this file or an identical instrument.

The doctor now gave a new suggestion. The finding of the towel and the duster near the deceased gave him the impression that they could have been used to stifle her cries.

Mrs Letitia Prescott Bossano had seen the deceased at about 10 a.m. going past Barclay's Bank on 29 November. She provided another important piece of evidence. She added that whilst on 27 and 28 November it had rained heavily, the morning of the 29th was a perfect day, but it started to rain at about 11.30 a.m.

Busy Morning of the Accused

It appears that the first person to see Ernest Opisso was Mr Joseph Bousquet, a Frenchman and a tenant of Miss Bossano's at 28 Cornwall's Lane, who testified that he had seen the accused on Saturday morning in the house where he lived and that he was measuring the water cistern with a piece of string and a lead weight. The accused had shown him the string and had pointed out to him that there was yet another foot of water left to fill the cistern. He had explained to the accused that the entrance of the building was flooded. He left on an errand, and when he returned about half an hour later, the accused had already cleared the drain. The accused showed him what he had done. It was about 11 a.m. (This time is questionable, as it conflicts with the time given by the Canessas).

The second person to say that he had seen Ernest Opisso was Mr Joseph Canessa, who was the next witness, giving his full account of what had happened on the morning of 29 November. He added that he knew the accused well and that he was a handyman who had done jobs for him and the deceased. On Saturday morning 29 November, he saw the accused in his house doing some painting at about 11 a.m. He added that he went out and returned. He had also done some work for Mr Canessa's mother at her house, and Ernest was still there when he returned at about 12.30 p.m. He left soon after.

Third, the bread boy said that he saw Ernest opening the door to the victim's flat at about 12 p.m.

Ernest went home for lunch and, according to his sister and the charwoman, arrived there at about 1 p.m. After lunch he went to Mrs Canessa's house at about 2 or 2.30 p.m. to tell her he would be coming back to her on the following Tuesday. From there he went to Mr Teuma's house; he got there about 3 p.m. and left at about 6.30 p.m. Mr Teuma had given evidence that when he left his house at around 4.30 p.m., the accused was still there. Later he changed this observation to 5 p.m.

The only strange thing about this last visit was that the accused said he went there to play with the baby of the house. Mr Teuma had three girls

When the Hangman Came

aged twelve, six, and eighteen months and a boy aged ten. It is difficult to understand why he did not do any work there. Why would he stay that long at Mr Teuma's house? Was his fondness for children that great? Yet Mr Teuma testified Ernest was still at his house at 5 p.m., and he found nothing wrong or strange with this. He actually added that Ernest used to stay late at his house and had done this before.

Detective Constable Wahnon testified that he had been sent to the accused's house to look specifically for a raincoat, and he found it hanging in the corridor. The whole of the lining was wet, and it was rather wetter on the back. The accused's mother had told him in the presence of the accused that some of the accused's clothes had been washed a few days before at Catalan Bay. The detective took with him a shirt, a pair of trousers, and the overcoat belonging to the accused.

When cross-examined by the defence lawyer, the detective stated that when he pointed out the dampness of the raincoat, the accused told him that he had it washed and had only worn it about twenty times and that the raincoat had been given to him.

The detective said that he had not verified whether it had rained the days before he had gone to the accused's house, although he could have found this information in the *Gibraltar Chronicle*. Counsel for the defence then read the meteorological observations, which appeared in the *Gibraltar Chronicle* for the whole week of the previous December, when the damp coat had been retrieved from the accused's house. The detective on further cross-examination said that he had not found any stains (of blood?) on the raincoat.

The Chief of Police had previously said, when giving his evidence, that he had not verified on what day it had last rained before 9 December. He could have easily have found out, but he did not think this very important, and through an interpreter he had asked the accused when had he washed the raincoat. It had been verified before that the raincoat had been found to be damp inside and outside, that even the collar was clean, and that the raincoat was heavily wrinkled.

Following this witness, the prosecution brought forward several other witnesses. Joseph Caetano, the deceased's neighbour, was recalled and was cross-examined about seeing the bread boy. The boy's employer was also questioned, and he reaffirmed that he had been to Market Lane several times with the boy and that the boy knew several neighbours there. He was positive about the day and the time.

A new witness appeared, a Major E. O. Singer, SMC. He stated that, accompanied by Police Inspector Santos, he had gone to Catalan Bay village on Monday and had seen Juana Bonfiglio, a washerwoman who was seventy-eight years of age and a chronic invalid who would be unable to attend court as a witness on account of her health. She was the woman who had given evidence at the police court the previous February, when she stated that she had washed some clothes for the accused.

Inspector Santos said that he had taken a statement from the lady, and this he read out to the court, although it was rather brief. Yes, she had washed some articles of clothing for the accused and also for his family, and she remembered having washed a pair of striped trousers and a shirt but did not remember when she had washed them for the last time.

Then came the turn of Dr James Durante, who repeated what he had said at the police court. When questioned, he said that he did not think that the injuries could have been caused by a piece of mirror shown to him. He repeated that he had examined the piece of skull and the file and had observed two distinct depressions in the bone, which fitted the file exactly, or a similar one. He had also examined under the microscope a scale of bone found embedded in the teeth of the file and was prepared to say that it was consistent with the bone of the skull, though he could not definitely say that the bone was human. He did not think the file had been thoroughly brushed, as there were some other particles of different things on it, such as wood, a white substance, and iron, etc.

When re-examined by the Attorney General, he stated that fresh blood would be very easily removed with water, and had the file been used for the murder and washed soon after, the blood would have disappeared. On questioning from the judge, he said that the piece of bone in the file would have remained lodged even if washed. He was sure it was bone; it could not be anything else.

To corroborate this evidence, Doctor J.E.Deale, assistant surgeon at the Colonial Hospital, stated that he was unable to detect the presence of blood on the file after a search for it on two occasions.

But what was the white substance that was stuck to the file? The jury was shown the file in question, and on cross-examination by the defence lawyer, Dr Deale said that he had examined the file on three different occasions, twice in the police station and once at the Supreme Court, and he thought that the white substance on the file was lime.

The Chief of Police, W.S Gulloch, was recalled, and he identified a hairbrush produced in court as having been found at the flat of the deceased. In the opinion of the Chief of Police, the crime had already been committed when PC Macedo saw the accused going into the patio. When referring to some footprints found close to a chair, he said that it was assumed that the victim must have sat on it before she died, but no one could say who had left the footprints.

After this last witness, the Attorney General informed the court that this closed the case for the prosecution.

The Case for the Defence

Mr Serfaty, in opening the case for the defence, spoke earnestly and eloquently for one and a half hours. Owing to the length of the speech, it is only possible to give a summary of it here.

He started by stating that all the resources of the Crown were arrayed against the prisoner. The prosecution had the Attorney General, assisted by Mr A.R.Isola, one of the ablest barristers whom Gibraltar had ever had, the Chief of Police with all the forces at his disposal, the doctors of the Colonial Hospital—all these were against the prisoner, who was a poor man, lame and deaf, with an impediment in his speech. On the other hand, he (Mr Serfaty) bore on his shoulders all the weight of the defence of a man on trial for his life, with only the assistance of the most junior member of the Gibraltar bar, Mr Galliano.

Mr Serfaty then dealt in detail with the evidence of the various witnesses for the prosecution, which he alleged was in nearly every case conflicting; whilst on several points, witnesses were in entire disagreement.

When Mr Serfaty cross-examined the bread boy, who had said he had seen the accused opening the door to him. He asked the boy if he remembered the colour of the shirt the accused was wearing. The young boy replied that he could not remember.

According to counsel, Dr Durante, who had assisted at the *post mortem*, had never seen the piece of bone which, it was alleged, had the marks of the file on it, and which Dr Griffiths asserted fitted perfectly into the marks on the skull. This file, the most important piece of evidence, was not found by the police until after the accused had been arrested.

The mat, according to counsel, was not thoroughly examined for footprints until seven weeks after the murder.

Counsel stated that when he had cross-examined Dr Griffiths on a certain book dealing with footprints, the doctor seemed to consider it of small account as it was a German publication, Dr Griffiths, who was called as a police surgeon and not as a detective, appeared to have been more interested in investigating bloodstains and fingerprints than in examining the victim.

Counsel referred to the evidence of the Spanish baker's boy as most amazing. This boy testified that in the few seconds the door of the flat was opened by the prisoner, he could swear to the colour of the latter's shirt and the dirty mark on it, and also the way his hair was done.

Counsel criticised severely the methods used by the police to secure the identification of the prisoner. He was not at all happy with their methods.

In his summation for the defence, Mr Serfaty brought forward a few witnesses, one of which was Mr Stephen P. Wall, who identified the bone-handle umbrella produced earlier as belonging to his wife and stated that he had given this to the accused for repairs some time the previous year.

Did the next witness provide an alibi for the accused for the time of the murder? Again Mr E. F. Teuma, who was the clerk of the justices, stated that the accused was in his house on Saturday, 30 November around 4.00 p.m. and when he (Teuma) left his house at 5 p.m., the accused was still there. Mr Teuma added that he had not observed anything abnormal about the accused. Mr Teuma had taken down the depositions in the police court in December 1930 and had also acted as clerk to the coroner. He did not hear the accused say *'mentira'* (lie) in the police court. So what did Superintendent Brown hear the accused say?

Teuma also identified a bone-handled umbrella as belonging to his wife and stated that the accused had mended it. On questioning by the judge, he stated that he was sure about the time when he saw the accused in his house. The judge asked this question because Mr Teuma had given a slightly different time at the police court. Mr Teuma's statement introduced a dilemma for the prosecution. The timing Teuma was giving did not fit in with their theory, because it posed the question, when did Ernest have the time to commit this awful murder?

PC Macedo would have left his beat in Main Street punctually at 2.00 p.m. He had seen the accused shortly after 2.00 in the entrance hallway to the patio in Market Lane. Since the doctors had placed the time of the murder between 2.30 and 4 p.m., the accused must have moved like lightning up the stairs, knocked and waited for the door to be opened, been allowed in or opened the door himself, and talked or argued with the victim. All of these actions took time.

He must have carried the file with him in his pocket, so he must have gone with premeditated murder in mind, since he was not due to do work there. He then committed a most violent crime, washed his hands and the file, and then left the flat without making a noise. He had then limped his way to Mrs Canessa's house, which was about ten minutes away, and reached the house by close to 2.00 p.m. Was this timing realistic and possible, since he was not able to run or walk very fast?

The defence called another witness, Miss Luna Beniso, one of the neighbours, who happened to be looking out of her window on 29 November when she saw the hairdresser going into the patio at about 2.30 p.m. and saw her come back out almost immediately. She again saw the hairdresser at about 4.30 p.m., this time coming out of the building. She did not hear any shouts or screams. When cross-examined by the prosecution, this witness said that when she was at the window she was on the lookout for a friend to arrive. It was pouring with rain, the hairdresser was carrying an umbrella, and she recognised the hairdresser by her walk. On being asked by the defence about this sighting, Miss Beniso said that although it was raining the first time the hairdresser went in at 2.30 p.m., her umbrella was closed.

Opisso Testifies

The last of the defence's witness was, of course, the accused himself, Ernest Opisso. He said he was a handyman who did painting and carpentry. He knew the deceased, had a store on her property, and had done work for her. He mentioned that he had last seen her on Friday the day before the crime.

He gave a detailed account of all his movements and everything he had done—the procurement of the ladder, the entry into the victim's flat through the window, the breaking down of the door on orders from the superintendent, the switching on of the lights, the visits to the police station, the giving of statements, and the fingerprinting.

He added that he did not know the bread boy. The first time he had seen him was in the street in the company of a policeman who, he noticed, had nudged the boy to look in his direction.

On the Monday after the body had been removed, he went to the deceased's sister's house to condole with her, and that same day he informed the police about this visit.

He was asked by PC Wahnon to go to the hospital. When he got there, he was told by Police Sergeant Ferro to go and see the body, and he did so. After that, he went to the police station. Again at the police station, he was shown photographs of the deceased lying on the floor. This photo was shown to him several times.

He said that the coat belonging to the deceased was shown to him by Detective Sergeant Gilbert. He was sitting down, and the sergeant put the coat near him and touched his face with it saying, 'Do you recognise this?' Detective Sergeant Gilbert kept on showing him the coat and also putting his hand on his heart.

Then Detective Sergeant Gilbert and Mr Brown accused him of killing her. He replied, 'I have not killed her. I don't kill anybody.' He got indignant with this and other things that were told to him. He had even gone with the police to his house and had seen several articles of his clothing removed. Three searches had been carried out in his store before he was arrested.

When he broke open the door he had his raincoat with him.

When asked if he had worked on bone before, he answered yes, he had worked on bone before. He had repaired two umbrellas (these were produced in court and identified by him) and also a horn trumpet. He had used the file mentioned previously for this work.

He said that if PC Macedo stated that he saw him on Saturday in the patio of the deceased, it was not true. When he went to the hospital to inspect the body of the deceased, he met the charwoman who had given evidence in one of the corridors of the hospital. He concluded by saying that he had not killed Miss Bossano nor was he capable of killing anybody.

Then Ernest was cross-examined by the Attorney General. In answer to his question, he said that he was sure that he had left his raincoat hanging in his house from the Tuesday after he had viewed the deceased's body at the hospital until the police took it away. It had been left hanging from Tuesday until the following Tuesday, when it was removed by the police, a period of one week.

The prosecution continued the cross-examination. When he had seen the boy with the constable, the boy had looked at him and he had looked at the boy. He had heard that the boy was looking for a fair man and woman who had been in the deceased's flat. He did not remember seeing the boy at the police station, though he had seen many people there.

The bunch of keys shown to him was kept hanging on the wall in his store and had been taken by the police when they visited the store.

He went at 2.30 p.m. on Saturday to Mr Canessa's mother, and before that he had been to his store and had also passed Market Lane. He had gone to the Canessa house to discuss certain work that had to be done by him in her house. He stayed at Mr Teuma's house from 2.40 p.m. until it became dark but did not do any work.

Prosecution Winds Up

The Attorney General opened his final speech for the prosecution by telling the jury that he wished to speak to them not personally, but as a jury. As a jury, they had taken the oath, and that oath carried with it a great responsibility.

If they were satisfied on the evidence they had all heard and if there was no doubt about any benefit of the doubt, then they should decide guilty, but if there was any doubt, so long as it was reasonable doubt, then they should find the accused not guilty. They had a responsibility not only to everyone in Gibraltar but also to all courts of British justice, and they would be shielding a murderer if they did not do their job. Let it not be said by their consciences that they were approving what had been done because they had no courage. They must do their duty and let their consciences answer.

He continued that they had been told about the physical defects of the accused and this had been done to arouse their sympathy. One could not help feeling sympathy, but all that must be put out of their minds. Let them remember that down at North Front a poor woman lay buried with a battered skull, while a piece of it was an exhibit in court. Let them have sympathy with the prisoner, but let them do justice to the victim. They had to deal with hard facts, not sympathy and sentiments.

The prosecution said that Opisso's playing with Mr Teuma's children on the Saturday afternoon and his condoling with the relatives of the deceased was deliberate acts on the part of Opisso. The Attorney General referred to the famous local case of Calvo, where the murderer, who was afterwards executed, not only condoled with the relatives but also attended the funeral of his victims.

He said that the police had been attacked and ridiculed in this case from beginning to end, and a bad atmosphere had been created about them. But what about the file and the skull? There was no getting away from that evidence, which had hardly been touched on by the defence but there had been a great deal of talk about discrepancies. How was it possible for a busy man like the Chief of Police to remember dates and times exactly when he was interviewing hundreds of people? Was it not likely that an occasional slight mistake might be made as to a date?

The prisoner could understand a little English. He got the gist of what he was being asked; for he was no fool, and when the whole question had been interpreted in Spanish, he gave answers that were no reply at all. He answered questions as to events after the woman's death, but prevaricated at questions about his doings on the previous days. He said his mind was in a whirl when relating to facts about the time of the crime, but not about Sunday and the other days.

The Attorney General then referred to the evidence of the doctors, who were in agreement that the piece of bone was 'live' bone and not a particle from the bone of a dead animal. Dr Deale testified that the piece of bone in the file was a piece of human live bone, which could only have been obtained from bone, which had been shattered by a blow and not by filing. The file, which belonged to the accused, was found in his custody under lock and key. It fitted perfectly and absolutely into the piece of skull. No other file in creation could have caused the depression, unless it had happened to be cast in the same mould.

The iron file was shown to the jury, and the prosecution declared that it was the file that had been used in the commission of crime and that it belonged to the prisoner. Neither the tests done in Gibraltar or those done in the month of February at Scotland Yard had shown any presence of blood on the file. Deale was to report that the fragments on the file were consistent with being those from a skull, but he could not state definitely whether they were human, unless he examined this off the file.

The Attorney General then addressed the question of the footprints. He asserted that the man who stood in the box put all his weight on his right foot as a man with a short left leg and that the right footprint was clear although the left a little smudged. This was not coincidence but sheer hard fact and the man in the room who did the murder was a man with a short left leg.

There had been a great deal of cross-examination about the raincoat. He alleged there was little doubt that here had been bloodstains on the inside of the coat, so that the prisoner could wear it two or three days, and no one would realise that the stains were there. His assumption was that when the prisoner realised that the bloodstains were there, he had the coat washed, and that was why when the police took it away a week later the coat was still wet, not only outside but inside as well. The Chief of Police had said that the lining of the raincoat had been crinkled as if it had been washed and squeezed.

The Attorney General asked, 'what was the defence? An alibi up to 12 noon and after 2.30 p.m. on the Saturday.' The conclusive evidence of the file and the skull completed the case for the Crown there was no motive proved, they said that it was not necessary for the Crown to show a motive and that it made a case much easier, that was all.

He added that the file fitted the depression in the skull according to the evidence of three doctors, and there was the observation of their own eyes to back up the medical evidence. They had seen the bit of bone under the microscope.

He concluded his speech by again asking the jury not to be influenced by the fact that the man in front of them had certain disabilities, but instead to remember Miss Bossano and the future generations before them and to return such a verdict as would enable them on returning to their homes to feel that their consciences were clear.

Judge's Summing Up

His Lordship, the Chief Justice, then summed up the case for the jury. He told them that 'they were not concerned with the punishment of the crime. Whenever a verdict turned on capital punishment, a jury might let this thought predominate, but it was of no importance to them. They must concern themselves with facts alone. Gibraltar was a small place, and it was no doubt difficult not to hear discussion of the case before they came to court, but they must eliminate all that they had heard outside and concentrate on the facts they had heard in court.

The *onus* of proof was on the Crown, and if they had any reasonable doubt about the guilt of the prisoner, it was their duty to give him the benefit of that doubt.'

It was a difficult case with a mass of technical evidence, which had been very ably put forward by both sides. The court was always more satisfied when the case was well defended. He said that 'unfortunately the police were very often attacked in criminal trials, as has been the case in this instance; but the jury would have come to the conclusion that there was no foundation for these attacks. Possibly, things might have been done a little differently, but in his mind, the worst accusation that could be brought was that there had perhaps been a little excessive zeal in the conduct of the case.'

Mention had been made of 'third-degree methods.' There was nothing, however, to support this allegation except the word of the prisoner. If his statement were correct, it would be most scandalous thing. The police had no objective in bringing an innocent person to death.

His Lordship then dealt with the various evidences and concluded by reminding the jury once again that their duty was to deal with the facts as presented in accordance with their conscience and with what had been brought before them.

The Hung Jury

At 1.40 p.m. the Chief Justice asked the jury to go and deliberate all that they had heard. At 9.50 p.m. the jury returned, and the Chief Justice again took his seat on the bench. The Chief Justice asked the jury if he could be of assistance to them. The reply he received was in the negative, so he informed the court that as there was no provision in the laws of the colony for taking a verdict on a Sunday, he would be available again at 10 a.m. on Monday.

All of the previous day and throughout the present day, a huge crowd had gathered anxiously in the vicinity of the courthouse awaiting a verdict to the murder trial of Ernest Opisso. Under escort, the jury was marched from the courthouse to the Bristol Hotel.

At 5.17 p.m. on Monday, 11 May 1931, His Lordship the Chief Justice took his seat on the bench and sent for the jury. In reply to the clerk of arraigns, the foreman of the jury stated that the jury could not agree and that there was no probability of their coming to an agreement. His Lordship then stated that he did not see any object in keeping the jury any longer and discharged them after thanking them for their services. The foreman of the jury expressed to His Lordship the jury's thanks for the comfortable accommodation that had been provided them during the trial.

His Lordship ordered that the accused be put back for retrial at the next criminal sessions to be held on 8 June. The trial that had started on Monday, 27 April had now concluded on 11 May with a hung jury. The trial had lasted fourteen days, and the jury had been out for thirty-six hours.

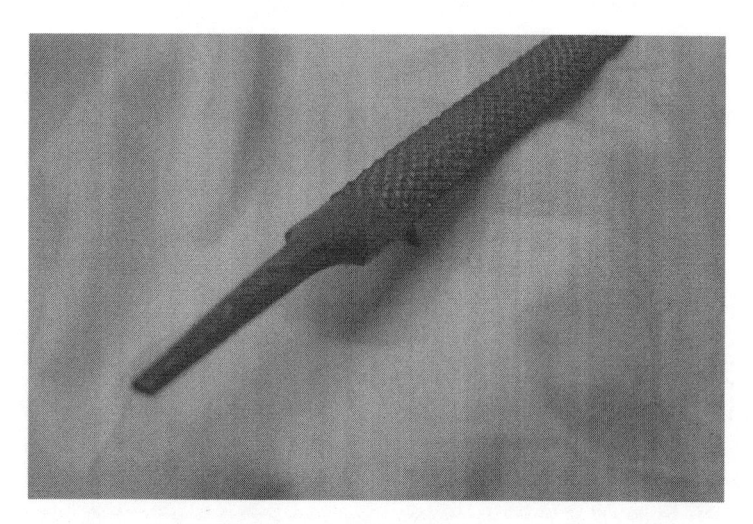

"ESCORFINA" – ALLEGED MURDER WEAPON.

KNIFE SHARPENER, POSSIBLE MURDER WEAPON.

UMBRELLA WITH PART BONE HANDLE.

THE SUPREME COURT

Chapter 6: Spectacular Parade and Naval Review

A large naval review was organised at the Alameda Parade Ground, now known as Grand Parade. A composite battalion had been formed from the ships' companies of *HMS Centaur*, the 5th and 6th Destroyer Flotillas, *HMS Lucia*, and the Submarine Flotilla. The battalion was over 500-strong, drawn up in parade column facing the saluting base. The senior officers who were not taking part in the parade stood on the platform behind the saluting base whilst the bank immediately to the rear was lined by crowds of spectators, amongst who were many naval and military officers and their families and civil officials.

The day was perfect for the holding of a ceremonial parade, and the glint of the sun on the swords and bayonets and on the gold lace of the officers' uniforms added greatly to the attraction of the spectacle. The precision of the movements with arms, the steadiness in the ranks, and the excellent alignment and distance maintained during the march past were specially remarked on by the onlookers, amongst whom were many well qualified to judge.

Grand Mediterranean Fleet Visits Gibraltar

The visit of one of the largest fleets to Gibraltar was a spectacular affair, both in the harbour and the streets of Gibraltar. This particular day, 18 March 1931, saw no less than twenty naval vessels in port. The flagship was the *Queen Elizabeth*, leading no less than three squadrons of fourteen battle cruisers, four destroyers, and two submarines, accompanied by several flotillas of frigates.

The crowded harbour was packed. Every possible available mooring and docking space was taken up. The dockyard and victualling personnel worked night and day, seeing to the various needs of one of the largest formations of battleships ever gathered during peacetime.

When the Hangman Came

The ships' crews had a schedule for shore and land activities, such as football games, tennis, and cricket. A schedule of inter-vessel tournaments had been previously been organised, and every available playing field and place was in use all day long.

However, the sailors' favourite pastime was going into Main Street. Viewed from a distance, the street was a sea of white caps. Sooner rather than later, the sailors entered one of the many 'honky-tonk' beer parlours that could seat over a hundred sailors at one time. There were about five of them and these honky-tonks were famous all over the Mediterranean region.

Some more adventurous members walked about through the narrow streets of the town, searching for a bit of skirt. There was one well-known district, called New Passage and Serfaty's Passage, where certain ladies, who came from Spain, offered their charms to the young sailors, some of whom were barely eighteen years old.

The honky-tonks provided entertainment in the form of a noisy band on a stage; some of these bands were composed of women musicians. Other friendly and much-painted females acted as hostesses and would join the sailors at the tables for a drink and a pinch! The drinks served to these ladies were usually coloured green to resemble a mint drink, but they contained no alcohol. In this way, they could order repeated drinks without getting tipsy. Those days turned out to be rather rowdy, and early in the afternoon the shore patrol started doing the rounds and encouraging those lads who had exceeded their limit to return to their ships. Some became so drunk they could barely stand on their own two feet, so they needed a 'taxi ride' in the patrol's 'Black Marias.' The worst time was at 9.45p.m. when 'Last Drinks, Gents!' was called for closing time.

At exactly 10 p.m., the customers would all be asked to leave the premises of the honky-tonk by some tough 'chucker out' (more nicely known as the doorman). Most of the sailors were unable to walk and tended to scuffle and shove. Many would sit on the road kerb sick as hell whilst others became belligerent and would invariably start to fight amongst themselves. The shore patrol and the local police had their hands full on these occasions. The cells at the police station would be full to over-capacity, and the poor, unfortunate fellows would sleep off the hangover.

One of the most popular military events on the Rock has always been the Trooping of the Colours. This time it was the turn of the resident

1st Battalion of the Lincolnshire Regiment. The ceremony took place at Alameda Parade Ground. The traditional ceremony dates from the seventeenth and eighteenth centuries. This particular one was marred by rain and a heavy Levant, but nevertheless the exercise went off with great precision. Spectators were not as numerous as on other occasions.

However, on the occasion of the visit of the Atlantic Fleet it was announced that His Excellency the Governor and Lady Godley were giving a dance for midshipmen and cadets of the Atlantic Fleet. There were about one hundred and seventy persons present at the dance. Music was provided by Miss Doris Lockey's band from the Royal Hotel. The excellence of its music was much appreciated and commented upon by all present.

The most spectacular view of the port and bay of Gibraltar was when the combined fleets of the Mediterranean and the Atlantic and the Home Fleet came to port at the same time, possibly consisting of over 100 naval ships. This gave an impressive show of power. Britannia certainly ruled the waves. A naval review marched down Main Street, consisting of no less than 4,000 navy personnel.

Gun practice was always notified to the public two days in advance. These practices were extremely regular.

Another report in the Gibraltar Chronicle informed us that Sydney Franklin, a matador from the USA, who achieved popularity in Spain in those years and who had taken part in the billing at a bullfight in Algeciras, had been badly gored in a bullfight in Nuevo Laredo, Mexico. He was supposed to have fought four bulls, but he was gored by the first and was taken out of the bullring unconscious.

The Spanish Revolt

Heavy snow in northern Spain had closed down railway lines, and many services had been interrupted. The snow was reported to be six feet high in some of the mountain passes. The snow was so heavy in Santander that sleighs pulled by donkeys were being used as transportation.

Four years earlier, there had been an alleged plot to kill King Alfonso. Finally those involved in the plot were brought to trial. It was believed that the King would be killed when he attended the funeral of the Marques de Estella.

From Santander, Spain came the announcement of the shipment of £1,000,000 in gold to London. This was the second shipment of the year.

Late in 1930, there was a revolt in Spain. The rising was put down, and martial law was proclaimed in Algeciras, La Linea, and other places in the neighbourhood by the placing of placards and the sounding of drums and bugles. His Excellency General Mario Muciera, Governor of Algeciras, also issued a proclamation to this effect. An uprising had occurred at the Aerodrome of Cuatro Vientos, but the rebels, led by one Major Ramon Franco, and the others flew to Portugal and arrived safely at Lisbon.

A Spanish transport arrived in Algeciras with a battalion of the Spanish Foreign Legion, who soon took a train for Madrid. It was understood that further units of the foreign legion and detachments of the civil guards were expected from Morocco on that same day. The legionnaires were unwilling to go to Madrid, but promise of double pay soon solved this problem.

Several arrests of persons believed to be ill disposed to the government had been made in the neighbourhood. Algeciras and La Linea remained quiet, and an attempt by the representatives of the revolutionary committee to call a general strike was frustrated by the prompt action of the authorities. Meanwhile in Spain, the Bank of International Settlements was attempting to set out a programme to stabilise the peseta.

A political revolt had been crushed, and General Quell de Llano, the leader of the revolt at Cuatro Vientos Aerodrome the previous December, had been dismissed from the services as a deserter. A decree had also been published expelling from the army Major Ramon Franco and five other officers at present in exile.

It was reported that Sr. Alcala Zamora, the ex-Minister for War, before the court that was conducting the preliminary examination into his conduct, had accepted full responsibility – for the air raid over Madrid. He said the Republic was to be proclaimed on 15 December, and one of the revolutionaries had been detailed to conduct the royal family to the frontier. The revolutionaries had relied on seventeen garrisons to revolt, but the hastiness of Captain Galan at Jaca upset the whole movement.

Steady progress towards a return to normal conditions was reported from all over Spain. A proclamation issued at Madrid ordered all arms to be surrendered. The province of Alicante produced the most serious incidents, and peasants completely dominated several small towns for some time.

The liberal organ *El Sol* complained that it had not been allowed to publish recent leading articles from the *Times* and the *Manchester Guardian*.

Madrid had a night of terror. The city was seething with excitement, and a squadron of troops had been called out in consequence of collisions between republicans and monarchists on the occasion of the latter opening an election campaign. Civil guards fired, inflicting casualties on a crowd attempting to storm and set on fire the office of the newspaper *ABC*. Two republicans and one member of the civil guard were seriously wounded when the civil guards fired A machine gun was reported to have been installed to repel possible invaders and subsequently, the crowd angrily demonstrated before the Ministry of the Interior.

In view of this recent political unrest, King Alfonso of Spain proposed holding a general election as soon as possible with universal suffrage.

15 April 1931 was one of Spain's darkest days. Eventually, the Spanish Republic was proclaimed, and the King of Spain for a while became a puppet king of the Republican Party's Primo de Ribera. Soon afterwards, he abdicated and was shown the way to Paris. Owing to the political instability, there was a run on the Spanish banks. The prelude to a civil war was in the making and one day, the rightists in Spain would seek revenge.

What happened next in Spain is told in brief in the first chapter of this book.

Meanwhile, one of the world's most popular comedians, Charlie Chaplin, was awarded in France the Legion of Honour Award of the Insignia of a Chevalier by Philippe Bertelot, Premier of France.

And at home in Gibraltar, life continued its normal very colonial course. The Calpe Tennis League was coming to the end of its season, and the Gibraltar Tennis Club needed to gain a decisive victory in their next and final match to prevent the Royal Engineers Tennis Club displacing them from their position as holders of the trophy.

The Calpe Hunt

In Gibraltar, the Calpe Hunt seemed to have a very active agenda. Towards the end of the year of 1930, they announced several hunts, almost on a weekly basis. Two meets were announced, one to meet at Guardacorte and the other one at the Almoraima.

One particular hunt was held in the second-to-last week of the year. The description of that day's hunt was extremely interesting and exciting, very quaint, and very English. When reading about this hunt, one almost gets the impression that it was taking place in some corner of the English countryside and not in the south of Spain.

The club, of course, colourfully designated the hunting areas in the nearby region with English names. In the Palmones district, there were 'draws' with the names of 'Matthew's Gorse' and 'Rocky Cavern' that held a 'brace' where hounds were unable to push on out of the thicket and cold-scenting covert. Then came 'Badger's Town,' which drew a blank. Further down were 'Dyers' and 'White' coverts. Then came 'Connolly's Hollow,' where a fox must have been scented that took them all the way towards 'Hankey's Gorse,' but the fox turned very sharply left and then went away in the open from the northeast corner, where Miss Larios viewed it from the high ground.

(Miss Larios was the daughter of Paul Larios, a very wealthy anglophile resident of Gibraltar who had the title of *Marques*. The Larios family had come to Gibraltar from northern Spain to escape the French. In time, they family settled in Gibraltar and did very well in many commercial ventures in the colony and in the surrounding Spanish region. They owned all the Cork Woods around Los Barrios and Jimena de la Frontera, and they became involved in the production of wine and spirits in the Malaga area. They lived at Connaught House, the present City Hall where Miss Larios was born)

As the *Gibraltar Chronicle* reported, the hunt continued on its way, and they ran at great pace pointing towards 'White's,' but the fox never entered this covert. It appeared to go towards 'Winton's' and then they raced towards 'Pine Ridge.' From there they went towards the Cortidera Farm on the right and onto the hills that mark the southern boundary of the Castellar Estate. Here the pack divided, but the main body, sticking to the hunted fox, ran on over the Castellar Bridge to a point about two miles west of Almoraima Station.

The *Chronicle* noted that a word of praise should fairly be given to the kennel huntsman Pecino, whose hounds put up a first class performance, rendered possible only by the first-rate condition in which he had turned them out that season. Eighteen couples went out on the hunt.

It must be remembered that the Royal Calpe Hunt Club had been pioneered by the high-ranking officers stationed on the Rock and that its executive committee was composed, for a very long period, of British military officers. When a few wealthy civilians tried to break this tradition, a serious feud developed between Governor Godley and Paul Larios, the main exponent of civilian participation, over who should be the next head of the Royal Calpe Hunt Club (whose chief patron was His Majesty, the King of England). So severe was the disagreement that those involved were known as the 'Godleys' and the 'Ungodly.' Paul Larios got the thick end of the stick, and the Governor's wishes were carried through. However, Larios owned most of the hunting grounds over which the Royal Calpe made their runs, so he soon placed restrictions on the use of his lands. The club found itself in a dilemma.

The King himself advised Governor Godley to find a peaceful way of resolving the dispute soon. At the first opportunity that arose, Paul Larios became chief huntsman of the club.

It was said that Lady Godley was a very jolly character, totally different to her serious and formal husband. On one occasion it was said that she road down the staircase in the Governor's Palace sliding on a tray! (*Hounds are Home*, Gordon Ferguson).

High Society

Among society events, we learn that His Excellency the Governor gave a dinner party at Government House and the following were the guests: Sir Sidney and Lady Nettleton, Surgeon Commander and Mrs Button, Mr A. C. Carrara, Mr G. Bowen, Mr Greenwood, Mr and Mrs Gulloch, Mr and Mrs Cardona, Major and Mrs Tealf and Miss Johnson, Major and Mrs Scovill, Major and Mrs Custance, Major and Mrs MacNally, Mr and Mrs

Luke, Mr and Mrs Discombe, Captain And Mrs Doig, Captain and Mrs House, and the Revd. Sheehan

A rather successful dance was held at the Assembly Rooms for the naval warrant officers. Rear Admiral and Mrs Curtis were the guests of honour. The dance band was the 'Imps' from the Lincolnshire Regiment. The decorations and lighting effects had been most tastefully carried out and the catering arrangements were all that could be desired.

The City Council of Gibraltar

By 1931, the City Council finally had local representatives, but not without colonial control. Among the names on the agenda of the meeting on 5 December 1930 were Lt. Col H. W. Tomlinson (Chairman), E. P. Griffin (Vice Chairman), A. J. Baldorino, Commander H. Biron, J. Discombe, Em. Gonzales, F. J. Silva, Commander R. L. Wiles (RN), and A. E. Heart.

One important item on the agenda that was that 'white lines would be drawn on the roads to help traffic.' A letter was handed in by the city engineer, which he had received from Mr A. Serfaty informing him that he was resigning his post as junior draughtsman, since he had obtained a position with Messrs Pearson Mechanical and Civil Engineers in the U.K. It was mentioned that it was noteworthy that a local articled pupil from the city engineer's office could get away from Gibraltar and into the much wider field of opportunity in the United Kingdom. Having been articled, Mr Serfaty could now sit in England for his qualifying examinations in civil engineering and surveying.

In time, Abraham Serfaty returned to his beloved Gibraltar and practised architecture. Later he joined the AACR and became a very distinguished politician, and for a while he was the Mayor of Gibraltar.

The Executive Council, of which the Governor was the head, included two Gibraltarian names, albeit as 'unofficial members,' the Honourable J. J. Russo, JP and the Honourable Andrew Speed, CBE, JP, as well as two non-local unofficial members, W. H. Smith, JP and His Honour Sir Kenneth James Beatty.

Meanwhile, the Law took its affairs seriously. As the town's people slept, some took the law into their own hands. Emilio Maria, a Portuguese, was arrested and appeared at the police court for collecting house refuse without the permission from the City Council. Poor Emilio, who was caught red-handed, was cautioned by the magistrates not to continue his filthy trade without a licence!

We no longer get this kind of medical advice on our modern medications. The following was part of an advertisement in the *Gibraltar Chronicle* on the 'Bronchitis Peril.'

> When stripped of its protective wrapper and dissolved in the mouth, a Peps tablet gives off valuable medicinal fumes. These fumes pass naturally with the breath through all the delicate air passages direct to the lungs. Peps speedily remove congestion. They soothe the throat, banish the stubborn cough, allay irritation and inflammation in the breathing tubes, and comfort and strengthen all chest sufferers.
>
> Keep Peps always handy. They are invaluable for coughs, colds and chills, sore throat, laryngitis, bronchitis, bronchial catarrh, asthma, etc. All medicine dealers sell Peps in handy size boxes. Full directions enclosed.

A footnote: One of the main ingredients of Peps was cocaine!

The Home Fleet in Port

Home Fleet 5,000 strong parade along Main Street

The 'pack' of hounds

Chapter 7: The Retrial

Opisso had been tried in the criminal courts with a judge and a jury of twenty-three persons. That jury had not come to a definite decision on whether Ernest Opisso was guilty or not guilty, and so the Jury had been dismissed. The 8th June 1931 was the appointed date for a retrial of the murder charge against Ernest Opisso.

There is little doubt that Opisso was still confident that the result of this trial would produce a favourable outcome for him. Opisso had naturally been kept at the civil prison inside the Moorish Castle since 11 May, the day that the last trial produced a hung jury.

The Moorish Castle in Ancient Times and Today

With the undecided verdict of the previous trial, Ernest's treatment at the prison had been somewhat more relaxed. There was a possibility after all that he could be found not guilty of the murder. In any case, he had brooded over his fate and destiny. Conditions at the Moorish Castle were in general rather bleak. The cold and damp passages and the small, uncomfortable cells, with their thick iron doors and peep-holes, were rather depressing even to those strongest in spirit. The place resembled the deepest of the dungeons in the Tower of London of the fifteenth century. In fact, the Moorish Castle quarters pre-dated the Tower's dungeons, since they went back to the eleventh century. If he went free, he would never in his life forget his stay at the Moorish Castle.

Curiously enough, the Moorish Castle of Gibraltar was not a castle at all. It was, in fact, a square Moorish Tower of Homage, built by the Islamic Moors after the year 705 following the invasion of the Iberian Peninsula by a strong wave of Islamic power with expansionist ideas in mind that eventually conquered half of Spain for over 700 years.

The orders of the invading force were in fact to land at a place called Ghezeira-al-Thadra (present-day Algeciras), but somehow Tarik-ibn-Zeyad, with a force of 7,000 men and 500 horses, came to the Rock on 27 April in the year 711 (the Fifth Rjab according to the Islamic calendar). Ever since, the Rock took on this general's name, Gibel-el-Tarik, Tarik's Mountain, Gibral-tar.

Up to that moment, the rock had not been properly inhabited. Its terrain and living conditions were not ideal for habitation; water, in particular, was almost unavailable. It was what its name inferred, Calpe a white limestone rock almost completely surrounded with sheer rocky cliffs.

However, the ingenious Moors, with their vast experience of living in arid lands and with their advanced techniques in water management, and under the orders of the one-eyed Caliph of Damascus, founded a small settlement, called Mersa Ashajarad (the First Village), with fortifications on the sheer northwest side of the rock and all along the cliff-face. (George Palao, *Genesis and Evolution*, 1982).

They saw the Rock as a natural fortress requiring very little extra to defend it, should it become necessary, but they did fortify it and took no chances. The ancient Moors described the surrounding fortification that they built thus: 'surrounding it on all sides as the halo surrounds the crescent moon.'

It became, truly, a citadel of Islam, where the black and green banners of the Kingdom of Granada, now in the hands of the Caliph, proudly fluttered. (Ibid)

The original Tower of Homage was destroyed during the siege of 1333, and the present structure, then called *La Calahorra* (the Granary) by the Spaniards, was re-constructed by Abu'l-Hassan. It was bombarded with stone missiles propelled by huge catapult machines during several sieges. One of these was led by Alfonso XI in 1333, when the attacking forces positioned themselves high up on the rock above the tower, the indentations of which can be seen to this day on the sides facing west and north. This Arab individual was a highly ingenious person and he also constructed a giant windmill in the vicinity to draw water. (George Palao, *Genesis and Evolution, 1982;* Tristan Cano, *Historic Walking Guides*)

Medina Sidonia the elder tried unsuccessfully to capture the Rock from the Moors. In one of his attempts he was captured and beheaded by the Moors, who placed his head in a wicker basket called *una Barcina*. This

When the Hangman Came

basket, with the head in it, was hung for all to see at the entrance to the village in an archway which is known today as Water Gate.

Eventually another Medina Sidonia, the son of the unfortunate beheaded warrior, invaded and conquered Gibraltar, so that from 1462 till 1502, Gibraltar belonged personally to the Medina Sidonia family. They had a great devotion to Saint Mary the Crowned. Therefore the Sidonias, wherever they established a village, town, or city, invariably constructed a church and named it the Church of Saint Mary the Crowned. near by.

In the proximity of the tower once stood the governor's palace, as well as fantastic gardens, vineyards, and woodlands where the governor would have hunted deer and wild boar.(Tristan Cano, *Historic Walking Guides*).

It is said that one of the Sidonias actually lived in the Moorish castle or its proximity.

On the top of this enclosed settlement of Mersa Ashajad, a tower was strategically built, which we know today as the castle. This tower had a variety of purposes, the first of which was that it could be used to call the faithful to prayers three times a day, much in the same manner as a mosque's minaret.

The second purpose was that it would serve as a lookout tower. It had a great and uninterrupted view of the Spanish mainland, stretching all the way north to the Sierras Carbonera, then west to Algeciras and the eastern coastline of the mainland, as far as the Guardiaro River, and on clear days even beyond.

The third purpose was that, since the African coast was visible, this high point could be used as a communication or signal tower with predetermined codes. Fire was used at night, mirrors or smoke during the daylight. Messages would quickly be sent through a relay system of predetermined towers at prominent points from coast to coast.

The castle's east gate, also known as the Moorish Gate House, is considered to be the oldest man-made structure in Gibraltar. The gate is made up of two towers, which controlled a vaulted entranceway and offered extra protection from enemy attackers. The gatehouse was built during the Nasrid Dynasty, and an inscription above the door in Arabic, no longer visible, once recorded a dedication to Yusef 1st., the Sultan of Granada, and mentioned 744 as the year the original castle structure was completed.

Some historians speculate that construction commenced not long after Tariq's landing at the beginning of the eighth century. This would probably make Gibraltar's castle the first Moorish fortification to be built on European soil.

The structure built in 1160 was badly damaged during the fourteenth century and was rebuilt in its present form around this time by the Merinids. The Nasrids of Granada completed further alterations to the tower when they retook Gibraltar around 1374.

There is still evidence that the whole castle had a white plaster exterior finish, which gave it the name of *la Torre Blanca* or the White Tower. This white tower must have looked impressive from a great distance.

Inside the tower was a stone staircase that led downwards into the castle's inner keep, which is inaccessible as it is presently used as Gibraltar's civil prison. The first floor contains a stunningly preserved medieval bathhouse not dissimilar to the type found in the basement of the Gibraltar Museum. Many of the features of the baths mirror the museum's bathhouse, such as the high vaulted ceilings and star-shaped cavities, which allow light into the rooms. There is also a series of underground canals for circulating hot air and a furnace room, adjacent to the dressing room, which has blackened walls that betray the room's former use.

The large rooms at the southeast end of the building were used as the living quarters of the governor. Although it was not his permanent residence, he would probably have retreated to the castle during times of crisis. The small prayer room, with its ornate ceiling mouldings, is probably the most impressive in the tower. The sealed archway at the far end of the room was the former entry to the tower, accessed by a timber walkway. Many graffiti can still be seen, scratched into the wall by the many sentries of old who guarded the gates.

A final ascent leads to the roof of the castle. The Tower of Homage is the largest remaining tower of its type in the Iberian Peninsula, and it is here, at its summit, that a magnificent view of the bay of Gibraltar, the Straits, and the mountains of Africa and Spain can be seen. (Tristan Cano, *ibid*)

When the Hangman Came

The village settlement itself was a small one, protected by its sheer limestone cliffs that provided a perfect natural fortress and further re- inforced by a massive thick wall. The lower part of Mersa Ashajarad was the place the Spaniards called *La Barcina*, remembering the wicker basket where the head of Medina Sidonia was once kept.

A pier was constructed from the edge of the fortification into the bay, facing west for easy disembarking and for unloading a variety of essential cargo needed by the invading forces that would come from North Africa, which was a mere ten miles away. The British later reinforced and lengthened this pier outwards towards the west, and this became known to the Spaniards as the Devil's Tongue because of its devastating effect on Spanish vessels.

By 1931, this Tower of Homage was just a piece of historical interest, a piece of heritage, in which the newly formed tourist bureau had started to take an interest and which they were trying to restore.

The earliest attempts to restore it for tourist access came during the early 1930s with the opening of an entrance to the tower, on the near side of the rock close to the entrance to the modern water catchments system and this entrance was only about 100 yards away on the rock side of the tower. Tourists visiting Gibraltar in those days could go and visit the middle galleries, the Moorish Castle, and part of a huge and complex waterworks system with reservoirs holding millions of gallons of fresh rain water. The newly established tourist bureau started to train special tour guides for this purpose. This was a great step forward in making Gibraltar a tourist attraction in post-war years. (*Gibraltar Chronicle*, December 1930).

But now, within the silent walls of this historic Moorish Castle and outer patio that once enjoyed so much activity, a jail had been built. The putrefaction of centuries clung to the stonewalls of the castle, filling the air with a dank mildew smell, the telltale sign of neglect. From the eaves and gutters sprang clumps of snapdragons that seemed to suggest that nature wanted to decorate the ancient monument in an endeavour to restore its once glamorous past.

Sunlight barely penetrated the high walls of the castle-cum-dungeon. Only at midday, when the sun was perpendicular with the tower, did the sun manage to sweep stealthily over the ramparts like a thief, but just for a short while only. Then, in what must have seemed a brief moment to the residents, the whole interior once again was covered by the shadows of the high wall. In the heat of the July and August summer, this process was a blessing, but the rest of the year it was bleak. The prisoners tried to enjoy the small luxury of basking in the sun and followed the sun's track until it finally disappeared.

For countless years, the criminals who frequented the Moorish Castle were petty thieves, brawlers, small-time smugglers, and the like. No hardened criminals or serious criminal offenders had yet lived in this jail. Such were the temporary companions of Ernest, petty thieves, brawlers, and small time law-breakers.

To be sent to the Moorish Castle meant that you had been sent to jail! At the moment, Ernest Opisso was one of its inmates. The first Gibraltarian civilian to be imprisoned for murder was now awaiting his second trial. At exercise time, he moved freely and spoke to his fellow prisoners. There is no report that he ever gave any serious trouble. His main complaint was that he was innocent and that he did not belong in there.

Ernest Opisso, a somewhat mentally subnormal 29-year-old man who had been lame since he was a child, was deaf and therefore had a speech disability, and who could obviously not express himself properly. All of this no doubt worked against him. His birth certificate shows his father's name as Luis Opisso, and his mother's as Amanda Gonzalez, but he never knew his father. On top of this, he was now a prisoner in jail, accused of a murder that he claimed he did not do. This unfortunate person was now charged with a vicious and brutal murder that, if he was found guilty, would take him to the gallows.

The Special Jury

This first trial had ended on 11th May 1931. On 21th May, the Attorney General applied for an order for a 'special jury' for the next trial. When the defence lawyer Mr Serfaty heard about this, he resigned from the case protesting against this special session with a special jury.

In the meantime, Opisso had to go through the ordeal of a second trial, but this one was a very special trial. Only once before in the history of the courts in Gibraltar had the Chief Justice, with the Governor's consent, called for a special jury.

The original trial of Ernest Opisso had been convened with a jury of twenty-three jurymen. (There were no women called to the jury at a time when women did not have the right to vote either.) The jury had been selected from a public jury list that was posted, and both prosecution and defence had the opportunity of accepting or rejecting any of the individuals called to serve as jurymen. If one or more of the persons selected were challenged by either side, the prosecution or the defence, that person was dismissed and another juryman selected in his place. In the first trial, the media had not reported this part of the court's process, but it must have been so. On the other hand, this process was reported at the time of the retrial.

The reports do not explain what a special jury consisted of, or what made it 'special.' But on enquiry it is clear that a special jury meant that in the published public jury list, certain individuals—those considered to be of great integrity, including property or land owners, businessmen, and professionals—would bear a suffix of ' SJ' alongside their published and listed names. The Chief Justice for 'Special Supreme Court' cases could call these people forward. Fortunately, this system was done away with soon after.

By today's standards, this form of selection would be totally inadmissible as being undemocratic and discretionary. No person, especially in a murder trial, could be considered more special than another for a jury by virtue of the fact that that person was a property owner or land owner, businessman, or professional. However, this was the prescribed law at the time, and it remains to be seen whether this special jury selection system may have been a total miscarriage of justice in the circumstances of this particular case.

Again, Chief Justice Sir Kenneth Beatty sat as judge. Public interest in this case had apparently dwindled, as was evident by the small numbers that assembled outside the court or who had sought admission to the trial.

The selection of jurors begun by calling persons from the jury list as posted in the *Gazette*, but only those whose name bore the suffix SJ. Naturally, this selection process was so furiously contested by Mr Serfaty, the defence lawyer, that he exhausted his ten peremptory or obligatory challenges. The Hon. C. F. Cox, the Attorney General, aided by Mr A. R. Isola, challenged six times those allowed by Mr Serfaty. Consequently, the original list of possible special jurors was somewhat shortened. It became even shorter when five of those who had been called presented medical certificates and were therefore excused. So desperately pressed for jurors was the clerk of arraigns that he later recalled and empanelled two of these persons with medical certificates. However, from an original list of forty-eight names drawn up by the registrar, the number of persons now left on the 'SJ' list had been exhausted.

There was no one else left to call, and the jury bench was short of jurymen, so the court had to resort to the unprecedented action of calling additional members from the public gallery in the courthouse, persons who had come simply to watch as spectators and to follow the trial. One of these was Mr W. D. Piccone, who was called by the clerk of arraigns. Mr Piccone, speaking from his seat in the balcony, stated that he had not been summoned as was customary, but the clerk of arraigns replied that this did not matter—he was called to be a juryman anyway.

Mr Charles Danino whose name also did not appear in the list of jurors, was sitting in the public gallery on the ground floor, and he too was called. When about to be sworn, Mr Danino stated to the court that he was about to join the Royal Air Force and was expecting a letter at any moment ordering him to proceed to England. His Lordship sympathised with him but felt sure that the Royal Air Force, under the circumstances, would undoubtedly excuse him. There was laughter from the public gallery.

The special jury was eventually formed and consisted of only twelve members This Jury was in fact eleven jurymen less than had sat in the first trial. The jury was composed of the following: Alfred T. Cochrane (foreman) James Restano, John Cruz, A. C. Savignon, Jerome Casaglia, Joseph G. Imossi, Humberto Podesta, Francis J. Aonso, A.,F. Imossi, Alfred Bassadone, William Piccone, and Charles Danino. The social standing of these individuals was rather impressive. There was no doubt that they all naturally qualified for the 'SJ' category of jurymen; there was no blue collar worker or bricklayer in this group.

Since I have already reported to the reader an account of the coroner's inquest, the police court proceedings, and the first trial at the Supreme Court, and since, obviously, most of the procedure followed almost the same line of questions and answers as these previous hearings, this account will limit itself to pointing out those points and issues which are either new pieces of information, new evidence or new revelations, of which there were a few

The Retrial Begins

The Attorney General, Mr Cox, opened the case for the prosecution. He stated that in the course of their evidence, they would prove without a shadow of doubt that the accused Ernest Opisso was guilty of murder.

He then went on to call his first witness. Mr John Coelho was Assistant Crown Surveyor and Engineer at the public works department, and he testified that he had made a plan of the victim's flat and added that the day he did this was a very clear day outside. However, he found the room next to the kitchen was in complete darkness, and this was at around 2 or 3 p.m.

Abridged Evidence by PC Bacarese

The next witness was PC Bacarese, who gave a full account of how he was called, how he fetched a ladder in the company of Mr Canessa and Opisso from the fire station close by, and how he later entered the flat through the window. The most revealing point, other than finding the body, was that he could not turn on the electric light even with Opisso's instructions.

When they finally broke down the door on orders from Superintendent Brown, who was present by now, he asked Opisso where the switch was. He noted that Opisso stepped back at this question, and he said to Opisso, 'Don't be afraid. I am with you.'

Bacarese did add that the accused had shown no hesitation in going up the ladder and was quite ready to help, and he did not notice him (Opisso) to be nervous.

The List of Articles of Evidence

Many articles were produced as evidence. As listed in the court's register, they were as follows:

The notebook, evidence, 'L'

Entries in the notebook,'L1/L2/L3'

Piece of bone from the skull, 'M'

Mat, 'N'

Lock, 'O'

Bunch of keys, 'H'

Raincoat, 'P'

Photo of lady, 'Q'

Piece of linoleum, 'R'

Sketches of injuries to the head, 'T/T1/T2'

Abridged Evidence of Superintendent Brown

Brown was the next witness. He too explained how he had ordered the accused to break the door down. As they entered into the flat, Opisso turned the electric mains on, and in turn he also turned the light switch on.

He told how he found the lady in the next room on the floor with her head towards the door. He bent over the body and found the woman was dead.

He ordered PC Bacarese not to let anyone into the flat and ordered him to call the Chief of Police and the doctor. He was present when Dr Griffiths examined the body. The mat was on the floor on the right-hand side of the bed. Across the mat was a double line of footprints in blood running diagonally. These footprints were very distinct.

There were also two electric bulbs on the chest of drawers in the bedroom. A small black book and a pen and ink were on the dressing table in the bedroom. He noticed some spots of blood on the dressing table. He also noticed some bloody fingerprints on the woodwork inside the drawing room.

Low down on the dividing wall between the dining room and the kitchen he saw three blood splashes. Some of these splashes reached ten feet in height, and they had splashed onto the glass door. Once again, he said that when he gave this evidence at the police court, the accused again said *'Mentira.'* ('It's a lie.')

The superintendent seems to have made a big thing about this interruption by Opisso. It is difficult to understand what he was concerned about or what bearing this *'Mentira'* had on the case. In any event, both the interpreter and the clerk of the court verified that they did not hear Opisso say this, and they were closer to the accused than he was.

Brown recounted how the arrest of the accused had taken place and how they had searched his house and store, adding that when the accused was arrested, he had a bunch of keys, and one of those keys unlocked the door of the stores. They opened the accused's store and inside they found another bunch of keys. One of these keys had been identified by the cleaning lady as being the same as the key owned by the lady

Then he described how some young kid had found another key on a window sill belonging to Mr Cohen's shop in Engineer's Lane on Saturday morning at 8 a.m. It was assumed that this key was the key of the deceased's flat.

He continued that Dr Griffiths had measured the footprints on the mat the day after the body was found. In his opinion, the toe print on one of the exhibits shown was that of the victim's shoe, but the imprint on the linoleum was part of the heel of a man's shoe.

He further added that before breaking the door down, the accused had tried to open the window that led to the corridor next to the entrance of the flat, but without success.

The inspector said that he asked Mr Benjunes, the photographer, who happened to live in the same block as the deceased, to take photos on two different occasions. He did add that whilst the first trial was in progress, they had taken more photos while the accused was in prison. His shoes had been wrapped inside a wetted blanket, and then the accused was made to walk on a stone floor whilst photos were taken, Dr Giraldi, the jailer, and others, including Mr Serfaty, the defence attorney, were present when the photos were taken. The accused knew what was happening.

Abridged Evidence of the Chief of Police

The Chief of Police, William Sutherland Gulloch, repeated his previous statement but added some new bits of information.

He said that on the dressing table there was a bottle of ink with the stopper out and also a small black book. In this black book, on a page marked 'L1,' there was a reference to Opisso's rent, and on another page marked 'L2' was a further reference to work done by Opisso. On the page marked 'L3' of the book, there is a reference to payment made to the accused for the measurement of the underground water cistern. There were bloodstains on either side of this page. These marks were not seen until after the accused gave evidence before the coroner.

He explained that the mat produced with the bloody footprints on it came from the right-hand side near the bed in the bedroom. The footprints were fading, but when he had first seen it, it was bright with blood. Such was also the case for the towel and duster (or handkerchief?) removed from next to the body.

On 27 February, he had asked Superintendent Brown to go to Opisso's store and try to find a bunch of keys. No doubt Opisso had told the Chief on questioning that his keys were at the store. When Brown got these keys, he found that one key in the bunch turned the lock. He noticed that it was the cleanest key in the bunch.

But now there were three keys that fitted the lock of the deceased's flat the one found in Engineer's Lane, the key on Opisso's bunch, and the one found on the lady's chest of drawers.

He then added that he had tried to show the accused the photograph of the victim lying on the floor for the purpose of ascertaining whether the furniture was in its normal position. He said that the accused turned his head away and said something in Spanish, and he told the accused, 'Take it man, it won't bite you.'

He continued that he had carried out some experiments at the police station to verify how the accused walked. He observed it when the accused walked twenty three or twenty four feet through the yard, which was wet, and then was brought in through the charge room, where he had left fourteen or fifteen footmarks across the wet floor. The accused walked with his toes turned inwards and took a longer step with his right foot than with his left.

When the piece of linoleum with heavy bloodstains was produced in evidence, he indicated the footmarks in the blood. The footmarks shown were by the legs of a chair that had stood in front of the dressing table. This was a man's right foot. It was eleven and a half inches long. It was made with a worn heel. Near that footprint there is another indistinct footprint. He added that the measurements of the shoes taken from the accused's house correspond with the footprint shown.

Because a lady's footprint was found close to a chair, they presumed that the victim might have sat on it before dying. Yet the dimensions taken were of a toe print that corresponded in size with that of the deceased's shoe. On the other hand, some tests carried out on sawdust two days before were not very distinct, but they did show that he turned his toes inwards in walking. In the pool of blood by the slain lady were some of her hair and several hairpins.

It is worth noting that all these pieces of evidence had been taken to Scotland Yard in early February by Sergeant Gilbert and were examined by the experts there. What is of extreme concern in this case is that the Chief of Police did not divulge the results of these examinations and analysis in court. Not a single trace of blood was found on any of the clothing or shoes. No fingerprints were identified as belonging to any of the known persons.

When the Chief of Police was cross-examined, he said that he had only seen the accused walk on one occasion at the guardroom in the police station. The accused walked across the charge room, and as far as he could recollect there was more inversion of the left foot than of the right.

He observed that the accused had suddenly altered his way of walking. He stated that one person in 10,000 walked with the foot inverted. The drawing of the footprint was certainly that of a man's shoe, much larger than a woman's shoe.

The Chief of Police was later to admit that he had not measured the footprints on the mat when he first saw them but that it was after 16th January when he made his examination. When he talked about the fingerprints found on the red glass door panel and the black book, he confirmed what he had been told at Scotland Yard, that the material in their possession was not sufficient to definitely identify these fingerprints as being of those of any particular person. Again, the fact that Scotland Yard had been unable to come up with a positive identification was not brought out during the trial.

The Chief of Police offered a new piece of evidence. He said that when he had questioned the accused at the station on 2nd December for close to an hour, the accused had given the impression that there was someone else in the room on the Friday evening when she asked him up to her flat to speak to her.

Inspector Ernest Santos, who had been translating for the Chief of Police when Opisso was being interviewed, contradicted this statement made by the Chief of Police. Santos said that he had not got the impression that the accused had said that there was someone in the flat when he called. So who was right, the Chief of Police or Inspector Santos?

The Chief of Police added that PC Macedo reported to him on 5th December that he had seen the accused inside the patio of 7 Market Lane on the 29th November. Yet another contradiction is revealed here by Inspector Santos when he said that he had been present at this meeting, which he translated, that took place on the 6th th. As a consequence, he and Superintendent Brown saw the accused for the second time on the 9th. At this meeting, he told the accused what Macedo had reported, and the accused immediately denied that he had been in the patio on the Saturday in question. On that same day, he also showed the accused the photo of the victim.

Before this, he had asked through the Press for people to come forward with information concerning the murder should they have any.

The inquest had terminated on 19 December. If Brown had said that the photo was shown to the accused to verify exactly what the victim was wearing, then either Brown or the Chief of Police was wrong. The real purpose, according to the Chief, was to see if the position of the furniture was the normal one, particularly the chair.

When asked if the position of the chair was important, the Chief replied that it was. This was was because the Chief of Police held the view that the victim had sat on the chair during the assault and had then been assaulted again and killed?

He first started to suspect the accused whilst the inquest was going on, and he had asked for an adjournment of the inquest as he was getting more information from Macedo and the baker's boy.

The Chief of Police was asked if he knew that the accused had said that third-degree methods had been used in dealing with him. The Chief of Police said that this was untrue. He was also asked why the victim's coat was shown to the accused. He answered that he did that to find out if it was the coat that she was in a habit of wearing indoors. The accused had not been accused with the murder at any of these interviews. He added that he took a large number of exhibits, including the coat, to England.

It appears that the police did not have the iron file at the time that the accused was arrested. Furthermore, after the arrest, there was no identification parade for the bread boy to identify the accused. Instead, the boy had been on the Monday in the same room all day long with the accused after the murder had been discovered.

When the Chief of Police was asked about what time he would say the murder was committed, he said between 12 noon and 2 p.m.

How and on what evidence did the Chief of Police arrive at such an early estimate of the time of death of 12 o'clock? Perhaps based on the witness account from the bread boy who said he has seen Opisso at the apartment at 12 o'clock?

Abridged Evidence of Doctor Griffiths

An interesting account is given by Dr Griffiths, the assistant colonial surgeon, of the degree of the wounds suffered by the victim.

When Dr Griffiths first saw the body of the victim on the night of the 30th November at Market Lane, he had estimated that the victim had been dead thirty-eight to forty hours. He said that he and Dr Durante had performed a *post mortem* examination on 1 December at the mortuary. This confirmed his opinion as to the time of death.

Dr Griffiths explained how he undressed the lady, removing her earrings and the rings from her fingers. She was wearing a dark blue coat. The collar was soaked with blood behind the right shoulder. Under the arm and back were lots of stains of blood. Under the coat, she had a woollen cardigan, which was open in the front, and under the cardigan she was wearing a purple dress. The coat and dress were lifted as far as the hips. There was, however, no evidence of sexual assault, and this possibility had been definitely ruled out.

He then proceeded to shave the head of the victim to better examine the wounds. He removed sixteen hairpins from the lady's hair. After shaving her, they counted about fourteen wounds to the back of the head, some horizontal, some oblique, and others vertical.

The lady, he said, had a small heart and healthy lungs. The stomach was rather extended, containing twelve ounces of food recently taken and traces of cheese, noodles, and peas were clearly apparent. In answer to a question, he said that this food had been eaten about twenty to thirty minutes before death occurred.

They prepared a scaled diagram of the head injuries. There was a groove in the wound, which must have been caused by a blunt instrument. Another diagram was produced of the crown of the head. It was from the centre of the crown that the piece of skull was missing. A sketch was made of the interior of the skullcap and the skull, which was divided into six sections. They found that the cone of the skull had been splintered, and some of the splinters had been driven into the membranes of the brain. Death was due to fracture of the skull, laceration of the brain, and haemorrhage. She died on the spot where the body was found.

A duster found under her nostrils was covered with mucous, which showed that she had breathed after being placed in that position.

At the flat, they had seen blood on the wall between the dining room and the kitchen and blood on the wall of the drawing room. These marks were consistent with having been thrown from a bloody weapon, which in his opinion was used several times in striking the crown of the head. As the piece of skull was knocked off, death would be instantaneous.

When the doctor first saw the piece of skull close to the body, it was covered with fresh blood. In the piece of skull, there was a V-shaped cut. This he had compared with the shape of the file. Similar marks on the file were reproduced in the depressions in the bone, and he restated that the corresponded exactly with the shape of the file. There were a large number of blows struck on the floor of the drawing room where the body was found.

In reply to a question from the Attorney General, the doctor said that the deceased could have lain in several places before the final blow broke the skull, and she had died where she lay.

Could the file cause all the injuries on the head of the deceased? Griffiths had answered most definitely that it could.

Had the doctor observed something else on the file? Yes, he answered, 'a scale of bone.'

The soft part of the bone on the file was on the inside of the file. Fresh blood was easily washed off with pure water.

There was a mat on the right hand side of the bed in the next room. There were footprints obliquely across this mat in the direction of the dressing of the dressing table. The marks were fresh and distinct. The doctor had examined this mat several times. The police took the mat to his house on 1 January, and he made a reproduction in paper of one of the footprints, the one nearest the drawing room. The rolling of the mat had damaged the footprints to some extent.

On examination, there were no signs of any sexual assault on the deceased, apart from the injuries described.

He was of the opinion that the accused was normal except for his bodily ailment. This statement was to be crucial after the accused was sentenced to death.

The Court adjourned for the day.

At the end of each day, the entire jury was taken to the Bristol Hotel, where they were isolated from the outside world. They walked the short distance from the courthouse to the hotel, a mere one hundred and fifty metres, escorted by two police officers, one leading at the front and another keeping the rear secured.

One of the jurymen later said that they felt as if they were the prisoners and not the accused. This juryman was, at the time, courting his girlfriend, who would come around to the square and wave at her boyfriend-juryman from the square. A policeman saw this and soon put a stop to this love sign language. (Conversation with John Restano).

Abridged Evidence of Mr Joseph Canessa

When the Court convened on the following day Mr. Canessa was called to give evidence.

Joe Caruana

Mr Canessa was married to a niece of Miss Bossano, and he now reported that on 30 November, which was a Sunday, he and his family were concerned that they had not seen Miss Bossano, who was a regular churchgoer. Her absence from Sunday Mass worried them somewhat. He assured his wife and mother-in-law that he would call on Miss Bossano, and so he went to 7 Market Lane and called at Miss Bossano's flat but got no reply.

He started walking towards the house agents in the hope of getting a key from them. On the way he met the accused. He told him to wait whilst he went for the key. When he got back from the agent's, he asked the accused to accompany him to Miss Bossano's flat. He tried to open the flat with the agent's key, but it did not work, so he decided to go to the police station for a ladder. When the ladder came, he went to tell his wife and relative. He returned immediately and found that a policeman had climbed the ladder and was in the house already. The accused was sitting astride the windowsill. He himself went up the ladder, and when he got to the level of the window sill, the accused pointed to a basin and said, 'There is blood there.'

The policeman came out looking rather concerned and went to the police station to inform his superior. Inspector Brown came. He (Canessa) was there when the inspector ordered the door broken down, which the accused did with the aid of a hammer. When the door was opened and the inspector had walked in, he heard PC Bacarese tell the accused, 'Don't be afraid. Go in.'

Canessa said that he next saw the accused on Monday, 1 December, and they talked this over and the accused told him, 'I took my coat off,' or 'I was going to take it off, as someone might have been in there and I would have to defend myself.'

On cross-examination, Mr Canessa said that the deceased used to do the measuring of the underground water cistern herself. She did this with a piece of string with a weight at the end.

He was asked if he attached any importance to the constable's remark about Opisso hesitating to go in. He answered that he was excited that night.

His fingerprints were taken at the same time as that of the accused.

He had known the accused for about two years. The accused was doing some painting at his house on the morning of Saturday, 29 November. He had seen the accused at his house at 10.30 a.m. and thought that the accused had left at about 12.30 p.m.

The accused was rather slow but a good worker. He often worked quite late, and he had no idea of time.

Abridged Evidence of Joseph Busquet

Busquet, who taught languages and was a tenant of Miss Bossano at 28 Cornwall's Lane, had heard of Miss Bossano's death on Monday, 1 December. He said in his statement that he had seen the accused on the previous Saturday morning. He saw and spoke with him when he was measuring the water cistern where he lived. He said that this was about 11 a.m. He went out, and when he returned, the accused had cleaned an obstruction in one of the drains and was still there at about 11.30 a.m. He was sure it was Saturday because it was a very rainy day and because he worked on weekdays and was not occupied that day.

Here we have another discrepancy in times as to where Opisso was that day. Mr Canessa also claimed that Opisso was at his house from 10.30 a.m. till about 12.30 p.m. How could Opisso be in both places at the same time? Was Busquet wrong?

Adelaide Canessa, wife of Joseph Canessa, confirmed Opisso's presence at Canessa's house. She said that the accused was painting at her house on Saturday, 29 November and that he had come at about 10.30 a.m. and left at 12.30p.m.

Abridged Evidence of the Bread Delivery Boy

Antonio Carretero Arjona, aged thirteen, testified that he was a bread delivery boy and that on Saturday, 29 November between 12 noon and 12.30 p.m. he mistakenly called several times at the door of the deceased's flat to deliver a loaf of bread. A man opened the door. When asked who that man was, the boy pointed to the accused.

When asked what the man was wearing, he said that he was wearing a shirt with black and white striped trousers and was wearing a tie. He also noticed that he had paint on his coat.

The young boy later admitted that he had been in the same room with the accused and twelve or thirteen other persons at the police station. This was on the following Monday, when he had gone to report that he had been at Market Lane on Saturday.

Abridged Evidence of PC Eliot Macedo

The new piece of evidence that this constable provided was that he finished his beat in Main Street at about 2 p.m. This time was later than that given by the Chief of Police, who had said 1.45 p.m., meaning the constable was leaving his point of duty early and he would reach the police station before 2.00 p.m.

He said the accused had an overcoat hanging from his shoulders. He was about three steps from the entrance when he first saw him. He stopped to look, since the shop in the street next to the entrance was a money-exchange place that was closed on Saturday. He said that the accused walked about eight steps and then turned round. He recognised the person as Opisso.

Eight steps from his first observation would put Opisso close to the stairs. An earlier version of this sighting, given to Scotland Yard by the Chief of Police, was that the constable had seen Opisso 'coming out' of the building at 1.45 p.m. How could the Chief of Police contradict Macedo's evidence so greatly concerning time and location?

He said *adios* and carried on walking as Opisso, he alleges, nodded at him. He added that he had known the accused for over twelve years, but he was hard of hearing and spoke in a peculiar way, and was also lame. The coat he was wearing was thrown over his shoulders Spanish-fashion, meaning like a cape. However he noticed nothing unusual about him. He saw him clearly because the entrance to the patio was not dark.

Abridged Evidence of the Hairdresser

The lady hairdresser testified that she first knocked at the deceased's flat at 2.30 and later at 4.30 p.m.

But could Opisso have been inside the flat when the hairdresser called the first time? If the timing of the murder and the timing giving by the Canessas and Teuma were correct, there was only one conclusion. Opisso could not have been inside the flat at 2.30 p.m., as about this time he was either already at or close to Mr Teuma's house.

Abridged Evidence of PC S. Wahnon

PC Wahnon was the constable who was present when the door was broken down by the accused. He stated that after the door was broken open, he went to put his hand on an electric switch inside of the door of the flat. The accused called out to him, 'Mind! You are going to get a shock. I had orders to repair it.' He then noticed that the porcelain of the fuse on top of the switch was broken.

On 9th December he had gone to the accused's house, accompanied by the accused himself, who had not complained about missing his lunch. He went to fetch the raincoat that PC Macedo had seen the accused wearing, thrown over his shoulder Spanish-fashion. The coat was hanging up in a corridor, and he noticed that it was wet both inside and outside, but the day before it had not rained. (This was nine days after the murder and Opisso had not yet been charged.) He noticed that the collar of the overcoat was also clean. The tape at the top of the coat was new and not damp. He had not noticed if the coat had dripped water where it was hanging. This evidence agreed with what the Chief of Police had said.

The accused has shown him his room, and he also went in there and picked out a shirt and trousers and three pairs of shoes.

Abridged Evidence of Mr J. Caetano

Mr Caetano was the deceased's next-door neighbour. He said he heard nothing strange next door, but he did say that when he came out of the toilet in the corridor at about 12 noon or 12.10 p.m., he saw the young bread boy who asked him, 'Do you know if the lady is in?' He answered, 'I don't know. Why don't you knock?' It was dark in the corridor, and then he went into his flat.

Abridged Evidence of Doctor James Durante

Since Doctor Durante had assisted Dr Griffiths at the *post mortem*, his medical report was almost the same as the other doctor's. All the details of the injury and the description of the sketch they had drawn of the injured skull were explained in detail. He had not seen any sign of rust in the skull bones.

He placed the time of death at between 11 a.m. and 4 p.m. on Saturday. His evidence differed from Dr Griffith's description of the *post mortem* only in one small detail. He said that he found macaroni and cheese in the remains in the stomach and that he saw no peas in the stomach as reported by Dr Griffiths. He had formed the opinion that death had taken place within two hours of taking the meal.

He demonstrated that the shape of the file fitted the indentations in the skull. When he was shown the file on 26th February, he noticed a flake of bone lodged in the teeth of file, but the flake was too small for him to say definitely that it was human bone.

Abridged Evidence of Doctor Edward Deale

Dr Deale, assistant surgeon at the Colonial Hospital, had been asked by Dr Griffiths to examine the skull injuries and the file that was alleged to be the murder weapon. He was the third medical person to give evidence for the prosecution.

His overall medical and technical evidence coincided with that of Doctors Griffiths and Durante, but it also firmly affirmed several important points. This doctor had for seven years been a Professor of Histology, which was then the science of examining tissues and their origin. He said that he first saw the piece of bone at the end of January and that this piece was a piece of a skull bone.

His first statement was very firm and categorical. He said, 'I found on examination that the file very accurately fitted into a depression on the surface of the bone. On the file there is a piece of bone adhering to it. I carefully examined the fragment of bone on the file both under a microscope and otherwise. I am of the opinion that it is skull bone. It has all the characteristics of human bone.'

He was asked if filing could have caused the chip of bone on the file.

'No,' he firmly answered.

'Then how could a flake of bone like that be caused?' he was asked.

'It could be broken off by a blow. The hard surface of the bone is on the outside. The soft tissue is in contact with the file. It had obviously been driven on the file,' was the doctor's reply.

Could he say whether the flake of bone was fresh or old when it went on the file? He answered 'Yes'. It was living or only dead a day or two when impacted into the file. Washing would not remove this piece of bone from the file.

He continued, 'In order to test that chip of bone for blood, it would be necessary to take it off the file. It is unlikely that I will find blood under the chip of bone, as the file has already been tested for blood. It is not possible for the flake of bone on the file to have come from filing the bone on the umbrellas that had been exhibited.'

On the application of the Attorney General and with the consent of counsel for the defence, the witness showed the scale of bone on the file under a microscope to the Jury. He was asked to remove the flake of bone off the file and test it for blood. Counsel for the defence offered no objection to this test being carried out in court and added that Dr Giraldi would be present and would watch the test on behalf of the defence.

This was the first time that Doctor Giraldi came into the picture in the trial, although as a young man he was considered to be something of an authority on medical matters. It was a move by the defence to counter the strong medical opinions of the previous three medical officers.

'In order to carry out the test, I must remove the scale of bone and drop it into the test tube', said Doctor Deale. 'If blood is present, the piece of bone will turn a dark blue or blue green. If there is enough blood, you will find some of the colour rising from the bone. The colour will appear immediately. Bone easily flakes when it is living.'

The doctor proceeded with his experiment, but it so happened that there was no colour change in the chemical and, therefore, the test was negative. There had been a very slight indication of blood, but not sufficient to say definitely that blood was present. The doctor said he would not use a wire brush on the file. If a wire brush had been used, the piece of bone would have probably come off.

At this point, the prosecution handed in the statement of the accused made in the lower court and closed the case for the Crown.

Once again, there appeared to be a weakness in the case made by the prosecution. So what if they did establish that a tiny piece of bone was in the file and that the file had been removed from the accused's stores? Curiously enough, the prosecution had terminated their case and there had been no attempt to establish a motive or a reason for the murder to explain why Opisso would kill Miss Bossano.

Or why would he take a file with him to the flat and surreptitiously enter the building and the flat at Market Lane and move like lightening to be somewhere else within minutes of the time of the murder?

One wonders why the intended killer would not take with him a heavier weapon such as a piece of pipe or a hammer. A file is not a very heavy weapon, but deadly if the point end is used.

It was now time for the defence to make its case.

Statement by the Defence

Mr Serfaty made his summary reply to the prosecution's statements. He forcefully put his summary in bullet points as follows:

- The prosecution only offered circumstantial evidence.
- Their case had a number of weak links.
- They had shown no motive.
- The accused assisted the police in every way possible.
- The accused is difficult to understand.
- Footprints were not examined till several weeks after the crime.
- The police had used improper and incorrect methods of search.
- PC Macedo had been late in reporting that he had seen the accused on the day of the murder, and there was no doubt that he had made a mistake.
- The accused says it was on Thursday and not Saturday that Macedo saw him.
- The bread boy had been made by the police to make an improper and incorrect identification of the accused.
- Defence would produce evidence that the accused was wearing the overcoat on the night the murder was discovered.
- Defence would provide witnesses to show the whereabouts of the accused on Saturday afternoon.

Abridged Evidence of the Accused, Ernest Opisso

Of the twelve witnesses for the defence, the first to be called to the stand was Ernest Opisso, the accused.

Ernest Opisso said that he was a painter, an electrician, and carpenter. He knew Miss Bossano and used to go to her house in Market Lane. He had last seen her on Friday, 28 November in the evening at about 7.30 p.m. as he was passing by when she happened to be at her window. He looked up and spoke to her, telling her that the Frenchman, her tenant at Cornwall's Lane, was becoming a nuisance.

She told him that she did not hear well and asked him to come up. He went up and told her that her tenant had complained about the flooding and the drain. He said that she had told him to tell the Frenchman not to tell the City Council, and also to inform her if the Frenchman made any further complaints.

It was at this point that she asked him to measure the water level of the underground water cistern at Cornwall's Lane and gave him a lead and a string to do it with. He said that he then left.

'On Saturday morning I measured the water in the tank at Cornwall's. When I measured the water level, the tank still needed another three feet of water for it to be full'. He said that for this reason he did not return to Miss Bossano to report.

(If and when the water level showed that the tank was full, there would be a change in the down pipe that delivered the water to the tank. With the addition of an angled elbow pipe, the rainwater was redirected to the overflow pipe that emptied into either the sewer pipe or the street.)

Since it had continued to rain overnight, he said he had gone and measured the water level again on Sunday.

Ernest's Movements

He was asked if he had gone to Miss Bossano's flat on Saturday, to which he replied that he had not. On Saturday morning, he had gone to Mr Canessa's house to paint a child's cot. He got there between 10.30 and 10.45 a.m. and then left at 12.30 p.m.

This did not coincide with the time given by the French tenant at Cornwall's Lane, who said that he had seen Ernest at Cornwall's at about 11 a.m., though this time is not crucial, since Miss Bossano was seen in Irish Town at exactly 10.00 a.m. At the exact time that Barclay's Bank was opening its doors, she was heading towards Commercial Square. Again, we do not know where she was actually going, probably to 10.30 a.m. Mass at the

When the Hangman Came

Cathedral, or how long she stayed away before returning to the flat, though a witness said she was seen at her flat at about 12.00 noon, when the bread boy called by mistake. However we have now reached the vital point where the timing is absolutely critical.

Opisso said that when he finished at the Canessa house at about 12.30 p.m., he went from there to his store to drop off some paint via Market Lane, passing under the window of the flat where the deceased lived, carrying the pots of paint. From his store he went to his house, which was only about two hundred yards away, for his lunch. His sister said he arrived at about 1 p.m., and he was actually seen entering his house by the charwoman who was cleaning the place. She also gave the time as about 1.00 p.m. The cleaning lady said that she stayed there till 2.45 p.m. washing the stairs.

Later Ernest was to say that he stayed at Market Lane with the police until the body was removed from the premises.

On the following Monday 31st he went to the deceased's relative's house to express his condolences. From there he went to the police station, and there they told him to go to the hospital to see the dead body. This was a very strange request by the police, since it was not until 9th. December that he was questioned by the Chief of Police about his movements on the 29th (Saturday) the day of the murder. The questioning took place ten days after the murder and four days after PC Macedo had informed the Chief of Police that he had seen Opisso at the scene of the crime.

Visiting the relatives and the corpse would be cool and cold-blooded behaviour on Opisso's part, and it can only be explained in two ways. Either he was a cunning, calculating, cold-blooded murderer with no conscience, or he was so out of himself mentally that he carried on as if nothing had happened, and he was showing no remorse at all.

Or perhaps he had not committed the crime.

This was a man who seemed to be dutiful in his work as a handyman, doing precise carpentry, electrical work, painting, and taking measurements. It seemed a rather uncharacteristic behavioural change. If he had not done his work properly, it is quite probable that neither Mr Canessa nor Mr Teuma would have put up with him. They obviously found him at least trustworthy.

The examination of Opisso continued. The police had asked him why he had not gone to Miss Bossano after he had measured the water cistern on the Friday. His answer was a very logical one since the tank was not yet full, there was no reason to bother the lady. He intended, if it continued to rain, to measure the tank again on Sunday, which he said he did, and that's why he kept the measuring string and weight.

He had been asked about the clothing the deceased was wearing when he last saw her, and the photograph of the dead lady had been shown to him at least three times. He found their insistence in getting him to look at the photograph rather upsetting.

The defence continued to question Ernest. His lawyer asked him, 'Where you told by them (the police) you did not go on Saturday because you knew she was dead?'

The questions were put in English and were simultaneously translated by the Spanish court interpreter. In his stammering speech, which was difficult to understand, he answered as follows.

'Y- y- yes, s- sir. Sergeant Gilbert said this. H-e insisted that I k-n-new something. He said, 'You will not leave here for twentyfour hours.'

'I said, 'I-f y-ou ke-ep me a m-m-onth, I can tell you nothing more.'

'Th- th- the coat of the d- d- deceased was produced by Sergeant Gilbert. It was bloodstained. Sergeant Gilbert said, 'Do you know this coat?' I replied, 'Yes.' Sergeant Gilbert brushed the coat against m- m- my face. Th- th- then he put his hand on my h- h- heart while he was asking me about the coat.'

'Then I heard the Chief of Police give Sergeant Reyes orders to shut the door and windows.

'Sergeant Gilbert said, 'Why didn't you go on Saturday? '

'I- I- I said there was n- n- no need. He then said, 'You didn't go because you killed her.'

His lawyer asked Ernest, 'Have you ever worked with bone or horn?'

Nodding his head, he replied, 'Yes. I repaired a gramophone and two umbrellas, one belonging to Mr Wall, and the other to Mr Teuma. I took a bone out of a dustbin to do the repairs to the umbrellas. I don't remember repairing any bone-handled knives. I used a file in repairing the bone parts of the umbrellas. It was not horn-bone, because this would have split on nailing the piece to the stick,'

'Where did the plaster of Paris on the file come from?'

'I was repairing a doll. I had a tin of plaster of Paris. The end of the file went accidentally into the tin. This was about two months before the file was seized.'

Ernest told of the first two jobs he had done for the deceased when she first moved into Market Lane last August.

'I put up the electric light and also put the linoleum on the floor of the deceased's flat when she moved in. I cannot read or write, but I can sign my name.'

'Did you work on Friday?'

'Y- y- yes, I- I- I went to Mr Canessa's house.'

'Where were you coming from when you passed Market Lane on Friday?'

'I had been to see a young lady. It is not correct that the deceased called me and asked me to measure the tank.'

'Did you go into the house on Friday?'

'Yes, into the dining room.'

'Have you ever been into the deceased's bedroom?'

'Yes, when I laid the linoleum. I have only been in that house three or four times.'

'When did you do the electric light?'

'B- b- before the deceased went to live there.'

'Did you see some electric light shades?'

'N- n- no.'

'Do you remember telling Constable Wahnon that you had orders to repair an electric switch?'

'No. It was only on the Sunday that I noticed that it was out of order.'

'Why didn't you tell Canessa on Sunday night that you had seen the deceased on Friday night?'

'I- I- I did.'

'Canessa said it was on Monday.'

'Yes, Monday too.'

'On Sunday night, you knew a crime had been committed?'

'I knew something had happened.'

'Why didn't you tell the police that you had seen the deceased on Friday night?'

'They didn't ask me. I told them on Tuesday when they asked me.'

'What time did you leave Canessa's house on Saturday?'

'The l- l- lady said it was 12.30 p.m.'

'Did you have anything to do at 12.30 p.m.?'

'N- n- no.'

'Why did you not go from Mr Canessa's house to Mrs Canessa's house?'

'Because it was raining, and I had pots of paint when I left Mr Canessa's house. I always have lunch between 12.30 and 1 p.m. I had to pass Mrs Canessa's house on the way to my house.'

Ernest's sister, Amanda Cassar, in reply to questions from Mr Isola, gave evidence saying that he left the house at 1.45 p.m. She remembered the day well, because that was the day that her other brother had moved from the south district and came to live in the town area.

'You went up Market Lane at 12.30 and returned at 2.30 p.m. on the Saturday?'

When the Hangman Came

'Y- y- yes.'

This route is not an unusual one. The Canessas lived at 53 Irish Town, and the accused had two routes he could use. He could either take a left up Tuckey's Lane or continue on Irish Town and then take a left at Market Lane to go through Horse Barracks Lane to 28 Cornwall's Lane, where he had his store.

'Did you have the overcoat in Market Lane about 2 p.m. on Saturday?'

'N- n- no.'

'You went to Mr Teuma's house that day?'

'Y- y- yes.'

'You know how important it is that you should not be seen in Market Lane about 2 p.m. with a raincoat?'

'I did not have the coat at 2 p.m.'

'You saw PC Macedo on Friday?'

'Yes, about 2 p.m. I said to him "Hurry up. You will be late." If Macedo had not made a mistake and the police knew it, I would have been arrested six or seven weeks earlier. It was Thursday when I saw Macedo. I was cleaning the drain at Cornwall's Lane at the time.'

'Macedo is mistaken when he says he saw you on Saturday?'

'Yes.'

'When did you first see the bread boy?'

'I-I-n t-he street w-with a po-liceman. I-I saw the policeman nudge the boy when they passed me. That drew my attention to him. It was before I gave evidence at the inquest. It was in Irish Town that I first saw the bread boy. There was something in the papers about a boy.'

'You knew the boy was looking for you?'

'Wh - Why should he?'

'You mentioned the boy to some other person?'

'Y- y- yes, to a clerk. I-I had never seen the b-b-oy b-b-efore.'

'How many times did you go to your store on Saturday?'

'T-t-hree t-t-imes. N-oo, f-f-ive times. I-I- was at m-m-y store a-a-bout a-an hour on S-S-unday. Y-Y- es, there is a tap o- f w-w-ater o-o-utside m-m- y store.'

'Before you were arrested, did you go to Mr Teuma to remind him that you had been there on the Saturday?'

'Y-yes I spoke to Mr. T-euma about that. B-ut I did not speak t-o the lady a-a-bout t-his.',

Now follows a very curious piece of information by Opisso concerning the keys.

He said, 'I-I o- ffered to go t-t-o my store o-o- n the Sunday night to g-g-et my b-bunch of k-keys, but Canessa said t-t-o never m-m-ind because he had s-s-ome keys.'

What keys was he referring to? Was Canessa referring to the house agent's keys? Since the question of the key and of entry into the apartment was an important and crucial issue, why was his statement not disputed in court? If Ernest offered to go to his store for his own bunch of keys, presumably because he knew it would open the flat's door, why was the door to the deceased's flat broken down when a ten-minute walk would have fetched his keys?

Did this not show that Ernest was not hiding the fact that he had some keys in his store, so, therefore, there was nothing sinister when the police located Ernest's bunch of keys?

The Chief of Police was very premature in saying that the key that he took to Scotland Yard was 'the only key of its kind', when the key that Opisso was referring to had not yet been found. It is very strange that the defence did not follow through this line of enquiry. And it is rather odd. Why did Canessa not take up Ernest's offer and thus avoid going to so much trouble? There would not have been any need to go for a ladder or the need to break down the door. No one is to blame. Canessa's must have been very worried at the time, but no finger can be pointed at Ernest for not producing the keys.

Prosecution lawyer Mr Isola continued to further cross-examine Opisso about the key.

'Hadn't you made keys for the deceased?'

'Y- y- yes, for a drawer while sh- sh- she was in the other house.'

'Have you ever seen the key of the flat?'

'N-N-o.'

This may sound contradictory, but it could be a truthful answer. Ernest may have had a key to the same flat that did not belong to the deceased, but it could have belonged to a previous tenant. So he could truthfully say he had not seen the deceased's own keys, but he did offer to go for them when Canessa first mentioned the problem of the locked flat to him.

So far Ernest's answers to the questioning appear to be precise and intelligent. There doesn't appear to be any hesitation or fumbling.

'Were you paid by Miss Bossano for cleaning the drain?'

'N-N-o. S-S-he paid me o-o-nce while she lived a-a-t C-C-ornwall's L-L-ane.'

'Were you paid one peseta for cleaning the drain?'

'N-N-o.'

'Why didn't you ask on Friday for payment?'

'I-I owed her r-r-ent a-at the that t-t-ime. T-The file produced is my property. I-I- have had it f-f-or over t-two years. Mrs Canessa g-g-ave it t-to me. I-It is always k-k-ept in m-m-y s-s-tore, and this is l-locked all t-t-he time. I m-m-ade the e-end to the u-u-mbrella o-out of a piece of marrowbone. I-I-t is not h-h-orn if it was horn, it would have b-b-roken when n-n-ailed on'.

'What is the substance on the umbrella?'

'O-O-ld bone. I-I did the work on those u-u-mbrellas o-o-ver a y-year ago.'

Prosecution lawyer Mr Isola continued the cross-examination. He got annoyed with the accused and reprimanded him, telling him, 'Look at me when I am talking to you'. The accused was behaving flippantly and had been looking back and making faces at the spectators in the back gallery.

It also seems that Opisso was annoyed with his own defence lawyers, because he saw that the defence was not taking notes in the same way as the prosecution lawyer was doing. The judge asked the press not to publish these exchanges, but it is certain that Mr Serfaty was at times annoyed with his client's frequent interruptions, which in a way showed that Ernest was diligently observing and following every word in the proceedings.

'How did you know they wanted to observe your footprints?'

'T-The first time, because the s-awdust had not been w-alked on. I saw the Chief of Police hiding b-ehind the door.'

'You knew at the time that it was important to know how you walked?'

'Y-Y-es, I had heard that the p-p-olice were looking f-for a l-lame man.'

'Had you seen the mat before the police court?'

'N-No.'

'Did you see footprints on the mat or linoleum on the Sunday night?'

'N-No. I never walk with my f-feet turned inwards.'

'There is nothing wrong with your right leg?'

'N-No. I had heard in court that I-I walked with my t- toes turned inwards. I-I knew that b-b-efore the photographs o-o-f my footprints were taken at the prison.'

'How long have you been lame?'

'T-Twenty four years.'

'You have changed the position you point your feet because you knew that there were footprints in the deceased's flat when you were there the night the murder was discovered.'

'T-T-hat is not possible in the first place, a-a-s the flat was in darkness, and I was t-told to remain at the d-doorway'.

When the Hangman Came

His defence lawyer, Mr Serfaty, asked the judge leave to re-question his client.

'Does the wire brush produced belong to you?'

'Y-Yes.'

'Where did you keep it?'

'I-In my store.'

'Does the black and white shirt produced belong to you?'

'Y-Yes, Mr Wall gave it to m-me for work I-I had done. It has no collar.'

'Do you wear a tie with working clothes?'

'N-No.'

This last question was very pointed, but it appears that that the defence did not press this issue further. Sometime earlier in the proceedings, the bread boy had given evidence saying that at the time when he made the mistake of knocking at the wrong door to deliver a loaf of Spanish bread, the man who opened the door to Miss Bossano's flat was wearing a tie.

Ernest was a working man who almost always went about with his working clothes, and it was most unlikely that he wore a tie on that Saturday, given that he was painting at the Canessa house. Who was the man with the tie who opened the door to Miss Bossano's flat? Could he have been someone she knew?

It is also highly improbable that Miss Bossano, a lady of means who came from a well-off family, would allow the lame handyman to open her house door. Opening the door was an act of confidence or intimacy with the flat's owner. That person must have been a person Miss Bossano trusted and knew well for him to take the liberty of opening the flat's door. Could this be the fair haired man the bread boy was trying to identify?

Defence lawyer Mr Serfaty continued questioning his client.

'You have now given evidence three times?'

'Y-Yes.'

'You gave two written statements to the police?'

'Y-Yes.'

'You were called many times by the police and asked many questions?'

'Y-Yes.'

'What is the distance between your store and your house?'

'I-It is n-not far. These experiments of taking m-my footprints at the prison w-were after I-I had been c-committed for trail.'

The second witness for the defence was Mr Canessa, whose evidence we have already reported.

The third witness for the defence was Mr Emanuel Teuma, who was clerk to the justices.

'I remember Saturday, 29th November. I saw him at my house that day when I returned to lunch between 2.30 and 3 p.m., and I spoke to him. He appeared quite normal and spoke of the Chappory case, which had ended the day before. When I left my house again between 4.30 and 5 p.m., the accused was still there. He had been employed by me previous to this to do some painting.'

The Attorney General asked leave to ask the witness some questions.

'Has the accused ever spent a whole afternoon at your house when not working?'

'No. It may have been nearly 3 p.m. when I returned home on the Saturday. The accused repaired the umbrella for me. He put on the piece of horn at the top of the umbrella.'

The defence lawyer now returned to questioning the witness.

'No, I saw nothing extraordinary about the accused idling his time away at my house. He often came there.'

The Attorney General again cross-examined the witness.

When the Hangman Came

'Before Opisso was arrested, had he gone to you and asked you if you could or could not remember that he had been at your house the whole of Saturday afternoon?'

'Yes, he came to me on 24th December. He said his lawyer had asked him to account for his movements. He said he thought he had done some repairs putting in panes of glass for me.'

The defence lawyer questioned his fourth, fifth, and sixth witnesses, Mr Anthony Lombard, William Davis, and James Warne. It is not strange to note the fact that these last two Gibraltarians, who lived and worked in this British colony, had English names. These witnesses had all been together on the evening of 29th November.

'Between 6.30 and 8 p.m., the accused joined us, and we went as far as the Cecil Hotel. He spent the evening with us. He was dressed in working clothes. The accused complained of having a pain and said he would go home.'

They did not expect Opisso would join them, since he said he was a bit sick. One of his friends said that he did not notice that he looked sick. He appeared much as usual. They had gone to La Linea that night and had asked the accused to go with them.

Attorney Mr Serfaty questioned his seventh witness, Mrs Amelia Bear, the charwoman at Opisso's house.

'Did you see the accused on Saturday, 29th November?'

'Yes, I was scrubbing the corridor where the accused lives, when I saw the accused pass. I made room for him to pass. This was about 1 p.m. I said to him "Here comes the only one left. You are always in a hurry." He went up, and I heard him knocking on the door. When I finished cleaning the passageway, I went to wash the stairs. I afterwards saw him again and asked him to lend me a brush to paint with.'

'What made you remember this?'

'Because of the paint brush.'

Mr Isola for the prosecution asked this witness when did she see the accused 'At 12.30 p.m.'

'When did you leave?'

'At 2.45 p.m.'

'Why did you say Opisso was in a hurry?'

'Because he always is. The accused's mother asked me about giving evidence.'

'When?'

'I don't remember. It was this year.'

'Was the accused in prison then?'

'Yes. The accused asked me to scrub the store. I did not do so.'

The ninth witness for the defence, Mr Obdulio Goodman, was called to give evidence. This was another witness with an English surname and a Spanish first name.

'I went to Market Lane the night of the murder. I saw, amongst other persons, the accused. I spoke to him. I was present when the door was broken open. Opisso gave me an overcoat similar to the one shown to me.

Mr Serfaty applied to recall the police superintendent.

'Do you remember whether the deceased had a handkerchief in her hand?'

'When Dr Griffiths turned the body over, I saw a small white handkerchief drop from near her hand. It appeared as if she had been holding it.'

'You heard me tell the accused to say nothing at the time he was arrested?'

'Yes.'

Evidence of Dr James Giraldi

The defence's tenth witness was Dr James Giraldi, MRCS, LRCP, MB, who was a medical practitioner in Gibraltar. This witness was the defence's answer to the other three medical experts used by the prosecution, Doctors Griffiths, Durante, and Deale.

Dr Giraldi was a young man at the time, only 27 years old, but even at this stage in his career his reputation, as a medical professional, was widespread and much respected. He had specialised in several fields of medicine, which had gained him much recognition, including the treatment of tuberculosis and coronary problems. Though young, he was a forceful and authoritative person who commanded much respect when he spoke. At this young age he was already a fellow of the Royal College of Physicians and a member of the Royal College of Surgeons.

He gave his evidence.

'I heard Dr Griffiths give evidence about the contents of the stomach. The age of the deceased would affect the time of digestion. In my opinion, it would not be justified to place the time of death within two hours of taking the meal described. Since the victim was fifty-nine years old, I think it would probably be longer than that. The stomach empties within six hours.

'The intestines should be opened in any *post mortem* examination.' (Was Dr Giraldi implying that the intestines had not been opened for examination?)

'I saw the mat at the police station sometime in April. There were some blood smears on it. The length of the stride on the mat is said to be twenty-seven inches. That is short for a man. I examined Opisso's way of walking at the prison on, I think, 24th or 29th April. I made him walk on sand and on clay. I measured the length of his step, which was about twenty-nine inches. His footprint was about eleven and a half inches long. He took a longer step with his right foot outwards in walking. I don't think the accused could have made the marks on the mat.

'I was present when the photographs were taken on 29th April. They show that the accused points his foot outward when walking. The footprints on the mat measure twenty-four inches, yet Opissos' have a twenty-nine inch spacing.'

Doctor Giraldi then produced a medical book showing two photos of persons with the same ailment as Opisso and described how the right foot points outwards.

'His lameness is due to old tuberculosis trouble in his left hip. The stance of a person is usually the same as his walk.'

'Is the diagram of the footprint shown smaller than the accused's footprint?'

'I think it is. It is only ten and a half inches long.'

'Does the file show any evidence of having been cleaned?'

'No, it has not been cleaned recently.'

'What is at the end?'

'Plaster of Paris. Blood would be difficult to remove, particularly from the plaster of Paris. There was no sign of powder or paste of this plaster in the wound. For the same reason, blood would be soaked up by the plaster of Paris, it being a highly absorbent substance.'

'You saw the piece of bone on it?'

'Yes.'

'Is it consistent with any bone other than skull bone?'

'Yes, it is so small that it would be difficult to say whether it was human bone or otherwise.'

'Could the notches on the piece of skull as shown have been caused by any other instrument than the file?'

'I think so. The soft part of the bone was adhering to the file. I should have expected to find signs of blood under the scale of bone, had it been driven onto the file as suggested by the other medical witnesses. I would not describe the file as a rounded instrument.

'The measurements of the footprints should have been taken immediately in order to be of value. The mat was negligently treated. The footprints on the mat are more or less in a straight line, which is the normal type of walk.'

Dr Giraldi was implying that the mat should have been kept stretched tight and not rolled or folded, as had apparently been done.

It was now the Attorney General's turn to cross-examine this witness, who had so far devastated all the prosecution's theories. He had challenged and contradicted no less than eleven vital points of the prosecution's evidence.

1. He gave the time of death from the time of having had lunch as about six hours, not two hours

2. The length of stride on the mat was twenty-seven inches—short for a man; it should have been twenty-nine inches.

3. Opisso's toes pointed outwards, not inwards.

4. The footprint was only ten and one eighth inches, not eleven and a half inches.

5. He did not think the footprints belonged to the accused.

6. The file did not show signs of having been cleaned.

7. The file was not the only instrument or weapon that could have caused the injuries.

8. A long steel knife-sharpener that is round and has file teeth was a likely weapon.

9. Blood would have stuck to the plaster of Paris on the file and discoloured it.

10. Notches on the skull could have been caused by another instrument or weapon other than the file.

11. He would have expected blood to remain on the inside piece of skull bone on the file.

The Attorney General cross-examined the witness.

'You would not say that the accused always took the same length of stride?'

'No. If the person were walking backwards, there would be a tendency to turn his toes inwards. The accused could walk with his feet turned inwards. The marks shown on the mat of footprints is not a normal walk. The accused's left leg is four inches shorter than his right. I do not agree that it would be difficult for the accused to turn his right foot outward in walking.'

'Isn't the footprint usually smaller than the shoe making it?'

'Yes.'

'Do you agree that the file is a rounded instrument?'

'No.'

'You examined the flake of bone under a microscope?'

'Yes. It is consistent with being skull bone. I agree that it has the characteristics of human bone. It is recent bone. It was live bone about October or November. I expected that blood would have been found under the scale of bone. The hot weather might have affected it. The file fits into the groove on the piece of bone. The bone of the umbrella produced is quite different to the bit of bone that was on the file.'

Mr Serfaty, lawyer for the defence, asked the witness about another possible weapon. This was the first reference made in the transcript of the trials of any other weapon.

'Does the knife-sharpener produced as evidence also fit the groove on the piece of bone?'

'Yes.'

The defence brought forward its eleventh witness, Mrs Amanda Cassar, sister of the accused.

'I am a nurse and midwife. I live in Castle Street. I remember 29th November. The accused is my brother. He came home to lunch that day. We had lunch together at 1 p.m. The accused left the house again at 1.45 p.m.

'When the police searched my house, they looked at my shoes. They took a pair of shoes belonging to my late husband.'

Mr Isola for the prosecution asked the witness, 'What makes you remember that Saturday?'

'Another brother of mine who works in the dockyard had gone to live in a government-owned house that day.'

'What time did you arrive home that day?'

'Between 12.30 and 1 p.m. The accused arrived a few minutes later.'

'What time did your brother come home on Sunday night?'

'I don't know. We usually have dinner at 5 p.m. None of the shoes shown belonged to my brother or my late husband.'

This could certainly explain one reason why Scotland Yard found no bloodstains in Opisso's shoes taken to Scotland Yard by Sergeant Gilbert in February.

The defence calls their twelfth and last witness, Mr Gustavo Mascarenhas, but it seems that because of the implications of his testimony this witness should have been the first of the defence's witness'es.

Mr Mascarenhas said, 'I remember Saturday, 29th November. At the time, Miss Caetano, my fiancée, lived at 7 Market Lane and I went there on that date at 4.10 p.m.'

We recall that a Mr Caetano, no doubt the young lady's father, lived next door to the deceased.

'When going up the stairs, I met a man and a woman. They were coming down from the direction of Miss Bossano's flat.'

'What nationality did they appear to be?'

'The woman appeared to be Spanish. The corridor was dark, and I did not see the man very well. I informed the police about this two or three days later. I did not see what sort of shoes the man was wearing.'

Here once again is mention of another man and a woman near the scene of the crime at the crucial time of death given by Doctor Giraldi when he said the murder was probably committed at about 4.00 p.m. How strange that this evidence did not appear before at the inquest, nor at the police court, or for that matter at the first trial. Mr Mascarenhas said that he had given this information to the police two or three days after the murder. What did the police do with this eye witness account?

Why would the police ignore this crucial piece of evidence? There can only be one logical reason. They were convinced that Ernest had committed the murder by 2 p.m. and ignored all other possibilities after this time. The Chief of Police was immovable in his theory, as he wrote to Scotland Yard's CID Commissioner, Mr Ashley, that he hoped that 'Opisso would not get away with it.'

But why did the defence not press this matter further? The reason will remain an enigma, even though Mr Serfaty did state that the defence did not have to prove innocence, but rather that the prosecution had to prove the guilt. But following this late testimony would have created the thought that other people would be under suspicion of having committed the crime.

Guilty Of Murder and Sentenced to Death by Hanging

The defence had finished presenting its case, and Mr Serfaty asked the court for an adjournment on the grounds of ill health, which was quickly granted.

When the court reconvened on the following day, Mr Serfaty, having fully recovered from his indisposition, made a strong argument on the improper way that the identification of the accused had been carried out. He quoted various precedents on the identification of a defendant by a witness. The identification must be absolutely independent, and it was improper that in order to identify the prisoner, the prisoner was set apart from other persons to be identified by witnesses. He quoted *Rex v. Dickman*, *Rex v. Chapman*, and *Rex v. Smith*.

And again no mention was made by the defence of the possibility that the murder could have been committed by other person or persons unknown in order to argue the case that reasonable doubt might exist.

The Attorney General then made his final arguments and his finishing statement for the prosecution.

Sir Kenneth Beatty, the Chief Justice, summed up and again advised the jury that it was their responsibility to take into account only the facts and evidence as given in court. It was their prerogative to judge whether or not there were any reasonable grounds for doubt. If there were, it was their duty to pronounce the accused not guilty. Their decision had to be a unanimous verdict, guilty or not guilty.

On Saturday, 13th June 1931, the jury retired at 5 p.m. to consider their verdict. The jury returned into court at 6.40 p.m. It took a mere one hour and forty minutes of deliberation.

The only thing that broke the intense silence was the whirring of the electric fans. His Lordship the Chief Justice took his seat shortly afterwards and adjusted his wig. Placing both hands flat down on the desk he nodded and said "Mr. Discombe if you please."

Mr Discombe, the clerk of arraigns, asked the foreman of the jury if they had found the accused, guilty or not guilty. To which the foreman announced that they found the prisoner guilty of murder but with a strong recommendation to mercy.

Their verdict was a unanimous one—guilty of murder.

Discombe was now obliged to ask the accused through the court interpreter, Mr Norton Amor, if he had anything to say as to why judgement should not be passed upon him according to Law.

Opisso at this point rose excitedly from his seat in the dock and shouted at the top of his voice, 'I am innocent! I am innocent!' and, looking towards the jury, shouted that they were mistaken. Why should he want to kill her? He also said that he would appeal to England.

The transcript states that the prisoner when the prisoner was asked how he pleaded that he answered, "Not Guilty", but in Discombes notes on his register he quoted Opisso as saying, " will someone explain to me how he could have killed the lady." In Spanish, he would have said '*Que alguien me diga como yo pude matar a esta mujer?*' Correctly translated, the sense of that question should actually read, 'Will someone tell me *why* I would have killed that lady?'

The judge placed the silk black cap on his head, straightened his wig and solemnly addressed the prisoner, 'Ernest Opisso, in accordance with the powers conferred upon me by His Majesty the King, I hereby sentence you to death by hanging, in accordance with the law.'

Immediately the prisoner became extremely violent, shouting and struggling to get out of the dock. The constables on duty at the sides of the dock at once grappled with him, but so violent did the prisoner become that further officers, eleven in all, had to come to their assistance, and Opisso was dragged out of court shouting and screaming.

As he was taken across the courtyard still struggling and kicking to the cell, members of the public, who were standing on various roofs and balconies overlooking the yard could be heard shouting at the police, *'Criminales, Criminales,'* ('criminals, criminals'), whilst the same words were heard being used in conversation by women in the public gallery This was in great contrast to the reception Opisso received when he was first brought to court following his arrest.

When quiet was restored in court, His Lordship discharged the jury and thanked them for their services, excusing them for further jury service in any criminal case for a period of three years. He informed the jury that their recommendation, about 'mercy' would be forwarded to the proper quarter.

Crowds attempted to remain in the neighbourhood of both the front and back entrances to the court, but this was not permitted by the police. Thousands of people then proceeded towards Castle Street where Opisso lived and they stood outside the house excitedly discussing the case for some time.

In fact the general public were not pleased with the way that this case had gone.

A further postscript to the sentence was that members of the Opisso family insulted and threatened the members of the prosecution, in particular Mr Albert Isola, who had assisted the Attorney-General. The threats to Mr Isola's family were taken seriously, and Sergeant Gilbert was assigned for a period of three months as a special guard to the Isola family, the sergeant accompanied the family wherever they went. (Conversation with Dr Cecil Isola).

When the Hangman Came

On 15th June 1931, the Chief Justice wrote to the Governor informing him as follows:

> The Case of *Rex versus Ernest Opisso* concluded at 6.40 p.m. on Saturday the 13th June. The Jury returned a True Bill against the accused at the last General Sessions of the Supreme Court, which commenced on The 27th April, and the prisoner was put on trial on a charge of Murder the same day.
>
> The trial lasted 14 days and the Jury, after being out for 36 hours, failed to agree and were discharged the prisoner being put back for trial at the next Session of the Supreme Court.
>
> On the 21st May the Attorney General applied for an Order for a Special Jury to be struck for the trial for the case.
>
> Mr Serfaty, who was then appearing as Court Defence Lawyer, opposed the motion.
>
> After hearing arguments, I granted the approval and a Special Session of the Court was fixed with the Counsel for the accused, for Monday 8th June.
>
> Mr Serfaty subsequently withdrew from the case and the accused applied for Counsel to be assigned since he was without sufficient means to employ one.
>
> Mr Serfaty was asked to accept an assignment by the Court to defend the prisoner at this trial, which he did.

However things were not to be as clear-cut as they appeared. A current of unease came upon the community. The death penalty was not acceptable to the vast majority of the population.

On 22nd. June 1931, Chief Justice Beatty from his chambers at the Supreme Court. wrote another letter to the Governor

Your Excellency,

I have the honour to inform you that in answer to an inquiry by the Registrar of the Court, the foreman of the Jury in the case of *Rex v. Opisso* stated that the Jury recommended the accused to 'Mercy' on the grounds that they considered he was not normal.

The accused gave no indication of mental weakness during the trial, and Dr Griffiths, who had the opportunity of observing him on several occasions, expressed the opinion that he was normal mentally.

I have the honour to be your obedient Servant.

K. Beatty

Chief Justice

Actual scene of the crime – Victim's bedroom. (Courtesy of Royal Gibraltar Police)

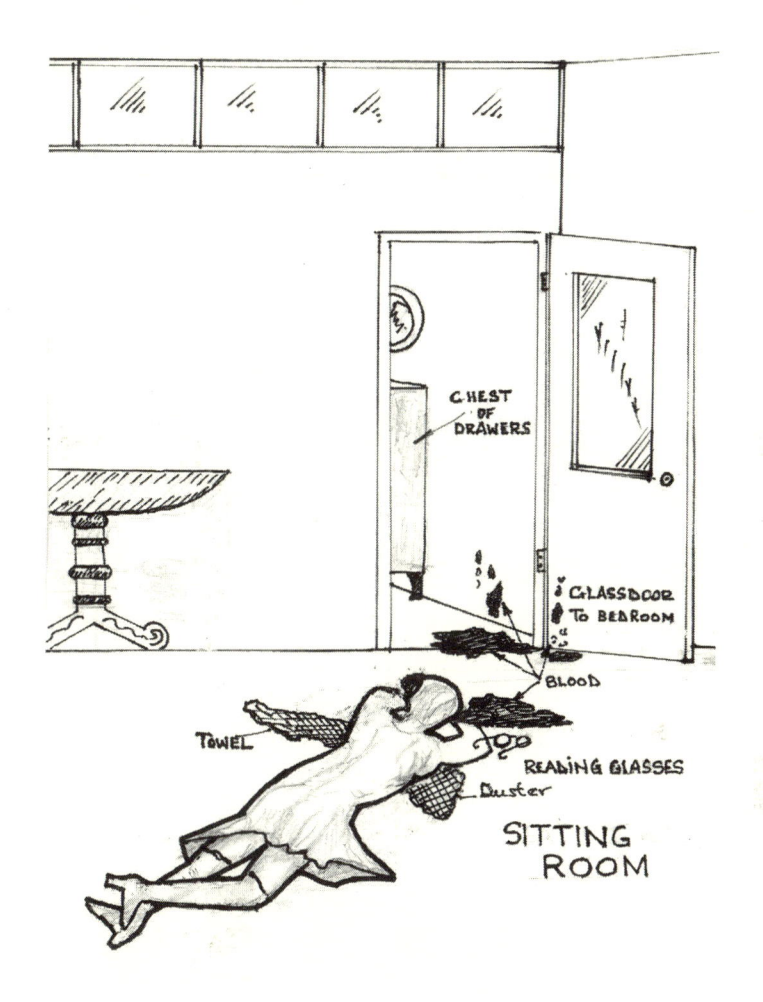

Sketch taken from Exhibit 'J' – Actual photo take by M.Benyunes (courtesy RGP)

Author's sketch of the corpse from the original photo.

MARKET LANE IN 2010. MISS BOSSANO'S FLAT,
FIRST FLOOR, BLACK SHUTTERS

ENTRANCE TO NO.7 MARKET LANE.

OPISSO'S HOUSE, NO.2 CASTLE STREET.

N0.28, CORNWALL'S LANE. MS. BOSSANO'S PROPERTY & OPISSO'S STORE ROOM.

POLICE STATION AT IRISH TOWN. IRISH TOWN ONLY STREET WITH WOODEN COBBLES.

Chapter 8: A Mother's Plea

The Public Petition

Had Opisso been convicted in England, he would have appealed to the Court of Criminal Appeal, but in Gibraltar the prisoner had no such recourse. So the next best alternative was a public petition, called a 'memorial,' the gathering of signatures from the general public.

A most successful petition was organised, and a staggering 13,018 persons signed. Though it was not crucial to the success of the petition, it is important to note that in some instances, the same writing could be observed in multiple signatures, and in several cases even the same name appeared more than once. Gibraltarians resident in Tangiers and in Spain also signed the petition, along with many Spaniards not resident in Gibraltar. But even allowing for some fraud and for some irregular signatures, the number of signatures was impressive by any standard, especially in a place where the population oscillated around 20,000.

Once this public petition had circulated throughout Gibraltar, the organizers gave it to Mr Serfaty, the prisoner's defence lawyer. He in turn arranged to deliver the petition to the Governor.

> TO HIS EXCELLENCY GENERAL SIR ALEXANDER JOHN GODLEY, CCB., KC. M.G., AIDE-DE-CAMP-GENERAL TO HIS MAJESTY THE KING, GOVERNOR AND COMMANDER IN CHIEF OF THE CITY AND GARRISON OF GIBRALTAR.
>
> The Humble Memorial of the undersigned Inhabitants of Gibraltar.
>
> SHEWETH
>
> That Ernest Opisso was tried on the 13th day of June, 1931, at a Special Criminal Sessions, held at the Supreme Court of Gibraltar,

Joe Caruana

on the charge of murdering Miss Maria Luisa Bossano on the 29th day of November,

That previously he was tried by a Common Jury at the Criminal Sessions which were held at the aforesaid Supreme Court and that the said trial which began on the 27th April, 1931 ended on the 11th day of May, 1931, with a disagreement of the said Common Jury.

That the Special Jury strongly recommended the prisoner to mercy.

That the absence of motive, the crime itself, the manner in which it was committed and the weapon used, all point to an unpremeditated sudden impulse.

That the prisoner has suffered since childhood from several ailments, which if looked into would tend to show that the prisoner might be mentally unbalanced or not in a right state of mind.

That the demeanour of the prisoner at both his trials and generally points to the conclusion that he is not normal.

That for a very large number of years, greater than any living person can remember, no Gibraltarian has been executed in Gibraltar and that there is no record of a fellow townsman being executed within the precincts of the Civil Prison.

That it is thirty-five years ago that a man, a foreigner, was executed by process of law.

That in 1918 and 1927 petitions for reprieve was successfully obtained on behalf of two utter strangers to this town and then for crimes, which revealed careful preparation and premeditation.

That your Memorialists understand that all the facts of the case are to be laid before Your Excellency they abstain from going into them. Wherefore your Memorialists humbly pray that their appeal, their entreaties to save the life of this young man be graciously acceded to and that this law-abiding town be spared the horrible feeling that an execution is carried into effect within its wall upon a man of whose normality they entertain very great doubts.

For the sake of a young Gibraltarian who has gone through the unusual ordeal of two prolonged trials, one of which was abortive and who is now preparing his soul to meet the Creator, Your

Memorialists entreat Your Excellency that of your mercy, you may, as representative of His Majesty the King, be pleased to exercise the prerogative, which has been placed by His Majesty in your hands, and grant the pardon which herein so eagerly requested.

For the sake of the poor mother and the family of the prisoner who are now suffering the excruciating, awful, horrible torture of counting the moments that are still left of life to one of their own kith and kin and to whom Fortune has so frowned that he has been afflicted since childhood by the calamitous deformity and impediment, which have deprived him of the pleasures and of the education that are afforded to normal persons of his age, your Memorialists humbly and earnestly pray that the hope of regeneration, that eternal spring, be not abruptly cut by sending the prisoner to his irrevocable doom, that the mother, who is suffering the most anxious, agonising, maddening moments may be able always to bless Your Excellency as the gracious Gentleman who has spared her son's life and who has caused the consolation, which is afforded by mercy, that gentle drop that falls from heaven for the quality of mercy not to be strained may be gracefully heard and acceded to by Your Excellency to whom your Memorialists will always be grateful for saving their cherished town from the sadness and mourning that would be caused by the knowledge that a fellow townsman, for the first time within living memory, has fallen at the hands of the executioner.

And your Memorialists will ever pray etc., etc.,

The Request for a Medical Board

On 22nd June, the defence lawyer Mr Serfaty sent the petition or memorial for the reprieve of Ernest Opisso to the Governor with an accompanying letter that said,

> I also enclose copy of a report published in 'The Gibraltar Chronicle' on the 24th day of March, 1926, with reference to proceedings at the Police Court against the said Ernest Opisso for larceny and wherein it is stated that the Chief of Police produced a certificate signed by two local medical practitioners stating that the accused was mentally deficient. This report supports the views put forward by the Memorialists as to the state of Opisso's mind. I may point

out that similar reports of the aforesaid Police Court case were published in the other two local papers of the same date

The Memorial is signed by thousands of persons of all classes of Society.

As you are no doubt aware, within an hour after sentence was known, people started signing for a reprieve and lists for the purpose were spontaneously placed at several shops. This fact and the rumour, unfounded as far as I can gather, that one of Opisso's brothers who wanted an appeal to England, had torn several lists of signatures may account for some people signing in two places.

The insanity defence could not be raised at the trial, as Opisso denied having had anything to do with the commission of the crime, a denial in which he persisted after sentence. However, at this point Mr Serfaty raised it with the Governor.

I venture respectfully to suggest that, in view of the statements made in the Memorial and Opisso's medical history, His Excellency be pleased to appoint a medical board to examine Ernest Opisso as to his mental condition.

Trusting that His Excellency will graciously and mercifully accede to the petition of reprieve of Ernest Opisso.

I have the honour to be, Sir, Your Obedient servant

A.B. Serfaty.

At the same time, the Registrar of the Courts wrote to the Chief Justice pointing out that the foreman of the jury in the case of *Rex v. Opisso* had stated that the jury recommended the accused to 'mercy' on the grounds that they considered he was not normal.

On 22nd June, the Chief Justice wrote to the Governor informing him of this recommendation, but in a second paragraph, which some may consider out of place, he added, 'The accused gave no indication of mental weakness during the trial, and Dr Griffiths, who had the opportunity of observing him on several occasions, expressed the opinion that he was mentally normal.'

The Governor's Concern

On 23rd June, the Governor sent a handwritten memorandum to the Colonial Secretary expressing his concerns. He made just two points: 'Is the mental deficiency mentioned in the *Gibraltar Chronicle* still existent?' and 'Is the abnormality suggested by the recommendation of the jury and by the petitioners such as to make it an extenuating circumstance which would justify me in reprieving the individual?'

The report of 1926 in the Gibraltar Chronicle referred to an instance when Opisso had been charged with breaking and entering a sports club and was initially charge for robbery and BAE. At the time the defence lawyer pleaded that Opisso was slow minded and had obtained a medical report from two different doctors testifying to the effect. The full charge was reduced to simple breaking and entering and he was only charged with breaking and entering and not with robbery, therefore he was fined but otherwise he would have gone to prison.

Nevertheless and under pressure the Governor, on 23rd. June, ordered a medical board to look into the matter. The Colonial Secretary selected the board members. Two doctors, Dr L. H. Gill and Dr J. A. Durante, and an army major, Major A. E. Singer, were appointed to the medical board.

A memorandum was attached to the order setting out the functions and terms of reference that the board was called upon to exercise, and it made it clear that it was most important that their report should reach the Governor as early as possible.

A room was made available at the judge's chambers as their headquarters. They were assured that on application to the judge's office, any further evidence that had been given at the trial or any other information that was on record would be supplied to them as required. The Superintendent of The Prison had been authorised to grant them all facilities to interview and examine the convict.

The Colonial Secretary promptly replied to the Governor that same day. He sent the Governor an extract copy of the *Gibraltar Chronicle* report, which said 'The Chief of Police confirmed the statement and produced certificates signed by two local medical practitioners certifying that the accused was mentally deficient.'

It was this information that led the Governor to take the following step.

The Medical Board: Normal or Abnormal?

On 24th June, the Executive Council met. (The Executive Council was the highest governing body of the City and Fortress of Gibraltar. It was, in fact, the government of Gibraltar).

An extract from this meeting said that His Excellency stated that he was not yet in a position to consider the Chief Justice's report (which had previously been circulated to members) on the case of *Rex v. Opisso*, which was the first item on the agenda, as he had received a letter from Mr A. B. M. Serfaty the counsel for the defence, attaching a memorial praying for the reprieve of the convict now under sentence of death, one of the main grounds being that Opisso was not mentally normal. His Excellency informed the council that he had in consequence convened a special medical board to enquire into and report on the mental condition of the convict and that it would be necessary to await the report before the matter could be usefully discussed.

A handwritten memorandum, Instructions 541/30 dated 23rd June, from the Colonial Secretary to the special medical board stated as follows.

> The Board is directed to the following points.
>
> The statements of Dr Griffiths during the trial, 'I am of the opinion that the accused is normal except as regards his physical ailment.'
>
> The statement in the letter from the Chief Justice dated 22nd June that the Jury recommended the accused to 'mercy on the grounds that they considered he was not normal.'
>
> The statement by the Chief Justice in his report dated 18th June that 'no motive was suggested for the murder which was a particularly brutal one. Dr Griffiths stated that there was nothing mentally abnormal with the accused and he gave no indication during the trial to suggest that he was not criminally responsible for his actions. I am therefore unable to associate myself with the recommendation of the Jury'.
>
> The statements in the Public Memorial (a) That the demeanour of the prisoner at both his trials and generally points to the conclusion

> that he is not normal, and (b) That the prisoner has suffered since childhood from several ailments which if looked into would tend to show that the prisoner is not normal.

The judge's qualification, 'I am therefore unable to associate myself with the recommendation of the Jury', was, to coin a phrase, a deathblow for Opisso.

The Governor was to add a note to this memorandum saying that the terms for this board were far too vague and that in his opinion the board ought to be asked to 'pronounce on whether the prisoner was sane or insane.' Regrettably, there is no indication that this wise suggestion was followed through. As we will read below, the report did not answer this question.

On the following day, 24th June, the medical board reported back to the Colonial Secretary, who passed the board's report to the Governor. The following is an account of the board's findings. The emphasis in italics is the author's.

> Following the instruction laid down in order 541/30 of June 23 1931, the board proceeded to the Civil Prison, where they interviewed the jailer, who produced the night reports on the convict, Ernest Opisso. Neither the jailer nor the reports mention any unusual behaviour on part of the convict pointing to mental disease.

> The board then had a lengthy conversation with the convict, which took place in Spanish, as the convict did not speak English. In consequence, one of the members of the board, Major Singer, was unable to follow the answers and statements made by the convict, which did not lend themselves to literal translation.

> 'The answers and statements made by the convict were *involved and rambling – he frequently went off the main theme under discussion and branched off on to side tracks, where it was difficult to follow what point he was driving at. He was in a state of suppressed excitement.*'

> From their conversation with the convict, the two Spanish-speaking members of the board, Dr Gill and Dr Durante, came to the conclusion that *'they were not dealing here with a man that, from a medical point of view, was mentally normal.'*

While they were unable to convince themselves that any action committed by the prisoner was done either without his knowing what he was doing or his knowing whether what he was doing was right or wrong, yet they came to the conclusion that '*his mental capacity is far below the average,* and while possibly not lacking in some low form of cunning, *his behaviour cannot be judged by ordinary standards.*'

How should the report's conclusion and comments be interpreted, since they are so clear? They said that they had not been asked whether they should recommend the convict to be sent to a lunatic asylum, yet they state that they came to the conclusion that they were not dealing here with 'a man that, from a medical point of view, was mentally normal.' 'His behaviour cannot be judged by ordinary standards'. Such phrases would seem to be the perfect assessment to send someone for treatment and rehabilitation.

With reference to convict's previous appearance in the police court in March 1926, the board were unable to obtain definite evidence as to any medical certificates produced at the time certifying the convict mentally deficient. This was an astonishing statement, since the Colonial Secretary had only two days previously sent a confirmation of the *Chronicle* report wherein they quote the Chief of Police on the matter of the case against Opisso four years early, when the two local doctors had produced a certificate testifying to his mental condition. Was not the trials transcript available?

This was an extraordinary confusing report by the board. In the first place, Opisso maintained to the end that he was innocent. How could these medical men say that 'any action committed by the prisoner was done so by him either without knowing what he was doing or whether what he was doing was right or wrong'?

In his letter accompanying the memorial, the defence lawyer had written to the Governor saying that he had not pleaded the prisoner's mental condition throughout the trials because he had held to his innocence.

Reported in the court records, the accused's behaviour in court was one where he often interrupted his own lawyer. Also, not recorded in the records of the proceedings was that he had several confrontations with the prosecution lawyer, Mr Isola, who apparently scolded the prisoner abruptly, telling him to look at him when he was talking to him and complaining that his 'antics' and his body language were deriding the prosecution. It appeared that this is what the memorial refers to as 'his demeanour in court.' (Conversation with Dr C. Isola, son of prosecution lawyer)

These statements alone should have been sufficient to pronounce mercy, but it was becoming increasingly clear that because of the brutal and savage nature of the murder, there was no will in the executive to show any mercy. The strong hand of the law and the unshakable course of justice must be allowed to prevail, and justice must be seen to be done at any cost, since such a savage murder could only be committed by someone who was a madman.

When referring to the police court case of theft in 1926, the medical report said 'the board were unable to obtain definite evidence as to any medical certificates produced at the time certifying the convict mentally deficient.' What an extraordinary conclusion! This last statement baffles the mind and logic. Why? Because no less than two medical practitioners who knew Opisso had testified in court in that case that the accused at the time of the theft was 'mentally deficient.' This evidence was surely at hand, and so were the medical practitioners. Why were these medical practitioners not called to give evidence?

However to demand a certificate certifying the prisoner 'mentally deficient' was totally impractical. Many mentally deficient persons lived outside an asylum without formal certificates of being 'mentally deficient.' It was common practice for parents to keep their mentally retarded children at home and out of sight of the public.

The medical report, even with its apparent contradictions, raises the question whether the Governor should have come to a conclusion of reasonable doubt as to the mental condition of the prisoner, sufficient to have declared a reprieve. This he could have done based on the discretionary powers that he had received from a memorandum from Downing Street on 22nd November, where the recommendation was not to send a convicted killer found insane to death or to a lunatic asylum, but rather to send him to a mental home and keep him under observation. But this was not to be so.

This memorandum was the subject of discussion between the Attorney General and the Colonial Secretary. In a memo of 15th December 1930, exactly fourteen days before the murder of Miss Bossano took place, the Attorney General wrote the following to the Colonial Secretary.

'It looks as though a man can still be detained after recovering his reason and that the form and period of his detention in the mental hospital should be determined by the Governor when he was insane.'

The Executive Council met again on 25 June.

> On Council resuming the case of Ernest Opisso, all documentary evidence being available including the Chief Justice's report and notes on the case, the public petition, the report of the medical board were considered. After His Excellency had briefly reviewed the various factors of the case, the Colonial Secretary stated that Dr Gill, the President of the medical board, had stated to him, in amplification of the Board's report, that although the Board was quite satisfied that Opisso was not normally minded, they were equally certain that, were they asked to certify him for admission to a Lunatic Asylum, they could not do so. The members of the medical board were then summoned and unanimously and unhesitatingly confirmed this view.
>
> After lengthy consideration and careful deliberation, the Council unanimously advised that in their opinion there were no extenuating circumstances which would justify His Excellency in extending a reprieve to the convict. His Excellency concurred and the decision was arrived at to allow the Court's verdict to be implemented.

In the meantime, several individuals had written to the Governor encouraging him to continue with the execution, informing the Governor thus:

> Attempts are being made to defeat the ends of Justice in the form of signatures to obtain a reprieve for this cold-blooded and brutal murderer and that the Governor was already aware that the greater part of the population shudder at the perpetration of this mostly ghastly crime and at the same time fully concur with the sentence of death passed. Lists are being carried about and children from ten and twelve years of age are signing their names without fully understanding the seriousness of the matter. The lists are being sent to La Linea and besides being signed by British subjects residing there, Spaniards have also signed these lists when they are not entitled to sign. Also the lists at Commercial Square were

being signed by American naval ratings from the American Ships of war in the Bay.

There is a pencilled item, dated 2nd July 1931, from the Colonial Secretary, with a very pointed note he wrote, no doubt to the Governor.

> I understand that Opisso has several times remarked today that, the fact that he is where he is now is due to his mother, presumably referring to the fact that he is a bastard and has been allowed to run wild.
>
> The Bishop commented on this remark to Gerrard and said that he thought that it was the equivalent of a confession.

This is the first and only time that we hear of a reference of Ernest Opisso being a child born out of wedlock, and it probably explains why, in his birth certificate, his father is named Luis Opisso (born in Gibraltar), but his mother's name is given as Amanda Gonzales also (born in Gibraltar). Yet throughout her life until she remarried, and even in all the documentation on record, she had always been known as Amanda Opisso. Ernest's baptismal certificate showed that he was baptised by the Reverend C. Mortiner, his godfather was Robert Smith, and his godmother was Catalina Opisso.

We assume that the 'bishop' must have been the Roman Catholic Bishop, Patrick Fitzgerald. Frankly, the last opinion, allegedly coming from the Bishop, is a little far-fetched. Whether right or wrong in doing so, Opisso had every personal reason to attribute his several infirmities, his unfortunate existence, and his bastard status to his mother, but not the brutal crime.

In any case, as we will gather later, the Bishop had gone in person to the Governor and made his own appeal for a reprieve based on what Father Salvador de Julian had communicated to him.

Yet in spite of all these appeals for clemency, on 27th June Mr Serfaty published a letter he had received from the Colonial Secretary.

> Sir,
>
> I have the honour to acknowledge the receipt of your letter of the 22nd of June, transmitting a Memorial, alleged to bear the signature of thousands of persons of all classes of Society, which has been duly laid before the Governor.

His Excellency in Council has given the fullest consideration to all the representations made, and inter alia, the Governor caused a special medical board to be convened.

All the points referred to in the various passages of the Memorial and in your letter, together with all possible evidence and all documents connected with the ease received full and careful examination and investigation.

The requirements of the Royal Instructions and the Law were carefully followed, and after consultation with his advisers His Excellency has regretfully come to the carefully considered conclusion that there are no sufficient grounds to warrant his interference with the sentence of Court.

There is no objection to the whole of this letter being communicated to the Press.

I have the honour to be, Sir,

Your obedient servant

Reprieve was not granted. The hanging would therefore take place on 3rd July 1931.

On 1st July, accompanied by the Attorney General, the Chief of Police, the Crown Surveyor and Engineer, and the gaoler visited the prison, and they inspected the scaffolding and the proposed burial place.

Eleventh-Hour Appeal by Father Salvador

The Roman Catholic chaplain, Father Salvador de Julian, who belonged to the Clarentino Order or more accurately to *Los Misioneros los Sacrados Corazones de Jesus y Maria,* was performing his duties at the prison, and he urgently asked the Colonial Secretary for an interview. The Secretary agreed to meet in his office immediately.

Father Salvador went to the office and found there not only the Secretary but also the Attorney General and Inspector Santos, who had been asked to act as interpreter. Father Salvador informed them that he was a Spaniard and had been in Gibraltar for the previous nine months, having been previously a priest for twenty years serving in Portugal and Spain. He started by explaining that he had now known the convict for twenty-one days and that, in his opinion, he was 'abnormal.' He was convinced that although Opisso might have committed the murder, Opisso did not know what he was doing. He emphasised to the Secretary the fact that Opisso had been abnormal since childhood, and he pointed out that the way he had acted since he had been in prison, that is, playing and joking, showed that he had no conscience.

The other points the priest made were that on the previous morning when he had visited the convict, he had found him asleep. He got up, washed himself, was quite calm, and showed no emotion. He then went to confession and Holy Communion and kissed the crucifix. When he was told that the reprieve would not be granted, he showed some excitement but afterwards became quite calm again.

He said that Opisso continued to maintain his innocence, and that in his opinion Opisso gave the impression of having the brain of a child. As a priest, his conscience told him that *if* Opisso had done the deed, he was not responsible for his actions. The priest said that it was his duty to mention this. Opisso, he continued, had shown no signs of bad temper during the time that he had been in prison.

The Colonial Secretary made notes, and in the margin beside this part he wrote that this statement was of some importance, as the Roman Catholic Bishop had informed His Excellency and himself that for some days after his conviction, Opisso had shown very violent temper and had refused to see the priest.

The priest continued to say that he was satisfied that Opisso was not pretending to be abnormal. He himself was an admirer of British justice, and he and all the priests were fully satisfied that British justice had been and would be done in this case. He added that, as a priest, he must do everything he possibly could.

It must be remembered that this spiritual man had been visiting Opisso for twenty-one days, so his evaluation of the prisoner should be taken seriously, whereas the medical board had decided upon their own opinion in a matter of one day and in a single visit of less than a couple of hours. Father Salvador's observations should have been taken more seriously but they weren't.

The Colonial Secretary informed His Excellency the Governor of all that Father Salvador had said. However, the Governor felt that 'there were no new grounds to justify any reconsideration' and accordingly signed the warrant.

Mother's Plea to the Governor for Mercy

In the afternoon following the visit by the Colonial Secretary to the Prison, Opisso's sister, E. Opisso, called on him at three o'clock to hand him the petition from her mother. This was addressed to His Excellency the Governor. The Secretary promised he would submit it to the Governor forthwith, so he immediately translated the mother's petition, and the Governor came from his cottage to the Colonial Secretary's office to read it.

The Colonial Secretary also took the opportunity of telling the sister, so she could tell her mother, that His Excellency and his advisers had been continuously and earnestly looking out for any good and satisfactory reason to justify the death sentence being commuted, but that much to their regret, such reasons had not been forthcoming. They were full of sympathy for the family in the painful situation in which they had been placed.

With the retrial now over and the death sentence pronounced, an undercurrent of unrest started to move through an unhappy city. Why should the Governor hold out, when the jury itself, though reaching a guilty verdict, had recommended mercy?

Now as a last resort the prisoner's mother had decided to write a heart-rending letter asking for mercy. The letter was handwritten in Spanish but a translation was prepared by the Colonial Secretary's office. Everyone in town knew about this letter and the mother's grief, and there was much sympathy for her, because Amanda Opisso, the very well-known midwife, was widely loved and respected by everyone. In particular, women were very fond of her and my mother was a good friend of hers and I personally met her on several occasions.

To His Excellency the Governor.

> Pardon me for taking the liberty of addressing Your Excellency, but it is the last recourse of the most unfortunate of mothers. I desire from Your Excellency the favour of postponing for two months the execution of the sentence that is impending over the

head of my son. During that period, on the assumption that Your Excellency will grant this permission we could try to find something to save the life of my son. We would leave my son some time under observation, for the doctors who examined him could not have appreciated the state of my son in one visit; or else we would write a Memorial to his Majesty the King, asking for the pardon, basing our statement on the fact that on the anniversary of his coronation we sent a Memorial to His Excellency the Governor of Gibraltar.

If His Excellency the Governor grants us this wish, we know well that the people of Gibraltar would bless him and in particular this unfortunate family, and more than anybody else this poor mother who prays kneeling in your presence that the last wish may be granted.

Signed

Amanda Opisso

Except for the sympathies conveyed verbally by the Colonial Secretary, there is no record that the Governor replied to the prisoner's mother.

Petition by Mr Serfaty and S. P. Triay

The Chief of Police made an urgent telephone call to the Colonial Secretary informing him that Mr Serfaty and another lawyer, Mr S. P. Triay, were in his office and would like an interview with the Secretary as early as possible in connection with the case.

The Colonial Secretary saw them at once. Mr Triay acted as spokesman and explained that they had called to see him on behalf of the relatives, as there was in their minds considerable doubt as to the mental state of the convict, and they did not feel that the special medical board 'had had sufficient time to make a thorough examination.'

The Colonial Secretary, with the Attorney General now present, explained to the deputation that the medical board had stated categorically that they had had all the time they required.

Mr Triay left two questions for the Colonial Secretary to communicate to the Governor. Unfortunately, these questions are not available in the record files. However, the Colonial Secretary did communicate them to the Governor, but again with no success. He then telephoned Mr Triay to inform him of the Governor's decision, and Triay promised he would pass this on to the family.

Appeal from Casablanca, Morroco

Another late appeal came from Mr Alex Gache, who wrote to Mr Serfaty on 27 June telling him of his great efforts to collect signatures in Casablanca. He now sent this to Serfaty, who in turn delivered it to the Colonial Secretary to add to the 13,000-plus signatures that had accompanied the original public petition.

Despite these pleas, the *status quo* remained in force.

Moorish Castle or Tower of Homage

Eleventh Century Moorish Castle as seen today.

Main Entrance to Moorish Castle Prison

Entrance to Civil Prison, Moorish Castle.

Aerial View of Moorish Castle Prison from the top

Entrance to Condemned Man's Cell

Lime Pit

Lime pit where Opisso's corpse was "washed clean" before burial.

Chapter 9: Preparations For The Hanging

The Governor's Warrant for the Execution

The Attorney General's office was extremely busy. They now had the task of ordering and organising all the formalities associated with a public hanging.

Capital punishment in Gibraltar was governed by sections 27-39 of the UK's *The Civil Prison Ordinance, 1889 (No. 8, pp. 378-380, vol.1)* and was based on the imperial Capital Punishment Amendment Act of 1868. This ordinance gave powers to the superintendent of the civil prison (it used to be the police magistrate who gave the orders) to make rules to be observed in the execution of judgement of death. However, no such rules had ever been written for Gibraltar, and so the Attorney General took his guidelines from the imperial Act, wherein the Secretary of State made the rules in England.

They found out that there was no copy of this UK ordinance available in the book shelves of the courts of Gibraltar, so one needed to be brought over from the UK. Because time was of the essence, it fell upon the appointed executioner to bring it with him when he sailed for Gibraltar.

The rules established the following guidelines.

1. Execution should take place in the week following the third Sunday after the sentence on any weekday except Monday at 8 a.m.

2. Public notice under the hands of the sheriff and governor of the prison of the date and hour appointed, should be posted on the prison gate not less than twelve hours before the execution and should remain until the inquest on the body has been held.

> 3. The bell of the prison or of the parish or a neighbouring church should be tolled for fifteen minutes after the execution.
>
> 4. Persons engaged in the execution should report themselves at the prison not later than four o'clock in the afternoon preceding the execution and remain there until the execution has been completed and permission has been given for them to leave.
>
> 5. It is the duty of the sheriff to notify the date of execution to the Home Office and also to the coroner to enable him to make arrangements for holding the inquest.
>
> 6. The omission to comply with any of the provisions of this Ordinance shall not make the execution of judgement of death illegal in any case where such execution would otherwise be legal.

The Attorney General added that he was of the opinion that they did not have to follow any set rules but ought to try to follow as far as practicable what were known and recognised as satisfactory rules.

On 30th June, the Attorney General wrote to the Colonial Secretary confirming that, the Colonial Secretary and the Chief of Police, and he had consulted together, and he was now submitting an original copy of the Governor's Warrant for the Execution of the Sentence of Death upon Ernest Opisso. He mentions that he had sent copies of letters to the superintendent of the civil prison, to the coroner, and to the prison surgeon. He had enclosed also a copy of a public notice informing the public of the time and place of execution. It had been agreed in fact that the notice would be posted as soon as the time was definitely fixed. He drew attention to the fact that the persons engaged to carry out the execution should report themselves at the prison not later than four o'clock in the afternoon of the previous day.

There remained two points to be settled the flying of the black flag and the tolling of the bell. The Attorney General was satisfied that the former was not indispensable and thus might not be necessary. The latter might be the subject of an agreement with the chaplain of the religious denomination to which Opisso belonged, who no doubt would be ready to arrange for

Joe Caruana

this rite to be performed at one of the neighbouring churches of Opisso's denomination.

The Hangman, Mr Baxter

There remained one important and vital question. There was no hangman in Gibraltar, so who would perform the execution? This was no task for an amateur. No one had an inkling of how a hanging was to be carried out or how the prisoner was to be prepared for the occasion. A hanging could be a very messy affair in the hands of someone with no experience.

On 25th June 1931, the Colonial Secretary wrote the following memorandum to the Governor.

> The Chief of Police has reported to me that a Spaniard recently arrested on a charge of larceny had volunteered to act as executioner in this case provided that the charge was withdrawn against him.
>
> The Chief of the Fire Brigade is also reported as having volunteers for the task

However, His Excellency decided that it was preferable in every way to arrange for qualified man from elsewhere to do the job. An urgent telegram was sent to the Governor of Malta on 23rd June that read,

> Gibraltarian charged with murder has been sentenced to death by hanging. Greatest difficulty in finding hangman here. Is it possible for suitable person to be sent from Malta? Must arrive not later than 2nd July.
>
> Reply urgently required.
>
> Colonial Secretary.

But Malta too drew a blank. A telegraph was returned saying that the colony did not have a hangman available. So the Governor had no alternative but to send an urgent request to the Secretary of State in London. By 24th June the Governor received the following telegram from the Secretary of State.

No.26. Your No.19, hangman. I am in communication with Prison Commissioner and hope to send suitable person by boat leaving Friday 26th June. Telegraph as early as possible if you do not want him.

Secretary of State

By 30th June the Governor had received a letter dated 25th June from the Secretary of State, Lord Passfield in which he told the Governor that a Mr Baxter was the official selected by the prison commissioners for the required duties He would, upon arrival, hand the Governor a printed Memorandum of Conditions to which he would, when acting as an executioner in that country, be required to conform and with which he has agreed to comply in the present instance. He would also deliver instructions regarding the carrying out of the execution and the burying of bodies of executed persons. The Secretary of State told the Governor that he would be glad to receive a report of the trial of the prisoner now under sentence.

This information was followed by a telegram from the Crown Agents for the Colonies saying that they were directed by Lord Passfield to refer to telephonic communications with Mr Reynolds of Gibraltar's Passage Department regarding the services of a hangman required for duty in Gibraltar. They stated that they had booked a second-class passage on the *SS Maloja,* sailing on the following day (Friday 26th), for Mr Baxter, the official who would have to travel 1,300 miles and was now on his way to the colony for the purpose.

Baxter's name was kept a secret known only to the officials. He would be travelling and known in Gibraltar under another name.

The Foreign Office told the *Gibraltar Chronicle* that the hangman was not one who was usually employed at executions in England. but when the Gibraltar authorities made the request to the UK, an executioner was soon found and sent out. They could not reveal his name. The *Chronicle* reported that it was probable that the execution would be undertaken by a colonial hangman who, having been on leave in England, was instructed to break his journey and go to Gibraltar instead. This person was a highly experienced hangman. He had already carried out no less than 122 executions.

It had been agreed with Mr Baxter that his remuneration should be £15 for the performance of the duty required of him, to which would be added £5 if his conduct and behaviour was satisfactory during and subsequent to the execution. The Colonial Secretary was authorised to pay Mr Baxter the amount due (including any incidental expenses) and the Crown Agents would repay the Colonial Secretary.

Mr Baxter arrived as scheduled on 1st. July and he brought with him the official instructions for carrying out the details of an execution. These included details for the preparation of the scaffold, which had been constructed by the Royal Corps of Engineers. Next, there should be meticulous testing of the mechanism with a bag of sand of the same weight as the prisoner. After completion of this testing, the scaffold and all appliances should be locked up and the key kept by the Governor until the morning of the execution.

Two hours prior to the execution the mechanism was tested again and all appliances checked to ensure that there was no malfunction of any of the components of the gallows.

Chapter 10: The Riot

On 3rd July, the day of the execution, one of the local newspapers, *El Calpense*, reported as follows.

> Last night Gibraltar became the theatre of grave and serious events; as much as for its form as for its makeup and never seen before in this peaceful and law-abiding place—the wave of humanity that descended from the upper parts of the Rock to the town centre—what happened last night was no more no less than a spontaneous reaction by a great mass of people, aided by the excitable shouting of youngsters and screams from many women—we regret what happened but at the same time we are grateful that it did not turn out to be far more serious than it was.

Just before 8 a.m. on 2nd July, the Colonial Secretary went to the Cathedral of St. Mary's the Crowned in order to see Bishop Fitzgerald regarding the question of tolling a bell upon the execution of the convict. The tolling was discretionary, but he wished to ascertain from the bishop whether he desired it on religious grounds. The bishop was not in, but he left a message that he would come to see him later.

At about 8.30 p.m. there was much activity in the vicinity of Main Street. A crowd of people of all sexes and ages lined both sides of the street. It appeared that they were following Mrs Opisso, the mother of the prisoner, who was naturally very distressed when she found out that her son was to be hanged the following morning. A huge crowd, particularly many women, went along with her in the direction of the Governor's residence.

Soon it was possible to see a crowd coming down from City Mill Lane, with individuals going into establishments and asking the shops to close their doors. Some descriptions of the composition of the crowd say that they came from the upper town and were stevedores, taxi drivers, and coal haulers. This was a very derogatory observation, implying that the composition of this crowd was the 'rougher elements of society' who were involved in this 'melee.' Writing of his observations, the Colonial Secretary said that so far as he could ascertain, the crowd consisted mainly of women and children, with the children cheering at odd intervals.

Another independent group was coming from the direction of *El Martillo* or Commercial Square and met with the first. Together they formed an impressive mass of people.

The Bishop's Activities

As it happened, on the evening of 2nd July, Bishop Fitzgerald went for his customary evening walk carrying, as usual, his walking cane. He loved his daily evening stroll. As the enlarged and noisy gathering approached the Golden Eagle, not far from the Governor's House, they saw the bishop. They all went towards him and surrounded him, imploring him to intercede for them with the Governor to grant the reprieve from the death sentence for Opisso, which had been petitioned for and signed by so many thousands of citizens. The bishop explained to them that he could do nothing because he had already done everything within his power, but without any result.

The crowd started to chant in front of the Governor's House and tried to enter through some smaller doors. They could not do so because the Sergeant of the Guard at Government House had his guard turned out in full with fixed bayonets surrounding the Governor's House. The Sergeant informed the Colonial Secretary that there had been an attempt to break into one of the entrances at Government House.

Quickly the crowd dispersed from the Governor's residence and moved down Main Street as the bishop, who had been detained by several well meaning persons, slowly continued his way to the cathedral. Unintentionally, the crowd was pressing upon him, and four policemen came to escort him to the entrance of the cathedral, avoiding some rough handling of the bishop.

He went into the cathedral, not without much hassle, and the doors were eventually closed shut behind him. The crowd could not go through the main entrance, so they went to the rear of the cathedral to try to enter through the back entrance that led to the sacristy.

My father often told us about this incident and the commotion and how he and a few other men stood between the angry, clamouring, and violent

When the Hangman Came

crowd and the bishop as they attacked the entrance. He said he got kicked and punched. The crowd were trying to get at the bishop, and my father and a few like minded individuals stood in their way. Consequently, he himself was pushed to and fro as matters had got out of hand Those in the front were extremely aggressive, but he stood his ground.

A few individuals managed to get inside the church. Soon the police were forced to intervene forcefully with drawn batons and repulsed those on the front line of the crowd and those inside the church. Stones were thrown at the police and many picked up sticks from the trees in the area and used them as clubs. Some continued to shout vociferously for the bishop to come out.

In the meantime, the Colonial Secretary recorded that he returned to his house in order to call the Chief of Police and shortly afterwards returned to the front of Government House, where he found that a goodly proportion of the crowd had dispersed.

Unknown to everyone including the Press, was the fact that Bishop Fitzgerald had gone to the civil prison to visit Ernest Opisso the day before. Ernest confessed with him, and a rather strange reference is made in *El Calpense*. It appears that Ernest had been baptised but had not received the sacrament of confirmation, so the bishop, in addition to hearing his confession, had also dispensed the sacrament of confirmation on Opisso. This was noted in the church's registry. Ernest also received Holy Communion, and the bishop gave Opisso a short talk. The bishop took to his grave the knowledge of whether Ernest had been or not the killer of Miss Bossano.

Following this visit to Ernest, there was another gratifying action by the bishop. He went to see His Excellency the Governor to ask him personally for the commutation of the death sentence on Opisso. No one knew about this until this was made public four days later.

The Colonial Secretary also wrote that when he was returning from the cathedral, he noticed a procession passing at the top of Governor's Lane. As he proceeded there, he was informed that the crowd was following Mrs Opisso, who had come to Government House in an endeavour to see the Governor.

According to the Colonial Secretary, a few spasmodic groups of youths and young boys came dashing into the Square. (The Secretary appears to have been playing down the significance of the event). The Colonial Secretary questioned one of the noisiest members of one of these groups, who informed him that he had just come from the cinema, that all the other boys were shouting, and that was why he too was shouting, but he did not know why they were shouting. Another group of boys, according to the Secretary, came from the direction of the Cathedral and in answer to his question about the noise, the boy answered 'It's nothing.'

Yet another youngster, quite well dressed and aged about seventeen or eighteen, must have recognised him and went up to him and said 'You would not hang Duffield because he was an Englishman so why do you want to hang Opisso?' This made the Colonial Secretary look into the Duffield case, which had happened almost four years earlier.

About 9.30 p.m., the Chief of Police telephoned him, informing him that a very large crowd was gathering outside the Roman Catholic Cathedral and that he was afraid events might become serious. He asked that a request should be made to fortress headquarters for troops, armed with sticks only, to stand by to render assistance if necessary. In the meantime, the Chief got pelted with all kinds of garbage, stones and even a basket were thrown at him. About thirty policemen stood their ground against this overwhelming crowd. Colonel Crichton happened to be with the Secretary at the time and at once took steps accordingly. Arrangements were made for a party of fifty soldiers to be held available at Casemates Barracks.

Later the Colonial Secretary went along and had a look at the crowd in Cathedral Square. The crowd was certainly thick, but so far as he could see, a greater number of those present were there out of mere curiosity. A voice was haranguing the crowd. He was informed that the name of this person was Juan - Asquez. He was told that he was protesting against the execution of Opisso on the grounds that Duffield, an Englishman, had been reprieved. The fact was that Juan Asquez was an active union member of the stevedores and no doubt a shop steward of the union who carried a lot of influence with the workers.

What the Secretary seemed to have missed in his report was how the groups of boys had suddenly merged into a crowd of adults, being urged by one who was to become no less than a member of the *Socorro Rojo International* or the 'International Red Auxiliaries.' This man was not only a trade union activist but also belonged to the extreme Left, something that would affect the thinking of the Governor when he finally wrote to the Secretary of State as to who might have been behind the disturbances. How important and what part did the communists play in this demonstration?

The situation at the cathedral had grown ugly. People were throwing stones at the cathedral windows and were attacking the police with sticks. The police rushed the crowd and managed to push them back. A figure of 3,000 people is mentioned by one periodical and the crowd extended from the cathedral all the way to Commercial Square. The Chief of Police notified Colonel Crichton, asking that the party of troops should be sent up there immediately. Several policemen were injured, amongst them Constables Flower, Tonna, and Dudly. (Notes written by PC Tonna on 4 July 1931)

The Chief of Police reported to the Secretary that the crowd had broken into the back entrance, breaking the door and locks off and going into the sacristy. Others were throwing stones and breaking the windows of the cathedral and were attacking the police with sticks. He had thereupon ordered the police to draw their truncheons, and this had had the effect of causing a goodly part of the crowd to disperse somewhat. Luckily, no sacrilegious acts were committed inside the cathedral and the crowd went out the same way they had gone in.

The Chief of Police had already called for help from the military who had been at the ready at the barracks at Casemates Square. In formation, the troop of about fifty soldiers, carrying hockey sticks held across their chests, stomped at the double along Main Street towards the cathedral. When the crowd saw the company of soldiers from the Staffordshire Regiment trotting in formation towards them and carrying hockey sticks at the ready, they slowly dispersed.

Police and protestors alike were injured, several of whom had to be taken to hospital with various types of wounds. By midnight, matters had quietened down. The party of troops were withdrawn and replaced by a patrol of fifteen men under an officer, their instructions being to patrol into the early hours of the morning.

Father Grech, the Vicar General, then called the Colonial Secretary to come to the cathedral. There he found the bishop very upset. Amongst other things he asked the bishop about the tolling of a bell at the time fixed for the execution, and after consulting Father Grech, the bishop expressed the view that from the religious point of view there was no necessity for such a course.

There were rumours that Mr Jaime Russo had been assaulted by the crowd, but these were soon dispelled when the Press interviewed Mr Russo and the full story was known. It happened that Mr Russo was approached by some of the leaders of the crowd to request him to lead the crowd to ask for the reprieve. They asked this in a most courteous manner. When Mr Russo learned of their intentions, he told them that he felt it was pointless to do anything, since the highest authorities had already turned down the public petition. The whole case had been diligently looked into without finding any grounds for a reprieve, and the Governor's powers did not reach that far. The prerogatives given by His Majesty the King have their limits, but he could assure the people that Sir Alexander J. Godley had been very sad since the day the petition had been turned down.

However, he told the crowd that he would lead them anyway to consult with the authorities, so they all went to the police station where he knew that the Colonial Secretary was waiting. He spoke at great length with him, and when they finished talking, Mr Russo came out again and told them that the Secretary confirmed everything he had said, adding that if the Governor had the remotest reason on which to base his decision, he would have granted the reprieve.

Governor's Report to the Secretary of State

This is another official account of the disturbance from the Governor to the Secretary of State, Lord Passfield.

The evening before the execution, a noisy crowd of several hundred persons had gathered outside the Governor's residence to see the Governor. In front of the crowd was Ernest's mother.

> The demonstrations of which I have forwarded an account in my despatch No.106 of the 7th July, were conspicuous by the fact that they appear to have been started by a number of youths and children parading the streets with a cry of 'We want a reprieve

for Opisso. Duffield was an Englishman and was reprieved; why should a Gibraltarian hang?'

Later these cries were taken up by some of the rougher elements of the Town, including Spaniards from La Linea.

The demonstration culminated in a large gathering in front of the Roman Catholic Cathedral where various speakers harangued the crowd, whose main theme was that a townsman must not be permitted to die when Duffield, an Englishman, had been reprieved. It is significant that the general tenor of the speeches was to draw comparison between the Duffield case and the present one emphasising the fact that the former was an Englishman. I am convinced that a great deal of the feeling amongst certain section of the local community was engendered by one of outraged pride that a Gibraltarian should suffer the death penalty.

The Governor conveniently omitted the fact that the crowd first gathered outside his place of residence, the Convent, also known as Government House. Here the crowd chanted away in unison clamouring for a reprieve. No mention is made of the disturbance that took place at his residence and that the crowd tried to break into it, forcing the guards to come out with fixed bayonets.

The Governor immediately gave orders for soldiers to be sent out, and these surrounded the Convent with fixed bayonets until the crowd were talked down and the crowd went away, though they did not disperse.

Curiously enough, this fact was reported in the British Press, the *Morning Post* and the *Daily Mail*, but this same fact was not reported in the *Gibraltar Chronicle*. The *Chronicle's* report was as follows.

> There were considerable disturbances in the town in connection with the approach of the execution. A crowd of several hundreds, a large proportion of which consisted of coal heavers and labourers, assembled and visited the various café's and shops demanding a general closing, which was complied with. They also called upon taxi and cab drivers to come out on strike and very soon there was not a vehicle obtainable in the city.
>
> The crowd marched down Main Street. Having seen steel, the crowd was now incensed and provoked and redirected their intentions to the Cathedral, and the Bishop in particular. Maybe

they felt there was one last chance for a reprieve if the Bishop intervened. The Governor had pointed out to the Secretary of State that none of the clergy has signed the Public Memorial and this included the Bishop.

The demonstration then proceeded to the front of St. Mary's Cathedral where their numbers were largely increased by passers-by and others who had heard that there was a disturbance afoot. A number attempted to enter the Cathedral but were prevented by a cordon of police, which was drawn up in front of the entrance. After this, cries were raised for His Lordship the Roman Catholic Bishop to come out, the idea apparently being that they wished His Lordship to head the demonstration and proceed to the Government House in order to make a further attempt to obtain a reprieve.

The non-appearance of His Lordship further excited the crowd and a small party of them actually succeeded in breaking down the back entrance to the Cathedral in Cannon Lane but were fortunately prevented from entering by the police.

The temper of the mob now seemed to be thoroughly roused and they made several attempts to rush the police cordon and the constables, who throughout had behaved with admirable restraint, where at this point and were compelled to draw their batons whilst a number of the rioters armed themselves by tearing up the young trees growing by the cab stand.

In the ensuing melee' a number of constables and rioters received injuries, two of the former being admitted to hospital.

Eventually a detachment from the North Staffordshire Regiment under the command of an officer and armed with hockey sticks approached the crowd, their arrival was received with hostile shouts. The Police then commenced to clear the streets in the vicinity and eventually succeeded in restoring order, the crowd dispersing in all directions.

The *Daily Mail* also reported on the riots.

A half company of the North Staffordshire Regiment then arrived armed only with hockey sticks. The crowd began to move backwards, and the police seized the opportunity to charge, although they only numbered 20. They dispersed the crowd in all directions and the streets were quickly cleared.

The Duffield Story

Incidental to the riots was the mention of a reprieve that a governor had given to a Lieutenant D. Duffield of the 2nd East Surrey Regiment stationed in Gibraltar at that time.

The murder occurred on the morning of 7th April 1927. Lieutenant Duffield had asked to see his commanding officer, 48-year-old Lt. Col. J. S. FitzGerald. He went to headquarters and was soon shown in to see the CO. The adjutant closed the door and shortly afterwards heard two shots in quick succession coming from the colonel's office. He heard the CO say out loud, 'Duffield!' He quickly entered the office and found the colonel holding his left shoulder. He said 'Dolland, arrest this man. He has just shot me.'

Duffield stood still and silent as the adjutant called the guards and arrested him. Duffield's service revolver and two spent cartridges lay on the floor. The CO was attended to at his office by some medics who rushed to the scene, but he died of the bleeding wound.

Duffield was tried at the Supreme Criminal Court with a jury. When questioned as to why he had killed his CO, Duffield replied that since their arrival from Jersey, the commanding officer had given up all ideas of soldiering, and all he was interested in was painting and eye washing.

He said, 'I decided to put a stop to this. Better that one man dies than the whole regiment is ruined. I missed the first shot, so I had to use my second bullet, which I had reserved and meant for myself. I was told I had a 'mark' on my hand, and because of this I would someday commit a murder.'

Duffield's assistant mentioned that he had been depressed for the last few days because of the situation of his general military duties.

The court found Duffield guilty of murdering Lt. Col. FitzGerald and sentenced him to death by hanging, but the governor of the day gave him a reprieve on the grounds of insanity. He was sent to the UK, where he completed his term of imprisonment in a mental asylum.

The public in Gibraltar was aware of this since, it had occurred barely three years earlier, and the case was relatively fresh in the minds of some people who decided that there might be a parallel here with the Opisso case. The only problem for Opisso was that he had pleaded not guilty all along, and his defence had not been based on his mental condition, which probably turned out to be a serious misjudgement.

The Arrests and the 'Red Brigade'

Nine individuals were arrested during the disturbances seven being Spanish nationals from La Linea and two Gibraltarians.

This led the Governor to send a despatch to the Secretary of State, marked 'secret.' After reporting on the details of the Opisso trial, the verdict of the jury, the public petition for a reprieve, the special report by the Medical Board, and his issuing of a warrant for the execution, he adds that he now had to refer to one important point concerning the disturbances of the evening of 2nd.July.

He informed Lord Passfield that the neighbouring Spanish town of La Linea is well known as a hot bed of syndicalism, and there was every reason to believe that communist propaganda and money was circulating there freely. There was grave suspicion that alien agents had seized upon this opportunity to stir up trouble in Gibraltar. This applied particularly to the closing of shops during the whole of the day of the execution, which was undoubtedly due to the instigation of these agents, and the lack of courage on the part of local shopkeepers, who, although promised every possible protection, feared reprisals, if not immediately, then at some later stage. He added that it was extremely difficult to get Gibraltarians to come forward and give evidence in cases of this nature.

In the police court proceedings, Mr M G. Corsi and H Bado, JP, presided over seven Spaniards on a charge of disorderly conduct. These were Juan de Rio Sanchez, Luis Rojas Tenveries, Miguel Lopez Garcia, Adolfo Loronga Pelaz, Juan Portilla Ruiz, Victoriano Villanueva Moreno, and Salvador Rodriguez Bernal. They were represented by Mr S. P. Triay.

The defence lawyer made the case that these individuals had never appeared in court before and it was their first offence. He added that the court must take into account the excitement of the situation and that everyone was caught up in it. It was difficult to say who had started the trouble.

The court did not agree with this argument and fined six of the accused two pounds sterling each or fourteen days in prison. The other prisoner was fined four shillings or twenty four hours in detention, simply because he was a minor. The judge advised them that they had got away very lightly in view of the gravity of the charge. He also added that just because they were foreigners, they should have refrained from joining in a local disturbance.

The Chief of Police had written to the Colonial Secretary on the matter as follows. 'The seven Spaniards involved should be expulsed on completion of the sentence and as soon as payment of fines are made. I consider that they are not desirable persons to be allowed to enter the garrison, especially during the present state of affairs in Spain.'

The two Gibraltarians, John Dyer and Joseph Duo, were each fined two pounds sterling, but one of them was additionally charged with attempting to wound Constable Samuel Wahnon with a knife when the latter was trying to arrest him. The accused pleaded guilty, was tried in the same court, and sentenced to four months imprisonment with hard labour.

The charge was the strongest charge that the forthcoming evidence would permit, and it resulted in the infliction of the maximum penalty. The Governor proposed to issue expulsion orders against those Spaniards who had been charged with disorderly conduct, since it had been established that they had intimidated shopkeepers to close down their establishments. There was obviously a weakness in the local law as regards dealing with the situation of these aliens.

A Spark of Gibraltarian Identity

Two items disprove the claim that there were no Gibraltarians as such until after World War Two. The first is the official reference above to Gibraltarians. The second is the community unity that the mass demonstration had provoked prior to the riot. The comparison by the crowd of case of Opisso, 'a Gibraltarian,' with that of Duffield, 'an Englishman,' shows strong sentiments of ethnic distinctions.

The Governor told the Secretary of State to rest assured that the communist movement in the vicinity and any possible danger to the fortress and colony was engaging his closest attention.

The night of the 2nd remained relatively quiet, but restless dissatisfaction remained. Throughout the silent city, there were murmurings about the disturbances and the interference by the military as it waited for the morning of the dreadful execution.

By now, Ernest would have been moved to the condemned man's cell, very close to the gallows. With him inside his cell, a prison warden would stay for that last twelve hours until execution time.

There is a saying in prisons, 'the number thirteen is unlucky for some.' This is because in some UK prisons, it takes exactly thirteen steps from the condemned cell to the gallows. The prison wardens in Gibraltar were astounded when they counted the strides from the condemned cell to the gallows. It was exactly thirteen strides!

No Gibraltarian within living memory had been executed, and certainly no townsman had been executed within the precincts of the civil prison. Irrespective of the brutal murder, the Governor's lack of mercy was obviously not acceptable.

On Sunday 5th July, His Lordship Bishop Fitzgerald gave a public address at the Cathedral of St. Mary the Crowned and then published this address in the newspapers. He wrote:

> It is my duty to condemn, in the most forceful terms, the most shameful scenes that occurred around the Cathedral on the night of last Thursday.
>
> A crowd stood in front of the Cathedral for several hours. I have the greatest sympathy for the motives and reasons for the demonstration, but I have every right to protest publicly and forcefully against the gross and indecent language used by some directed at the Clergy and me.
>
> I protest against the violent and criminal breaking in through the back door. I protest against the attempt to break down the front gates that lead to the patio, where the police showed a superhuman

effort of restrain and patience, which eventually led them to charge against the attackers.

I have been filled with shame and indignation at such language and spectacle.

I thought it impossible that a group of British subjects, in any part of the Empire, would turn their backs on their education and traditions and lower themselves to such a level, wishing to imitate the savage and repulsive communism that exists across the border and which has given such a bad name to Spain throughout the civilised world. (I wish to add 'the uncivilised.')

Ernest Opisso's family will be the first to condemn this criminal and reprobate type of exhibition on the eve of the mournful and tragic day.

They know very well that I had done everything possible within my power about this sad case. Only last Tuesday, I revisited His Excellency the Governor in order to put before him new information that had been supplied by the Prison Chaplain in favour of the prisoner. I could do no more, yet my dignity as a man and my dignity as a Bishop did not allow me to take part in a street demonstration so disorganised, so late, so stupid, so counter-productive, and so far from a true representation of the People of Gibraltar.

I would have never imagined the events as they developed, especially in front of the Catholic Cathedral, if I had not seen them with my own eyes. We should all feel ashamed about the occurrence, and myself more than anyone else. I am convinced that the true People of Gibraltar must be deeply sorrowful about these shameful occurrences since it has blackened their good name.

It is inadmissible that the People of Gibraltar will tolerate riots of this calibre, influenced and promoted by outside influences, and so opposed to our education and civil ways. It will fight if it is necessary for its religion, its culture, and its civil ways. Let everyone take note.' (Author's translation from the Spanish taken from *El Calpense*)

Members of the International Red Brigade

Group photo of members of the International Red Brigade.

Chapter 11: The Day of the Execution

The Execution

The appointed day arrived for the hanging of Ernest Opisso for the murder of Miss Maria Luisa Bossano on 29th November 1930 at 7 Market Lane.

The execution was to be carried out within the walls of the prison, in keeping with the new Act in Britain called the Capital Punishment within Prisons Act passed on 29th May 1928. The first person to be executed in the UK inside the four walls of a prison was Thomas Wells, aged eighteen years, and the hangman then was one William Calcraft, who had been a public executioner since 1929. 'Wells' execution was not a clean one,' reported the London *Times*. 'Wells died hard after three convulsive struggles.'

At exactly 6.00 a.m. on the morning of the 3rd, the executioner Mr Baxter again carried out a complex inspection and test of the gallows and the equipment. He had taken a precise measurement of the rope when fully stretched with the aid of two flat heavy plates of metal, which were imperative and had been got ready.

At the end of the rope, which forms the noose, he had measured thirteen inches from the centre of the noose and marked this with another chalk mark round the rope. This mark was particularly important, because it fixed the stretching point of the rope with the lengthening of the neck and the body of the culprit, as well as the constriction of the tightening of the rope around the neck with the weight of the body.

Once again the executioner tested the hanging mechanism. He measured off the required length of the drop from the painted line on the rope, and then he measured off the distance of the sandbag from the ground.

He then went to the 'pinioning room.' This room had been conveniently chosen close to the scaffold. The prisoner had already been moved from his cell to this room. A close watch was kept on the scaffold whilst the executioner went to the pinioning room so that no one could tamper with the mechanism.

The culprit was then pinioned. We are not told how this particular culprit was pinioned. Two methods come to mind. One is that he might have been dressed in a 'restraining jacket' with his hands pinioned behind his back by the long sleeves of the jacket. Alternatively, he might have been strapped with a wide belt around his upper arms around the elbows and with his hands tied behind the back with smaller straps. (A heavy leather belt is currently held as an exhibit at the present prison, together with the noose, the handcuffs, and the heavy metal plates).

His neck was bared, a collarless shirt was put on him, and no gold chains were permitted. Ernest must have been medicated with a mild tranquilliser. Nevertheless, there is no doubt that his feeble mind could not comprehend what was happening to him. Everyone was in agreement that his mental ability was way below normal. He was probably shaking, sobbing, and uttering in his unintelligible voice his protestations of innocence.

In the notes written by P.C. Tonna he describes how four prison wardens had to escort Opiso from the Condemned Cell to the scaffold. It is probable that one of the prison Wardens gave this information to the policeman

With the help of the prison officers, the hangman finally pinioned Ernest in his cell. It was now 7.55 a.m. Once the pinioning was done, he was taken quickly to the gallows. The prison chaplain, Father Salvador de Julian, accompanied and comforted the prisoner and prayed with him till the very end. *(El Calpense)*

The executioner placed him in position under the beam to which the rope was attached. He strapped the prisoner's legs tightly. He put the white linen cap over his head. He put the rope over his head and tightened it around the neck, with the cap between the rope and the neck. The noose was placed so that the rope was under his chin. The noose was kept tight by means of a leather ring. Finally, the executioner bent down and tied the heavy metal plates to the foot straps. The extra weight ensured a heavy pull and therefore a quick death.

When he was sure everything was in order, he went quickly to the lever, made sure the culprit was standing on the marked spot, pushed the lever

When the Hangman Came

forward, and let down the trap doors. The heavily oiled trap door hinges gave way smoothly.

The body disappeared into the depth of the pit with a sudden jerk.

There was no further movement.

Ernest hung on the spot at the end of the rope for one hour. This was the time specified by the regulation of 1891. Then the body was carefully raised from the pit. The rope was removed from the neck, and also the straps from the body. The white cap was removed. The body was made ready for the inquest and the head was raised three inches by placing a small piece of wood under it. (1891 Regulations)

El Calpense makes a reference that a grave nine feet deep had been dug for the purpose of burying Ernest Opisso, but this was not to be his final burial place.

Ernest Opisso, aged twenty-eight, was pronounced dead by the prison surgeon, Dr Leopold H. Gill. *El Calpense* carried the following final message,

> May God receive the soul of the unfortunate Ernest Opisso, giving him eternal rest, and his aggrieved mother in her grievous pain and also his brothers the resignation to bear such a bitter test.

3rd July 1931

From about seven o'clock in the morning of the 3rd, a crowd of about a hundred gathered in the vicinity of the prison, whilst many others could be seen at the windows of houses in the neighbourhood and the neighbourhood of Willis's Gate. There was, however no repetition of the previous night's disorder.

At about 8 o'clock a loud piercing scream was heard, and those close by thought it had come from the prisoner, but this turned out not to be the case. It was simply a hysterical woman in the neighbourhood reacting spontaneously to the appointed hour.

At 8.25 a.m. the official notice that judgment of death had been carried out was posted outside the prison door. In addition to the signatures of the prison officials, Mr Joseph Olivari, John Smith Wilkinson, Sergeant of Police, it also bore those of Commander H. Biron, JP, and Captain of the Port, Mr W. S. Gulloch, the superintendent of the prison, Doctors L. H. Gill and G. H. Griffiths, and the Revd. Salvador de Julian CMF. No one saw them entering or leaving the prison. They must have left the place through a back entrance.

Reporters were not allowed in to witness the execution, and some bad press about this was published.

Following the execution, the Coroner, Mr J. King, had to perform the official *post mortem* and give the cause of death. For this inquest, a jury was named, which was comprised of the following persons: Mr Joseph L. Cazes, Joseph Noquera, Anthony Gareze, Adolfo Montegriffo, Alexander Simpson, Judah Balensi, Arthur de la Paz, and William J. Ellicott.

Before the inquest started, Mr Anthony Gareze complained to the coroner that when Policeman Constable Neal had gone to his house, he was told that he was not in, but the policeman insisted in searching the house. The coroner undertook to take the matter up with the proper authority.

The *post mortem* had to be carried out at the prison, and the Press was allowed in as well. They saw the corpse in a cell, lying on a low bed that was almost at floor level. The face was peaceful and appeared more asleep than dead. The face muscles were not tight and showed no sign of contraction whatsoever. The left leg was slightly bent at the knee and his left hand was upon his chest. The body showed no signs of violence and appeared peaceful as if in a profound sleep.

At the entrance gate to the prison, they saw a notice signed by Dr Leopold H. Gill, surgeon to the civil prison, that he had on that day examined the body of Opisso and had found him to be dead and that he had died an instantaneous death.

The Coroner thanked the jury for their attendance and hoped they would never again have to serve on a similar jury.

The civil prison, like the Colonial Hospital, was equipped with a lime pit or well. This well was filled with quick lime, and the corpses of condemned prisoners were lowered into these cavities so that the quick lime would dissolve all the flesh and biodegradable parts of the body. Only the skeleton would remain and would be washed clean and placed inside a niche in the wall.

Contrary to the report carried in *El Calpense*, Opisso was not buried in a grave, which, it claimed, had been specially dug for him. Opisso's remains were introduced into this niche in the wall. Then the hole was covered with a small white marble slab with the prisoner's initials, his prison number, and the date of the execution. Ernest Opisso's niche bore the initials 'E. O.,' and below the letter 'E.' was the date '3/7/31' the date of the executin. Above the initials was his registered prisoner's number '17.27.1.31.' (See Photo).

No Flags, No Bells Tolled

No flag flew at half-mast, no black flag flew from the Moorish Castle, and no bells pealed from any church. Ernest Opisso was no more.

It was a day of general mourning. All shops and entertainment places were closed for the whole day. The streets were deserted, and a strange calm and quiet prevailed on that ominous day. The same was true in the town of La Linea. The Governor had hinted that the shops had closed for fear of reprisals and in the face of intimidation from certain quarters, but he does not say who was in that quarter.

In commiseration with the family, thousands gathered around the Opisso residence. The newspapers reported that a great depressed silence had fallen all over the town, and that the topic of conversation was nothing else but the terrible execution.

El Calpense added a rather pessimistic analysis of the situation in Gibraltar. It wrote:

> As if our unfortunate community does not have enough problems of its own with the paralysis of commerce and unemployment, the high cost of living, and the effect of the rate of exchange, we now have this sad situation of the trial and the terrible execution. God grant that all these calamities will stop and that all the suffering over the few last years will finish and Gibraltar will stop to be so distressed as she finds itself today. (*El Calpense*, 3 July 1931)

Mr Baxter, the executioner, was expeditiously sent on board a naval vessel *HMS Sandhurst* the night of the 3rd and was due to arrive in Sheerness on or about 10th. July.

The Coroner Gets into Trouble

The inquest had to be carried out at the civil prison in the Moorish Castle. When the Coroner arrived, the press were waiting outside the entrance to the prison. They were all anxious to hear what had happened. They attempted to enter the prison, but the jailer stopped them from entering. When the coroner saw this, he overruled the jailer and ordered him to allow the reporters to enter.

According to the Colonial Secretary, as a consequence of this decision the Press had published unnecessary and inaccurate details as regards the proceedings. In what appears to have been an angry note, the Attorney General wrote to the Colonial Secretary, Alexander Beatty, informing him that it had come to his knowledge that the Coroner had allowed members of the press to view the dead body of Opisso. He told the Colonial Secretary that the Coroner's Court is an open court, and as such the Press should be allowed to attend. But 'the court' meant the proceedings that take place at the magistrates' court, where the evidence was taken, and does not include the viewing of the body. Therefore, in his opinion, the Coroner was very wrong in allowing press representatives to enter the prison and view the body, especially as no evidence was taken there.

The Colonial Secretary lost no time in writing to the Coroner and explained in detail the Attorney General's opinion. He added that the government was advised, therefore, that his action in allowing Press representatives to enter the prison and view the body was wrong. In its intent this was a strong official reprimand that the Coroner received.

The Coroner replied that the Coroner's Court was normally held at the Magistrates' Court, but it was necessary to adjourn the court to the civil prison for the purpose of taking the usual evidence of identification, and in this respect, therefore, such part of the civil prison as the Coroner and his jury made use of in connection with the proceedings became the Coroner's Court for the time being.

In these circumstances, therefore, and in the further exercise of his discretion, he had decided that as the Press representatives had attended the first part of the proceedings, he could hardly debar them from attending such part of the proceedings as were to be held in the Coroner's Court when it was held at the civil prison, more particularly in view of the principles laid down in legal authoritative text books and prescribed by statute.

He added that it had always been the practice in proceedings held before the Coroner in such places as the Colonial Hospital, to which inquests are sometimes adjourned, for Press representatives to attend both the court and the mortuary. The Coroner pointed out that in these exceptional circumstances, he had spared no pains to ensure that the investigation was conducted with full regard to law and practice.

In accordance with the Memorandum for Executions of 1891, the dead culprit was supposed to be buried within the prison's walls.

Recognition of the Jailers

Nine days after the hanging, on 12 July the Colonial Secretary wrote a letter addressed to the jailer of the Moorish Castle civil prison, Mr Olivari. He wrote:

> I fully realise how this case has caused a great deal of extra work to the small staff of the Civil Prison and some members of the staff, including yourself, remained on duty for 14 and 15 hours a day.
>
> I am desired by His Excellency to convey to you an expression of grateful thanks and high appreciation.
>
> Yours truly,
>
> Colonial Secretary

A reward of two pounds was paid to each police officer and the Chief.

The first public execution of any kind in Gibraltar was that of Private George Shaw of the Fusiliers. It took place in 1896 at Casemates Square.

Jose Martin Munoz was hanged in 1942 for wartime crimes, including espionage, and Luis Lopez Cordon Cuenca was hanged in 1943 for attempted sabotage. He was caught just in time with a bomb, which he was trying to introduce into the ammunition stores inside the Rock.

The wooden scaffold of the gallows used on Ernest Opisso's execution was still in place until 1982, and during a visit to the prison by Governor Sir Peter Terry, he ordered, to the chagrin of all prison officers of the time, the structure to be dismantled. The officers saved the wooden beams, and several years later they were used as ceiling beams for the prison officers' social club inside the prison complex.

The rope noose, the handcuffs, the pinioning belt, and the weights used at this execution are still on display as you enter the main offices at the civil prison.

Within this complex there is a distinction between two sections, the civil prison and the military prison. (Visit to Moorish Castle Prison).

Military Hanging 1893 at Casemates

Military public hanging in Gibraltar in 1893.

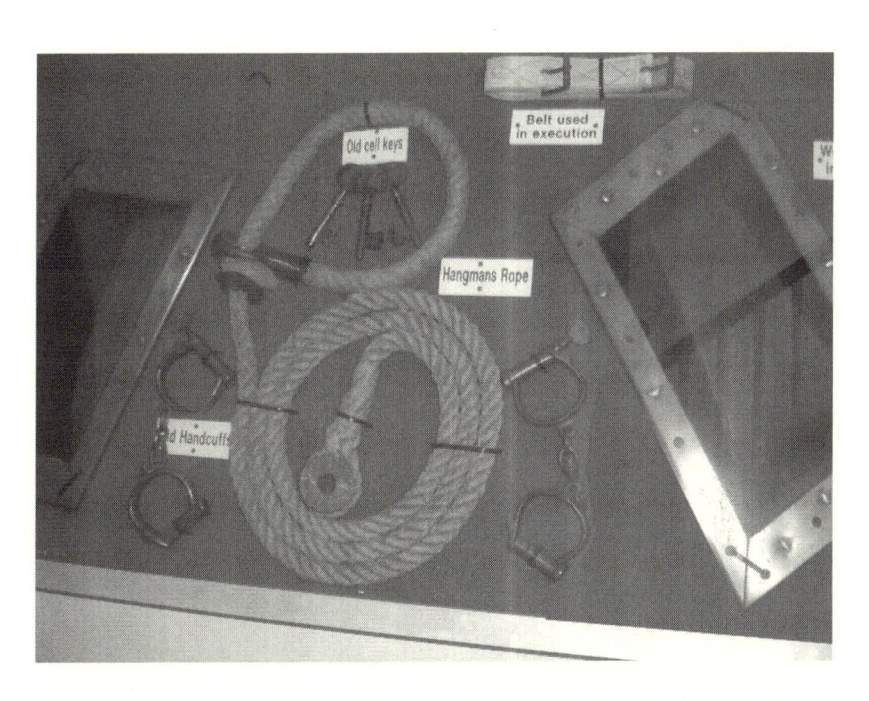

Actual noose and paraphernalia used on Opisso's hanging.

What Scaffold Would Look Like

What Opisso's scaffold would have looked like.

Chapter 12: Where Was the Motive?

Motives are very important in a murder case. Hate, money, jealousy, vengeance, and fear are some of the most common motives. If there is no motive, then there must be a reason for its absence.

Curiously, the trials had not established a motive. In fact, the prosecution made a statement that it was not necessary for them to establish a motive. However, without a motive the murder would have been a senseless, maniacal, brutal act of violence. Since there must have been a reason for a brutal murder I shall theorise three possible 'hypothetical' motives. There are definitely no concrete evidence for any of the theories only what can be deduced from the transcripts of the trials and some hearsay.

First Possible Motive: Jealousy

According to a note in the Colonial Secretary's own hand writing, Ernest was born out of wedlock, a child worthy of pity because he had several several other disabilities with his deafness, speech impairment, and lameness. PC Ernest Santos testified that he had known Ernest Opisso since he was a small boy and that it had always been difficult to understand what he said. The lameness, as stated by Dr Giraldi, was the result of a rare case of tuberculosis in the left hip, a very rare medical condition.

A child with those conditions would have had a tough life and possibly have been the object of fun at school from his peers. Children can be very cruel to other children who are not 'normal.' He may have been called names such as 'freak,' 'hoppy,' even 'bastard.' Not having a father around like all the other children in his neighbourhood must have produced a deep hole of resentment, feelings of not belonging, of insecurity, and of not being loved.

Psychologists would say that all these shortcomings would normally lead a person to develop an inferiority complex and to carry a chip on his shoulders, a grudge against society. With such a background, a young child would eventually wish to 'get even' with society, to show that he was important, or even to show 'who was the master.'

In some extreme cases of murder, there is a classical condition called 'slow-burn syndrome.' This can result from continuous harassment and threats, physiological or physical, and the victim eventually reacts violently against his or her tormentor.

In the criminal robbery case in 1926, when Ernest was twenty-five years old, two doctors produced medical certificates in court testifying that Ernest was not mentally stable. What did they mean? He had the mind of a child? He was simple-minded? He was bi-polar? He did not know what was right from wrong? Good from evil?

Ernest's behaviour in court during the trials had been rather childish and flippant, as can be gathered from a few comments in the transcripts. But his replies at the inquest, at the police court, when he was not yet under suspicion, and at the first trial and the retrial, he answered lucidly and intelligently. The prosecution set several courtroom traps for him, and he sensibly (not cunningly) avoided them. More so, his answers were totally rational. For example, he was asked, 'Did you know the boy was looking to identify you?'

His gestures in court could have been interpreted as 'antics' and appeared funny, but a person with hearing and speech impediment could appear to act in a strange way.

'Why should he?' he replied.

Ernest has been described as 'slow' and 'mentally below normal,' but never was he described as an idiot, stupid, foolish, or unintelligent. So can lunacy and insanity be ruled out? Could there have been a moment of temporary insanity brought about by some provocation or insult and an arousal of passion or even jealousy? Ernest had a mind and a brain of his own. He also had feelings, human and manly feelings.

In one of his answers when he was asked where he was coming from on Friday, 28 November when walking up Market Lane, he replied, 'from seeing a girl.' It was at this point that he saw Miss Bossano at the window, they exchanged words, and she asked him up to her flat. Although this

When the Hangman Came

must have been a surprising revelation in court, neither the prosecution nor the defence made much of this statement.

Now we find out that Ernest, the short fellow with a limp, deaf and impaired speech-, had a lady friend. This is extremely surprising. Was not this an obvious and reasonable line to probe into further? Who was this lady friend? Where did she live? What did she do for a living? Was she local or was she a Spanish lady? And importantly, did he actually come from seeing a lady? Curiosity alone would have been sufficient to expand on this revelation; it showed another side of the accused murderer.

The next question would be what kind of lady would encourage or respond to close friendship or affection from Ernest. Maybe this lady herself was in need of companionship and friendship, even from a young fellow with Ernest's physical disabilities. As they say, 'love is blind.'

It was not uncommon for a few Spanish female day-workers to make a little extra money on the side by granting small personal favours to male friends.

Ernest was a young and virile male. It is highly possible that he would have had a desire to visit a friendly lady and that he would be likely to easily succumb to this desire. He lived not far from Serfaty's and New Passage, streets well known for their local brothels, but it is highly unlikely that he would frequent those areas, simply because they were too close to home.

Ernest said that he had met with some friends in Main Street during the evening of the Sunday, the day the murder was discovered, and he mentioned that his friends were going to La Linea, a town next to Gibraltar to which they could easily walk. La Linea was not without its facilities for young men. There was the notorious Calle de Gibraltar, often frequented by males from Gibraltar of all ages. This place was visited for its economy and anonymity, in preference to Serfaty's and New Passage, which catered mostly for the military and naval personnel, who could possibly and regrettably be rewarded with an unwelcome dose of something undesirable.

However, I was now in search of some facts or even rumours as to what the motive might have been. During a visit to the Elderly Persons' Residence of Mount Alvernia, I spoke to a very lucid centenarian, my mother-in-law, and I asked her.

'Carmen, do you happen to remember the Opisso murder case where a Miss Luisa Bossano was killed?'

'Why, yes, I do remember the case. I even remember the lady in question, though she was much older than I. I was twenty years old at the time'.

'What can you remember of the reason for killing her, what were the rumours at the time?'

'I think they were saying that he had gone with someone else.'

Of course I was surprised. I was flabbergasted! This recollection by this hundred year old lady could have knocked me over with a feather.

Luisa Maria Bossano was a very devout spinster lady, well bred, a lady of means and well liked by everyone. A kind hearted, charitable, and lonely lady like Miss Bossano would probably encourage, out of pity, a prudent and proprietary friendship with her handyman, and poor Ernest, with his bagful of personal mixed emotions and longing for some kind of affection, might have misinterpreted it as something more than friendship.

So assuming that Ernest was the murderer, could the motive have been jealousy? Could this have been the cause of an argument?

Ernest knew the victim from before, when she lived at another address, so their acquaintance went back some time. He rented from her a store, and he carried out odd jobs for her.

He may have gone up Market Lane on Friday the 28th, not coming from seeing a lady friend, but wishing to see a lady friend, Miss Bossano. She happened to be looking out of her first-floor window, and when they starting talking, she asked him to go up to her flat because, she said, she could not hear him from the street. However, unless the lady was deaf too, it is most improbable that she could not hear him from the street below which was so near her window and only a few yards above street level.

Ernest could have read more into that invitation to go up. It may have possibly touched him in a sentimental way, though it was purely kindness on the part of the lady. Under such false impressions, Ernest would possibly demand more. In the old days, well-off ladies tended to be prudish and reserved. 'Strait-laced' was a common description. It was just not the 'done thing' to have a man coming to your house, but if this man happened to

When the Hangman Came

be someone everyone recognised as the handyman, his visits would be perfectly acceptable.

Ernest said he only stayed there for five minutes, but then again, if he did stay longer for a cup of tea and biscuits, it would be highly improbable that he would have volunteered this information.

Did some kind of discussion take place on the Friday, which remained unfinished until Saturday? Sometime on Saturday, possibly at around 4 p.m., he again visited the lady, this time in a surreptitious way. The time is difficult to determine because several witnesses, in particular Mr Teuma, had provided what appears to be an almost watertight alibi for the whole of Saturday, but the afternoon was a more likely possibility. He could have left the Teuma's house when Mr Teuma was away and returned before Mr Teuma came home from work at 5 p.m. Mr Teuma would have been left with the impression that Ernest had not left the house. However, this late timing conflicts with two medical approximations and fits in with the time of death given by Dr Giraldi and the alarm clock mysteriously stopped at 3.55 p.m.

When he called, the lady opened the door for him, rather surprised. It was Ernest's opportunity to confront the lady. When he had gone up on the previous day, there was someone with her in the flat. Ernest had surmised that she was entertaining a man. He was jealous about this, so he questioned her directly in his stammering and halting way. Who was that man? What was he doing there? What was his business there? A discussion developed which evolved into an argument, which in turn blew up into a fight.

Raised voices and accusations of duplicity may have followed. The lady called Ernest several offending names, and he got mad. He reached out to the table in the kitchen and grabbed the knife-sharpener that was handy. He pushed and shoved the lady, but she ran away from him from the entrance room through the glass door into the bedroom. By now she was had reached the far end of the bedroom and could go no further.

He had got the long, pointed steel knife sharpener with the intention of frightening the lady, but she was not that frightened and told him to leave her house. She wanted nothing more to do with a good-for-nothing person like him.

Blind with fury, he lifted the heavy sharpener and struck her, once, twice, three times. The lady staggered a few steps. She went down on one knee, bleeding from a wound to the left side of her head. She got up and tried to go to the window to shout for help, but Ernest got her from behind, gagged her with a duster, and pulled her further into the house towards the inner sitting room. There, by the glass door, he hit her again with the heavy sharpener. She grabbed him by the hair and pulled some off, but for such a small person he was very powerful. Again he hit several heavy blows, and then she collapsed by the door with her eyeglasses falling off. Blind with fury, he hit her again whilst she was on the floor, this time dislodging a piece of skull bone. Blood and brain matter came away with the weapon.

He noticed there was blood everywhere, on the floor, on the furniture, on the carpet, and on the walls. The lady, once his friend and employer, lay motionless on the floor. She was dead. He had killed her.

In disbelief he looked at both his bloodstained hands. For a moment he panicked, but soon he came to his senses. He poured water into a basin and washed his hands on a towel nearby. He made his way to the door silently opened it and listened carefully, making sure no one was coming up the stairs. With his own spare key he locked the flat. He hoped that it would take time to open the flat and he would gain time to return to Teuma's house before he returned from work.

Fortunately for him, no one saw him leaving the flat, and he made it to Teuma's house fifteen minutes' walk away and resumed playing with the children there.

This hypothesis is only possible if Ernest was the killer. But one other big question arises. What if the true weapon was the file and not the knife-sharpener? Where did the file come from, and what was it doing in that apartment?

There could be two simple answers to this question One was that Ernest had left a bag of tools in the flat from a previous job or else had brought it with him with murder in mind The other was that the murder was committed with another weapon similar to the file, like, for example, the knife sharpener, and the file was not the murder weapon.

It had been suggested that a piece of glass, just like the one produced as evidence during the trial, could have been a possible murder weapon, but a piece of glass was an unlikely weapon since it would have left cuts and scratches on the murderer's hands leaving clear evidence. Dr Giraldi suggested the knife-sharpener, because it was a tool similar to a file, and it had a semi-circular shape. This was a likely weapon, because knife-sharpeners tend to be rather heavy, heavier by far than a carpenter's file.

Could the three doctors, who agreed that the file was the likely weapon, have been wrong and one doctor right?

Robbery was not the apparent motive, since Miss Bossano's relative Joseph Canessa found more money in the top drawer of the chest of drawers than he expected. A thief would have rummaged the house for money, but it was not done. No money was taken! Even her jewellery was there. Nothing was missing, and nothing had been taken, except the life of poor Miss Bossano.

So was jealousy the possible cause of an argument and the motive for murder?

Second Possible Motive: Money

From an examination of the evidence given at the trials, a second hypothesis for a motive, assuming that Ernest was the killer, emerges. This second hypothesis was the one that the prosecution thought was behind an argument over money that developed into a murder. Even so, the prosecution did not press this theory at all. We know of it because the Chief of Police mentioned it to Scotland Yard in London, and this theory was included in Scotland Yard's early report following the Chief of Police's statement to them.

However a question arises with this theory. Was Ernest's and Miss Bossano's disagreement over money that serious and bad enough to have led to such a violent conclusion?

Both individuals had their reasons not to get into conflict. The lady, in the first place, was well known for her charity and good nature, but Ernest was also very useful to her. She had property that constantly required maintenance and work. If Ernest owed her rent, then she could have easily made arrangements for him to pay her off in kind. Ernest, on the other hand, needed his store and the work that the lady occasionally provided him with. It is highly probable that he would have agreed to pay the lady over a period of time with his services. Therefore, why should a situation over money lead to such an uncharacteristic discord that eventually led to violence and murder?

Nevertheless, for the sake of completeness, let us assume that the motive was a serious discussion over money that took place between Ernest and the lady.

It so happened that Ernest owed Miss Bossano two months' rent. He had not paid his October rent, and the lady must have been reminding Ernest and asking him when he was going to pay her the rent money.

On the evening of the previous day, she had asked Ernest to go up to her flat. Ernest said all along that the purpose was to give him the piece of string and weight to measure the water level of the underground water cistern at the Cornwall's Lane property and that he had taken the opportunity to tell her about the complaints of the French tenant at Cornwall's Lane.

At first she had talked to him from the first-floor window, but she then asked him up, not because she could not hear him, a most unlikely thing, but instead because she wanted to talk to him in private, out of earshot of any nosey neighbour.

'Ernest, I've asked you to come up to ask you again. When are you going to pay your October rent? You realise it is now the end of November, and you now owe the October and November rents.'

She had taken out her little black book and showed it to him, the book where she kept note of all her receipts and payments, pointing with her finger at the rent page. Because of his deafness, she addressed Ernest very slowly so he could understand what she was saying. He could see she was very annoyed.

'Ernest, you are not keeping to our agreement. You owe me now two months' rent. Do you have the money ready to pay me?'

A very embarrassed Ernest replied, 'Sorry, Miss Bossano, I don't have the money with me at the moment, but I'll fetch it for you tomorrow. I have to be paid by Mr Canessa and Mr Teuma for a couple of jobs I've done for them, but in any event you too owe me. How do you expect me to pay you, when you owe me money for several jobs I have done for you?'

'That's beside the point, Ernest. I expect you to pay on time. I want the money by tomorrow and not later. Do you understand?'

'I understand you, but you are a mean lady. You expect me to work for you for nothing. It has been like this for a long time. I'll come tomorrow with the money. Goodbye, and go to hell!'

'You insolent man, how dare you talk to me in that way? How ungrateful you are! I give you work to help you, and this is the way you repay me.'

That night, an embittered Ernest did a lot of thinking. He wished this old lady would not take advantage of him just like everyone else did. How could he get rid of this mean woman who was abusing him and treating him unfairly, even robbing him of his money? Just like everyone else, she was taking advantage of him.

By the following morning, Saturday the 29th, he had figured a way out of his dilemma. He could remove the pressure that this old spinster was placing on his life.

He was clever enough to know that if he was going to 'do her in' and get away with it, then he needed a good alibi. He figured out that the timing was important. He needed to do it at a time when there were few people around and when neighbours would not be looking out of their windows, as they usually did. That perfect time was lunchtime, two o'clock in fact. People would be sitting down to lunch or relaxing after lunch, listening to the radio and nodding off.

However, he did not take into account the fact that policemen finished their beat in Main Street at precisely 2 p.m. and that one common route from Main Street to the police station was Market Lane. It so happened that one such policeman would testify that he saw Ernest go into Market Lane as he passed by on his way to the nearby police station.

Ernest had thought that his alibi would be two of his regular clients whom he intended to visit. He had scheduled two jobs, one in the morning and another in the afternoon. He would somehow sandwich the murder in between these two jobs. First he would go to the Canessa house, not too far away from the lady's flat Conveniently, they were also relatives of his proposed victim. From there, he would go at his regular time to his house for lunch at one o'clock, where his sister would have lunch ready. He knew that on a Saturday the charwoman would be there as usual and would see him, so much so that when she saw him she would tell him, 'You are always in a hurry.' The fact that he was rushing was an interesting remark, because this lady added in court that Ernest was always in a hurry. Therefore, no one would think anything about this rushing behaviour.

He calculated that he should end his lunch break very early. Since the charwoman did not wear a watch, he mentioned as he passed her that it was already ten minutes to two, when in fact it was only twenty minutes past one. He was calculating that he would be at Market Lane by 1.30 p.m.

He would wear his raincoat and carry the iron file in the pocket of his coat. Why he would take a file and not a hammer, or a heavier weapon, is a puzzling question. The file, after all, is not a very heavy tool, yet, in all probability, he never thought the file would cause so much damage.

Miss Bossano had finished her lunch not long before at about 1 p.m. She was a very disciplined and correct lady who kept to a regular routine. She was also very generous, except when it came to paying for work, as she was rather frugal. This was evidenced when she went to the second-hand marketplace to buy her curtain rods, and she felt it was an outrage that Ernest expected payment for just lowering a piece of string to measure the water level. Surely, that only took a second? She was also angry with him for his insolence, as she was not used to having her correctness questioned. At this moment, she was lying down and resting, on top of her made-up bed, thinking about the embarrassing incident of the previous day and looking at her black book.

Cautiously and silently, Ernest went through the pitch-dark first-floor corridor where the flat was located and carefully peeped through the closed kitchen window in the corridor. He saw that there was no light showing in the flat. He was ready with some kind of excuse should he be unexpectedly surprised by some neighbour turning up at that critical moment, although his presence would not arouse suspicion. He was known by all the neighbours as the handyman and would just pretend he was on a job.

Ernest knew Miss Bossano's daily routine. She always rested after lunch for about half an hour. He stealthily produced from his coat pocket a spare key that had belonged to a previous occupant, which he had kept. Silently he turned the key in the lock and opened the door very slowly. He reached to his right and turned off the electric mains switch, which was at shoulder level, and with difficulty, because of his limp, he crept inside on tiptoes.

The first glass door that led from the hall to the sitting room was no problem as it stood open, but the other glass door that led into the bedroom was only partially open. With his fingertips he slowly pushed the glass door open. Miss Bossano heard a sound, a very slight sound. Propping herself up on her elbows, she said into the darkness, 'Who is it? Is anyone there?'

The shutters of the two windows in the bedroom were closed, so in order to see better she tried to switch on the bedside lamp, but the light did not come on. Now, that was strange. A little frightened, she sat on the edge of the bed.

Ernest stood as frozen as a statue on the other side of the glass door. His silhouette could not be seen because of the darkness. Instinctively, Miss Bossano felt a presence in the house. She got up and moved two paces as far as the dressing table, but Ernest pushed the door fully open and rushed across the room at the lady. Miss Bossano tripped backwards on the mat by the bed.

File in hand and fast as lightening, Ernest reached the lady and hit her on the head with the flat part of the file. This first blow stunned and injured Miss Bossano badly. Her head bled severely and profusely, the blood dripping onto the mat by the bed. Ernest saw that he had not achieved his aim with the first stroke. She was trying to get up, supporting herself on the bed. With his free hand he stuffed into her mouth a duster. Quickly he turned the pointed file to hit her again. She was too stunned and surprised, and all she could do was stagger forward, trying to push her assailant away.

Now he knew no fear. He was in a rage, as this person, a woman, was abusing his kindness and taking advantage of his disability. She was no better than all the others, always putting him down and asking him for more.

The poor half-dazed woman managed to stagger. In the process she stepped on the pool of blood by her bed. She was half getting up, supporting herself on the bed, and she was able to move a few paces towards the door. She managed to get a good hold of his hair and pulled it. A clump stayed in her hand. In a frenzy, Ernest hit her another blow, this time with the pointed end of the file, and this penetrated the skull.

Again and again he hit her head as she was falling down towards the glass door. Blood and brain matter splashed in all directions, onto the walls and other items. A small piece of the skull came off and fell beside the now-dead woman. Miss Bossano had been holding a handkerchief at the time and had reached up to touch her bleeding head, handkerchief in hand. But now she lay motionless on the floor of the sitting room just past the glass door.

Ernest had finished his job. It was done. No more pestering, no more ordering, no more ridicule.

He moved to the washbasin, washed his blood-smeared hands, and immersed the file to rinse the blood off. The file, he thought, was now clean. He took a towel from the washstand, dried his hands, and threw the towel in the direction of the fallen woman. He was totally unaware of the blood that had splashed onto his raincoat.

He listened as intently as he could before opening the door. He cracked it ever so slightly, and when he was sure that there was no one around, he stepped out, locked the door, and crept down the stairs into the street, where he made his way to Canessa's house. He was there by 2 p.m., and made sure that he was seen there. Shortly afterwards, he made his way slowly to Mr Teuma's house to play with the children. At the Teuma house, Ernest continued as if nothing had happened. According to Mr Teuma, he acted very naturally until way past 6.30 p.m. when he left.

As Father Salvador de Julian said, 'If he did commit the crime, he is not aware of what he has done'.

The Third Possibility: Persons or Persons Unknown

That 'persons or persons unknown' committed the murder was the verdict given at the inquest hearing before Ernest was charged with the murder almost two months later.

This third possibility is that Opisso did not commit the murder, that he was innocent all along, and the authorities, in particular the Chief of Police and the prosecution, when all the circumstantial evidence pointed at this unfortunate person, were too keen to name him as the killer.

One of the witnesses was Miss Amar, who lived next door to the left of the victim's flat .She had reported to the police that several months earlier someone had broken into her flat and stolen two watches, one opera glass and several Argentinean gold coins.

The verdict at the inquest was one of wilful murder against some person or persons unknown, and the jury added that 'they considered that owing to this unprecedented murder and recent robberies committed in such a short time, which have so far been undiscovered, vigilance at night is insufficient as it is actually done by the police.' The jury at the inquest made this statement, and they hinted that the police were not doing their job.

Who was committing these robberies that were raising so much concern? No one had yet been caught, and therefore the Chief of Police was in a dilemma, since his department was being officially and openly criticised.

Was it possible that Miss Bossano had become the target of a robbery scheme that went sour? Was this scheme devised by someone who knew the lady well, someone who was in her confidence, who had possibly obtained a copy of the house key and had seen that the lady kept a lot of money in her flat?

Two individuals had been seen at the scene of the crime by the fiancée of the victim's next-door neighbour Miss Caetano. This young man was Gustavo Mascarenhas, who happened to be inside 7 Market Lane at the critical hour of 4.10 p.m. and who testified that he saw two individuals coming from the direction of the victim's flat. As soon as the murder had become public, he reported this fact to the police, but we do not hear much about this until the defending lawyer brings him forward as the defence's last witness.

According to Dr Giraldi, the most probable time of death was close to 4.00 p.m. This time was also indicated by Doctors Griffiths and Durante in their widest estimate of the time of death from their observations prior to the *post mortem* report.

The witness, Mr Mascarenhas, said that the lady he saw looked Spanish and that her male companion was probably also Spanish. Identifying these two individuals shculd have become a high priority for both the Attorney General's office and the defence lawyer, and a search for them should have been made so that they could be questioned. Who were they, and what where they doing there? The records show that no attempt was made to locate and question them.

The scenario could have gone something like this.

Someone who the victim knew came to visit Miss Bossano, and a male accomplice secretly accompanied her. This person came frequently to the apartment and had the confidence and trust of the victim. She knew, and had seen on several occasions, that Miss Bossano kept lots of money in her handbag and that the handbag was kept in the chest of drawers.

The plan was an excellent one. The idea was that the female visitor, whilst Miss Bossano sat on the chair in front of the dressing table, would be doing her hair and keeping her occupied and distracted with conversation. She would stand behind the lady, endeavouring at all times to impair the line of vision in the mirror and obstructing any movement taking place behind her. She would keep the lady occupied and distracted. Probably, she sat the lady on the stool at the dressing table and started to do her hair, talking to her about this and that.

In the meantime, the male companion had silently gone into the flat and had stealthily and unseen crept into the dark areas of the flat past the first glass door of the sitting room and then the second glass door that led to the bedroom. There he waited for the right moment. This occurred when his accomplice, obscuring the victim's vision, gave him a signal, perhaps a light cough, at which point he would reach out open the dresser's top drawer and get at the handbag.

The chest of drawers with the handbag full of money was close to the glass door that led into the bedroom. Carefully timed, the operation could work. The thief would stealthily conceal himself in the darkness of the hallway and the sitting room. Then, crouching, he would creep in. This would only take a split second.

However, the manoeuvre backfired. The lady must have seen the intruder in the mirror, and turned to confront the thief in the act of robbing her.

Miss Bossano was no coward. Nevertheless she was startled and jumped up. To her surprise the woman tried to hold her down. Now that the occupier had seen them they could be identified, and they would go to prison. She would certainly recognise them and report them. The sentence for robbery was very severe. The penalty was not one they could afford. The thieves panicked and fear set in. The male person, who had previously picked up the long and heavy steel knife-sharpener from the kitchen table, hit her over the head to silence her.

When the surprised Miss Bossano reacted to them, the female visitor tried to hold the injured and bleeding lady as she struggled for her life. This could explain the footprints of a woman and a man on the floor mat that stood by the bed and the clock stopped at 3.55 p.m. The footprints could not be matched with anyone else's.

Miss Bossano stood up, but she was literally cornered in the farthest corner of the bedroom between the dressing table, the bedside table, the chair, the bed, and the window. She tried to open the window to shout for help, but the two robbers were intent that she should not be heard and were stronger than she. Together they overpowered the more fragile lady. They gagged her with a duster that stood on top of the chest of drawers. They dragged her away from the window to the interior of the flat.

At this point Miss Bossano managed to get a grip on the assailant's hair and pulled, tearing away a small amount of black hair in the process. By now the robber was frantic, and he hit the lady several times with the heavy, pointed weapon, bringing her to her knees. The man's final blows were mortal. They penetrated poor Miss Bossano's skull. When she finally fell limp on the floor and they saw the blood gushing from her head, they realised it was time to flee, but first the murderer washed his hands and the weapon in the hand basin and wiped his hands dry on a towel.

Frightened by the failure and the fatal outcome of their attempted robbery, they quickly left the flat. They locked the door behind them and took the key with them to delay the discovery of the body whilst they escaped across the border to their home in Spain.

After they had closed and locked the door they did not count on meeting a man who was coming up the stairs. They acted normally as they passed the man on the first floor landing. As the new comer came up, the male robber carefully leaned back into the dark corner of the staircase landing.

The new arrival got a fleetting glimpse of the woman, saw the man but could not see his face. Why would the witness say that he did not see the man's shoe? This is rather curious.

In their panic, they left without the money. The money remained in the handbag and was found the following day by a very surprised relative of the victim, Mr Joseph Canessa. To his great surprise there was more money in the handbag than Mr Canessa expected.

Could these have been the real circumstances that led to the murder?

Chapter 13: What Was the Evidence?

At the end of the first trial Judge Beatty in his summing up instructed the Jury that 'The onus of proof was on the Crown if they had any reasonable doubt about the guilt of the prisoner it was their duty to give the prisoner the benefit of the doubt.'

There is no doubt that the same instructions were given to the 'Special Jury', so with this instruction in mind we make the following assessment because so many important points seem to have been overlooked. And after a close examination of the facts and the evidence, we are left with a list of questions and doubts as to whether or not Ernest was the murderer.

We also ask.

Was the jury system a just one that led to a fair trial?

Why were the reports from Scotland Yard not revealed during the trial?

Was all the evidence that came to light used fairly?

Did the process overlook important evidence that pointed away from Opisso as the murderer?

Could there have been another other person or persons unknown involved?

Could there have been a reprieve granted by the Governor? There is a maxim in forensic work that says ' every perpetrator either leaves or takes with him/her some form of evidence from the scene of the crime'

The Special Jury System: Fair or Unfair?

Our question here is, 'Was the jury system a just one that led to a fair trial?' The key words here are 'just' and 'fair.' The 'special jury' system in itself, although the law at the time prescribed it, was an unjust system. Because of its unfairness and discriminatory nature, it would definitely not be

Joe Caruana

tolerated in our more enlightened times. That is why this system of 'special jury' was done away with and never used again thereafter.

When the defence lawyer, Mr A. B. Serfaty heard of the appointment of a special criminal session with a special jury, his objection to this led to him resigning from the case. It appears that after much persuasion and pleading, he relented and took the case back on.

Later in court when the special jury was being selected from the special list, Serfaty exhausted every available option open to him. It was obvious that he was not happy with this system, and his objective of recruiting or selecting an impartial jury did not materialise. It was no fault of the defence lawyer, but rather the colonial system of the day that prevailed. The defence, according to the rules, was allowed only ten challenges. It used up its limit of the ten challenges available to it and was unable to challenge further. Even so, the prosecution challenged six jurymen whom the defence had allowed. No less than sixteen of the 'special' prospective members of the jury were dispensed with or disallowed from service.

Nevertheless, it appears that the remaining twelve, including the two picked from the court floor, still presented a severe setback for the accused. An examination of the names of these jurymen indicates that in such a close-knit community like Gibraltar where everyone knows everyone else, all these gentlemen were obviously very well acquainted with the victim, Maria Luisa Bossano. She was, after all, one of their own social circle.

. The jury was special because those selected or nominated by the Chief Justice were persons who owned property or were landowners, professionals, or businessmen. There was no ordinary man of the street therein, such as clerks, shopkeepers, or tradesmen. So in 1930 this list of 'SJ' jurymen came exclusively from the upper classes, wellborn, well placed, well-off, well-educated individuals, as was Miss Bossano.

This is not to say that these persons were not fair persons, just, law-abiding, God fearing persons. Indeed, they were good people and totally above reproach, but in the sensitive trial of a brutal murder of a victim who was, to all intent and purpose a friend or an acquaintance, the make-up of the jury was not, as it were, totally neutral. Unintentionally, they had been placed in a highly unenviable situation not of their own making.

When the Hangman Came

Whether the accused was guilty or not guilty, the special jury system was drastically unjust. With the best of intentions, could the system produce a possible miscarriage of justice?

How different were the deliberations of the jury at the first trial! This jury taken from the published jury list contained persons from all walks of life and took over thirty six hours of deliberation, only to arrive at a split verdict.

In contrast, the special jury took just one hour and forty minutes' deliberation, even though there was no drastic addition of new evidence. Substantially and materially the case was the same, except for the last witness, Mr Mascarenhas, who saw two persons, a man and a woman, leaving from the direction of the victim's flat.

Maria Luisa Bossano was known to be a church going, charitable lady of means and a property owner who came from a prominent family. She knew all these gentlemen, and all these gentlemen knew her, some more intimately than others.

Under the circumstances, how could Ernest Opisso, the deaf, lame, unintelligible handyman who, it appears, made faces at the public, who was wanting in his demeanour, and who could not express himself well, receive a proper trial?

In an endeavour to answer Opisso's question, 'I would like someone to tell me how I could have killed the woman?' our duty is to try to look into the following mysteries.

Mystery that Shrouded Scotland Yard

Scotland Yard was involved in the investigation and forensic testing of much of the evidence that was obtained from Ernest Opisso. Almost every piece of clothing and fingerprint was investigated, all except the alleged murder weapon, the file.

Both Chief of Police Gulloch and Sergeant Gilbert made the first visit to Scotland Yard at the end of December 1930. But later Sergeant Gilbert made a further visit alone in February of 1931.

During the trial the defence lawyer mentioned that he knew that Scotland Yard had been visited with some of the evidence, and he asked, 'But where are the results?' No answer was given to this question, and the matter of Scotland Yard's involvement is not mentioned again. The prosecution and the police knew that absolutely no positive results had turned up either from the first or the second visit to the Yard. No fingerprint matched the accused, no bloodstains found on any of the clothing or, for that matter, on the shoes.

We are not informed that the defence counsel was informed of this important and vital fact, the fact that Ernest Opisso could not be associated with any of the evidence taken to Scotland Yard. Neither was the defence shown or given the two negative reports that came from Scotland Yard. We assume that, had the defence been informed of those negative results, their case would have been strengthened and their claim that all that the prosecution had was circumstantial evidence would have been exploited to the fullest and would have planned its defence differently.

The question or mystery to be answered is 'Should the prosecution not have made the defence, the judge, and the jury aware of Scotland Yard's reports? Surely in a murder case where the life of a person is at stake, all evidence or lack of evidence should have been placed on record. The mystery remains, was this part of the investigation deliberately kept from the court?

The file, as the alleged murder weapon, had not yet been obtained, and therefore it was not taken to Scotland Yard for analysis. Medical persons, producing several differing opinions, examined the file in Gibraltar. For logistical reasons it was not examined by the Scotland Yard forensic experts.

Mystery of the Time of Death

Early into the investigation and without much scientific corroboration, the Chief of Police stated to Scotland Yard that he believed the murder was committed between 12 noon and 2 p.m. The twelve o'clock timing was not corroborated by the medical reports of Dr Griffiths and Dr Durante, but even then the lady was seen at her door at 12 p.m. by the bread boy, yet the two o'clock timing was the earliest time of death estimated by Dr Griffiths. When Dr Griffiths first saw the body of the victim at approximately midnight on Sunday, the night of the 30th, at Market Lane, he had estimated that the victim had been dead thirty-eight to forty hours, which placed the time of death between two and four o'clock. However this was only based on *rigor mortis* observations.

Both Doctors Griffiths and Durante, as a result of the *post mortem*, estimated that the time of death was between two and four hours *after* the lady had her lunch.

So since the lady usually had lunch close to 1 p.m., the hours of between twelve o'clock and two o'clock could not have been an accurate time of death. So where did the Chief of Police get the notion that the murder had taken place before 2 p.m.? Therefore it also means that by the time that PC Macedo saw Opisso entering 7 Market Lane at 2 p.m. was she dead or not?

If the lady had lunch close to 1 p.m., the two-to four-hour timing would place the time of death at between 3 and 5 p.m. Dr Griffiths in his testimony said that some peas were found in the stomach of the lady and that these would take about two hours to digest. This contradicted his previous assessment that what he found in the stomach would have taken twenty minutes to one hour to digest. However, the timing given for the peas would also place the time of death no earlier than 3 p.m. Other food found in the victim's stomach was macaroni, and some cheese There was no mention of the sardines.

In answer to a question, Dr Griffiths had said that the remains of the food found in the victim's stomach must have been eaten about twenty to thirty minutes before death occurred. This was a far shorter time than previously given by himself and Dr Durante of within two hours before death. This meant that if this was a more accurate time of death, the murder must have taken place at around 1.30 p.m., once again making it difficult to place Opisso at the scene of the crime, since he was seen arriving for lunch at his home at about 1 p.m. and still there at 1.45 p.m.

To make the time of death even more dubious and difficult, Doctor James Giraldi challenged the speed of the victim's digestion, because he reckoned that since the lady was advanced in years (she was over 59 years old), perhaps the time of death would be more like four to six hours from the time she had lunch.

However if an average of the timings of these three medical persons were to be taken, it would place the time of death more surely around 4 p.m. This would coincide with Dr Durante's later evidence when he revised his estimated time of death to four hour after the lunch was eaten. His broad estimate had been that time of death could have between 11 a.m. and 4p.m.

Was it coincidence that the alarm clock had stopped at 3.55 p.m.? And a greater coincidence that a witness saw a man and a woman, who looked Spanish, coming from the direction of the lady's flat, at 4.10 p.m.?

But it appears that the prosecution had discounted any and all events that took place after 2 p.m.

Was Opisso the Murderer?

The original pronouncement at the inquest was that 'person or persons unknown' had committed the murder. It was two months before Ernest Opisso was arrested and charged with murder.

Several pieces of evidence came to light late in the retrial. Doctor Giraldi, appearing for the defence, put into question eleven vital pieces of evidence, which devastated the case for the prosecution.

The first was the original time of death as given by Dr Griffiths and Dr Durante. These last two maintained that death occurred about two hours after the victim had eaten lunch, which could have placed the murder at around 3 p.m. if she had her lunch at around one o'clock, which was her regular lunch time according to her relative, Mr J. Canessa.

Even the Scotland Yard report, with the scant information available at that stage ' described the lady as having a peculiar temperament and was very methodical in her ways and had a "religious turn of mind." Death had probably occurred not later than 4 p.m.'

In the evidence given by Superintendent Brown, he states that they found five fried sardines on a plate on the kitchen table. There is no doubt that the lady ate some sardines as her first course of her lunch as sardines are best eaten and are nicer when hot. The *post mortem* mentions the detection of peas by Dr Griffiths and macaroni by Dr Durante. Neither of them mentioned detecting any residue of sardines in the stomach, which could possibly mean that the sardines, the lady's first course, would have been digested by then into the upper intestine. All of this evidence pointed to the fact that the murder did not take place immediately after she had lunch. In fact, we have noted elsewhere that Miss Bossano a meticulous person had time to wash and clean up and put everything away after she finished her lunch, supporting the idea that a later time of death was highly likely. Dr Giraldi seems to have disapproved of the whole *post mortem,* because he believed that the intestine should have been examined as well.

Dr Giraldi also mentioned that the weapon could have been a 'knife-sharpener,' which was circular, just like part of the file produced as evidence. He further added that the notches on the skull could have been made with this weapon or a similar one, not necessarily the file.

The piece of bone removed from the file and tested for blood in court did not produce signs of blood residue as the experts expected and the test carried out in the courthouse was negative with the assistance of Dr. Giraldi.

He also added that the piece of plaster of Paris on the file produced would have absorbed blood if it had come into contact with it and would not have been washed out.

Dr Giraldi said that he did not think that the footprints on the mat were those of the accused. The measurements were not correct and they were shorter than the accused's. He also deplored the fact that the mat with the footprints had been treated negligently when it was rolled and folded instead of pinned flat to some surface.

The Question of Third-Degree Methods

When the defence lawyer accused the police of using third degree tactics during the questioning of the accused, this was refuted by the judge, who said that he was satisfied those methods had not been used and that to use them would have been totally unacceptable.

There may not have been third degree methods used, but there was definitely irregular and unlawful treatment in the interrogation of the accused.

First the raincoat was waved in the accused's face.

Then he was cajoled in looking at the horrendous photos which any squeamish person would find offensive.

However it transpired that during the interrogation the accused said that while he was being questioned by Sergeant Gilbert, this policeman asked him, 'Why did you not go on Saturday to report to the lady about the level of the water cistern?'

Opisso's reply was that it was not necessary because it was not full and that he was waiting for more rain to come and then take another measurement and report to the lady.

The Sergeant, according to the defence, insisted and said, 'You did not go because you already knew the lady was dead.' The defence held that when this accusation was made, the Sergeant placed his hand on the accused's chest as if to determine whether the accused's heart beat increased or not. In this way, it was assumed, they could tell if the accused was lying or not. This was a crude and primitive lie detector test no doubt practised during interrogation.

This action by the Sergeant was strange, and one wonders what conclusion was reached. It appears that it did not change the police's suspicion of the accused.

Though the methods used for identification were critical according to the defence lawyer the normal police methods were not followed,. There was the incident when Detective Sergeant Gilbert took the bread boy to the police station and, pointing through a window at Ernest Opisso, he asked the boy, 'There, boy, have a look. Is that the man you saw at the door?' To which the boy replied, 'Yes'.

By the police's own admission the bread boy's evidence was inadmissible. We read in Scotland Yard's report, 'But he could not be relied upon in the absence of any other independent corroboration apart from the police constable, particularly in view of the alibi put forward by Opisso.' Yet even at this stage the above reference to the police constable's evidence did not appear to them to be that strong, why else would they have added 'in view of the alibi put forward by Opisso'.

When the Hangman Came

Mystery of the Timing of Ernest's Movements

Ernest's timing, on the day of the murder went probably something like this.

Around 10 a.m. he measured the water tank at Cornwall's Lane. The Frenchman saw him—an erroneous time, if we are to believe Canessa's evidence as more reliable.

At 10.30 a.m. he went to Mr Canessa's house, where he stayed until 12.30 p.m. Canessa lived at 53 Irish Town, four or five minutes from Market Lane. The Canessas had three children; a boy one aged ten and another aged five years and three months, and a one-year old girl.. (Register of Electors, 1930)

From the Canessa house, he took a ten-minute walk (unless he stopped to talk with someone on the way) to his store, getting him there at about 12.40 p.m. He opened the store, placed the paint pots in place, and locked up, probably taking about eight minutes. It is now 12.48 p.m.

From the store, he went to his house 300 yards away, walking up the steps of Castle Street. If you allow five minutes for this, the time is now 12.55 p.m., very close to the time of 1 p.m. given by his sister and the charwoman. Allowing for a fifty-minute lunch break, it puts the time at 1.50 p.m., corroborating what the charwoman said, that she saw him there about 1.45 p.m.

After lunch he went to his store again to fetch a foot rule. This would take him at least another eight minutes, or until 1.58 p.m.

From there Ernest said that he first went to the Canessas' house to tell the lady there that he would be coming back to her house on the following Tuesday. Allowing another ten minutes for this diversion, it is now 2.20 p.m.

The Canessas were relatives of the victim, and had this statement not been true, the Canessa family would surely have challenged it. This suggests that it must have been true. This is a highly significant detail.

From Canessa's he went to the Teumas' house, again via Market Lane. It takes fifteen minutes to walk this distance, so this placed him there at 2.50 p.m. Teuma's evidence verifies this when he said he saw Ernest there just before 3.p.m. Considering his walking disability and the fact that it was an uphill walk at that, it would make the time gap even tighter, that is closer to 3 p.m.

If we follow the prosecution's line of reasoning, one highly notable point is that, if Ernest Opisso had committed the murder and then walked all the way from Market Lane to either the Canessas' or the Teumas' house, his coat would have been blood-stained, and he would have been agitated after such a brutal killing.

The walk to Mr Teuma's house would have taken about fifteen minutes. His route would have taken him from Market Lane across Main Street, through Horse Barracks Lane, up part of Cornwall's Lane, about 150 yards up City Mill Lane, another 100 yards up Governor's Street, and finally up another 200 yards to 17 Prince Edward's Road, which in fact is not a road but a hill, making it harder going for a lame person.

The important point about this itinerary is that this route is a very busy thoroughfare and there are at least thirty small shops and businesses along the way. All these businesses would be open between 2 and 3 p.m., and in 1930 everyone worked a six-day week that included Saturdays. However not a single person came forward as a witness to say that they had seen the highly conspicuous person of Opisso agitated and rushing and limping his way uphill to his destination, which was Mr Teuma's house. That he made this trip totally unseen is incredible and highly improbable.

The same applies if he had left 7 Market Lane before 2 p.m. and walked the shorter distance through busy Irish Town to Mr Canessa's house. If this were the case, Mrs Canessa would have seen a bloodstained and agitated Ernest and would have detected something strange in him and she would have reported this to the police, given that she was the victim's sister. But no such unfavourable and damning report was made. Why? Because Ernest must have appeared perfectly normal and his usual self, which was precisely the remark that Mr Teuma made when he gave evidence; he said, 'I did not see anything unusual in Ernest that day.'

But if Ernest was the killer, when did he have the time to go from any of these places to Market Lane, walk down a corridor and open the flat with his own key, surprise the lady or have an argument, we presume, struggle with Miss Bossano from the bedroom to the sitting room, clean the blood off the file and his hands, dry them clean on the towel, exit the victim's flat

When the Hangman Came

without being seen, lock the door, make his way to the Canessa's House and afterwards to the Teuma's house to be there before 3 p.m.? This seems to be a rather rushed and highly impractical time frame.

In practice, as a rough estimate the crime sequence could not take less than twenty minutes from start to finish, that is from the time of entering and leaving the building after having committed the crime So how does one explain Opisso's presence in this equation? What if we assume, as the Chief of Police said, that the lady was attacked and killed between 1 and 2 p.m. and was dead by the time that Macedo saw Opisso at Market Lane? How is the alibi given by the sister and the cleaning lady explained? The police checked and double-checked, at the suggestion from Scotland Yard, all his alibis and nothing was challenged during the trial.

He was not condemned on the basis of this lack of alibi.

If the time of death is moved forward, another question arises. How could Opisso kill her at 3 p.m. when Mr Teuma saw him about 3 p.m. at his house, a good fifteen minutes away from the location of the murder? Did Ernest really have time to commit the murder during either of these time periods or for that matter during the afternoon period?

Again, Teuma saw him at his house at about 5 p.m. but knew Ernest had stayed until later, more likely closer to 6.30 p.m. Ernest said that when he left it was dark. So Ernest had been at the Teuma house from 3 to after 6 p.m. this also puts him outside the time frame of a possible 4 p.m. murder.

It was said that he was seen at 2 p.m. at Market Lane, but it was also said that he had been at the Canessa's house at 2 p.m. and at 2.55 p.m. at Teuma's house. We have to accept that if he was at Teuma's house at 2.30 and if it takes five minutes plus fifteen to walk there from Irish Town to Market Lane and then to Teuma's house, then Ernest had less than ten minutes in which to go through the whole ritual of an argument, a struggle, the murder itself and washing, and locking the flat. This is a most impractical timetable?

Surely a reasonable doubt exists. Did or did not Opisso commit the murder?

Although it appears that Opisso had the perfect alibi for both periods, neither the prosecution nor the defence nor even the police seem to have spent any time exploring the accused's movements.

The defence lawyer insisted that PC Macedo had made a mistake about the day on which he said he had seen Opisso. Could this have been a genuine mistake?

Leaving Teuma's house at about 6.30 p.m., he went to his store and from there to Main Street, where he met some friends between 6.30 and 7 p.m. It was raining at the time, but when it stopped, he walked down the street with his friends between 7 and 7.30 p.m. He was still in his working clothes. If he were still in his working clothes, these people would have noticed any bloodstains. No such statement was made.

The time frame is now outside the latest possible time of death given by Dr Giraldi, who had challenged the time given by Dr Griffiths, placing the time of death closer to four to six hours after the lady had lunch, which put his estimated time of death at around 4 p.m.

There could have been a possibility that Opisso's sister was lying and covering for him, but what about the charwoman who saw Opisso enter his house at about 1 p.m. and made no mention of seeing him go out early. Was she too covering up and committing perjury? Could Opisso have skipped lunch, walked out in a hurry to Market Lane, and killed Miss Bossano between 1.30 p.m. and 2.00 p.m.? Again this was not possible for the same reason as before, the charwoman's eyewitness account said she stayed cleaning the stairs until 2.15 p.m. and saw him there at 1.45 p.m.

However, if someone was lying and covering for Opisso, this is the only gap when he had an opportunity of committing the murder, and two persons would have had to commit perjury. The prosecution, however, did not press this possibility, home.

Who Else Could Have Done It?

If Opisso did not commit the murder who did?

If Opisso took the file with him, he must have gone to Miss Bossano's flat with premeditated murder in mind. However, Opisso does not seem to have had a quarrel with Miss Bossano. No relative of Miss Bossano mentioned any problems between him and her. Miss Bossano had visited the Canessa family on the previous day. This family played a significant part in this story, and still no one there mentioned any discord whatsoever between Miss Bossano and Ernest Opisso. If they had known of any problem between them or if Miss Bossano had mentioned to them any incident concerning Ernest, they would have surely said so at an early stage in the case. As it happened, no one mentioned anything negative or accusatory about Opisso.

Living relatives of Mr Canessa say that at the very beginning shortly after the murder, when the murderer had not yet been named, Mr Canessa himself feared that he was high on the list of suspects.

The Late Witness

One late yet crucial witness to appear in the retrial was Gustavo Mascarenhas, whose girlfriend was the daughter of the elderly gentleman who said that he saw the bread boy knocking on Miss Bossano's flat. Gustavo's fiancée lived with her father next door to Miss Bossano.

Mr Mascarenhas made one of the most revealing and important statements of the whole trial. It was far more important and credible than PC Macedo's late testimony. He said that he went to visit his girlfriend on Saturday, 29th. November, the afternoon of the day of the murder, at around 4.10 p.m., and as he went up the stairs, he came face to face with a woman and a man coming down from the direction of Miss Bossano's flat. He said the woman looked Spanish, but because the corridor was dark he did not see the man very well. Mascarenhas said that he told the police about his sighting of these two individuals a few days after the murder was discovered.

Extraordinarily and strangely, no importance seems to have been given to this remarkable encounter, and no effort seems to have been made to locate these two persons who had been seen at the scene of the crime prior to the discovery of the corpse.

Why was this critical piece of evidence overlooked? One assumption is that by then the Chief of Police and the prosecution had decided that that the time of death was 2 p.m. They therefore continued following only the circumstantial evidence that seemed to point to Opisso.

Important too is the evidence given by the neighbour who said that she saw the hairdresser entering 7 Market Lane at around 4.00 p.m. Could the neighbour have been too approximate in the time she gave, and might her sighting of the hairdresser going in have been closer to 3.50 p.m.? Certainly, the neighbour did not testify to seeing either Mascarenhas, at 4.10 p.m. or the unknown gentleman going in (that is, the man who Mascarenhas said was with the Spanish lady). Nor did she testify to seeing any of them coming out. There is nothing strange in this, since any neighbour leaning out of their window needs only to move away from the window just for one minute and the scenery changes completely in that time.

It appears that no less than four persons went into 7 Market Lane at around 4 p.m. Was the lady that Mascarenhas saw going out at 4.10 the same person the neighbour saw going in at around 4.00 p.m. ?

Why would Mascarenhas say that he saw them coming from the direction of the victim's flat? Very simply, because as he was coming halfway up the dark stairs, he could see the couple's legs coming frontally towards him from the location of the victim's flat. If they had come from another flat on the same floor or from one on the upper floors, the approach would have been from his back, and since he was facing the other way, he would not have seen them had they come from some other flat. The only flat beyond Miss Bossano's was that of Mrs. Amanda Amar who said she never used it since she lived elsewhere.

Why did he see the woman's face and not the man's face? The reason could be that if the woman was walking ahead of the man, she would have reached the landing and the steps ahead and in front of the man and would have been at the same level as Mascarenhas. On the other hand, the man would have remained at the top of the stairs landing with the woman in front, thereby blocking his view of the man's face. He would also have had to move back to allow Mascarenhas to pass. Doing so would have placed the man further into the dark corner of the landing with his back to the little light that came down the well and through the opening on the wall. Mascarenhas, on reaching the top landing, would make a sharp turn right to reach the door of his fiancée's flat, missing altogether a glance at the man's face.

Who were these two people? What were they doing at 7 Market Lane? Why were they coming from the direction of the victim's flat? The time of their departure from Market Lane was highly critical to the time of the murder. This visit was closer to the time of death, as given by Dr Giraldi, than any of Opisso's other windows of opportunity, i.e., around the lunch hour and the early evening.

Who did this people come to visit at 7 Market Lane? Was it possible that these people could have killed Miss Bossano? If so, why? The verdict is left to the reader to decide.

Was there a miscarriage of justice, or did Ernest Opisso commit the murder?

Was PC Macedo's Account Accurate?

PC Macedo was a policeman of two years' experience, and yet even though the Chief of Police had made public appeals asking for anyone who had information to come forward, it took one whole week before this officer disclosed that he had seen Opisso at Market Lane around 2.00 p.m.

On December Tuesday the 2nd El Calpense newspaper carried an appeal that read, " Any detail and data however insignificant it may appear will be of great value to the police, nothing is lost in reporting it, to keep quiet could affect the whole investigation. It could be that someone may have noticed something abnormal, heard something, seen some strange person or seen some movement of someone that may have appeared insignificant or seem unimportant to the crime would be of great assistance." Naturally this piece of information must have circulated in the police force from the day the murder was discovered.

However, the Scotland Yard report stated that 'the Chief of Police told them that Ernest Opisso had been seen leaving the building at around 1.45 p.m.' This appears to be another confusing error on the part of the Chief of Police, because from the explanation we have given about the routine change of police shift, the constable would not have seen Opisso inside the

Joe Caruana

patio and *leaving* at 1.45 p.m. since he would not have left his point duty in Main Street until 2.00 p.m.

In answer to questions about PC Macedo the Chief of Police dismissed the delay in reporting saying that at first he did not suspect Opisso and secondly that Macedo was an inexperienced policeman

Another discrepancy was that Macedo's evidence stated that he saw Opisso walking *inside* the entrance with his back to the door *walking in* the direction of the stairs, not just entering However in the Scotland Yard report the Chief of Police is quoted as saying that the eyewitness had seen him *leaving* the building.

Who was right and who was wrong? Was Macedo's evidence of Ernest *going in around 2 p.m.* correct, or was the Chief of Police correct that Macedo saw him *coming* out at 1.45 p.m.? Did not the Chief of Police get this information from the constable himself? Why would this important bit of information clash so disparagingly? A very curious contradiction indeed in a serious murder investigation.

In the end it was Macedo's belated evidence that surely convicted Opisso of the crime. Yet it is clear that it was almost impossible for Opisso to be that close to the scene of the crime, since, according to the first medical estimate the shortest medical timing, the crime occurred at the earliest, between 1.30 p.m. and 2 p.m. and, possibly, within two to four hours after the lady had lunch, about 3 and 4 p.m.

Even if Opisso walked up Market Lane at about 12.40 p.m. as he himself said he did he had been seen before that at the Canessa house at 12.30, and later he was seen at his house at 1 p.m. and at 1.45 p.m. But suppose that Opisso had not gone to Mrs Canessa's at 2 p.m., someone in the Canessa family would have denied this as a blatant lie since Mrs Canessa was the sister of the deceased. But no one denied this timing, making it more difficult to accept that Opisso did the murder and that the lady was already dead by 2 p.m. as the Chief of Police said. If that was so, how could Opisso have committed the crime by that time since Opisso was somewhere else?

Likewise, the policeman's late testimony comes under question because when PC Macedo was asked why he took so long to report seeing Opisso, he said *'at the time I did not think it important.'*

When the Hangman Came

We come back to PC Macedo's account. This account was more difficult to explain because Opisso admitted walking down Market Lane, not just once but twice, during the lunch hour. The first time was when he was going home at 12.40 p.m. and there after seen by the cleaning lady both arriving at his house at 1 p.m. and later at around 1.45 p.m. and then, after lunch, went to the Canessa house where he was seen at about 2.00 p.m.

Was it possible that the constable saw him on one of these two occasions, not necessarily inside the building but passing by? Could the Chief of Police's zeal and determination to make sure that Opisso '*did not get away with it'* place the constable's observation not outside but inside 7 Market Lane? It was also very strange that PC Macedo was not asked, within the first 24 hours of the murder, by Detective Sergeant Gilbert and his superiors to report on everything and anyone he may have seen during the time that he was on point duty in Main Street on the actual day of the murder.

If Opisso was the culprit, it is difficult to allocate sufficient time for him to have carried out all the movements and activities necessary for such a brutal crime and still be at different places almost at the same time and in places where others testified he had been. Difficult, very difficult to attribute the crime to him! His alibi was very much secured, but?

That is why in its report Scotland Yard advised the Chief of Police, during his visit to on 24 and 25 December 1930, to check Opisso's alibi, which we know the police did. Yet how strange it is that no strong debate took place by the prosecution in court destroying those alibis? Could it be that they were unable to do so?

In any event, in light of the time of death as surmised from the added testimony of Dr Giraldi, and the two-hour digestion period given by the other two doctors, the murder could not have taken place before 2 p.m.

According to PC Macedo's evidence, Opisso was seen i*nside* the corridor of the patio and *not going into* the victim's flat, shortly *after* the PC finished his point duty. Traditionally, police constables came off point duty punctually at their scheduled time, when they were relieved by another policeman. Those of us who lived in the vicinity could set our watches by the change in the policemen's beat change. In this case, the time was always precisely 2 p.m. Therefore, Macedo would pass 7 Market Lane between 2.01 or 2.03 p.m. How could Opisso have been there at that time?

Another question. If, as Macedo stated, he said *'adios'* to Opisso when he saw him in the corridor and Opisso turned back to look at him, would Opisso, now that he had been seen and identified, still have carried out the murder?

But suppose that Opisso did manage to get up to the flat and kill the lady, the time would be closer to 2.10 p.m., thus contradicting the Chief of Police's contention that the lady was already dead before 2.00 p.m. His contention that the murder took place earlier than 2.00 p.m. was probably based on the 12 o'clock sighting of Opisso at the lady's door by the bread boy.

But this testimony, by the bread boy, was totally false because Opisso was still at the Canessa's house painting the baby's cot until 12.30 p.m.

Yet, to repeat, there was another contradiction in the timing which appeared in the Scotland Yard report, no doubt from information provided by the Chief of Police. The report stated that the constable had seen Opisso coming out of the building at 1.45 p.m. yet the cleaning lady, where Opisso lived, said she had seen him there at 1.45 p.m. again, who was right and who was wrong?

How then can these two differing and contradictory pieces of information coming from the Chief be reconciled? Opisso had always maintained that PC Macedo had seen him on Thursday and not Saturday.

Mystery of the Bread Boy

The baker's delivery boy could not have seen Ernest at Market lane around 12 or 12.15 p.m. Mrs Canessa's evidence said he was still at her house till 12.30 p.m., so how could he be at Market Lane at around 12 noon? Are we expected to believe that this lame man, who walked with great difficulty, could make a quick transfer of locations from the Canessa house about two to three hundred yards away to Miss Bossano's flat? Even allowing for some small inaccuracies in time by the bread boy or by Mrs Canessa and Mr Canessa, it was still almost impossible for such a change of location to be achieved.

The bread boy said that the man went in and called out to someone inside, *'The bread boy!'* A lady came out. The boy recognised her as the lady in a photograph later shown to him. The lady told him, *'I don't take bread.'*

The bread boy further said that he had not seen Mr Caetano, the next-door neighbour. From there and after correctly delivering the bread to the second floor neighbour, the boy went straight back to the bakery.

This last statement contradicted what the next-door neighbour Mr Caetano had said, when he stated that not only had he seen the boy but he had also spoken with him. Under the circumstances, the old man's version is more credible than the boy's, who was likely to be more of a scatterbrain. In a matter of about an hour, he had forgotten which floor he had to deliver the extra loaf of bread to. The boy was obviously not a very credible witness. That is why, no doubt, the police had hesitated to bring him forward. Funnily enough, no sufficient debate or discussion took place about this important issue of timing.

In the report from Scotland Yard, no doubt based on the Chief of Police's verbal report and theories before any charges had been made, they reported that the Chief of Police had said that 'he did not have sufficient evidence to prove his case as the most important witness was the baker's boy who saw him (Opisso) at the flat at 12 noon, but he could not be relied upon in the absence of any other independent corroboration apart from the police constable, particularly in view of the alibi put forward by Opisso.'

It has been shown that the account of the prosecution's 'most important witness,' the bread boy, was not only unreliable but also totally incorrect. Opisso could not have been at the lady's flat opening the door to him.

By now the case against Opisso was slipping through the Chief of Police's fingers. What was needed was someone else to corroborate the delivery boy's evidence. P.C. Macedo's late evidence came in handy.

Mystery of the Man Who Answered the Door

Who was the man that opened the door at about 12 noon when the bread boy called? It could not have been Ernest because he had been clearly seen at the Canessa's house between 12 noon and 12.30p.m.

However, the bread boy later identified Opisso as being the man he saw. His identification was faulty. The boy described the way the man dressed and what he looked like and that the man was wearing a tie. However, the boy said that the man at the door said out loud, 'It's the bread man.'

Since Ernest Opisso had severe speech impairment, the best way to identify him would have been when he shouted out to the lady behind him, 'It's the bread man.' His stammering, halting, and difficult to understand speech would have been a sure giveaway, but no mention is made of this man's speech. In fact, the impression is given that that man said the phrase in a normal conversational way, he did not say anything about the man having a limp.

Wrong person, wrong time. Yet again the Chief of Police's case was weakening.

Mystery Of the Stopped Clock

The clock found in the victim's bedroom was stopped at 3.55 p.m. Was this purely coincidence? Or was this clock dropped during the struggle that took place in the farthest corner of the victim's bedroom on the right side of the bed, where the clock had stood on the bedside table and where the experts deduced that the first assault took place?

But the question that follows is more serious. Why did the clock stop? Why was this not an item of discussion during the trial?

This lady was a woman of habit and routine. There is no doubt that she would not allow the clock to wind down and stop. She would wind the clock last thing before going to sleep and first thing when she woke up. This was the regular habit of everyone who used wind-up clocks. Being a woman who ran her life 'by the clock,' she would need to know the time at all times.

The answer could be that the Chief of Police had made up his mind that the murder had taken place before 2 p.m. Could the clock indicate the exact time of the assault and murder?

Mystery of the Keys

Scotland Yard's report stated, 'the only key in existence, as identified by the cleaning lady, was that found on the bunch of keys at Opisso's store.'

This was a rather premature statement, again based on the early information given by the Chief of Police. As the case unfolded, there were no less than three keys, two of which opened the lady's lock: Firstly the one on the lady's bunch of keys taken from the chest of drawers, Secondly the one taken from Opisso's store, which at one point he offered to fetch for Mr Canessa, and thirdly the one found in the street by the son of the egg vendor. This last one presented a further mystery. It worked in the lock of the flat, but it was found at 8 a.m. on the Saturday morning of the murder. Therefore, this key could not be relevant to the crime, because it was found far too early in the day. The lady was still alive at 8 a.m. and was seen leaving her house at about 10 a.m., implying that this key had nothing to do with the murder case.

Was there a fourth key that was used by the persons who entered Miss Bossano's flat and left at 4.10 p.m.? This type of old-fashioned lock had a long neck and was not a thief-proof design, having an uncomplicated, flat, serrated design on the end. It was not that difficult to open one particular lock with a similar type key, but not necessarily the correct key.

The Fingerprint Mystery

The Chief of Police told Scotland Yard that 'he relied principally on the expert examination of the footprints,' and of course the fingerprints but as these proved negative, it was agreed that the other points did not carry the case much further 'so far as the suspect was concerned.'

In any event, in so far as the defence was concerned, there was very little issue made about the fingerprints. Was it because the defence was not sure what the outcome would be and they therefore avoided the matter? So, the question that arises is whether the defence was fully informed of the full results of all the tests done by Scotland Yard during both the December 1930 and the February 1931 visits to London.

We hear very little about this—in fact hardly anything. Yet both of the Scotland Yard reports stated that they could not identify any of the fingerprints on the various pieces of evidence, not only on Opisso but on any of the other fingerprints taken to London of which there were quite a few. Specifically a blood smeared finger print on the frame of the glass door and another on the wash basin could not be matched with known finger prints, so whose finger prints were these?

Also, none of the articles of clothing or shoes belonging to Opisso showed any signs of bloodstains.

What kind of clean-up and cover-up had Opisso, a mentally slow individual, carried out that even the greatest crime detection experts in the world could not find a single trace of any kind to pin-point the murder on him?

The Footprint Mystery

The Chief of Police in one of his appearances said that the female footprint shown in court on a piece of linoleum that had been cut from the victim's bedroom could not be said with certainty to belong to any specific person. He also testified that no one could guarantee who made the footprint found close to a chair where, it was assumed, the victim had sat before she died. If they could not attribute these two female footprints to the victim, to which female did these footprints belong? Could they have belonged to the Spanish lady seen leaving the flat at 4.10 p.m. by Mr. Marcarenhas?

Dr. Giraldi had said, ' The length of the stride on the mat is said to be 27 inches, that is short for a man', meaning no doubt that it was a woman's footprint. He had also stated that the mat had been negligently treated by the police.

Both the above statements the first one by the prosecution and the other by the defence negated Dr. Grifith's original argument that the footprints that he examined when Superintendent Brown brought them to his house were definitely those of Opisso.

One wonders what was the condition of those pieces of evidence, the linoleum and the rug, when the doctor and the sergeant were examining the blood footprints on the linoleum and mat six or seven weeks after the event?

It was highly unlikely that the prim and proper Miss Bossano would allow Ernest Opisso to enter her bedroom. The likeliest possibility is that she would receive him at the entrance hall and would not even show him into the sitting room. From the bloodstains on the bedroom mat and the dressing table, it would appear that the first assault took place between the bed and the dressing table. If Opisso was the murderer, how did he get to the other side of the lady's bed, which was at the extreme end of the bedroom almost next to the window and the dressing table? Did he meet

When the Hangman Came

the lady by the bed? This was most unlikely, because it would have shown some level of intimacy between them. Or did he make a dash from the entrance hall through the sitting room and the bedroom round the bed to where the dressing table was and assaulted the lady as she sat down at the dressing table? At this position in the bedroom, the lady would have been next to the window that looked out into the street. If Opisso were running to attack her, would she not have screamed out of the window, calling for help?

So how come the experts could not attribute the lady's footprint in the blood to that of the victim at this precise spot? A most likely possibility is that the lady was surprised and assaulted at her dressing table in her bedroom and was most probably gagged with the duster to stop her from screaming.

Again the Scotland Yard report says that the soles of the lady's shoes had ample evidence of blood. Yet none of Opisso's shoes showed up any traces of blood. Could Opisso have been so thorough in the cleaning of the shoes as well?

But the Scotland Yard Report went further. It said, 'The Chief of Police, Gulloch, stated that he relied principally on the expert examination of the footprints, but as these proved negative it was agreed that the other points did not carry the case much further so far as the suspect was concerned'. So it appears that even at this stage no connection was found between Opisso and the crime.

After Opisso had been arrested, the police tried to figure out the pattern of his footsteps whilst he was at the police station and later at the prison. Opisso's footprints were never definitely and authentically linked to those footprints on the pieces of linoleum. In fact, one expert also said that the footprints on the linoleum were not those of the accused. This was Dr Giraldi who said that the pieces of linoleum had also been badly handled and stored. He also said when giving evidence "the footprints were certainly not that of the accused for 3 reasons 1) His steps were too short and there was a big difference in the spacing 2) the steps on the mat were in the same line and the accused could not walk like that because he was lame and finally 3) Because the accused turned his right foot outwards." These observations by Giraldi devastated all the work done by the police to proof without a shadow of doubt that the footprints belonged to Opisso.

Mystery of the Hair

During the first visit to Scotland Yard it was noted that Gulloch mentioned that he had not brought the black hair found with him that was the same colour as the suspect's hair, because he did not attach much importance to this as nearly every other person in Gibraltar, being of Spanish extraction, had black hair. We will never know what was Scotland Yard's reaction to this statement, since hair can be as important as fingerprint in forensic investigations, but here could have been additional proof or otherwise of Opisso's guilt.

But we hear again from the Scotland Yard report, though not during the inquest, that when the victim was examined, there was found clasped in the hand of the deceased a small quantity of black hair, and they added that this was the assailant's, since the deceased had grey hair, some of which was intermingled with blood on the linoleum.

The hair was apparently taken to Scotland Yard on Gilbert's second visit to London, and Scotland Yard kept this hair for further examination. There is no doubt that, in one way or another, the local police obtained a sample of hair from the suspect for comparison. The fact that no mention of the hair occurs throughout the trial indicates that obviously Scotland Yard drew another blank on this matter. If they had found a positive connection, it would have become a big part of the prosecution's case, but it was not.

Mystery of the Washed Clothes

The evidence given by Juana Bonfiglio was short and sweet, it may appear rather unimportant, but in fact, on examination it revealed much to support Ernest's innocence.

She said that she could not remember if there had been blood on the clothing that she washed for the Opisso family. The lady was old and, it appears, not very bright, yet the fact that she could not remember could imply that there was no blood on any of the clothing. The slightest hint that she had seen dried bloodstains on any of the clothing would have been detrimental to Ernest's case.

If there had been blood present on any of the clothing she had washed she would not have forgotten. Why? Because she would have had to wash the clothing laboriously by hand on her wooden washing board, and bloodstains are stubborn stains that do not come out that easily. The clothing may need to stand in cold water, and possibly, if the clothes are white, some powdered bleach must be applied to the dried blood spots and then they must be rubbed vigorously together. This would have entailed much extra work for the washerwoman, and she would not have easily forgotten this extra work.

Therefore, Juana did not remember that she saw blood spots on the clothing. Why? Because, logically, there had been none.

Mystery of the hairdresser.

Rosario Villatoro was the hairdresser who had given her service to Miss Bossano for the last 13 years and would do the lady's hair several times a week.

On Friday 28th she went to Miss Bossano's flat at around 2.30 p.m. knocked on the door and got no reply. Yet we know that Miss Bossano was very much alive since she was seen on Saturday morning on her way to Commercial Square and no doubt to the Church.

On the following day, the Saturday 29th, she did the same at the same time and again she got no reply, meaning that Miss Bossano was not expecting her either on the 28th or the 29th, it appears there was no previous appointment and the hairdresser turned up hoping to find the lady in. On both occasions she failed to make contact.

However when Rosario said that she went into the patio at 2.30 p.m. on Saturday she was seen entering the building by Miss Luna Beniso. Miss Beniso said it was raining hard and Rosario had her umbrella closed, she saw her go in and then go out, she could not tell whether she actually called at and entered Miss Bossano's flat or not.

Miss Beniso said she was at her window at about 4.00 or 4.30p.m.when she again saw the hairdresser, this time coming out of the building, it was pouring with rain and the hairdresser carried her umbrella opened, she recognised the hairdresser by her walk.

Esther Beniso, sister of Luna, also saw the hairdresser around 4.00p.m. This meant that three witnesses possibly saw the hairdresser leave the building, Luna Beniso, Esther Beniso and Mr. Mascarenhas.

Bishop FitzGerald and Father Salvador's Appeals to the Governor

There is no doubt whatsoever that Ernest Opisso, after relenting and accepting Father Salvador as a friend, went to confession with him. Also, since the bishop went to the prison and confirmed him into the Catholic Church and gave Holy Communion, the prisoner must have also gone to confession with the bishop.

There is also no doubt that neither the bishop nor Father Salvador would ever break their vow in the confessional and divulge what Ernest must have told them, either by action or insinuation. Their priestly vows would prohibit any such thing.

But both the bishop and the priest had an option open to them that in no way broke their priestly vows. This was not only to appeal to the Governor in the way they did, but to at least ask for a reprieve of the death sentence. If these two religious persons had heard in the confessional that Ernest Opisso had indeed admitted to killing the lady, they could never tell anyone. It would remain a sacred secret of the confessional. Yet they both made private appeals to the Governor for clemency. This in spite of the fact that the Colonial Secretary had pointed out that no clerics had signed the public memorial.

Should the Governor Have Granted a Reprieve?

Governor Godley was reputed to be a strict disciplinarian, cold and aloof. The following are matters of fact that the Governor simply overlooked.

It is apparently clear that the Governor listened and therefore relied more towards the report by the Chief Justice and Dr. Griffins than on the twelve Jurors and even the Medical report itself. The Jurors' observation and the Medical Report contained strong evidence that Ernest Opisso was not mentally normal. This is what the report said, "while unable to convince themselves that any action committed by the prisoner was done by him either without knowing what he was doing, or whether what he was doing was right or wrong, they yet think that his mental capacity is far below the average and while not lacking in some low form of cunning, his behaviour cannot be judged by ordinary standard. Major Singer associates himself with this view, arriving at this conclusion by observing the behaviour of the Convict and hearing him making long rambling statements".

How strange that the Chief Justice, in his final trial report to the Governor, which we have quoted in full earlier, said that he did not see or notice anything untoward in Opisso's behaviour in court, when in fact the transcript contains several mentions of unusual outbursts, gestures and movements that obviously disturbed the court and, which agree in many ways with the statement made by the Medical Board. But not only this, when the Special Jury of 12 persons delivered its verdict of 'guilty' it added a strong recommendation for 'mercy' on the grounds that they thought the individual was not mentally normal.

It was alleged that Opisso's demeanour in court was not that of a normal person. His constant interruptions during the trial annoyed both the prosecution and even his own defence lawyer and these were far too frequent. His own lawyer instructed him on a number of occasions to be quiet.

Four years before, in a previous case when Ernest appeared before the courts on a breaking and entering charge at a football club, two medical practitioners had given evidence testifying that Ernest was mentally subnormal—so much so that in this case the Chief of Police reduced the charge to simple burglary. Yet these two medical practitioners were not called to give evidence in the murder trial. Was this an oversight by the defence? In this case, the defence lawyer in a letter to the Governor, said that he had not used the argument of diminished responsibility simply because Opisso claimed he did not commit the crime.

Defence rightly objected to the terms set out for the medical board, claiming that the special board should have declared Opisso sane or insane. The outcome of the medical board could have been different, because to be 'insane' did not mean to be mad or a lunatic. The word 'sane' comes from the Latin word '*sanus,*' which means 'healthy' or 'whole.' The word 'insane' therefore would refer to a person not being 'mentally healthy' or 'mentally whole.'

There is no doubt that this was what the medical board wanted to say and in their own words, he was 'not mentally normal.' However, the Governor and his other advisors did not see it that way. From the information provided, there is every indication that the reports reaching the Governor on Opisso's mental condition were suspect.

Furthermore, the Colonial Secretary informed the Executive Council that Dr Gill had informed him by way of amplification of the Board's report 'that although the Board was quite satisfied that Opisso was not normally minded, if asked to certify him for admission to a lunatic asylum, they could not do so.' But the Board had not been asked to certify him to a lunatic asylum. Rather, they were to determine whether his mental ability was normal or not, and they did admit that they were 'not dealing with a normal person.'

The jury, who had witnessed the accused's behaviour in court, had strongly recommended, together with its verdict of guilty, a plea for mercy, which again the Governor overruled. It appears that the jury's recommendation should have been followed.

Governor Godley had enough reasons to have shown mercy. *El Calpense* incorrectly reported that:

The prerogative that has been conceded by His Majesty has its limits, and the Governor cannot depart from them, and that is regrettable because he cannot cede to the desires of the Gibraltarian.

In the first place, the prerogative that was given by His Majesty to the Governor in a letter of 22 November 1930 guidelines precisely on this kind of situation and these guidelines did *not* have any limitations. He was actually informed and directed that he could act on his own discretion and did *not* have to refer such matters to the Secretary of State.

Mysteries about the Chief of Police

On 2 February 1931, the Chief of Police wrote a note to Chief Inspector Collins of Scotland Yard saying, 'I am hoping that when Dr Lynch examines the articles I am now sending him, it will be impossible for Opisso to get away with it.' This was in reference to a second batch of evidence that did not include the file.

When the Hangman Came

It becomes very apparent that from the very beginning the Chief of Police was intent in proving Opisso's guilt.

Even in the early days of the investigation the press was hard on the heels of the police. On 2nd December only four days after the murder the newspaper El Calpense wrote that the whole nightmare and the ramifications surrounding this event was affecting the general population and everyone was wondering at the incredible state of the vulnerable state in which Gibraltar found itself. It wrote *"What with the daring robberies committed recently in the vicinity of the crime on Saturday, it looks like that area close to Main Street and its small lanes and alleyways is a favourite spot for criminals with several robberies that has startled the population creating a state of great insecurity in such short a time leading to such an extreme as this last brutal murder."* To add insult to injury this newspaper went on to compare the level of crime in Gibraltar to be worst than that of the Spanish neighbouring town of La Linea, known to be a cess-pool for petty crime. The newspaper went on to appeal to the police to protect the city from known criminals, it asked where was this situation leading too?

Observers may query if this kind of public criticism could have driven the Chief to produce results in a shorter time than he may have otherwise taken under different circumstances.

And we wonder if this kind of public criticism drove the Chief to having to produce results quickly"

In addition to this pressure Scotland Yard had also noted that after the negative assessment of all the tests and analysis, 'Mr Gulloch suspected that he did not have sufficient evidence to prove his case, that the important witness was the baker's boy who saw the suspect at 12 noon.'

So it appears that at that point the only evidence to prove the case was in fact the testimony of the 'important witness' the baker's boy, whose testimony in fact was totally inaccurate and unreliable.

The mystery continues. Why was the Chief of Police, at the time when he was at Scotland Yard, so sure Opisso was the culprit and so determined that he should not get away with it? The file had not yet been produced in evidence and he did not have any other evidence by his own admission, two of the witnesses were unreliable. And in the end this boy witness was totally mistaken.

The first batch of evidence examined by Scotland Yard over the Christmas period of 1930 all produced negative results, no matching fingerprints, no bloodstains in any of the clothes and shoes and no identifiable footprints Neither did the second batch of evidence produce any damaging implications against Opisso.

Why did the Chief of Police, or for that matter the prosecution, not inform the defence counsel about the lack of any positive report from Scotland Yard? No mention about this is made during the trial. Was he wilfully keeping information away from the defence attorney?

The question arises, since the Chief of Police was keen on proving that the murder was committed by Opisso, as he stated in his letter to Ashley at Scotland Yard, did the Chief of Police call PC Macedo to his office for questioning about what he had or had not seen during his beat around Market Lane, and to think hard of what he had seen? There is the logical possibility that PC Macedo was first questioned by Sergeant Gilbert from CID and then by Superintendent Brown, prior to his final interview with the Chief of Police, which on its own would have been an intimidating affair for a young officer. Otherwise, Macedo's delay in reporting his sighting to the Chief of Police was rather strange.

Still stranger is the fact that Macedo's evidence was in conflict with the Chief of Police's testimony. regarding the time and the direction of the sighting?

The Judge, in his summing up when he was referring to the accusation that the police was being unduly harsh on the accused said that

"The police had no object on bringing an innocent person to death." But? On the other hand the defence was rather wanting about this detail.

The Mystery of the Black Book.

The black book, the property of the victim in which she recorded all her transactions, was produced totally unannounced by the prosecution. In it was recorded what the lady had paid Opisso for his work and also what Opisso paid or owed her for the rent of the store. Its significance was that it had blood splashes on those pages, which referred to Opisso. The circumstantial possibility is that the lady was sitting at her dressing table revising Opisso's recent work when she was attacked. Someone had handled the book because it had fingerprints on it.

Could the lady have been reading her notes whilst the hair dresser worked on her hair? Did the police take the hairdresser's fingerprints? The reports do not indicate this.

The Chief of Police when giving evidence had stated that, he was satisfied that the finger prints on the book did not belong to any particular person from whom they had obtained finger prints, Opisso's and the lady's included. So who, in heaven's name, did that fingerprint or prints belong to? The finger print test comparisons had been done by Scotland Yard, though in the trial he did not specify this fact.

Mystery of The Iron File and the Bone

The mystery of the iron file is the most puzzling piece of evidence. That the file was the murder weapon was obviously clear enough for the jury. The jury's reasoning was very logical. If the file fitted the broken piece of bone and had a sliver of bone in it, it must have been the weapon, and how did this weapon come to be in Opisso's store?

The iron file was taken from Opisso's store on 27th January, two months after the murder was discovered and one month after the Chief of Police and Sergeant Gilbert returned from visiting Scotland Yard and after the prosecution had decided they had a case against Opisso and after Opisso's arrest on the 26th January. The discovery of the file in Opisso's store by DC Wahnon and Superintendent Brown is significant for several simple reasons.

Firstly even with his feeble mind, if he had been clever enough to have wiped off all blood traces from his shoes and had sense enough to send his clothes to be washed so thoroughly that no evidence was left behind, surely he would have disposed of the file? Why would he leave the file, the murder weapon, in his store where it would sooner or later surely be found? This omission of Opisso does not fit in with his previous behaviour.

Secondly, why did Opisso take a file with him to murder the lady? If he took a weapon, this was a premeditated murder, so why did he not take a piece of pipe or a hammer, which would have been more appropriate and effective weapons with less likelihood of producing bloody wounds?

Opisso was a suspect, in the Chief of Police's mind, from an early stage, so why did the police not look for a murder weapon before Opisso was arrested instead of waiting till after he had been charged?

Worse still, why did Opisso leave the file untouched when he could have easily brushed it clean with a wire brush He must surely have had one in his store, which he could have used to remove any possible traces of evidence, as he had allegedly done with all his other items of clothing? He had plenty of time to clean off the traces of bone and even the plaster of Paris, before storing or hiding it, kept it or disposing of it. One of the prosecution's witness had testified that the file had not been cleaned?

This type of file was very common and could be bought at any of the ironmonger shops in town and there must have been scores of files of this kind around Gibraltar.

If the file was the supposed murder weapon that had penetrated the cranium and brain to a depth of about six inches, why did the file not produce any signs of blood during the blood tests in the courtroom, especially when the tiny chip of bone was removed? Could three doctors be wrong and one right, and the piece of human bone on the file was not human? There was much doubt at one point as to its true nature.

Why were no other pieces of tissue lodged in those fine teeth? Dr Giraldi, the medical expert for the defence, asked why, even if the file had been washed, there was no blood either in the plaster of Paris or under the small chip of bone?

In his evidence Dr Giraldi had said that he had carried out certain experiments with a similar file, which had had plaster of Paris on the point. He said that he had stained the plaster with human blood and after three minutes he had washed it and left it to soak for two hours, yet the bloodstains were still fairly visible. Soaking the file for two hours in water was far more rigorous a test than the file exhibit even if it had been washed.

The file had a very pointed and sharp end, which was where the wooden handle, would be located (see the illustration. The other end of the file would be a flat end that would have difficulty penetrating any kind of surface. Therefore, the sharp and pointed end of the file was obviously assumed by the Doctor to have been used to penetrate the skull, so the file would enter in the reverse direction, with the direction of the cutting teeth pointing upwards and not downwards. This has an important connotation: the piece of bone could not have lodged under the tooth on entry, since the sharp teeth were pointing in the opposite direction to the direction of the blow. The force of this blow would have been at its strongest on the downward stroke when it would have cracked and broken the skull. To corroborate the force of the blow Dr. Griffiths said that the piece of bone was deeply embedded in the teeth of the file. There would logically be less force when withdrawing the weapon from the skull, certainly not enough to enable a piece of bone to lodge itself on the way out of a skull bone which was already broken and moving. Therefore any bone or membrane would adhere itself to the top of the tooth and not in the cavity the tooth forms as its cutting edge. It would be very difficult, if not impossible, for the tiny piece of bone that was shown in court to lodge under the inner space of the tooth with an already broken piece of skull bone. Because of this any substance adhering to a tooth of the file, when the file was on the upward stroke, would not hold firmly it would be loosely held and vulnerable to dislodging itself easily.

One other puzzle was why there was no evidence of plaster of Paris on the edges of the piece of cranium that fell off, or for that matter on the remaining broken skull? If there had been plaster of Paris in the main part of the skull, the two doctors who diligently performed the *post mortem* would have probably spotted it, given that the doctors examined and made detailed sketches of the head injuries that were shown in court.

So the mystery now remains. How did the small piece of bloodless bone get under a tooth of the file that struck in the wrong direction?

Under the cross-examination of the defence lawyer, Dr Griffiths, referring to the tiny sliver of bone, said that in order to determine with accuracy whether the bone was human one needed to be a 'great expert.' Yet the doctor for the defence, Dr Giraldi, said that it was so small that it was impossible to tell. In any case, the test on the bone for blood proved negative.

The legal requirement when a piece of evidence is found is that its integrity relies on the fact that it has not been contaminated. The item of evidence must be provided with a proper chain of handling from the time that it is found to the time when it is presented in court. If there is a break in the chain, then the evidence may have been tampered with, in which case it may be inadmissible in court.

The Chief of Police had this file, as well as the piece of broken piece of skull, in his possession for some time, could the Chief of Police have examined and handled this file and the piece of bone for far too long before he gave it to Dr Griffiths and Dr Deale for examination? How else could a microscopic sliver of bone lodge in a tooth of the file with the direction of the file's teeth in the rasping position? How else can the unlikely choice of weapon be explained and the uncharacteristic negligence of the accused in keeping the murder weapon uncleaned in his store be explained?

It is difficult not to look back and recall the Chief of Police's zeal and letter to Scotland Yard, before the file had been produced saying 'It will be impossible for him (Opisso) to get away with it' when in fact none of the evidence he sent to Scotland Yard produced any evidence detrimental to Opisso's guilt.

One Last Observation

One last observation, Opisso maintained his innocence throughout his trials and even after sentencing. Even when knowing that he would surely be hanged, he still did not repent nor offer a confession to the murder. It would be perfectly understandable for the condemned to do this once he knows the inevitability of his fate and that everything is finally over and there is nothing to hide and no one left to trick. One wonders if, under the circumstances, Opisso would have confessed to the murder if he were really guilty.

Why would he walk on two occasions up and down Market Lane, making himself more identifiable? Would it not have been more likely for him to stay as far as possible from the scene of the crime? In fact he had two alternative routes to get to his house when he left and went to the Canessa's house. He had also informed the court that he had made five visits to his store on the morning of the Saturday in question, so it appears that he was not trying to hide the fact he was close to the scene or for that matter keep a low profile.

If Ernest killed the lady, why would he make himself so easily available? Why was he so cooperative with the police? Was Ernest Opisso that

When the Hangman Came

cunning, calculating, and cold-blooded, or was he that mentally deficient? Even though he was slow-witted, he was neither of the latter two.

Ernest Opisso's Burial niche

Francisco Cuenca's Niche close to Opisso's

Chapter 14. SHORT SEQUEL ABOUT SIR ALEXANDER GODLEY, GCB, KMC.

The role of Governor Godley's story was of paramount importance to the final fate of the accused Ernest Opisso so we may well ask what kind of a man was Godley, a man who attained so many prestigious honours and who had been mentioned in no less than ten despatches during World War 1?

During the period of his Governorship little had been written and therefore known locally about his earlier life. We are aware that when the Colonial Hospital in Gibraltar was enlarged during his tenure of office a medical ward was named Godley Ward possibly after him or his wife, the Colonial Hospital was later renamed St. Bernard's Hospital after the patron Saint of Gibraltar.

Godley and his wife always seem to have taken an interest in the social fabric wherever they were posted. An example of this was their active involvement with the Gibraltar Royal Calpe Hunt Society referred to elsewhere.

Godley's name appears earlier on in time in connection with the opening of a convalescent hospital opened in Alexandria Egypt by Mrs. Godley, formerly Louisa Marian Fowler, whilst the New Zealand contingent was stationed there getting ready for military action against Turkey.

Although the couple was childless their marriage was considered affectionate and happy and it was said that it was hard to envisage Godley's career without the constant support of his wife's involvement in their demanding social duties.

We read that in the first place he was a person that attended to his affairs in great detail and was meticulous with planning matters perhaps the main reason for his appointment as Major-General, in 1910, with the purpose of introducing discipline, routine and order to a bedraggled New Zealand army in New Zealand itself.

Two great well-known soldiers of the time, Col. Robert Baden-Powell and Lord Kitchener thought highly of his genius for military organisation but at the other end of the scale his men despised him for his nose-in-the-air or arrogant attitude.

Yet he did a remarkable job during his three-year term in New Zealand, he turned out a well-trained territorial Force equipping it with up-to-date equipment particularly machine gun platoons. Three members of the New Zealand Task Force received the highest honour a soldier can get, the Victoria Cross, awarded for valour over and above the call of duty in the face of the enemy.

Chroniclers however to not match his organisational skills with his battle skills as they developed during WW1 specifically during 1915 and 1917. In their accounts they describe his record as 'inept to disastrous'.

During the Gallipoli campaign when the British, New Zealand and Australian forces, under the command of Godley, landed in Turkey to get a foothold on the southern flank of the German forces who were then allied with the Turks, things went wrong when a bayonet charge was ordered by him against superior forces in well entrenched positions. When this battle was over there were so many casualties that it became known as "Godley's abattoir" and the Gallipoli Campaign offence was a total failure and the Allied Forces had to retreat. Godley was blamed for this failure.

It need to be added that the strength of the British and New Zealand forces was in the order of 9,000-15,000 men whilst the Ottoman forces numbered 20,000-30,000, representing odds of 2 to 1.

No wonder that in a battle at close quarters with hand-to-hand fighting with the enemy on high ground and the attacking forces on a steep climb the decision to attack was considered a great miscalculations

But that was not all, once again in October 1917 during the battle of Ypres, specifically at Passendale his weak leadership was blamed for the death, disappearance and injury of more than 2,700 New Zealand troops.

Again during that same year the battle of Messin although a success for the British forces under General Plumers, the latter wrote that the battle would have had greater success if Godley had better co-ordinated follow-up attacks to support the British Troops.

New Zealand's Minister for Defence, James Allen, was quoted as saying that it would have been better if some body else other than Godley had been placed in command once Godley had finished his training programme of his men.

When questions were raised in Parliament and elsewhere about Godley's performance in the field of battle he offered to resign.

However in spite of his poor record in the field, no doubt because of his organisational skills, his resignation was not accepted and was in turn appointed Military Secretary to the Secretary of State for War and in 1923 he was promoted to full General.

A comment by one chronicler said that Godley was known for his callous indifference to the plight of his troops. (Dictionary of New Zealand Biography - Wikipidia)

By 1928 at the age of 60, when the world was in relative peace he was finally but gently pushed sideways and was appointed Governor of the British Colony Gibraltar, where apparently he was at his organisational best in a society that was severely military and flourished on pomp and class distinction the perfect location for a man known for his stuck-up personality. His appointment to Gibraltar was certainly not valuable or beneficial to our friend Ernest Opisso who received no 'mercy' from Godley.

During WW2 he commanded a platoon of the Home Guard perhaps reminiscent of "Dad's Army".

Godley died peacefully in England in 1957. (Biography: Life of an Irish Soldier).

Joe Caruana

Appendix 1: *The Royal Gibraltar Police 1830–1930*

In their book with the above title, the authors Cecilia Baldachino and Tito Benady briefly mention the murder of Miss Bossano in 1930. I had finally finished my manuscript when I came across this interesting book, and one comment in it got my immediate attention. It was in the part where they refer to the riot that took place outside the Cathedral of St. Mary's and the intervention of the police in that riot. I must confess that in my research I had not come across this particular explanation as to why the crowd rioted.

'The crowd was indignant because it was felt that the condemned man had not been treated fairly, he was of low intelligence, and also because *he was condemned purely on the basis of circumstantial evidence which most people in Gibraltar did not consider adequate'*. (*The Royal Gibraltar Police 1830-1930, P39.* Author's italics)

Appendix 2: An Unsubstantiated Rumour—True or False?

After I had completed writing the whole story of this horrible murder case and having arrived at so many contradictions and doubts as to Ernest Opisso's involvement in the murder of Miss Maria Luisa Bossano, I came across a most astonishing piece of information.

It so happened that I had been seeking and exchanging information on this murder case with an influential person in the law profession and since I have learnt that this person had also gathered information on and had been interested in this case for some time now. I approached and told him that I was well advanced in the writing of the murder story and he told me that he was glad that I was writing it because he had no time to do so.

After several exchanges of views, to my great surprise, he told me that his 84-year-old mother had heard the news a few years ago that an elderly man, in the North of Spain, had confessed that 'Opisso did not kill the lady in Gibraltar. I killed her,' she heard him say.

I find myself at a loss as to how to go about finding the origin of this report heard by this elderly lady. I can assure the reader that the transmission of this information comes from respectable and reliable persons.

Should this sensational piece of information be true, then a serious miscarriage of justice took place in Gibraltar in 1930, and Ernest Opisso's body should be exhumed from its present resting place in a hidden, derelict, and remote hole in a wall of the dilapidated part of the old Moorish Castle and given a decent burial in sacred ground. Hanging by the neck for a crime, which he probably did not commit, may mean that an innocent man was hanged. Even if the remotest doubt exists that he committed this crime, then the same suggested course of action still applies.

Appendix 3: History of UK Capital Punishment and Its Abolition

The above recommendation is not without precedent. The following quotes taken from British Military & Criminal History in the period 1900 to 1999 shows just how many innocent persons were sent to the gallows and then subsequently found innocent.

In the years after the end of the war in 1945, there were several notable cases. Either due to the coverage given by the British media, the case's use by the pro- or anti-capital punishment people, or the innocence of the executed person, in fact since 1945 three people have received posthumous pardons: Timothy Evans in 1966 and in 1998 both Mahood Mattan and Derek Bentley. After the abolition of capital punishment, there have been several famous cases of miscarriages of justice, which would have resulted in executions, if that option had been available. A good example of this is the Birmingham Six case.

1908	People under 16 are no longer liable for hanging.
1922	Infanticide (mother killing her child) is no longer a capital offence.
1931	Pregnant women are no longer hanged.
1933	People under 18 are not executed but are sentenced to Her/His Majesty's pleasure.
1948	House of Commons suspends capital punishment. Overruled by House of Lords.
9 March 1950	Timothy John Evans hanged at Pentonville Prison.
28 January 1953	Derek Bentley hanged at Wandsworth Prison for the murder of PC Miles.
13 July 1955	Last women hanged in the UK (Ruth Ellis at Holloway Prison).
1956	The passing of Death Penalty (Abolition) Bill is overturned by Lords.
1957	Homicide Act 1957 restricts use of capital punishment.
23 July 1957	First execution under the 1957 act: John Vickers.
5 November 1959	Last execution for murder of police officer: Gunther Podola.
13 August 1964	Last executions: Peter Anthony Allen & Gwynne Owen Evans.
1965	Capital punishment in murder cases is suspended for 5 years.
1966	Timothy John Evans receives a posthumous pardon.
1969	Capital punishment for murder is abolished.
February 1998	Mahmood Mattan receives a posthumous pardon.
July 1998	Derek Bentley receives a posthumous pardon.

Parliament then voted to abolish the death penalty for murder for a five-year experiment in 1965. Just before the Murder (Abolition of the Death Penalty) Act 1965 received its royal assent, the Home Office allowed the reburial of Timothy Evans outside Pentonville prison. It was the start of a process, which led to Evans being granted a posthumous free pardon in October 1966.

In the State of Texas alone, in the U.S.A. and following DNA tests years after the event, no less than 21 persons have been exonerated for serious crimes and after serving long-term imprisonment for crimes they did not commit. According to experts most of these wrongful convictions were made on the grounds of wrongful identification.

In the same way, I call upon the authorities in Gibraltar to bury the remains of Ernest Opisso outside the prison walls in sacred ground and for the authorities to consider whether to grant Ernest Opisso a posthumous free pardon on the grounds of reasonable doubt.

Joe Caruana

Appendix 4: U.K. Press reports

The Daily Mail
Cutting from issue dated... 3 - JUL 1931

GIBRALTAR RIOTS.

BRITISH TROOPS TO QUELL EXECUTION DISORDER.

GIBRALTAR, Thursday.

Serious rioting broke out in Gibraltar to-night as the result of public feeling aroused by the news that a man named Opisso would be hanged to-morrow.

Thousands of inhabitants had signed a petition asking that he be reprieved, but the Governor had refused to grant it. There has been no execution in Gibraltar for 35 years and it is said that no inhabitant of Gibraltar has ever been hanged before.

A crowd gathered in front of Government House, and the guard turned out with fixed bayonets.

The crowd then paraded the main street, where they tried to break into the Roman Catholic Cathedral.

Police with drawn truncheons protected the cathedral until the crowd, which was armed with sticks and staves, began to force them back.

A half company of the North Staffordshire Regiment then arrived armed only with hockey sticks. The crowd began to move backwards, and the police seized the opportunity to charge, although they only numbered 20. They dispersed the crowd in all directions and the streets were quickly cleared.—Exchange.

The Daily Mail
Cutting from issue dated... 4 - JUL 1931

HANGMAN FROM ENGLAND.

GIBRALTAR'S FRENZY AT EXECUTION.

From OUR OWN CORRESPONDENT.

GIBRALTAR, Friday.

A HANGMAN came specially from England to carry out an execution here to-day—the first in Gibraltar for more than a quarter of a century. It was that of Ernest Opisso, who had been sentenced to death for the murder of an elderly woman.

The town has been in a state of frenzy since last night, when demonstrators had to be dispersed by British troops. A crowd gathered outside the Roman Catholic church demanding that the bishop should intervene on Opisso's behalf.

Although the crowds assembled outside the prison this morning, the execution passed off without disorder. All shops, however, have been closed, and no taxicabs are running.

Most of the officials connected with Opisso's trial have been threatened and a double guard has been posted at the summer residence of the Governor, Sir A. Godley.

Appendix 5: Telex to Malta requesting a hangman

> Telegram.
>
> ...lta.
>
> Gibraltarian charged with murder has been sentenced... Greatest difficulty in finding hangman here. ...possible send suitable person from Malta. Must ...e not later than 2nd July. Reply urgently required.
>
> ...6.1931.   Secretary.

23.6.31 at 14.40am.

Fortress Headquarters.
23rd. June, 1931.

Colonel,
A.A.G. A.G. I/c Administration.

Copy to :- D.D.M.S. Hon. Colonial Secretary.

Joe Caruana

Appendix 6: Letter of Public Petition of 3,000 signatures

SERFATY
BARRISTER-AT-LAW

TELEGRAPHIC ADDRESS:
"EQUITAS"

TELEPHONE A. 454.

6, City Mill Lane

Gibraltar _____ 22nd. June, _____ 19 31.

RECEIVED
22 JUN. 1931
COLONIAL SECRETARY'S OFFICE
GIBRALTAR

Sir,

   I have the honour to enclose, for the consideration of His Excellency the Governor, a Memorial for the reprieve of Ernesto Opisso, who was found guilty of the murder of Miss Maria Luisa Bossano, and sentenced to death, at the Special Criminal Sessions on the 13th inst.

   I also beg to enclose copy of a report published in "The Gibraltar Chronicle" on the 24th day of March, 1926, with reference to proceedings at the Police Court against the said Ernesto Opisso for larceny and wherein it is stated that the Chief of Police produced a certificate signed by two local medical practitioners stating that the accused was mentally deficient. This report supports the views put forward by the Memorialists as to the state of Opisso's mind. I may point out that similar reports of the aforesaid Police Court case were published in the other two local papers of the same date.

   The Memorial is signed by thousands of persons of all classes of Society.

   As you are no doubt aware, within an hour after sentence was known, people started signing for a reprieve, and lists for the purpose were spontaneously placed at several shops. This fact and the rumour, unfounded as far as I can gather, that one of Opisso's brothers, who wanted an appeal to England, had torn several lists of signatures may account for some people signing in two places.

   The defence of insanity could not be raised at the trial as Opisso denied having had anything to do with the commission of the crime, a denial in which he has persisted after sentence.

   I venture respectfully to suggest that, in view of the statements made in the Memorial and Opisso's medical history His Excellency be pleased to appoint a medical board to examine Ernesto Opisso as to his mental condition.

   Trusting that His Excellency will graciously and mercifully accede to the petition of reprieve of Ernesto Opisso.

          I have the honour to be,
            Sir,
          Your obedient servant,

TO.
  The Hon. Colonial Secretary.

Appendix 7: Medical report

The Hon. The Colonial Secretary,
    Gibraltar.

Sir,

    We have the honour to report as follows :-

    The Board following the instructions laid down in your 541/30 of June 23rd, 1931, proceeded to the Civil Prison where they interviewed the Gaoler who produced the night reports on the convict, Ernesto Opisso. Neither he nor the reports mention any unusual behaviour on part of the convict pointing to Mental disease.

    The Board then had a lengthy conversation with the Convict which took place in Spanish as Convict does not speak English. In consequence, one of the members of the Board, Major Singer, R.A.M.C., was unable to follow the answers and Statements by the convict, which did not lend themselves to literal translation.

    The answers and statements made by the convict were involved and rambling - he frequently went off the main theme under discussion and branched off on to side tracks, where it was difficult to follow what point he was driving at. He was in a state of suppressed excitement.

    From his conversation the two Spanish speaking members of the Board, Drs. Gill and Durante, came to the conclusion that they were not dealing here with a man that from a medical point of view was mentally normal. While unable to convince themselves that any action committed by the prisoner was done so by him either without knowing what he was doing, or whether what he was doing was right or wrong, they yet think that his mental capacity is far below the average, and while possibly

                                                                                 not

Joe Caruana

Appendix 8: Medical report

2.

not lacking in some low form of cunning, his behaviour cannot be judged by ordinary standards. Major Singer associates himself with this view, arriving at this conclusion by observing the behaviour of the Convict and hearing him making long rambling statements, even though unable to follow their purport.

With reference to convict's previous appearance in the Police Court in March, 1926, the Board were unable to obtain definite evidence as to any medical certificates produced at the time certifying convict mentally deficient.

We have the honour to be,
Sir,
Your obedient Servants,

Appendix 9: Negative report from Scotland Yard

METROPOLITAN POLICE.

CRIMINAL INVESTIGATION DEPARTMENT,
New Scotland Yard.

16th day of February, 1931.

1.

To Chief Inspector.

With reference to the attached:—

I beg to report that on the 6th February 1931, Detective Sergeant Gilbert of the Gibralter Police called at this Office with the attached letter of introduction from Mr W.S.Gullock, Chief of Police, Gibralter to Chief Constable Ashley, in which the former stated that Ernest Opisso had been arrested and charged with the murder of Miss Maria Louisa Bossano. He also asked that Sergeant Gilbert, who had come to this Country with various articles, the property of the prisoner, with a view to their being examined for blood by Doctor Roche Lynch, be assisted whilst he was here.

As directed, I accompanied Sergeant Gilbert to St Mary's Hospital, Paddington, on the afternoon of 6th February 1931, where he saw and handed to Doctor Roche Lynch, the articles for examination.

The Doctor stated that he would carry out an examination on Sunday 8th February 1931, and that he would be in a position to say whether certain spots on a pair of shoes and on a file, were human blood or not, by the afternoon of 9th February 1931. Upon this date Sergeant Gilbert again saw Doctor Roche Lynch, who informed him that the spots had been tested with a negative result. The officer immediately cabled the result of the examination to the Chief of Police Gibralter.

The exhibits, with the exception of some hair,

Appendix 10: Mother's Plea, letter to Governor

Excelentísimo Sr Governador

Perdoneme el atrevimiento de dirijirme a su Excelencia, pero es el ultimo recurso de la mas desgraciadas de las madres. Yo desearia la gracia de que su Excelencia concediera un aplazamiento de dos meses, para que se ejecutara la fatal sentencia que pende sobre la cabeza de mi hijo.

En ese tiempo siempre contando con la venia de su excelencia, podiamos intentar algo por salvar la vida de mi hijo, dejariamos a mi hijo algun tiempo bajo observacion pues los Doctores que le escaminaron en una visita, no han podido apreciar el estado de mi hijo.

O bien escribiriamos un Memorial a su Majestad el Rey pidiendole el indulto basandonos que el dia de su coronacion escribimos un Memorial al Excelentisimo Governador de Gibraltar.

Si el Excelentisimo Sr Governador nos concediera esta gracia sabemos bien que todo el pueblo de Gibraltar lo bendeciria y en particular esta desgraciada familia y mas que nadie esta pobre Madre que le ruega de rodillas que le conceda esta ultima gracia.

Amanda Spiteri

Appendix 11: Acknowledgement of Public Petition

541/30   26th June, 1931.

Sir,

    I have the honour to acknowledge the receipt of your letter of the 22nd of June, transmitting a Memorial, alleged to bear the signature of thousands of persons of all classes of Society, which has been duly laid before the Governor.

    2. His Excellency in Council has given the fullest consideration to all the representations made, and inter alia, the Governor caused a special medical board to be convened.

    3. All the points referred to in the various passages of the Memorial and in your letter, together with all possible evidence and all documents connected with the case, received full and careful examination and investigation.

    4. The requirements of the Royal Instructions and the Law were carefully followed, and after consultation with his advisers His Excellency has regretfully come to the carefully considered conclusion that there are no sufficient grounds to warrant his interference with the sentence of the Court.

    5. There is no objection to the whole of this letter being communicated to the Press.

                                I have the honour to be,
                                Sir,
                                Your obedient Servant,

                          (Sd) Alex^r. E. Beattie

                                Colonial Secretary.

A.B.M. Serfaty, Esq.,
    Barrister-at-Law

Appendix 12: Second Negative report from Scotland Yard

222/P.C./3616 (C.2.)

Sir,

    re Murder - Miss Marie Louisa Bossano.

    I am directed by the Commissioner of Police of the Metropolis to return herewith the raincoat and pair of trousers left by you with Dr. Roche Lynch for examination, and to say that the latter has not been able to trace any human bloodstains on the articles.

    It is understood that Dr. Roche Lynch has already communicated with you to this effect.

    I am, Sir,
    Your obedient Servant,

    Assistant Commissioner

The Chief of Police,
    Gibraltar

When the Hangman Came

Appendix 13: Hand written note from Colonial Secretary.

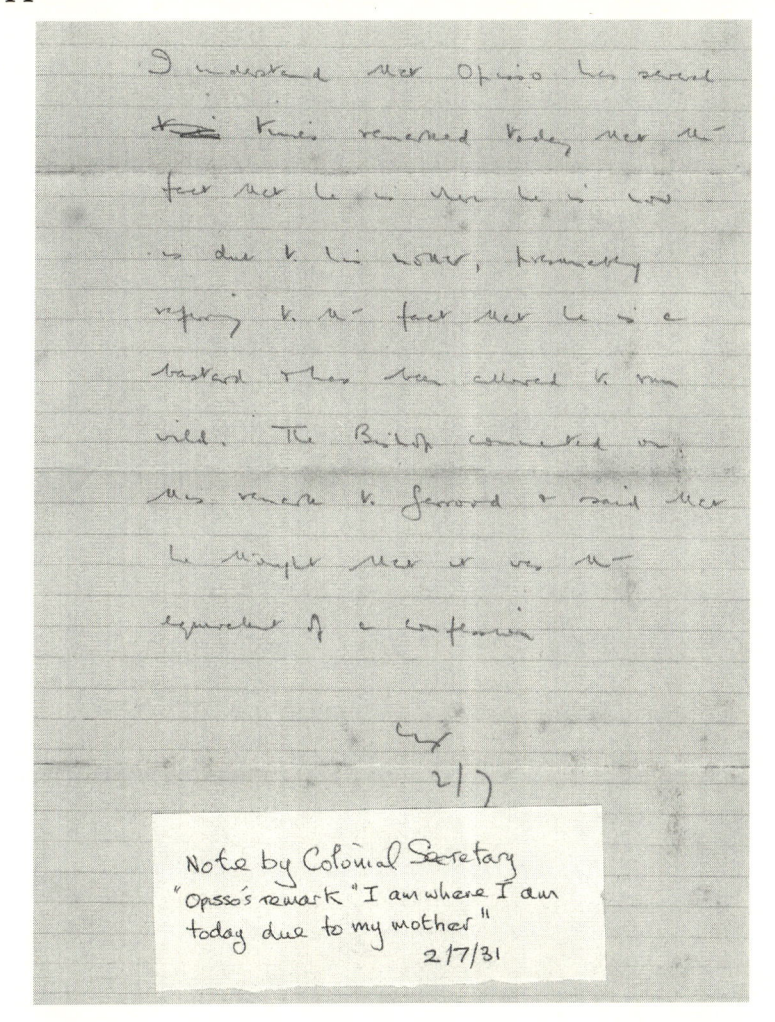

Note by Colonial Secretary
"Opasso's remark "I am where I am today due to my mother"
2/7/31

Appendix 14: Opisso's Baptismal details.

Baptismal Certificate

Ernesto Opisso

Child of Luis Opisso natus Gibraltar
Amanda Gonzales nata Gibraltar
born on 22nd January 1903
place Gibraltar

was reborn of water and the Holy Spirit as a child of God at the Sacred font of Baptism

on 24th May 1903 in

The Cathedral of Saint Mary the Crowned
Gibraltar

by the Reverend C Mortiner
Godfather Robert Smith
Godmother Catalina Opisso
issued by [signature] date 4th May 2010.

Confirmed in Prison on 5th July 1931.

Appendix 15: Executive Council's decision on Medical Report

25th June.   On Council resuming, the case of Ernest Opisso was further considered, all documentary evidence being available including the Chief Justice's report and notes on the case, the public petition, the report of the medical Board &c. After His Excellency had briefly reviewed the various factors of the case, the Colonial Secretary stated that Dr. Gill, the President of the Medical Board, had stated to him, in amplification of the Board's report, that although the Board was quite satisfied that Opisso was not normally minded, they were equally certain that, were they asked to certify him for admission to a Lunatic Asylum, they could not do so. The members of the Medical Board were then summoned and unanimously and unhesitatingly confirmed this view.

After lengthy consideration, and careful deliberation, the Council unanimously advised that in their opinion there were no extenuating circumstances which would justify His Excellency in extending a reprieve to the convict. His Excellency concurred and

Joe Caruana

Appendix 16: Court's Warrant for Execution

At a Special Criminal Court of the Supreme Court of Gibraltar begun to be holden at the Court House on the Eighth day of June and continued by adjournments to the Thirteenth day of June in the Twenty-second year of the reign of Our Sovereign Lord GEORGE THE FIFTH by the Grace of God of Great Britain Ireland and the British Dominions beyond the Seas King Defender of the Faith Emperor of India and in the year of Our Lord One thousand nine hundred and thirty-one.

BEFORE His Honour Sir Kenneth James Beatty Knight Chief Justice.

WHEREAS at this Special Criminal Court ERNESTO OPISSO stands and is convicted of Murder

IT IS THEREFORE ORDERED AND ADJUDGED by the Court that the said Ernesto Opisso be taken from this place to a lawful prison and thence to a place of execution and that he be there hanged by the neck until he be dead and that his body be afterwards buried within the precincts of the said prison.

By the Court,

John Discombe,

Clerk of Arraigns.

(L. S.)

Certified true copy :

Clerk of Arraigns.

Bibliography and Sources

Gibraltar Archives

National Archives, Kew

Gibraltar Chronicle (from November 1930 to July 1931)

El Calpense, (ditto)

El Anunciador, (limited publications)

The Hounds are Home, Gordon Ferguson

Life of an Irish Soldier, A. Godley

The Royal Gibraltar Police 1830-1930, Mrs C. Baldachino and Tito Benady

Genesis of Gibraltar, George Palau (deceased)

About the Author

Joe Louis Caruana, MBE

Joe Caruana was born in Gibraltar on 13 November 1937. He attended Gibraltar Technical College. He worked as a draughtsman at the Air Ministry in Gibraltar and the UK and studied Engineering at the London Polytechnic. He became a specialist in industrial diamonds.

Joe's public life started in 1966 when he became founding secretary of the Gibraltar Junior Chamber of Commerce. In 1967 he entered politics and joined the executive of the Integration with Britain Party in Gibraltar. The IWBP won the 1969 general elections, and he served as Minister for Medical Services from 1969-70, and from 1970-72 as Minister for Public Works). He served as a member of the Gibraltar Council and was chairman of several important committees including the Development and Planning Commission.

In 1975 Joe and his family went to Canada and stayed there for twelve years, starting a successful business in his old profession in the industrial diamond drilling industry.

Around 1984 Joe volunteered to help at a home that helped teenage prostitutes and drug addicts called Exodus House in Calgary Alberta, run by lay Franciscan brothers, an order he joined at the time.

In 1987 Joe sold his business and with his Franciscan spirit moved back to Gibraltar. With him he brought the idea of starting a rehabilitation centre, which he called Camp Emmanuel. Camp Emmanuel became very well known from 1987 till 1998. In 1991 Joe pioneered the Narcotics Anonymous group in Gibraltar and also assisted in starting another NA group in nearby Spain. That same year Joe started two other vital groups, 'The Family Group Meetings,' known today as 'Family Anonymous,' and the 'Drug Advisory Service,' a place where people could make contact and get support.

In 1999 he revived the Integration With Britain Movement, continuing the political ideal of making Gibraltar a region of the UK.

Joe is an accomplished painter, and his paintings have sold worldwide.

To this day, Joe continues to give valuable counselling to those who seek help and is a director of Nazareth House, that houses 'The Soup Kitchen' and where several self-help groups meet on a daily basis.

His first book, 'Spirit Of The Phoenician', is his own autobiography that starts with what he considers the roots of his family, the vastly travelled and ingenious Phoenicians—no doubt a reflection of his own life.

In 2010 on the occasion of Her Majesty Queen Elizabeth II's birthday Her Majesty made Joe a Member of the Most Excellent Order of the British Empire and awarded Joe the MBE.